BLACK LIST, SECTION H

Francis Stuart was born in Australia of planter stock, was educated at Rugby and has lived most of his life in Ireland. As a young man he married Iseult, the daughter of Maud Gonne, and began to make his name during the twenties and thirties as a poet and novelist. He was interned by the infant Irish Free State for joining the Republican cause during the Civil War.

A citizen of Ireland, he spent the war years in Germany, where he had been invited to lecture and to broadcast to Ireland. At the end of the war he was detained in Austria by the French occupying forces, pending the subsequent clearance of charges that had been made against him. Francis Stuart lives in Dublin.

Francis Stuart

BLACK LIST, SECTION H

A KING PENGUIN
PUBLISHED BY PENGUIN BOOKS

Penguin Books Ltd, Harmondsworth, Middlesex, England
Penguin Books, 625 Madison Avenue, New York, New York 10022, U.S.A.
Penguin Books Australia Ltd, Ringwood, Victoria, Australia
Penguin Books Canada Ltd, 2801 John Street, Markham, Ontario, Canada L3R 1B4
Penguin Books (N.Z.) Ltd, 182–190 Wairau Road, Auckland 10, New Zealand

First published in the U.S.A. by Southern Illinois University Press 1971
First published in Great Britain by Martin Brian & O'Keeffe 1975

Published in Penguin Books 1982

Made and printed in Great Britain by
Hazell Watson & Viney Ltd
Aylesbury, Bucks
Filmset in Monophoto Times by
Northumberland Press Ltd, Gateshead, Tyne and Wear

In memory of John Lodwick dearest of friends

1

His window looked on to a derelict mill half-hidden by a small wood above the three ponds, each on a slightly lower level. A last patch of vivid sunshine, coming in intense, isolated gleams in this northern county, caught the slope of grass close to where dusk was already gathering under the ruined wall, the wet ivy glinted against the black stone, and short, intense intervals of silence formed between the cawing of the rooks.

H started scribbling, scrawling through the lines and substituting others, his nerves vibrating to a new kind of rhythm. It was not another shy love note to one of his girl cousins that he was feverishly writing, but his first poem.

> The sun is dropped and shadows grow
> As swords for the world's overthrow
> And through the depths the lightnings crawl
> Each like a wounded nightingale.
> The flashing dreams of coming years
> Dance upon the heart like spears,
> Of burnings breaking into swans,
> Of sun-enchanted golden lemons,
> Of Ninevehs and Babylons,
> Whose stones are dark with future tears,
> Or of more homely, simple sights
> In gardens at the dim of nights
> When the white petal of the moon
> Throws every flower in a swoon . . .

After he'd finished it, he took a sheet of notepaper, went downstairs, embossed it in the little machine on his aunt's desk with the address, and wrote a letter to a Dublin newspaper on the subject of Home Rule. He guessed that, coming from the heart of the Unionist North, the letter would have a good chance of being published in spite of the not very original arguments for independence expressed in it. It was not for the sake of seeing his name in print for the first time that he had composed it. Not because in his heart of hearts – though what really went on there it would still take him years to grasp – he had any great interest in Irish, or any other kind of nationalism. What was behind it was an instinct, far from conscious, to cut himself off from the world of his cousins once for all. And the resolution to act on this impulse came directly from having just written his first poem, and, indirectly, from a kind of faith in himself and his confused instincts that the news of the Russian Revolution that he'd heard during his last term at an English public school, had given him.

A few days later H went to stay with his mother and stepfather who'd rather unexpectedly taken a house at the seaside. Henry still made intermittent attempts at family life and acting the father.

One morning in his ground-floor room that looked out, beyond the small yard, on to the branch line from Coleraine, H opened the paper and there was his letter. H was surprised and somewhat shamed at the satisfaction that seeing his name gave him, all the more as he knew that his poem, or another that he'd written since, had no chance of appearing in print, and it was only the political banalities, coupled with the family name, that had got him the publicity.

Later he met his stepfather walking back to the villa across the links from the golf club. 'Hello, Harry; I see you've a contribution in the paper.'

H realized by Henry's tone and the amused, quizzical glance he gave him, that Henry, unlike his own blood relations, was too much a man-of-the-world and a cynic (though this was a concept H couldn't have found the word for) to feel much real disapproval.

H said that yes, he had; and it was left at that as they walked together towards the row of houses overlooking the links. Next day he got a seat in the hired car taking his stepfather to Belfast as far as the crossroads in the wooded hollow of the Ballyboggy mill ponds (his mother was staying on at the villa).

The letter was mentioned, H thought rather grudgingly by Aunt Jenny, though for years he was to notice it, from time to time, put away, with newspaper clippings about her prize heifers, in the empty half of her silver cigarette case.

H had chosen to return to his aunt's house rather than wait with his mother till the end of the month at Rockport partly to avoid a chance meeting with his cousins and partly because of the books there. His first choice was of one at the farthest, darkest end of the top row in the case by the wall between the doors. Why he took out this one rather than another was partly because of its position on the shelf, partly because of the title, and had also something to do with the dark blue shade of the binding. Once open, the name of the author which he hadn't been able to read through the glass, Count Leo Tolstoy, and also the decorations on the fly leaf, seemed a confirmation of his instinct in taking it out.

For days H was absorbed in *Resurrection*. A great deal was obscure. He read on through pages that enclosed him in a solid, tangible kind of boredom that he didn't dream of escaping from by skipping. There was a dense, stuffy air about it, especially in the Russian courtroom between whose whitewashed walls he spent some days.

His participation became acute when the girl was being questioned. He was listening, listening, the rough wood of the bench under him, breathing the smell of warm iron from the stove, hearing the scratch of pens.

H had only a hazy idea of what the case was about. The girl whom the dead merchant had sent for to spend the night with him in a room at the inn was saying 'He'd been drinking heavily, your Honour.'

But it was the mention of the size of the ring that it seemed she was accused of having stolen (H couldn't be sure of the charge, there was too much to take in) that bowled him over.

'Why, the fellow must have been the size of a bull.'

'He was a big, heavy man, your Honour.'

The girl in her shabby thick jacket and head scarf and the huge, gold ring, passed from hand to hand in court, and whose weight he could feel in his own, were what H couldn't get over.

The early winter was very wet, there was rain all day; the old wooden sluices of the upper of the three mill ponds had to be fully drawn up to let the extra water through, and H was able to stay indoors and read or brood.

One dark afternoon, in a kind of trance, he took the mattress from his bed and dragged it up the narrow, uncarpeted stairway that led from just outside his bedroom door to a small attic where the zinc water tank was. Doubling it over he lay on the floor and hugged it to him. He was trying to make the mystery incarnate in calico stuffed with horsehair around which his arms just met. But the old What? How? and Where? were more insistent than ever. All he sensed was that the answer lay in the fold between the two halves of the unwieldy bundle that he could only keep from springing apart by a tight squeeze.

With difficulty keeping the mattress pressed together with one arm, he thrust his free hand into this cavity. But the touch of the coarse material through which wiry ends of hair pricked his fingers was not the revelation he was seeking.

One autumn morning, while no future plans for him had yet been mentioned, his aunt gave him a letter to take to her brother at Benvarden. Short and stocky like her, Major Geoffrey Quintillan was a favourite of his sister's. She had kept house for him until what she looked on as his ill-advised marriage. And it was largely to be near him when he was becoming more and more estranged from his wife that she had moved back to the North. And now she kept sending him notes which, H surmised, contained veiled criticisms of her sister-in-law.

As H rounded a corner near the gate of his uncle's estate the road dipped and disappeared into a shining level expanse that stretched far across the bogland in front of him. The water was shallow enough to ride his bicycle through as far as the entrance to the long drive that, bordered by laurels and raised above the excavated bog, was not flooded. Halfway along it the black plain of peat and heather emerged from the water, and, a little further on, where this gave way to cornfields, H ceased pedalling and came to a stop.

Still in the saddle, feet touching the ground, he was overcome by a sleepy lassitude in which he sensed that what he'd been seeking was going to be revealed. He was lifted on heavy strong wings off his bike and carried into the seclusion of the laurels that edged the avenue.

H bent forward, supporting himself with his forehead against a tree trunk, his back to the golden fields where, in the distance, women in coloured bonnets were gathering the reaped corn into stooks.

His hands, cool from the handlebars, had hold of the warm apparition from which, as in the story of Jacob and the angel that had haunted him in his Bible-reading days at school, he was wresting the secret.

O woman ... woman ... woman! Here she was at last in her shameful glory, his cousin Maida, the girl in *Resurrection* and, above all, the one who was to come. Amen! Alleluja!

By the time he seemed to himself to limp into his uncle's study (had the angel maimed him in a sinew as in the biblical story?) he realized that nothing had been finally resolved, that the answer had been postponed and the question sidetracked.

2

The arrangements for continuing his education were made rather suddenly. His mother took lodgings in a Dublin suburb for H and herself from where he went by tram daily to be prepared for the university entrance exam by a young tutor called Grimble.

H hadn't been in Dublin since the County Meath days when, sniffing up its impact through the smells of fresh horse dung from the waiting sidecars, the tang from the river or the brewery, he had stepped across the deep but narrow steamy chasm on to the Amiens Street station platform with a tight grip on his nurse's gloved hand.

Now it was the big yellow tramcars passing the windows of the lodging house that flashed and screeched the message that this was Dublin. Yet when he first made the trip in one of them, getting out at the corner of Grafton Street, he did no more than stand on the crowded pavement watching the tram disappear under a series of violet sparks around a big stone building and then, crossing the street, took the next one back in time for high tea served in their small sitting room.

It was the first time H had lived alone with his mother. He disliked many of her ways, especially her power of evasion, which among other things, had resulted in her delivering him over to Henry at a crucial and vulnerable period of his boyhood. Several other characteristics were hateful to him in her. Her lack, for instance, of a sense of decent privacy. She would sit and snatch the inside of her leg through her much-darned, grey cotton stockings in front of him with what he felt was a desire to bring him down to her own narrow strip of earth. There was also her lying, mostly to extricate her from awkward situations brought about by her incapacity to disagree with anyone, and that meant practically everyone more self-confident than she. He resented the weakness that was the cause of the lies, rather than their untruth, partly because he had to struggle against the same weakness in himself. He took pains to show his disbelief in many of her accounts of daily events, among them some which he knew were strictly factual. At the same time he was touched by the humility that made her in awe of the rest of the world, including himself. Above all he appreciated her store of patience, which communicated itself to him in her most instinctive gestures and movements, reflecting contentment with her lot. She was never nervy or waiting for a change for the better, as many people were. Sitting by the fire reading, knitting with her long awkward fingers, or merely keeping it up, she emanated a tranquillity that H was grateful for. He could share too in some of her delight in minute tasks (others were beyond her) as in the preparation of the evening cocoa for which there was a kettle on the hob of the coal fire watched over by her long before it came to the boil with quiet, if exaggerated, attention. The measuring out and mixing of the drinks was left to H, and one night he noticed that it was a different brand that she took from the cupboard. He spooned the paler powder into cups as she stooped over the kettle with a piece of cloth in her long hand, waiting while the steam had been lifting the lid for several moments before she dared take it from the fire.

After H took the first sip he knew that had he said that the flavour was too sweet or rich, she'd have agreed at once, making a face, and been vehement in her disgust, but when he commented favourably on the change, he sensed that her evident pleasure was because in this coinciding of taste was another proof of their kinship.

Taller than even H himself, and with a pallor that H related to scholarship, G. O. Grimble, whose initials were to H as much a part of his tutor as the pince-nez he wore, or his receding hair, taught him in a room with three beds in it in lodgings even more drab than those of H and his mother.

Unknown to H, his aunt had sent Grimble a few of the poems H had copied out for her some time ago. H, perceptive about what concerned him vitally, had noted the arrival of the long envelope with the university crest on the back and had later taken it from her desk and, extracting the accompanying letter, read that Grimble considered the poems showed neither talent nor the promise of any to come.

The verdict caused H one of the first violent sinkings of the heart that were to become so familiar. But he saw that the defeat was already causing a retreat not just from some hope of admiration but back into himself to force him in secret patience to perfect his gift for its own sake; it was pain that then, and later, made him discipline and temper his unruly and often capricious kind of imagination. Not that his use of this setback prevented H from scorning Grimble as somebody whose old-maidish precision was incapable of appreciating what he had written. Grimble's distinction, for H, was that he knew W. B. Yeats and other legendary figures such as Maud Gonne, to whom Yeats had written his love poems.

On an end-of-winter evening H and his mother met Aunt Jenny at the little suburban station down by the shore. She was coming to spend a week with them, and after her on to the platform stepped Grimble, his high forehead and pince-nez reflecting the platform gas lamps. He had met her at Amiens Street station and, besides her suitcase, was carrying a book whose title H's (at such times quick) eye read before they passed into the dusk of the street: *A Portrait of the Artist as a Young Man.* It turned out that Aunt Jenny had bought it at the Amiens Street bookstall on Grimble's advice while they'd waited for the suburban train.

At supper Grimble spoke of taking him and his aunt to one of George Russell's Sunday evenings.

The awaited moment came, and they climbed the steps to the front door that stood ajar, in spite of which Grimble knocked, not caring, H supposed, to walk in with two strangers in tow.

H waited nervously till a bulky figure with a pale, fleshy face, more than half-hidden by tousled hair and beard and steel-rimmed glasses, beamed at them and shepherded them into a room where several people were already gathered.

H's first contact was with the paintings on the walls. Unlike the pictures he was used to, framed and glazed and hung two or three to a wall with plenty of space between, these naked canvases crowded together side by side. At first H was aware of the profusion of misty blues and luminous shades of grey, depicting a dream landscape with hushed figures with faces lit by the glow of a cottage hearth or stooped over an oar on a mist-wreathed lake. In some, towering unseen over these bent forms was a being fringed by an aureole of lambent flames or plumes in yellow or violet brush-strokes, that struck H as false and invented.

12

When their host was introducing him, H heard him say, 'And this is Mr St George.' Sensitive to first impressions and tending at such moments to see omens everywhere, H concluded that, after all, such gatherings were not for him.

But a greater letdown was in store. Russell took a heavy book, the size and shape of an atlas, but bound in black, from the table where he'd evidently put it down before going to the front door to answer Grimble's knock. He was reading excerpts from it, pausing now and then to raise his shaggy head, in which the smallish eyes twinkled, and explain something to one of his guests.

At first H wasn't sure what the book contained. Only when Russell handed it, open at a page, to a fair young man, an English writer who had been living in Dublin to avoid the call-up, Grimble whispered to him, that H realized it was full of newspaper cuttings of reports of a lecture tour Russell had made to America.

Although Russell laughed, his lips pink and full against the surrounding hair, and might have been making light of the laudatory passages to amuse the company, H noted how he opened the big book at photographs of the large crowds assembled outside halls in Boston, Philadelphia, and other cities where he had appeared, and handed it around.

Could Russell really delight in being acclaimed by crowds in America? Where was the proud and lonely spirit H imagined all writers and painters as possessing?

Mrs Russell, her face seeming diminished by her husband's shaggy head whose skin, where exposed through the tangle of hair, was glistening, brought in a pot of tea. As cups and plates were handed round, a tall girl arrived all alone and Russell introduced her as Miss Gonne.

Was this the woman whom Yeats had loved and longed for hopelessly and for whom he had written the many lines that H knew by heart?

> Until the axle breaks
> That keeps the stars in their rounds,
> My breast shall not lie by the breast
> Of my beloved in sleep?

Having no firm grasp of time, H was ready to see Maud Gonne as still as young and beautiful as in the poems. He took the girl in as she sat talking to Russell's son, a youth whose hair fell in a fringe, like H's own, over his forehead. The young man had drawn up his chair towards her and was sitting just in front of her, his parted knees enclosing hers. Russell was telling her something, bending over her in his baggy suit with a plate of cakes, and she was smiling, the pronounced curve of her upper lip giving her an air of slight disdain.

Grimble accompanied H and Jenny to the centre of the city to see them on to the No. 7 tram that took them home. While they waited for it, H, standing behind the other two with his back to some area railings, heard them discussing the evening. His aunt was saying how struck she had been by Russell's lucid exposition of some political situation (Lloyd George was mentioned) of which H was ignorant. Then came what he'd been waiting to hear about since leaving the party.

'Yes, Maud Gonne's adopted daughter,' Grimble was saying, 'I believe the relationship is actually a little closer than that, though it wouldn't do for Madame to admit it in the nationalist circles in which she moves.'

3

H's mother gave up the lodgings and went to live with her sister in the North. And an arrangement was made through Grimble for H to lodge in the house of an acquaintance of his, a widow called Mrs Dennis.

Though H slept at the top of the tall, Georgian house, he was given a room in what once had been stables and coach house at the end of the back garden. Long and narrow, with a horseshoe-shaped window high up at one end, it was at last a place of his own. Added to this partial freedom was the relief that he need go no more for tutoring to Grimble.

What Grimble had told his aunt H could guess. As for Henry, since his heart attack, that H's mother had mentioned casually one evening at supper, he had broken his last links with wife and stepson and was living in a London hotel.

The books in the cream-painted bookcases in the big, pale first-floor sitting room, that Mrs Dennis called a salon, had brighter bindings than those of his aunt. The room itself with a grand piano and the formalized crucifixions and annunciations didn't appeal to him. He was homesick for the other, low-ceilinged drawing room even at noon full of dust and the glint of polished wood and small diamond-shaped panes of glass.

Here it was assumed because he wrote poetry he'd be glad to find himself in the bookish and musical swim. Leaving music out of it, for he thought he was tone-deaf, this wasn't his concern at all; it soon struck him that though he was obsessed by a few books, he didn't care for the literary milieu. The writers that Mrs Dennis spoke to him of, Zola, Stendhal, Henry James, he found it hard to read. Most of her friends, after a few attempts to engage him in conversation, ignored him.

But one young man, Dugdale, a dandyish medical student from South Africa with a small, alertly poised head, managed to penetrate H's slow-

14

wittedness. Instead of talking esoterically of books and pictures, he spoke of dress and hygiene, suggesting in his quick, nervous manner that H couldn't resent, that he take more care over these, and bringing H a cure for the acne from which he was suffering. This Dugdale himself applied one evening in the stable room to H's face, after removing his jacket and carefully turning back the cuffs of his silk shirt.

H was touched by this attentiveness and not very taken aback when Dugdale suggested, having invited him to tea at his flat, that H let him bathe him in the bathtub.

'Well no, I don't feel like a bath. Thanks all the same.'

'I'd like to show you the way to wash yourself properly which they don't teach you at an English public school.'

But though he liked Dugdale more than Mrs Dennis's other friends, H wasn't going to be pestered into becoming a daily bather and immaculate dresser any more than into joining a cultural clique.

H's lassitude increased; he gave up reading and lived for days and weeks at a time in his stable in idleness, lighting the gas ring in the winter afternoons and sitting for hours on end bent over the glowing crown which, when turned low, was set with ultrablue jewels in the dusk.

Lunch he ate with Mrs Dennis and her daughter; but he sucked his supper out of a tin of Nestlé's milk, punctured in two places, and afterwards washed his sticky mouth at the tap in the cobbled passageway between the stalls and dried it on a dirty handkerchief.

It was on one such evening that Dugdale called to take him to one of Maud Gonne's Tuesday at-homes. At first H declined, feeling no inclination to leave the seclusion of his retreat in spite of the haunting memory of the girl who had turned out to be Iseult. But in the end, not to disappoint Dugdale rather than with any feeling of enthusiasm, he said he would come, and went to spruce himself up at the tap in the dark stable, sluicing his semi-tranced face, wetting his hair, and brushing it out of his sleepy eyes.

The door of the house in St Stephen's Green was opened by a short stocky figure with whom Dugdale exchanged some words in French.

She wasn't what H had been expecting. Yet in his present state it was much the same to him whether this French cook with her broad sallow peasant face and hair caught in a scant knot at the back of her head, or Yeats's pearl-pale queen, had appeared. It was a state which was to overcome him through the years, which he defined to himself variously as one of passivity, idleness, acidity, or the spirit's sleep. At such times he spent most of the days on his bed, eating what came to hand, seldom shaving or even washing.

He followed Dugdale up the stairs and into the first-floor room where, instead of the gathering Dugdale had mentioned, there was only Iseult Gonne.

15

After H had been introduced, she told them that she and her mother, whom she called Moura, had only just returned from spending a few days in a remote Wicklow glen and, not having expected to be home in time for their Tuesday reception, had sent previous word to their usual guests.

H hoped Dugdale would say something about returning next week and depart. The tall girl in a sky-blue dress with a tasselled shawl had less impact on him than she had the evening at Russell's. He felt that nothing could burst the cocoon of disinterest and would have preferred to be back in his stall with Mrs Dennis's sleeping cat and the glow of the gas ring.

'Oh no, you mustn't go,' Iseult Gonne was saying, looking at H rather than Dugdale, 'Moura will be delighted to see you; she was regretting just now that we'd have no visitors.'

But H wondered whether Maud Gonne, if the news of their arrival that her daughter had gone to tell her really came as a pleasant surprise, wasn't in for a disappointment. Could Dugdale, for all his charm, which might not, H sensed, be quite the sort to go down here, keep up their end of the talk single-handedly? For he himself would be tongue-tied.

But when she sailed into the room in a long black dress whose line had an uninterrupted flow from widow's veil to foot, he saw that he needn't have worried. Her complete unselfconsciousness as, after shaking hands with them, she plunged straight into what she had on her mind: the planting of young apple trees in the plot that went with the Wicklow cottage she had just acquired, ruled out any awkward hiatus. She was praising Iseult for the help she'd been (surely not in the actual digging?), impulsively taking her daughter's hand and calling her belle animale.

From Maud Gonne, her single-minded obliviousness, and especially her effusiveness, H recoiled even further into himself. He felt his hair dry out and fall back over his brows, his toes turned awkwardly inward, and he knew that, if he wasn't careful, he'd drop a piece of cake or knock over a coffee cup.

Iseult's large brown eyes seemed to rove around the room, across the ceiling and back, before coming to rest on him, as if, for all her cosmopolitan upbringing, he was something strange to her.

As they were leaving, Maud Gonne (Madame MacBride was how Dugdale addressed her) looked right into H's eyes without, he thought, seeing him and invited, almost implored, them to come back one evening when the rest of the circle would be there.

Back in his stall H smelt the palm of his hand as he punctured a tin of milk and sniffed in the scent of powder left there by Iseult Gonne's as she'd said good-bye to him. It was a kind of contact between himself and the girl, the only sort which could then affect him: non-verbal, sensuous.

This tenuous link was still there the next day as he had purposely not

16

washed his hands, and caused the girl to loom up between his stable walls, apparitionlike in a kind of full-length tasselled halo of ultrablue.

Yet he wasn't anxious to present himself again, alone or with Dugdale, at the house on a Tuesday evening when she'd be in the midst of her mother's political friends.

It could wait; he felt patient and assured in spite of all that was unpropitious; his age, seventeen; his prospects, nil. He was emerging from the long bout of lassitude with, he imagined, new energies, and began attending Mrs Dennis's parties again. At one of these 'salons', H was attracted to a corner of the room by the gleam of red tabs on the shoulder of a khaki jacket. British uniforms weren't common in Dublin drawing rooms and an English staff officer was a rare bird indeed. Going over, with the excuse of handing around a tray, H found himself addressed by the young captain.

'Sit down a moment, if you don't mind being seen talking to me,' he said. 'I've no idea what your politics are, but you don't look as if you worried about what others thought.'

H smiled and took a seat beside him.

'I wouldn't be here at all if it wasn't for being a relative of our hostess. You're probably wondering why I came in uniform. Well, I'm not ashamed of it and I'm not going to try to find friends in Dublin, which is what I hope to do, by hiding what I am. But of course I feel rather out of it.'

H too had this instinct only to make friends with those from whom he hadn't to hide any part of himself, though by now he guessed how difficult this was going to be. It was the same obscure urge that had made him write the 'nationalist' letter to the paper.

Captain Richard Purcell, shortly to be demobilized, was spending his leave by getting to know the sort of people – writers, musicians, painters – that he planned to live among. Hearing from Polly Dennis that H was a poet (H imagined her mouth, dimpled at each corner, smiling its I'm-only-telling-you-what-he-told-me smile) he had probably thought that here he might find a younger brother. He told H that, though not in uniform, he'd attended a couple of Madame MacBride's soirées, as he called them.

Dick heard that the Gonnes had gone to stay in Wicklow and suggested that H and he made a walking trip through some of the glens ending up at their cottage, and, after studying maps and organizing the expedition with military precision, called for him one spring morning.

H had never before made a trip of this sort anywhere. It was the first in a widely spaced series of memorable trudges, pilgrimages, flights, and forced marches.

They took the road to the hills, Dick having exchanged his uniform for a tweed suit with a rucksack strapped on his back. H wore his one suit of

17

navy serge and carried an old attaché case of Henry's, imprinted with his stepfather's initials. All it contained was a packet of ginger biscuits and a volume of Yeats poems with a gilded pattern of leaves, scales, or hearts, embossed on the night-blue cover, with a long, tapering finger parting the golden thicket. No pyjamas, not even a toothbrush.

Windy roads up mountainsides festooned in coppery bracken and weighted with granite boulders. H accepted the discomfort as part of the hardships attendant on the quest, but he did not care for the scenery which his companion kept admiring. He was glad when midway through the day they dropped down into a sunny valley that Dick told him was Glendalough. They had another range to cross, climbing above the dark, forbidding lake, and through an endless-seeming expanse of wiry tufts of heather on the mountain ridge.

They descended into the sudden twilight of a narrow glen where a black silhouette of thorn tree beside a track whose white gravel gleamed ghostly, and Dick mentioned lead mines, lifted twisted arms out of the shoulder-high mist.

As they approached the farmhouse where the Gonnes were staying, the mountainsides drew closer together and the roar of waterfalls intensified the eeriness.

They were shown into a room lit by an oil lamp on a large table deep in litter among which H's embarrassed eye sheered off from a roll of toilet paper. A friend of the Gonnes, a small, plain woman, cleared a couple of chairs, saying, 'Pray sit down, Mr Ruark,' the old-fashioned turn of phrase coming helpfully into what H felt was the tense atmosphere produced by the arrival of Dick. And, indeed, quite soon Madame MacBride was denouncing, with agonized fervour, the British Empire.

Dick was not discomforted. He was admitting mistakes and injustices – in India, in Ireland, anywhere she liked to name – while all the time preserving an air of being on the enlightened side, the side of reason and decency. Madame MacBride was roused to an even intenser diatribe, but with what H began to grasp was a fury that had nothing personal in it.

He sensed in that moment, exhausted, sore-footed, disturbed by the presence of Iseult, that there were those who fastened on causes as an outlet for passions which weren't fulfilled through their senses and that they had a puritan lack of complexity in them that to him was alien.

Adroitly extricating himself from the one-way discussion, Dick suggested to Iseult that they take a walk before darkness fell. Left alone with the other two, H turned to Miss Molony, but Madame MacBride treated him gently and told him slightly ridiculous stories about Willie Yeats, as she called the poet.

When Dick returned with Iseult, he and H set off down the glen to the inn at the other end where they were to spend the night. The others came with them to a ford through the stream that flowed down the valley. Dick took off his shoes and socks before wading across but H, too tired and occupied by his thoughts, kept his on. As he squelched along beside his companion through the blackness, following the gleam of the gritty road, Dick told him of his walk with Iseult. They had sat down on a slab of rock. 'When I tried to kiss her she turned away her face.'

There was no guile in Dick. Nor was H sufficiently versed in the ways of love to feel the dangers that beset him. He was conscious neither of fear nor jealousy. Later, he told Iseult that all the way to the inn he'd felt a hand on his shoulder; a boyish romanticization.

Next morning they found the three women planting apple trees in a plot of stony ground beside the Gonnes' cottage. It was the last habitation in the glen and behind it boulders from the steep slopes on either side met in a drift that all but walled off the ascent to the pass beyond.

Shyly, but never doubting that she'd agree, he asked Iseult to come for a walk with him. They followed the track between the boulders towards the top of the pass, stopping halfway up at a rock against which they could rest and where H gave her the blue and gold book he'd brought and asked her to read out a poem. Iseult was only too ready to play the part he'd assigned her; he'd made a false move right at the start. He had placed his beloved in an unreal, Yeatsian world, instead of trying to take her into his which, however immature, was a very different one.

4

H made an exciting discovery. He could open the heavy old gates that led from the weed-grown yard at the back of the stables to the lane. By easing loose the rusty iron fastenings they creaked apart a couple of feet.

Almost as tall as he was, an astrakhan cap on her head and her hands in a muff, Iseult slipped through them one winter evening. As H turned up the gas ring, a black Persian cat crawled out of the hardly distinguishable muff in which she'd brought it; she told him that this was Minou about which Uncle Willie had written the poem. Again the magic of Yeats's shadowy world enclosing them before he had the strength to make her aware of his own.

Iseult talked more than H did, because she had more to tell him, having lived several years longer and in places like Paris and London, and because in the latter, while her mother (arrested in Ireland in the last year of the war) was in Holloway jail, she'd associated, as well as with Yeats, with writers about whom H was fascinated to hear.

'Moura's right about Uncle Willie, Luke' (she'd asked him what the initials on the brief-case that weren't his stood for and had chosen to call him by his second name), 'being mean and a snob. He was actually ready to accept a knighthood till we talked him out of it.

'He took the house in St Stephen's Green while Moura was in jail, getting it for a very small rent and then letting his pet rabbits eat up the plants in the back garden. Having just married a rich wife it wasn't as if he couldn't have paid her properly.'

But H, still thinking over the story of the knighthood, told her that there was a more vital reason for Yeats not accepting it than the nationalist one given by her mother.

'Dishonour is what becomes a poet, not titles or acclaim.'

She looked startled, not perhaps so much at what he'd said as at his expressing an opinion at all.

'What makes you say that, Luke?'

What indeed! Feelings and instincts were stirring to become thoughts so that he could express what was bursting to be said.

'A poet must be a countercurrent to the flow around him. That's what poetry is: the other way of feeling and looking at the world. There's the world as it is, I mean everything that keeps most people content and busy, becoming whatever they can – doctors, lawyers, politicians, priests, tradesmen, and so on, and as well, of course, husbands and wives with families. And however much they may disagree over things like politics or religion, they're all intent in keeping the whole thing intact and functioning.'

Was her proud upper lip curled in a smile? He didn't dare look at her but plunged on: 'If society honours the poet, he's tempted to say what those in authority expect from him. They wouldn't have honoured him otherwise, would they? But the poet will only come out with the sort of truth that it's his task to express when he lacks all honour and acclaim. Oh no, no honours, no prizes, or he's lost!'

'And you, Luke? If a delegation were to arrive here in the stable with some honour to confer on you, what would you do?'

H laughed; what, give him a prize for the poems that Grimble had returned to Aunt Jenny with the remark in his disagreeable cerebral script, thin as his receding hair and particularly revolting to H in the initials by which he signed the letter, that they were totally without talent!

'I'd be afraid to leave them alone while I filled the kettle at the tap to make them tea in case they changed their choice of candidate while I was out of the room.'

Was this true? He thought he'd given himself, with his extreme attitudes that she might think naïve and callow, away too naïvely just now and wanted to make a joke of it.

They went for walks in the hills, taking a tram to its southern terminus and walking out through dingy streets in one of which Iseult would leave him to slip into a huckster's and emerge with a small flat bottle of whiskey that took him by surprise. It kept out the cold, she told him, preventing her fingers turning yellowish blue as he'd seen them do on their first winter walk into the hills.

Coming back late one night into the city in a gale that was setting the shop signs wildly swinging and the branches creaking above the canal, she started to run, face raised to the stars and the small, torn clouds, and hair streaming.

He kept hold of her hand, drawn after her, afraid of her being blown away across the canal, or into it, though it was obvious that he was the less adroit one.

He didn't like the wind and couldn't exult in it. He liked best to have stillness around him with nothing moving and the shadows motionless, and her delight in the storm took her from him.

As they parted outside her mother's house she told him, 'Did you think I was running away from you, Luke? But it won't be me who'll do that. I'm the willow rooted on the river bank and you're the black swan gliding past.'

Another night in a clearing of pine forest above the city whose distant lights swarmed among the trees like shining bees, they sat on a felled trunk and talked. When it became too cold to stay there longer and they did not want to return to Dublin and part, they knocked at the door of the forester's cottage.

The son of the house offered Iseult the spare room (his parents had retired) but she preferred to stay with H in the kitchen by the log fire which the young man told them they could keep burning all night.

When they were settled on a rug on the stone hearth, she gave him what was left in the small whiskey bottle to finish, and although already too hot from the fire, he gulped it down and laid his head on her thigh. He felt her move her leg as if she didn't want it there, but she said she'd undo her suspender which must be hurting his cheek.

Undoing stockings was the start of things he didn't dare think of, at least in connection with her. How could he try to leap across the gulf between his body and hers without fatal disaster?

Her face reflected the magic twilight of Yeats's poems, proud, pure, and, he thought, contemptuous of the flesh with its concrete and detailed functions and urges. That might come from his having enshrined her from the first in the kind of poetry which, though it charmed and beguiled, had nothing vital to say to him.

To make the decisive move was impossible. Not only didn't he know how she'd take it, but he lacked the incentive of previous experience or any reliable knowledge of the kind of sensation he was seeking. He didn't even know the exact location of the goal, the thought of which when he tried to define it appalled rather than roused him.

The moment passed and, after some desultory talk, H gave her a peck of a good-night kiss.

Mrs Dennis came out to his stall, midway through the morning to tell him that Madame MacBride had been around inquiring for her 'niece'. She pronounced the word with distaste, for, as H knew, the Gonnes and everything to do with them were hateful to her.

After this the gates of the stable yard were padlocked and H had to visit Iseult at her mother's house (though Mrs Dennis had told him he was welcome to entertain his friends in her dining room). They were alone together most of the time as Madame was constantly out attending some meeting or other, with only Josephine coming shuffling in in her long skirt with the tea tray and in her Normand patois seeming to tease Iseult about having so callow a boy as a lover.

Her mother would sail in her black robes from some political committee meeting or other and stoop down to put her arms around Iseult and call her belle animale and, oblivious of H, enthuse over her in a manner he'd never seen anyone adopt before. Was it an act? Trapped in his own shy reserves he couldn't make it out.

Then she would start telling them about the rise of national sentiment throughout the country or of the amount of American help coming in, in dollars and also in parcels of clothing for the refugees from the North. H was equally ill at ease whether Madame was caressing Iseult or talking in her impassioned way about Ireland.

He didn't like her easy assumption of the absolute rightness and moral purity of the nationalist cause. His own feelings were confused. He honoured the 1916 men, as he did the Russians, particularly the poets Essenin and Mayakovsky (of whom he'd heard but hadn't yet read) as revolutionaries and, above all, as having suffered calumny and derision.

What really attracted him were not the doings of patriots but the reports of certain crimes he read in the papers. He delighted in hearing of riots, no matter where, in civil disturbances, even in bank robberies; also in assassinations and anything that diminished or threw doubt on authority. He hardly distinguished revolutionary acts from those committed by criminals as long as the result was like that of a stone dropped into a mill pond. He imagined the ripples of unease that must disturb the complacency, which was what he distrusted most, that stagnated in the minds of many people, especially those held in high esteem in their own closed circles.

'Iseult hasn't a father; you know that, don't you, Luke?' her mother told him one day.

H nodded, thinking of his own father, whose death shortly after H's birth, was shrouded in shame and mystery. This confiding in him he took as a sign that she had come to accept his and her daughter's relationship. Not that he and Iseult had yet spoken of marriage. He wasn't yet eighteen and had only the erratic allowance that his mother sent him, a pound or two at a time, in her letters. Of course, as well as that, there was whatever she paid Mrs Dennis for his rooms and midday meal.

As marriage appeared, a first small cloud on their horizon, heralding change, she mentioned some past indiscretion of hers in London which didn't register with him because he still hadn't become sensually aware of her and also because the sort of delinquencies that occupied his thoughts were of a different kind.

London kept coming up in their talk until it became clear that it was to be the place to which they would go to start living together.

In the end the arrangements were made with surprising ease and even a kind of casualness. H told his mother he was going to England for a time and asked her to send him while there the equivalent of what she was paying Mrs Dennis plus his indefinite allowance. And one day Iseult said, 'Moura will be out all afternoon tomorrow, so come for my suitcases and later I'll slip out and you can meet me with them at the boat.' She added that he could follow her the following night.

H didn't ask why. He left it all to her, though if she was pretending to go to London on her own, why the secrecy of departure? Was it a trip from which they'd return in a week or two? He wasn't quite sure and he didn't inquire. She had said 'suitcases' in the plural, but perhaps she didn't want to have it all cut-and-dried until she saw how it was going to work.

5

After the growing sense of expectation reflected back at him from the passing rows of houses and intensified at each window that was lit in the dawning greyness, came the shock of the final halt in the great, shadowy, echoing cave of Euston station.

H, dragging the half-empty heavy leather suitcase that had been a last-minute present from his mother, walked along the platform breathing the steamy, sooty air and looking for the Burne-Jones apparition amid the harsh light and shadow.

The stream of passengers diminished to a trickle and there wasn't a single figure facing his way. He was alone with the red vans into which mail bags were being loaded. He left the station and crossed the court to the big hotel, inquiring at the reception desk first for Miss Gonne, and then Mrs Ruark, but the clerk told him that neither lady was staying there.

H hurried back to the platform at which he'd arrived. A grim, deserted expanse, the lamps fading into the smoky fringe of day. He started to explore the rest of the station. In the main hall he put down the suitcase, itself heavier than its meagre contents, to ease his arm, and as he straightened up his heart leapt before his eyes had taken in the tall girl in the black oilskin, her oval face even paler than he remembered it.

He hardly understood what she was saying about having overslept because with her beside him and the whole day in front of them, and the unknown city just beyond the courtyard, the panic of the previous ten minutes when an answer to her absence had been his most crucial need was erased and entirely forgotten.

London, it seemed, was crowded with demobilized soldiers and with visitors still enjoying the easing of war restrictions, and the proprietress of the small hotel where Iseult had spent the night told them that H would have to share a room with a Captain Angus, and H foresaw that it was another of those incidental names he'd remember all his life.

The sensation of London was flowing over him from the wet, black shine of the wide roadway smelling of coal smoke and petrol and traversed by red buses displaying names of destinations that made him feel faint with the promise of strange places, each with a different kind of excitement, off-shoots of the central heart whose throbbing his nerves were interpreting as the distant roar of the ocean of life. And mixed with this mystery of place was one of time, the sense of unlimited duration, not in its nightmare aspect as had been revealed to him at school but in the blessed sense of there being no hour of the day when they would go their separate ways.

They wandered through a city-space of yellow plaster, by rows of Doric pillars, past deep, railed areas bridged by pale, scrubbed stone steps, lingering by windows with cards in them of rooms to let. They ate a frugal meal in the tiled electric gleam of an A B C café, and towards late afternoon were in Chelsea where Iseult had lived with her mother on first coming to London from Paris.

They dropped blissfully into a cinema and afterwards, instead of the usual sobering letdown, H had the thrill of emerging into a street (the King's Road) stranger than the film, and the impact of where they were, forgotten for a couple of hours, struck him all over again.

Most crucial of all the moments of that day was one in the evening back in Iseult's room at their hotel. Sitting at the dressing table, brushing her hair, she turned her head and suggested that he go out and fetch them supper from a fish-and-chip shop, ending with, 'Will you, darling?'

It was the first time the endearment had been spoken between them and what it signified he wasn't sure; it could be any of the miracles that he felt were about to be performed by them. It evoked for him intimacies accompanying the approach of night, not this one, but others soon to come, and in fact, next day they moved to a furnished room of their own at ten shillings a week over a small grocer's shop off Tottenham Court Road. The entrance was through makeshift double doors that looked as if they were discarded scenery from the Scala Theatre whose stage door H noticed further up Tottenham Street, with panels papered over to look like stained glass. The long, narrow room at the top of a narrow stairs, with the single bed at one end, was the most exciting and at the same time disturbing sight he'd ever laid eyes on.

For the rest of the day they were constantly on buses going from one part of the city to another, while Iseult showed him the places where she'd lived and worked (as a translator) and visiting a couple of tea shops (one on Chelsea Embankment called the Blue Cockatoo, the other in a back street off Euston Road near the house W. B. Yeats had lent her), delaying, he felt, the crucial moment of returning to the single room.

On the first of the crowded buses on which he got a seat beside her, and after gazing silently out at the passing scene for most of that particular journey, he told her, 'I can sleep on the floor.'

'That's not necessary, darling.'

Not necessary ... not necessary ... the words repeated themselves to him as they got out, strolled down a side street and entered a baker's where the woman proprietor greeted Iseult and, with a glance at himself, asked after the gentleman with the beard.

They only returned to the room when it was time to go to bed and H went out again almost at once while Iseult undressed. He walked round and round the block, one side bounded by Charlotte Street, past the shut-up Scala Theatre, aware of peculiar strains and stresses in his body (that next day turned to muscular aches), glancing up at the small lit window above the ramshackle double doors each time he passed the corner grocer's shop.

When at last he entered their room Iseult was in bed in her nightdress, her hair soft and loose over the pillow. H undressed quickly in the dark and got in beside her. He didn't dare put his arms round her flimsily clad body but lay frozen with desire so unexpected and extraordinary that it absorbed him without a need to go beyond the immediate experience.

In the morning she went to their landlady's kitchen and returned with tea, a tin of condensed milk, and a piece of Jewish bread, doughy and filled with marzipan, for which delicacies she'd been down through the back of the shop. The breakfast had a rich, exotic flavour on his tongue that merged with the other strange and intense sensations.

In the evenings they ate in a restaurant around the corner (how many darkly gleaming, rainy corners there now were, each revealing new vistas!) in Charlotte Street. Sitting at a table in a corner of the Cuisine Bourgeoise Iseult told him, to the background noise of orders shouted down the hatch in a seemingly exasperated French, about her time in the Pyrénées, in Paris, and in Normandy. Of Yeats sitting beside her in the villa at the sea, kissing her and asking her to marry him, of Wyndham Lewis coming by mistake into her room one night in the flat she'd shared with a girl friend of his here in London, and of other writers, several of whom, besides Yeats, had wanted to marry her.

H didn't ask her why she had chosen a boy like himself with nothing to recommend him, immersed in his separate dream, idle, negatively disposed towards her mother (and to much else besides that she held in esteem, though this might yet not be apparent), poor, whose father had died of delirium tremens and whose own mental capabilities had been seriously questioned by most of the masters at his various schools.

One night back in their room from the Cuisine Bourgeoise and a visit to a tiny dark cinema in Tottenham Court Road where a serial called *Elmo the Mighty* was being shown (the incredible ordeals of whose hero were for long after associated for H with his own subsequent distress) came the revelation that he had sensed the others leading up to. Iseult told him that while alone in Yeats's house with Josephine in the alleyway she'd taken him to see, she had become the mistress of the poet Ezra Pound.

Catching sight of his face, she said, 'But, Luke, I told you this long ago.'

She had told him something that he had failed to take in because it had been beyond his imaginative grasp at the time. How could he have understood that she, the hem of whose tasselled blue dress he hadn't dared touch, had gone through all the stripping, the shameful intimate postures that were part of coupling with a man, and which he still wasn't quite clear about.

He didn't want her to see his shock, but he couldn't help asking useless questions, the answer to each of which supplied a further painful detail to the picture that haunted him.

Without telling her where he was going he went out and spent hours over cups of coffee in cafés in Charing Cross Road that stayed open most of the night. He tried to sink into that state of apparent lassitude and apathy that overcame him involuntarily at times and during which his feelings in regard to the rest of the world became less acute. At such times he lost both his fears and his power of intense delight, in an obscure sense that nothing mattered except the spirit asleep (or hiding) within him that neither fortune nor misfortune could touch.

At last H went back. As he turned the corner of the dingy side street he caught a glimpse of white at the small dark window and guessed she'd been watching for him. He got into bed with her and she put her arms around him without asking where he'd been. He was being dragged down into the fevers of boyhood he'd thought were gone for good. Now there was nobody to turn to, as to his nurse, Weg, long ago in all his childhood miseries for comfort, except to her who was inflicting the pain.

He had the urgent need to destroy the image of her inviolability, and thus balance her own shameless discarding of it, it now being a source of anguish. To erase his dream of her, with its foolish fantasy of stripping away the veils one by one in fear and trembling, he must achieve the direct, brute act she'd shared as a matter of course with someone else (how many times a night?).

But inches were miles in the tricky geography of the body; where tenderness and loving trust would have guided him to the healing entrance, anguished desire, combined with Iseult's passivity in the face of his unhappy fumblings, prevented him. He became terrified of remaining outside with his hurt, unadmitted to the ravished sanctuary.

At last he lay quiet and started putting importunate questions to her in an even more futile attempt to exteriorize his pain by a detailed description of what caused it. She told him not only about herself and Pound, but to satisfy his curiosity or, by making fun of sex, to diminish its importance, about what she'd come across of it as an observer.

It now struck him she looked on sex as a kind of infirmity, the stranger symptoms of which it amused her to describe to him.

There was the case of her French father, Millevoye, who had tried to persuade her mother, with fantasies about her conceiving an Irish patriot hero, to let him make love to her before the altar of Joan of Arc in a Paris church whose sacristan he had bribed. There were stories of the libidinous ways of writers and painters she'd known in Paris and here in London which she'd observed from afar. But he brought her back to touch the wound.

'Did you have the rapture with Pound?'

'I've told you.'

'Tell me again.'

'No. I did not.'

All the talk about what he still hadn't experienced obsessed them both in their different ways, and the topic of sex was constantly being discussed.

Iseult would come back with their breakfast tray from the kitchen with

Mrs Abraham's complaints about the girl who had the room at the top of a second crooked stairway from theirs. 'Though they've forbidden her to bring Negroes to the house, she can't give them up. There's something about the way they're made that prolongs the act beyond the few seconds it lasts with white men.'

H was always the one being enlightened, and although the fact of her greater experience was horrible to him, he could not forgo making the most of it.

Her troubled eyes roamed over his face as once they had over the walls and ceiling of her mother's room before meeting his. But it wasn't only his unhappiness that worried her. She was concerned over the letters she'd been getting from Helen Molony telling her how hurt and disconsolate her mother was, and suggesting they return to Ireland.

'But we're happy here.'

Happy! Why was he saying what was obviously untrue? In the hope that in another few days all would be resolved? Or in a kind of perversity of desperation?

'Moura thinks we should get married.'

With him: the respected public ceremonial; with Pound: the private secrets!

H was shivering as they left the train at Westland Row and crossed the street to a café for breakfast. He'd never been so cold before. He hadn't taken note of things like the weather, food, or clothes. Was he, because of the blow to his pride, losing his natural invulnerability?

They took a train on to a seaside village where H's mother was staying. At the whitewashed Post Office she had taken a room for them with a view on the still wintry-looking shore, over sand flats through which a river cut its narrow, winding way seawards from under the railway viaduct.

His mother accepted H's coming marriage as she accepted everything that required resolution to oppose. Not that, he supposed, she had, in any case, anything against the idea. She got on with Iseult from the start, because, H thought, they were basically so far apart that there were no possible points of serious friction. Yet he saw they had their unworldliness in common, and when over minor household matters or in appreciation of sea and country-side, they appeared to agree, the illusionary contact seemed the fuller for being reached over such an intervening distance. When Helen Molony arrived as an emissary from Madame MacBride, the sensible manner (as if it was the most natural thing in the world) in which she discussed the wedding, completely won Libby Clements over.

Strolling by the winter sea, eating fat mutton chops by the fire in the overupholstered sitting room, or up in their room with its holy pictures and fake homely air that their London eyrie had never had, H was aghast at what was taking shape out of the dream in which they'd started.

Twice a week they went to Dublin, Iseult to see her mother and H to receive 'instructions' from a priest, a friend of the latter's.

Father Monaghan, handsome, with an ascetic brown face, beautifully brushed, white hair, in his long soutane, was suave and easygoing. It was soon understood between them that H was not an apt pupil, especially for the sort of teaching that treated religion as a cut-and-dried subject, with hard-and-fast rules to be meekly memorized.

When he said something like this to Iseult she screwed up her eyes behind the smoke of her cigarette (she was smoking more and more) and told him that it was presumptuous to talk like that of the theology in which the great saints and mystics had found their inspiration.

Her introduction of the mystics silenced him. As did her occasional mention of classics he hadn't read. All the same he wasn't satisfied.

On one of the last evenings before the wedding H and Iseult took a walk after supper along the road inland. They crossed some fields to a wood above the river. H saw this as the last chance they had to become lovers, and for him to taste the forbidden delight she'd bestowed on Pound. Neither the part undressing in the cold, nor the bed of damp leaves helped to arouse in him the blind urge that he needed to carry it through. As for Iseult, although she complied, she was more passive than ever, and H soon saw it was better to give up the clumsy attempt.

At the altar rails of a side chapel of the small church with its genteel air of good taste (Father Monaghan's parish was a wealthy one) H knelt beside Iseult. His Aunt Jenny was there with his mother, as well as Madame MacBride, looking more tragic than ever in her widow's veil and robes as she'd shaken hands with him, Helen Molony, who, in a few whispered words, somewhat reassured H by seeming to treat the ceremony as a piece of church bureaucracy not worth making an issue of by refusing to submit to, and an old woman who had hobbled in on a stick and taken a seat in one of the pews, someone H had never seen before.

A plump sacristan strutted about, setting vessels on a side table, sketchily genuflecting as he passed in front of the tabernacle with, H thought, the air of easy familiarity with which one greets an old acquaintance in the street.

H felt unease and distaste. Nothing in the ceremony had a bearing on the situation between Iseult and himself. It seemed put on for the sake of the relatives who would now recognize the relationship, whether they privately approved or not, as legitimized and one of those things which were to be accepted because established by custom and common consent.

They went alone to Helen Molony's room not far away for tea and cakes, and later in the day travelled by train and sidecar to the ugly, two-storeyed little house whose four windows all looked down the narrow, boulder-strewn glen to which spring hadn't yet penetrated.

Taking Iseult in his arms the first night there, H became aware that what all previous probings hadn't achieved was now happening. What hadn't before seemed to belong anywhere in the puzzle slipped into place, and it was suddenly perfectly simple. There was no getting used to it; he had to make sure at odd hours of the day the knack hadn't been lost and that it still worked. Iseult stayed in bed all morning with her paperbacked French novels and cigarettes while he made a fire downstairs, got breakfast, brought in water and turf, and made short excursions into the surrounding wilderness of bracken and stone. Clambering among the boulders with the box of matches he'd brought with him, he set fire to the gorse bushes. The dry, sharp crackle of the flames hidden in the heart of the thick spiky, sheep-cropped bushes, and the immense cloud of smoke drifting down the glen was his way of celebrating his coming to manhood and making a burnt offering to the great sensual spirit that had at last revealed to him its secrets.

It was in the night that their disagreements usually started. Ostensibly these were over Irish nationalism, the Church, or literature. As a newcomer to these things, H had to listen to her with patience. As far as the first two went, he felt her views reflected her mother's. By saying that an obsession with politics was a substitute for fulfilment in more complex and difficult activities, he was trying to detach her from her apparent dependence. He wanted to prove that having failed in her relationship to her three men (Yeats, Millevoye, and, later MacBride) her mother found in nationalist passion an emotion to fill the void.

Iseult's erudition when it came to the mystics irked him because she seemed to use it to support the sham pieties of others. But the violence of his own feelings in all this shocked and bewildered him. Only when it came to literature were their discussions calmer; if they still often disagreed, H was ready to listen with more patience. But as had happened with Mrs Dennis and others, when she spoke enthusiastically of books he didn't know, it put him off them. He even misinterpreted what she said and imagined them as either long and dull or plain lurid. Thus he was convinced that *The Brothers Karamazov* was a gloomy, unlikely fantasy about Siamese twins who, on a moor at night during a violent storm, are separated by lightning.

H would get out of bed and rush out of the house and across the plank footbridge over the stream in the pitch blackness that almost always shrouded the glen. In the outhouse on the other side he threw himself on a pile of bracken, used for bedding for cattle, in his pyjamas. There he was overcome by bouts of sobbing.

30

He had hung the plaster cast of a heron he'd made in art class – the only one at which he'd shone – at Rugby School, on their bedroom wall. He wasn't sure why he prized it as much as he did unless as a tangible reassurance from those years of failure. In the midst of one of their quarrels Iseult took it down and held it in her raised hand, hurt by one of his jibes, if jibes they were rather than blind, instinctive rejections of what she saw as enlightened and above discussion.

Break it, H willed her, and that will be the end, even if it comes sooner than expected, that we both foresaw (had they foreseen anything of the sort?). It will undo, in a flash of despair, whatever validity the marriage ceremony had. But the moment she sent it crashing to the floor he was beside himself with fury: it seemed to him she had deliberately destroyed a precious part of himself. He had pulled her to the floor and was kneeling beside her, about to strike her, but instead got up and rushed down to the kitchen for the paraffin tin.

Locked into the second upstairs room, he dragged her dresses from the wardrobe, threw them on the floor, poured paraffin over them and set them on fire. The top garment, made of a stiff tapestry material, started to smoulder and char. Directly beneath was the sky-blue dress and tasselled shawl she had worn the night that Dugdale had taken him to her house.

Leaving the dresses to burn, H ran out through the orchard of young apple trees and started setting light to the gorse bushes. Smoke gathered and drifted down the glen into which the sun, though it was a clear midmorning, hadn't yet shone. At last he leaned, exhausted, by a boulder at the stream in the dark pall that was blotting out the few distant dwellings.

After an hour or so Iseult loomed through the lingering smoke in his old camel-hair dressing gown (the one he'd been wearing that evening in the school sanatorium when he'd heard the news of the Russian Revolution) and taking him by the hand, led him, without a word, back to the house.

Clinging together, sobbing, kissing, sighing, whispering repentances, in a weariness of bliss, getting up to make sure the fire in the next room was out, as well as the other, more spectacular one, padding back to more love and forgiveness, the rest of the morning and afternoon passed in a moist, healing glow of reconciliation.

Trembling and humble, H dressed quickly and made a sketchy attempt at clearing up while Iseult washed in a bucket of cold water (the kitchen fire was out and the thought of the additional smell of smoke attendant on lighting it was too much for them). They embraced once more, locked the outer door, and started on the nine or ten miles walk to the town where they could get the evening train to Dublin.

They tramped down the white-gravel track past the ruined stone cottages of the former workers in the lead mines to the roar of waterfalls cascading from the steep hills on either side. Stopping for Iseult to hitch up a stocking, H saw two pricks of red in the shadowed flesh under her eyes where tiny blood vessels had burst.

They missed the train and had to stay the night at a hotel whose upper floor looked as if it had been abandoned and the derelict room at one end of it unlocked for them after remaining for years uninhabited. But the pub below was noisy long after they were in their damp bed. It was there, H was convinced, and not, as was far more likely, at the cottage in the glen that Iseult conceived.

6

After a couple of days at the house in St Stephen's Green, they moved to a furnished flat at the top of a Georgian house.

In the mornings, before they were dressed, they started playing card games that so absorbed them that at midday or later they were still shuffling and dealing, discarding and taking the number of substitutes allowed from the pack, with Iseult stubbing out her cigarette butts on the underside of the table to which they clung out of sight like stale-smelling limpets.

After spending a few nights in the big bedroom without making the bed, they moved to the small one and slept there till the clothes from that bed too were beyond a simple pulling over them when they got into it, and there was nothing for it but the general straightening up that Iseult had such an aversion to. Once when they had an early afternoon caller H had to ask the lady to sit out on the landing because Iseult was on the sofa in the sitting room, still in her nightdress, the cards beside her.

She was often at her mother's and sometimes she told H the things that Madame MacBride had said about him, laughing them off as her mother's failure to fit him into her over-simplified world.

His mother-in-law had said to Iseult that, at the time of the family conferences preceding their marriage, his Quintillan relations, who had come down from the North, had seemed to regard him as an imbecile. She also suggested, when there was a recurrence of the rash that Noel Dugdale had earlier cured, that he might be suffering from second-degree syphilis.

When the roar of the Black-and-Tan lorries were filling the nights and even in their backwater of a street there was hammering with rifle butts on the doors at night, Iseult told him she was pregnant and started paying regular visits to a well-known gynaecologist, a friend of her mother's. Sometimes she didn't keep her appointment because they couldn't be sure that the examination mightn't reveal that they'd made love that afternoon and that her mother, getting to hear of it, would regard it as a further sign of his degeneracy.

It seemed to H they were being hemmed in on all sides, by his mother-in-law and her wide circle of admiring acquaintances (one of whom, the lady he'd had to keep out on the landing when she'd visited them, lived in the same house and, he imagined, made her reports), by the curfew lately imposed on the city, and by some of their own habits such as the card playing and Iseult's general neglect of the flat, which he occasionally tried to straighten out in her absence.

They bought a tiny chess set with flat leather pieces that slipped into slits in a leather board that folded like a pocket book. Then, instead of cards in the morning, they played chess late into the night till, sometimes, when Iseult, her front beginning to bulge, half-undressed but too absorbed to go to bed, passed across the window to fetch herself one of the oranges she'd taken to devouring between cigarettes, they noticed they'd forgotten to draw the curtains.

When they'd fallen a couple of months in arrears with the rent Iseult remembered the pearl necklace that had been taken from the bank where, with other Quintillan heirlooms, it had lain for years and given to her, with Aunt Jenny's consent, at the time of their wedding. She had seldom worn it and she suggested that H should see about selling it.

They took it from the tissue paper and examined it for the first time on top of the grand piano (deep in dust), admiring the cunningly graded pearls, minute on each side of the gold clasp, swelling to the size of mistletoe berries round the loop till, at the bottom, hung the five or six in fully ripened bloom.

H took it to a shop in Grafton Street where he was offered thirty pounds for it and came home to consult Iseult who was sure they should get more.

'Go back and say you won't take less than forty, then they'll offer thirty-five and we'll end by getting thirty-seven pounds ten.'

H saw she would have haggled over it at the shop while preserving her cool, rather disdainful, composure, in the way that she could relate intimacies about her father or Yeats; there was also an anecdote about how her stepfather, John MacBride, had made advances to her as a child, with the same detached air. Whereas he realized he couldn't argue over money or talk of sex without personal involvement. But in one respect Iseult *was* self-conscious. She didn't like to display her pregnancy, and went out as little as she could.

H tried another shop where he was offered less. He then suggested that he take it to London and sell it there where he was sure they'd give him as much more as wouldn't only cover the cost of the trip, but leave them with something above the price they'd been offered. Recalling the outline of the great commercial blocks along the north sweep of the Thames as he'd seen them from Waterloo Bridge one evening, he, to whom money was still an unfamiliar commodity, was sure that there, at the financial heart of the world, the necklace would fetch its proper price.

Iseult agreed at once. She was even glad, he thought, of the respite, and would stay with her mother for the few days he was away.

H left the small suitcase of Iseult's in the station cloakroom at Euston, and while he had breakfast at Lyons was heartened to find in the newspapers he'd bought advertisements offering the highest prices for jewelry. It seemed that he'd been right in supposing there was a lively market here for such wares as the one he'd brought, and before the shops opened he was in the neighbourhood of Bond Street, outside one of the premises whose addresses he'd noted down.

By ten o'clock he had sold the necklace in a small back room containing a large, green-painted safe with brass fittings and a table with a baize top to it (a material he hadn't set eyes on since pulling down the articulated lid of his desk at Rugby for the last time) to a Jew in black jacket and grey, striped trousers. Returning from an outer office with a typed receipt which he asked H to sign, the dealer had laid eight five-pound notes and eight single ones on the green cloth.

H's next call was at a post office where he sent Iseult a money order for forty pounds. On the bus back to Euston for the suitcase he was exhilarated at the first business transaction he'd ever embarked on turning out so well. He made several calculations, subtracting the three or four pounds he'd spent on his fare, breakfast, buses, etc., from the sum he had sent Iseult, getting mixed up, but concluding that she'd still have more than they'd been offered in Dublin. With what remained he was going to do what had all along been at the back of his mind: spend a few days in London.

He took a large unfurnished front room in Charlotte Street, towards the Fitzroy Square end, whose attraction for him was that, leaning out of the window at night, he could see the reddish glow from behind the curtains of the Tour Eiffel restaurant at the other end, paying a week's rent in advance. He bought a big secondhand trestle table and with paint and brushes from Woolworth in Tottenham Court Road painted the deal top, which with a camp bed and a folding canvas chair was all the furniture he could afford, with a large golden star in the centre. That night he went to the Coliseum where Varvara Polenskaya was dancing in a ballet called *The Life and Death of a Poet.*

He shrank from the burst of applause that greeted the ballerina as she came running, with short steps, on the tiny stilts of her toes, on to the stage. As well as the darkness of the stalls, he needed absolute silence to take it all in. The short ballet was a new one to the music of Percy Grainger (the details, down to the names of advertisers in the programme were imprinted on H's mind) and the dancing of Polikov and Polenskaya, poet and muse, was a strictly formalized mime. The disciplined rhythm imposed on the uprush of sensuous magic seemed familiar to him, the poetry of Keats, Shelley, and the later Yeats, made flesh.

The image of Polenskaya's distance-blurred face and ebony head, a pale petal in the downward-opened sheath of black, and the stiff wreath of ballet skirt, tilting, spinning, rising, and sinking to the current rushing upwards from the charged, blocked toes of her shoes, cast a spell on H.

Late that night, at the black-topped trestle table, with the gold star in the centre, long after the illuminated sign on a warehouse opposite had switched itself off, he wrote a poem (his first in over a year):

> You were a young fountain, a mad bird
> And half a woman, a secret overheard
> In a dark forest,
> Setting the trees alive, the leaves astir.
> You were my joy, my sorrowful you were!

In the morning he went to the post office from which he'd sent Iseult the money order and, before putting what he'd written, with his name added, in the stamped envelope he'd bought, read it over.

Bad and good. Immature, yes; ungrammatic, possibly, but the words were limpid enough to let the light of his imagination through.

He wrote 'Varvara Polenskaya, Coliseum Theatre, St Martin's Lane,' on the envelope, but he didn't post it. He returned to his room and composed another, somewhat longer poem that ended:

> When men applaud another woman and I long
> For you again, will I not think how once
> I dreaded every night you danced because
> Your movements were entanglement to me?
> And of your flower-like name on every mouth
> When I was still too young to value youth
> And thought: In time, in time a way will come.

Trembling, but never doubting something would come of what he was embarking on, he let the envelope fall through the slit in the pillar-box in Charlotte Street.

H returned that night to the theatre and again the following afternoon, a

Saturday. Afterwards he went around by the alleyway to the stage door and asked to see Polenskaya, handing the doorman a slip with 'Luke Ruark' written on it. The man returned and (wonder of wonders! and yet not so wonderful, for he'd known that she would see him) said, 'This way, sir.'

Nor did H wonder what the ballerina would make of the clumsy youth with a fringe of burnished hair like a hawk's wing folded low on one side of his forehead. And as he'd surmised, she seemed to take him for granted, having no doubt had stranger visitors in the course of her fabulous career.

Besides her dresser, there was somebody else in the room, an elderly, female shadow who soon got up and left.

'I was touched by your poems,' Polenskaya told him.

Touched; that was a word to store up and think over, even if he didn't manage to preserve it in the faintly foreign accent.

She was telling him about Russia in reply to a question of his, transporting him to that great land of hers that he had tried to make his by the power of his dream. He listened and took her in and heard her say how much Petrograd meant to her, though Moscow was the more outwardly attractive city.

'Shall I go now? Do you have to dress?'

She paused in what she was telling him to wipe, with cotton wool swabs, greasepaint from her face while peering in the big, bright mirror.

'I'll tell you when to go,' she said, turning her head to him, and went on with what she'd been saying, and he saw that she liked him, extreme youth, awkwardness and all, and was ready to help him over his shyness.

Quite a long time later, though he couldn't tell whether time had speeded up or slowed down, she said, 'Wait for me outside, if you're not in a hurry.'

He stood in the corridor and quite soon she appeared in a grey fur coat and a fur bonnet beneath which her dark hair was hidden. They started walking down the street while H adjusted himself to this situation. In Trafalgar Square she stopped. Now it was up to him: she'd done all that she could.

'Will you come and have tea at the Hotel Cecil?'

He'd noticed the rather imposing entrance when passing along the Strand and it was the only place at hand he could think of taking her.

'Not now, I've got an appointment to keep. Come round to my dressing room one night next week; ring me first at the theatre before the performance, and we'll go out somewhere.'

H walked back to his room in the wintry dusk, his imagination soaring away to snowy streets at whose dimly lit corners ever more sensational promises were being whispered to him under the falling flakes.

Yes, but even if he could make the money he had left last over the weekend by living on ginger biscuits and tins of condensed milk, there still wouldn't be enough to take her anywhere on Monday or Tuesday but to a cheap café or back to his bare room, both of which seemed out of the question.

There were two possible (impossible?) solutions. Go and see his former nurse who lived with a rich married sister, a visit he'd originally intended making in any case and then shelved, and when he mentioned that Iseult was going to have a baby (his last letter to Weg had been one telling her of his marriage), Mrs Evans would hand him a five-pound note: 'Buy something warm and woolly for the dear little babe when it arrives, Harry.'

Or turn up at the hotel at Victoria where his stepfather was living when he'd last heard of him. Even less possible. H's silence at the time of Henry's heart attack and, later, about his own marriage, had made the break final.

He decided on Highgate and Weg.

Weg was ill, lying in bed in the room at the top of the house where, in the hushed, expectant, early dusks of the days before Christmas, he'd sat in the basket chair and sniffed the aroma that had been an annunciation, that he'd no longer the gift of receiving, as she had poured the boiling water on to the teaspoonfuls of coffee paste in the china cups.

H sat by her bed and she took his hand and told him, 'I've been dreaming so much about you, Boy, that I knew you'd come.'

H pressed the still capable-looking hand with the opal ring on one of the fingers, given her, as she'd confided to him long ago in a house by the sea (where was that?), by a gentleman friend in Brisbane when she was a girl lately arrived in Australia as a domestic.

H was aware of a greater loss than any he had yet experienced. He was appalled by a conflict within himself between an apparently profound but inexpressible pain and a total indifference. Time seemed the factor that allowed the great dichotomy.

Weg was dying and what once would have been the end of his small world was now no more than an event on the margin of his much larger one. He could tell himself that what she had once been revealed to him as was a vision formed and coloured by the child's great need. But was that a valid excuse? Had the child's egocentric image brought him no nearer her than his present detachment? Hadn't the intensity of that image communicated itself to her and to some degree transformed her into the child's concept; wasn't that part of the process of love, and wasn't there more of reality in it than in his present impression of a sick, not-very-intelligent, sentimental old woman?

His world was expanding all the time, growing richer, but there was this half-conscious fear that it was also being impoverished.

He'd never really seen the round, puffy face before, undistinguished now by any of the reassuring signs he used to find there. There was nothing to say, no more communication from him to her.

'I've the Holyhead boat train to catch, so I've got to go, Weg.'

'Thank you for coming, Boy. Give my kind regards to your dear wife. And God Bless you.'

7

Back in Dublin, H spent his time between their flat and Iseult's old room at her mother's where she was remaining till the baby was born, sometimes staying the night with her, surreptitiously because of Madame MacBride's disapproval, of which Iseult had told him, of his sleeping with her before the baby was born. He didn't think that this was because of possible ill effects, as she'd pretended to her daughter. During the few days they spent at his mother-in-law's between returning from the cottage and moving into the flat, he'd been puzzled by Iseult's own apparent wish to keep her mother from being reminded of their relationship. One night after Iseult had come to bed with him they'd heard her mother calling her in her emotional voice outside Iseult's old room, and he'd felt her wince in his arms at its being revealed that they weren't in separate ones.

H, in an access of goodwill which he had at times towards her, though never for long, invited Madame MacBride to come with Iseult by taxi to an early supper, so that they could return before the eight o'clock curfew, at the flat. He selected a piece of steak at the butcher's, waited till the pan was really hot, fried it in a smattering of butter and served it with finely chopped parsley sprinkled on the dark crust.

Madame MacBride was delighted. Her enthusiasm was turned on him for once, and he was overwhelmed with the warmth of her praise. 'I wish Josephine could cook a steak like that,' she said. 'I can't tell her anything. If I try to get her to ring a change on the two or three dishes she's used to, it's, "Oui, Madame; mais bien sur, Madame;" and she serves up the omelette fines herbes or choufleur au gratin we've been having for years.'

But the next day, when he was with Iseult in her room and Madame MacBride came sailing in, tragic-browed, with news of the latest Black-and-Tan outrage, she was as unaware as ever of him as, pressing her cheek to her daughter's, she murmured, 'Quelle belle bête!'

One morning when H arrived at the house, a baby was lying beside his wife in the bed, a fragile, raw-looking piece of wrinkled flesh in which the features were hardly discernible. A girl, she told him.

By the time of the christening H's antipathy to Madame MacBride was at one of its peaks and he didn't go to it. Instead, he wrote a poem beginning

> Today my child was christened but I was
> Elsewhere, in converse with my other kin ...

'What "other kin"?' Iseult asked when he showed it her.

H laughed. 'My muses, I suppose.'

'Well, it's no good, Luke. Nothing like the ones for Polenskaya.'

He had shown these to her on his return from London and, far from resenting them, she'd said they were his best.

'You should have come to the little ceremony with us. After all, it was you who thought of calling her Dolores.'

He was already sorry at not having gone. Many years later looking back on a life full of omissions and non-participations, it was one of those he most regretted.

At Easter, when the baby was a month old, they moved to a bungalow H's mother had taken at the sea not far from where they'd stayed with her before their marriage. But now both the view and the weather were pleasanter. There were signs of heat to come; the sea lay aglitter with long, pale wavelets frothing towards the beach. By summer the sun-drenched walls gave off a scent of warm, tarred wood and Snuff lay all day panting in the shade of the verandah. But louder than the dog's snortings or the bouts of wailing that came from Dolores's pram, was the sharp burst from the exhaust of the glossy new motorbike when H rode it the few yards along the central passage. He'd bought it with the money saved by living here with his mother and giving up the flat, but because motor vehicles were being strictly controlled, hadn't got a permit for it.

H kept it, the back wheel raised on its rest, in his room. He would sit on the saddle, the chrome controls and brake levers under his fingers on the handlebars, the shiny expanse of tank, topped by the oil drip-feed in its tiny, celluloid dome, between his knees, and envisage the trips before him. He heard (and didn't hear) the whimpers of the baby coming through the wooden wall from the next room.

Soon after dawn on a summer morning when the tide was out he took the bike down to the beach. Chugging along the wide, deserted strand, he hadn't the sense of power that had come from sitting on it in his room. Somewhat downcast, he rode back to the bungalow and wheeled the bike down the passage to his room. The place was quiet. He opened the door of Iseult's room softly without waking her and tiptoed in. The baby was lying on her back in the pram, her blue eyes open and darker than he'd expected.

She looked up at him, her arms crooked outside the coverlet, fists clenching and unclenching, in a long, unsmiling (unseeing?) stare. It was H whose gaze faltered. He returned to his room and laid his hand on the finned engine cylinder to let its heat reassure him.

That same morning as H was reading on the verandah that faced away from the sea and towards the road, he heard a two-stroke engine, his ears now attentive to such things, misfiring to a halt. Laying down the big book, a volume marking the Keats Centenary he'd bought with excitement and which he now realized was a collection of banal eulogies, he went to the gate. The motorcyclist, in the khaki uniform and black beret of the Auxiliaries, was bending over his machine.

Alert for any movement in the vicinity and catching sight of H out of the corner of his eye, he straightened up, and, as H didn't avoid his glance, called, 'Damned thing's conked out!'

H strolled over and contemplated the stranded machine. He guessed what was wrong, but he wanted to have a closer look at the Auxiliary before deciding whether to help him.

'Know anything about these?' the soldier inquired.

The closest H had seen an Auxiliary before was as they drove through the Dublin streets in armoured cars or inside the wire cages of their lorries. This man was looking at him as if he still expected him to turn his back and walk off.

'Sounded as though you'd run out of petrol.'

The Auxiliary, who'd been depressing the needle of the float chamber, indicated the overflow from the carburettor.

'Let's have it off the stand,' H suggested.

He was taking over, confident that he knew the cause of the trouble. When the bike was down and standing on the road, he tried depressing the needle again, but the petrol had stopped flowing.

'When the bike's propped up,' he explained 'what petrol there is flows forwards to the outlet pipe (stupid place to put it, really) but with both wheels on the road (there's a slight rise just here) it stays at the back of the tank.'

The Auxiliary tapped his forehead. 'Made of bloody wood! You've hit it, old chappie. Well, thanks for the helping hand.' He nodded to where the road reached the top of the incline. 'If I shove it up there I can push off on what's left.'

Their barracks was an old army training camp a few miles along the coast, but the road made a detour inland to join the main Dublin one where it crossed a river. It was the same that, spanned only by the railway viaduct, flowed into the sea near the little village where H and Iseult had stayed with his mother before their marriage.

Either the Auxiliary didn't know this or he hoped to find a garage on the way where he'd get some petrol, in spite of an order against obtaining fuel on the road because of rumours of places that kept a special supply mixed with sand or water.

Telling him to hang on, H went back into the bungalow. On his way out again with the can he met Iseult.

'You're not going to give that Black-and-Tan petrol?'

'Well, yes, I am.'

H emptied what was in the can into the tank of the bike and the engine started with a roar. The Auxiliary felt in his breeches pocket, not the one that bulged with the Colt revolver, and handed H four shillings.

'The marked price, old chappie, though it's worth far more to me.'

H handed him back one of the florins explaining that there had only been about half-a-gallon in the can. The Auxiliary saluted and rode off and H returned to his room with Iseult's accusation still unanswered in his mind.

The other day H had heard that a couple of girls, with heads shaved, had been found one Sunday morning chained to the railings of a church in the local town, a notice pinned to them with the word 'Traitors' scrawled on it.

These, everyone knew, were some of the women who associated with the British military. H himself had had glimpses of pale oval faces framed in head scarves high up in the cabs of Crossby tenders at night between the caps of the other two occupants.

H sat astride his bike in his room and reflected. Supposing it had been he with the chains that were padlocked to the railings around his wrists? Would he have met the surreptitious glances of the early Mass-goers with a haughty, unflinching stare, rejoicing not to belong to their complacent, church-going, patriotic fold?

Long ago when she'd visited him in his stall, he'd told Iseult that what the poet needed to keep him unspotted from the world was dishonour. It hadn't been a phrase he'd thought up. It had come out instinctively without pre-meditation. Now it was time to catch up and to come to a conscious grasp of his attitude.

He believed that nothing short of the near despair of being utterly cast off from society and its principles could create the inner condition conducive to the new insights that it was the task of the poet to reveal.

The girls tied to the railings symbolized for H the poet who is exposed and condemned for his refusal to endorse the closed judgements and accept the categorical divisions into right and wrong that prevailed. If he survived the ordeal there would flow from the depths of his isolation fresh imaginative streams to melt the surrounding freeze-up.

Yeats, for all his superb craftsmanship and intellectual passion, was not going to cause any real alteration or re-orientation in inner attitudes because he had not been forced to this point of extreme loneliness.

When, later that evening, Iseult suggested he'd helped the Black-and-Tan out of a sense of kinship for the British and a secret admiration for the powerful, he said nothing. She had an idea that he'd been tainted by his time at an English public school.

Wasn't the truth the very opposite? But there was still a degree of confusion in his thoughts. Hadn't he helped the Auxiliary because at that particular moment he was a despised and threatened person? There had to be an extreme flexibility of spirit and avoidance of all moralizing in order to associate with the losers at any given moment, who, for the poet, were the only suitable companions. This meant never holding to any political, social, or moral belief, because that would put him on the right or justified side where he would be cut off from the true sources of his inspiration.

The baby whom the woman doctor in Dublin had advised her to wean and feed from a bottle, grew more distressed. After several sleepless nights, Iseult drove off with Dolores in a hired pony trap to catch a train and H stayed on, with his mother, the panting dog, and the immobilized machine.

Telephones were not yet a general means of private communication and he walked every day or two the four or five miles to the steel-shuttered and sandbagged police barracks to see if the permit for the bike had arrived. He also awaited news from Iseult which when it came by letter was to say that Dolores was in hospital very ill.

H was learning that life developed in the manner of all natural phenomena: through static periods followed by a state of confluent events; and after the time of waiting, the permit came the same morning as the telegram from Iseult.

During the ride over dusty roads H was as much absorbed in learning to manipulate the controls of the little engine, keeping an eye on the oil feed, avoiding the potholes made by the military tenders, as by the death of the baby.

As he arrived at the house he saw two tall figures in black walking away from it and at first he didn't recognize Iseult in the mourning that made her, before he saw the white and haggard face, a counterpart of her mother. They were on their way to make arrangements for the funeral, but Iseult returned to the house with him and, up in her old room on the top floor, told him of the baby's agony.

While he'd been daydreaming of entering the isolation of truly imaginative spirits, more or less ignored by him in the room next door a fragile life was being destroyed.

As Iseult was talking she took from her handbag and gave him a metal crucifix. It was heavy as he held it in his hand waiting for her to explain its part in what she was telling him. Not that he didn't guess. He saw the infants' ward of the children's hospital which, with its rows of white cots filled with the spinal meningitis cases, had become a big bright and airy condemned cell and torture chamber. The crucifix had come from there, had been laid on the baby's finally still breast. His wife was speaking to him out of her grief that he couldn't share with her. He caught the chill whiff of misery that clung to her, a scent from the damp pit where hopes decay. But he hadn't loved the baby, had hardly taken her in, except for fleeting moments, and her loss couldn't reduce his sensations to a single unbearable one.

Iseult was saying that the matron, a nun, had told her how, as she'd stooped over the cot, Dolores had grasped the crucifix so tightly she had had to take it from its cord and leave it in the baby's clenched fist where it had remained. He saw that this was a straw of comfort she clutched at as a sign that what had happened was explicable in terms of her religious faith. But because this was not of the robust and primitive kind, he knew that, like him, she suspected that the baby would have grasped any similar object in her agony.

He stood dry-eyed beside the mound of yellowish clay and neat oblong hole under a yew tree while Iseult and her mother wept silently. When they went across the road to order the headstone – Madame MacBride and Helen Molony had gone back in the funeral car – he chose a pale grey slab the shape of a small upended coffin, while Iseult held his arm in silence, with the cross in low relief, and wrote under the name, on the slip of paper provided by the stone mason, the two dates, one in March and the other in July, to be chiselled on it.

A few weeks later, when the headstone was in place, they planted a rose tree on the grave. That, as far as H knew, was the last time Iseult ever went there though, he believed, it always remained at the back of her mind. As for him, he passed the cemetery countless times driving to and from Dublin when later they lived in the mountains, without giving it a thought.

It was thirty years before H visited it again, by which time Iseult was dead. By then he could see the pale headstone half-hidden by weeds and a lower branch of the yew tree as a steadfast rock in the flood of events that had flowed over him. He came at long last to realize that this and the other neighbouring tombstones, many of them overgrown with ivy, were speaking to him of a reality outside of time.

8

Sudden silence woke H. From the darkened compartment, where they'd switched out the main light and left a blue one burning, of the stationary train, he seemed to look far down, though he was uncertain of these new perspectives, on the marble, moonlight aisle of a huge ruined temple whose shadowed walls were crumbled in. This was the first stock of the unforeseeably foreign: the Rhine at night.

Opposite, Iseult and her mother were asleep. The idea of the journey had been Madame MacBride's; she'd thought it would help Iseult over the baby's death. By taking her to performances of Wagner at the newly built opera house in Munich she might manage to disperse some of the gloom that, left to herself, Iseult seemed unable to unburden herself of.

In his inside pocket, as well as the little leather chessboard and red and black leather pieces (he'd not known what to bring) were the crisp, new bluish mark-notes whose value was still ungrasped and the passport issued at Dublin Castle with the circular visa stamp, and another larger, square-shaped one to say that the first wasn't valid for the occupied zone.

Munich was at first the exciting smell of cigar smoke, low, coupled-together tramcars snakily twisted into streets of tall houses off the big station square down which were glimpses of a warm smoky autumn skyline pierced with saffron belfries and glowing towers.

H was soon engrossed in this new world as, with the two women, he strolled past long, palace-like buildings in shades of stained saffron that gave the avenues their tone of faded glory, under triumphal arches, with names (as his mother-in-law found out in her guidebook) from ancient Greece, into open spaces where spray sparkled from sprinklers over grass that indecipherable notices no doubt warned them to keep off. He absorbed the strangeness with silent zest, including the food at dinner in the hotel restaurant which, whatever he chose from the long menu, consisted of succulent portions of pinkish, porklike meat ribbed with bone, in thick, creamy sauce, and served with a variety of cabbage, green, red, and almost white, which he washed down with thick glass tankards of brown beer. Afterwards, when Madame MacBride had gone to her room, H and Iseult went out together, usually across the station square and into an adjoining one, the Karlsplatz, to sit on one of the benches at the fountain in its centre with the lit, single-deck trams crisscrossing the blue dusk beyond the grey pillarlike trunks and leafy canopies of the plane trees round the brimming stone basin.

The unaccustomed beer, and the violent impact of so many revelations, ensured that, as well as the sights sought out by Madame, he saw the inside of all the urinals in that part of Munich. Afterwards, hurrying after the two women, something was sure to catch his attention that they, on their way to more celebrated attractions, had no time for. One was a placard outside a theatre. In large red letters he read: Polenskaya; and in somewhat smaller ones, Serge Polikov. It took him a little while to puzzle out of the rest of the announcement the news that the Russian dancers were appearing there the following week.

What would she think of him after his appearance from nowhere in her dressing room at the Coliseum followed by his disappearance without a word? She'd had other things to concern her since then, having been much in the news, both because of her divorce and of the suicide of a diplomat the night of a party given for her in Sydney.

H went with the two women to the opera, sitting between them and thus in the way of all the effusive remarks from Madame to Iseult.

He was intent on what lay outside the concert hall and was impatient during the performance which he couldn't relate to any of the new impressions he had absorbed to saturation point. What had these white-bearded pixies banging away in exaggerated gestures with toy hammers on shaky anvils in time to the loud clanging of the orchestra (the fact of its being out of sight seemed to delight Madame although he'd supposed she'd come all this way to see as well as hear it) to communicate to him?

Down in the foyer during the interval his mother-in-law met a tall blond man in white tie and tails, whom Iseult whispered was Walter Rummel, a pianist friend of theirs and – she still liked recounting the love affairs of others with an indulgent smile – a former lover of Isadora Duncan.

This encounter seemed to crown the evening for Madame MacBride, adding memories of the old Paris days to her delight in what H, for all his ignorance of music, suspected was Wagner's oversimplified and under-motivated passion.

H took advantage of his mother-in-law's preoccupation with the pianist to slip away. When Iseult came back to their room she said that when her mother had missed him, which wasn't till the second interval, she'd remarked on a rash she had noticed on the backs of his hands and advised Iseult to take him to a doctor without delay in case it turned out to be venereal disease.

'What about the constant peeing, which I'm sure she's also noticed?' H couldn't help asking, although the excretionary functions were never mentioned between them. Neither ever used the chamber pot at night, a matter of delicacy that inconvenienced him more than her.

An old German with cropped grey hair looked at H's hand and wrote a prescription, becoming one of the very few members of the medical profession H was ever to have any respect for by remarking that he showed every sign of being highly *nervös*, and asking him whether, as well as his skin, his bladder ever gave him any trouble.

Informed by her daughter of the doctor's diagnosis, Madame said something in French that H didn't catch, and which, being otherwise preoccupied, he forgot to get Iseult to explain afterwards. That evening he wrote a note to Polenskaya to await her at the theatre, asking her to meet him the day after her first performance under one of the triumphal arches called the Propylaeon.

Madame spent her time at the operas, galleries, churches, shops, and cafés, with Iseult docilely, it seemed to H, trailing after her. Whenever he could without offence he would slip away by himself and wander the streets or, of an evening when they were listening to Wagner, sit on a bench in the large park that appeared to border two sides of the city.

As he sat there one evening he was preoccupied by the notion of time which had obsessed him before at periods when, through pain, he'd been more than normally perceptive. He'd left Iseult in the hotel examining, up in her mother's room, the Dresden tea set Madame had bought earlier in the day. Resentful at her apparent intention to spend the evening with her mother of whose influence on her he was jealous, he'd left without a word and was already sorry that he hadn't told his wife where he would be if she cared to come later and join him. But there were only a few streets between him and the hotel which he could get up and traverse again at any moment he wished.

It was not therefore her present absence that gave him his sense of foreboding, but an inkling he had of the power of time to change and to separate.

This moment would become the past which he couldn't relive or enter again. By then Iseult might be a chapter in his private history and all his present acute emotions about her, and his irritations with his mother-in-law, would have been erased. The thought was too painful to examine in detail but nor could he leave it.

Supposing he was in this city in years to come when time had long separated them. How would it feel to realize that he could no longer cross the Karlsplatz and the square in front of the station to the Hotel Deutscher Kaiser and find her up in their room?

He had had a dream the other night in which, during a voyage they were taking together, Iseult had died and been buried at sea. His sense of loss was the core of the dream, but what gave it the peculiar nightmare intensity was that on the return trip the ship had sailed past the spot where he imagined, in his bunk that night, her lying, sewn in canvas and weighted, not far below at the bottom of the sea.

How would he think of her across the vast tracts of time that he envisaged extending between them? Space separation intensified memory, but time separation, given enough, diminished it. Time lays everything waste. Not only his present intense little world, but the world around him, the outside area of bodies and buildings. This city too, though he had no foreboding about that, he would be present to see razed by fire.

There was also the other direction of time with its equal power to lay waste and obliterate. When he thought of his father, as he did with a frequency that he couldn't explain, he believed that had there not been this uncrossable expanse of time between them he could have shared in his father's despair. Not being sure in what it had consisted, this was, he saw, a somewhat doubtful conclusion, but at least he could have accompanied this being whom he felt so close to and familiar with to the room in the house in Townsville, Australia, that he kept having glimpses of during his own states of inner misery.

For the next couple of days H followed the women around, lingering before Greek statues while Madame enthused to her 'belle bête', falling in the rear when, in her black robes, she darted with sudden speed to the next exhibit. But thus left behind one afternoon halfway across the polished parquet floor of one large room, H turned and retreated to the hotel where he wrote a note for Iseult.

It was difficult to find words that wouldn't hurt her and, all the same would hint at his need of a breathing space. He couldn't write 'I'm taking a short break,' when that was what he was supposedly already having. In the end he didn't leave a note at all. She would see that he'd taken some, but not all, of his things and thus hadn't been run over or kidnapped.

H asked for a room at the Continental Hotel with the idea, should the situation arise, of having somewhere to take Polenskaya. But either because, as they told him, the place was really full, or because of his shabby air and unimpressive suitcase (the Germans, he saw, were sticklers for appearance and deportment) they didn't want him, he was directed to a nearby flat where a room was available.

Installed there, he spent the next couple of days writing poems, filling several pages of one of the exercise books he'd brought with him and only breaking off to cross the hall from time to time to the toilet. Two or three, addressed to Polenskaya, he copied out carefully on separate sheets of paper. On the evening of the second day he went out to look for a clock, there being none in the room and having no watch, and found there was no time for supper; he'd had no lunch that day nor the previous one; before going to the theatre. But from there too he was turned away, not having had the foresight to procure a ticket beforehand.

Next morning H was at the triumphal arch before the appointed hour. The sun was sparkling, the sprinklers were whirring on the wide lawns and half the world was passing along the broad walk. Amid the women strolling by in summer dresses it wasn't going to be easy to recognize her. He'd only seen her in a wrap, her face smeared with grease, in furs under a bulb in a tiled passageway and, finally, had a few sidelong glances as she'd walked beside him in a street at night.

H stood at the edge of the deep shadow cast by the monument watching those emerging from under it, though she might equally well approach it from the side where he was. Catching sight of an elongated black shadow bent slightly forward as it hurried towards him, he stepped back into the shade, just in time to avoid coming face to face with Madame MacBride.

He had taken a few uncertain paces after several passersby and faltered to a stop, before one of these looked round and then slowed her steps. H was very nervous and still not quite sure it was Polenskaya until, as he fell into step beside her, she started talking almost as if there had been no interruption of their walk that wintry London evening seven or eight months before.

'You left me in the lurch, but I don't expect poets to keep appointments. They just turn up again unexpectedly like this.' She herself had come from a tour of the Balkans, turned immediately for H into legendary regions, as would Belfast or Glasgow had she mentioned them instead. In Budapest she'd had a glimpse of what was happening under Bela Kun, whom H had never heard of.

H's nervousness had left him when she spoke of his having left her in the lurch and halfway down one of the main streets, where they were suddenly in the heart of the city again, he realized it was the continental lunch hour. Boldly he asked her to eat with him in a restaurant across the Platz from the hotel she'd told him she was staying, the one where he'd failed to get a room, and which they were approaching all too quickly. Polenskaya took the invitation, it seemed, as a matter of course and the next moment, with time progressing for H again quantum-wise in fits and starts, they were sitting in the dim elegance of the restaurant with a well-shaded lamp and gleaming cloth between them.

What was ordered he hardly knew until there appeared before each of them a small, thick steak on whose crisp, cracked crust was a poached egg and tiny wreath of water-cress. He was miles away from the big, busy dining room of the Deutscher Kaiser and the ribs of pork with vegetables and sauces, which he had finally grasped he always got because the 'do.' in do. garniert or do. mit Rahmtunke merely stood for 'ditto'.

Polenskaya's face was doubly shadowed by the dimness of the place and the wide brim of her hat as she inclined her head to eat. H had to slant the piece of paper towards the table lamp before he could read the poem to her.

> Remember, dear, if you have thought me careless
> I would have sought for you and found you too,
> Were I less proud and you less fair, less
> Impossibly the woman that we knew
> Had travelled to her lovers East and West
> With a long train of rumour and the rest
> The faithless have for gaudy retinue.
> You'd wish me start up now, determined, slowly,
> As if somehow or somewhere heroes were
> Successful still, and seek you, tranquil, holy;
> I a crusade and you a sepulchre.

'Ah,' she said, 'Luke, you're a regular Pushkin with your romantic feeling. But you've been reading newspaper gossip about me, haven't you? Do you know, when I was a young woman in Russia before the Revolution, they sent a monk, a pale young man who looked like Alyosha (Have you read Dostoevsky?) to my house to chide me for going about with a prince whose fat wife had left him.'

She took the poem from him and slipped it into her handbag, and H resolved to get hold of *The Brothers Karamazov* which Iseult had been vainly praising to him since before their elopement to London.

At the door of Polenskaya's hotel they parted. Though he might have gone in with her, H now wanted to get away before anything could dim, even by further intimacy, the perfect hour in the restaurant before he'd absorbed it into thought.

She said she'd have a ticket kept for him at the box office, not for that evening which might be difficult at short notice, but for the following night. They were only here for a week (this was something he hadn't deciphered from the placard in German) before going on to Prague.

In the evening H stood close to the theatre box office and waited for somebody to bring back a ticket they couldn't use. When the back of a bald head and bull neck was bent towards the guichet and he went closer to investigate, it turned out, after some difficulty in understanding what the woman inside meant, that there were prior requests to be dealt with before his.

He returned to his room and lay on his bed, content to be alone because now he had a link (and how precious a one!) with what was going on outside in the deepening evening. Someone at this moment in the very heart of it all would give him more than a passing thought, had her poet's slip of paper tucked away in her handbag.

The following night at the end of the show some young men ran onstage and carried Polenskaya on their shoulders into the wings after she'd taken several curtain calls, and when H got around to her dressing room there was a crowd of them outside the door. Suddenly downcast, he left the theatre and walked through parts of the city he'd never been in before, until unexpectedly, and by a circuitous route, he reached the Karlplatz. He hadn't been sitting on a bench at the fountain long when Iseult appeared through the circle of plane trees.

She'd come here, she said, at this hour each night since his disappearance. H held her hand and said nothing until he heard that Madame MacBride was returning to Ireland next day, when he suggested they go to Prague as soon as she'd seen off her mother.

'Early in the morning after you left, the police came asking to see the passports of foreigners and I had to tell them that I was on my husband's and I didn't know where he was,' she told him.

In the morning, after she'd been to the station with her mother, H met Iseult at the hotel. She wanted to spend a couple of days in Nuremberg on the way to Prague and they travelled there on the next train, buying a bottle of one of the sweet liqueurs that were sold on German stations, and drinking it while H showed her the poem to Polenskaya and one on the Karlsplatz fountain:

> The fountain falls from laughing mouth of stone
> In laughter through cigar-smoke-scented gloom
> And from the corner of the curved lip
> The drops like petals gather, fall and slip
> From carven lead to leaf. I am alone
> By the slim, white, unwitherable plume
> The water flaunts against the darkened sky.
> I, who found in mutability
> A lot of weeping and a little laughter
> See here before me Nature's strange hereafter
> The immortal ghost . . .

At Nuremberg their room was long and narrow and had a step dividing it into two, one half being on a slightly different level to the other. They went out to visit the places Iseult wanted to see, a couple of churches and an ancient torture chamber, though what fascinated H were the powerful white motorbikes in the streets with 'Mars' in red across their big tanks. It was after they'd returned to the room that what had struck him as merely curious about it began to seem sinister. He started looking around, examining the walls and wainscoting, for rat holes perhaps; he was not sure; or for any indication as to why it was on different levels. Later he realized that it recalled the sickroom at one of his preparatory schools, Bilton Grange, as he'd seen it in his fever which, in turn, he associated with a room in a mental home in Townsville, Australia.

As he was filling a tooth-glass at the tap at the handbasin, thirsty after all the cherry brandy he'd drunk on the train, Iseult exclaimed, 'Don't drink out of that, darling. They're used by men to wash their sexual organs.'

This remark, with its associations in which she seemed involved, added its minor horror to the place.

'I suppose your mother's afraid I'll take after my father. She's sure to have heard about him from some of my relatives.'

'Only that your Quintillan uncle told her he died in an asylum.' H said nothing and she asked, 'You didn't know that?'

'I'm not sure whether they hinted at something like that or whether I guessed it.'

'Moura wanted me to go home with her, but I wouldn't.'

'Why not?'

It surprised him that she had chosen to stay with him.

'Were you glad when you saw me last night at the fountain?'

'Of course.'

'You looked like a little boy who'd got lost. But you wrote a fine poem, I must tell you that.'

'The one to Polenskaya?'

Iseult nodded. He knew that jealousy didn't come easy to her. Was it partly because she felt superior to any possible rival?

'You don't mind coming to Prague to see her dance?'

'If you like.'

The weary note had come into her voice as if it was all the same to her where they went. And where they ended up a couple of mornings later was a frontier town called Marktredwtz on the edge of nowhere where they had to leave the Prague express because they hadn't visas for Czechoslovakia.

While they waited for a train back to Germany they walked out beyond the last of the houses where the dusty road ran between bleached wooden fences enclosing parched vegetable plots. But just as he was beginning to discover a kind of foreignness here more intimate and minute, in the vegetable rows, the texture of the soil between them, than that of cities, he glanced at Iseult and saw by the vague, distracted look in her eyes that she was taking in none of this.

He had now often a sense of her apathy pulling them down and diminishing his own delight in everything new. This town which she was transforming into something dreary and without interest he'd have gladly spent a few days in, absorbing the atmosphere. The other mode of living, discernible in some chance glimpse, that he knew about from his reading of Russian novels, might already have its beginning here. He imagined the fascination of merely gazing from his hotel room window towards the rolling plains of Bohemia, whether he could actually see them or not, that stretched eastward to the secret heart of Central Europe. As it was, they sat in a cinema until it was time for the train to Dresden, where he supposed she'd find the things that seemed to distract her: art treasures, ancient churches, and monuments.

They took a room in a pension between the station and zoo; he was economizing with the money that was left till the next sum came from his mother, for the trip to Prague.

They had their meals in their room which Iseult didn't seem anxious to leave, spending hours at the bamboo table in the corner writing long letters (to her mother? – H didn't ask), playing patience; he knew she'd have sooner played the old card games with him, but he'd got out of that indolent phase of their early days. Or she smoked endless cigarettes while leafing through illustrated magazines she found in another corner of the room.

Meanwhile H went to see about the Czech passports, which he was told would take a day or two, sat under the trees in the zoological gardens, where the entry cost very little, and, in general, just hung about.

With Madame's departure the purposeful flow of the days had slowed down. H was content for the time to do nothing, but he daren't ask Iseult what she was thinking all day in their room in the boarding house in case she suggested returning to Ireland.

During the spring and early summer she'd complained of soreness which, she'd heard, was quite natural after the birth of a first baby, and in the weeks of mourning sex had been ruled out. Now it was headaches that got worse, it struck him, when it was time to go to bed, and which she woke up with most mornings. She dosed herself with aspirins that, with the cigarettes, seemed to keep her in her state of semi-torpor.

It was on one of these afternoons in the Dresden pension that they returned to the subject of why her mother had been reluctant to leave her alone with him abroad.

'She thinks you're neurotic.'

By now he'd begun to grasp that this judgement wasn't a considered rejection of his personal world by those who inhabited better, more imaginatively conceived ones of their own. It was dawning on him that many, perhaps most people, including his mother-in-law and the school matrons and masters, were not after all judging between comparable states of consciousness. Themselves deeply involved in outward areas of existence, they had no way of truly assessing his kind of inward-turned attention. All the same these pronouncements filled him with dread.

For one thing he didn't know how universal and powerful their faction was, and although there were poets who certainly hadn't belonged to it, there were also madmen, like his father; and, of the poets, how many of them were now alive? H didn't think of Yeats as one of them. Surely Yeats had his feet, or at least one of them, firmly planted on solid rock.

Sitting on a bench in the zoo or in a park, he foresaw that it was only by what they called his neurosis becoming more profound that he could write the kind of poems that might lessen his isolation, or at least fully reconcile him to it.

9

What made the delay in the receipt of the allowance from H's mother more serious was that they'd spent the last of the money they'd arrived from Ireland with on the trip from Dresden to Prague and back.

Prague had eaten up everything. After Germany, where the value of the mark was falling, prices were ruinous. H disliked the place from the moment they left the station and saw the miniature French flags and Stars and Stripes in the shop windows, along with photos of a bearded patriarch whom he later learned was Masaryk, that were lit in mid-afternoon because of the fog. Then there was trouble with the taxis. The first H asked to take them to a cheap hotel and the driver, pretending not to speak German, drove them to a big place called the 'Princess Passage', another of those fortuitous names that stuck in H's mind for years; the second, to the theatre, overcharged them as did another to take Iseult back to the hotel while H went round to Polenskaya's dressing room. Finally, there was the taxi that brought him back, and whose driver, because it was after midnight, doubled the already excessive fare.

Polenskaya danced to Mozart's *Kleine Nachtmusik*, a composer whom (Iseult translated the part of the programme printed in French) the Czechs looked on as their own. But it was by another dance, to the music of Dvořak, in which she mimed a mechanical doll, standing stiffly on her toes, inclining her head in a series of jerks and moving clockwork arms in a manner more evocative of H didn't know what half-imaginable intimacies than any directly sensual gestures, that he was bowled over.

When she, her face an alabaster mask, with dark holes for mouth and eyes that were shocking revelations of human femininity, took short mechanical steps across the stage to the accompaniment of metallic clangs from the orchestra, he was both enthralled and tormented.

The ambiguity was unbearable, something he had to resolve by hurrying around to her dressing room afterwards, leaving Iseult to the fog and another taxi. Without a word of greeting, as she stood in front of the mirror in the wrap that the woman he recalled from the Coliseum had just put over her glistening shoulders, he took Polenskaya in his arms. She was hot, sweaty, and breathless as she kissed him.

'Now go and sit over there and calm down,' she told him.

As she settled herself before the big mirror H realized the sensuality of her exhaustion. Serge Polikov, small, fair, blue-eyed, kept looking in from the adjoining room and, ignoring H, addressing her excitedly in Russian.

'What's he want?'

'He doesn't like it here, that's all.'

'Nor do I.'

'No?'

She turned from the big, bright mirror, her face, from which she'd wiped the make-up, pale and damp, her black hair loosed from its bun at her naked shoulders from which the kimono had slipped.

'No! All this patriotism and profiteering!'

But he hadn't come all this way at such expense to talk like this to her! He sensed from her last exchange with Polikov, by the way she told him to wait, but more surely by what he saw of her in the mirror, the look of sweaty exhaustion and of passionate stillness, the clockwork doll run down and waiting for his hand on the key, that she expected him to take her to his hotel.

The knowledge of this and at the same time its impossibility was unbearable, the sense of the loss he was about to suffer seemed a new and terrible kind of pain. In the end, without mentioning Iseult, with no explanation at all, he left the dressing room as suddenly as he'd burst into it.

That night in bed in the wretched hotel they'd found for themselves, he heard Iseult sobbing and took her into his arms.

'Ah, what a horrible town!' he murmured, 'we should never have come to such a godforsaken spot.'

Had he known that Kafka was perhaps only a few streets away in his attic on the eve of his flight to Berlin and Dora Diamant, H wouldn't have thought of Prague in such terms.

Back in Dresden the twice-daily trip to the post office began. They didn't go hungry, though they had to leave the second week's bill for board and lodging owing, and went to a friendly little goldsmith with Iseult's wedding ring who, after touching it with a piece of cotton wool soaked in chemical to test if it was gold, paid them enough to keep them in stamps, tram fares, and a ration of cigarettes for another few days. It was during the time in Dresden of waiting for the money to arrive that they came closer than in all that period abroad. There was an anxiety that at last they could share instead of each being enclosed in his or her separate fear and longing.

Then one evening when H inquired at the guichet, the white-moustached official, who knew him well by now and always greeted H with a 'Guten Morgen' or 'Guten Nachmittag, mein Herr' and a smile from which H tried to extract the knowledge the postal clerk must have as to whether the letter was there, asked him for his passport. Having glanced at it, he pushed H the registered, reinforced envelope that looked exactly as he had been picturing it at all hours of the days and nights, and a slip to sign.

They had long looked up the train times and procured the visa, and now they rushed back to the pension, paid the accumulated bill, threw what was not already packed into a suitcase and, not finding a taxi, ran with the luggage to the station. After buying the tickets there was just time to get Iseult a box of a hundred cigarettes of a brand called 'Josef' before the train for Vienna left. After dinner in the restaurant car they went to the sleeper H had booked and lay on their berths, H on the upper, Iseult who had started making up for all the smokes she'd had to do without, on the lower. After the shared ordeal, it was one of the few hours of quiet bliss they'd yet shared during their time abroad, or indeed ever.

H had not yet undressed by the time they reached Prague and he got out and walked about the platform. He tried to get a glimpse of the city to see if the fog that he associated with it had lifted. Polenskaya had long left and where she now was and with whom she might be keeping assignations there was no telling. But he realized that it was the interposing of time, not space, between that was taking her from him and robbing him of the painful yet precious obsession that had made him sit all one afternoon and evening without moving in a deep trance in his room at the flat in Munich.

H read the word 'Wien' as they drew into the terminus. Although he'd pronounced the name at the Dresden ticket office, he hadn't expected it to be spelt like that, and it was his first sharp sensation in this city of sensations; he'd supposed it was written 'Vienne', because perhaps having seen over Iseult's shoulder as she sat at the escritoire in their room at the pension a few words of a letter to her mother in French. Like hearing a strange woman first called by her Christian name, it thrilled him as they drove along the Prater-strasse and over the canal in the early morning chill and the hush that descends at the end of long train journeys.

They sat in a big hotel room crowded with, as they were told by the waiter who brought them coffee, Rumanians and Yugoslavs, most of whom had been up all night and many of whom were drunk, though a few like themselves had just come from the station, not that which they'd arrived at but another on the other side of the city, attracted here by the collapse of the

Kronen which H hadn't heard about till now. The hotels were full and they were advised to try the smaller ones when they opened.

They got a room in the annexe of a hotel at the unfashionable side of the Danube canal, in a short, nondescript street of bakers, a garage or two, and blank walls, called Mohrengasse. Not far away was the longer Praterstrasse, wide, cobbled, and tram-tracked, flanked by run-down houses of no more than two or three storeys, full of shabby, crowded cafés, and an air, not of past grandeur but of having been intensely lived in, that immediately fascinated H.

While Iseult had her coffee, fresh rolls, and honey in bed, he breakfasted in a little café off the Stefansplatz. There, on the second or third morning, he got into conversation with a baldish middle-aged Englishman, or rather, Jew, for H soon saw that there was that further dimension to him that he'd discovered in the couple of members of that ethnic group, one the other occupant of his study at school, he'd encountered.

H began to look forward to meeting Mr Isaacs at the café where, in a back room heated by an iron stove, for the days were turning frosty, furriers examined the wares brought in from the forests, as H liked to suppose, and sitting with him at the table by the wide window. He regained his repose in listening to Mr Isaacs's comments about the falling exchange rate, the restaurants, the Viennese, while watching at the same hour each morning, a woman with a scarf around her head shake rugs from a balcony opposite. This punctual event he participated in from afar as in a rite commemorating a mysterious and wonderful era that, having just missed, evoked in him an intense yet vague nostalgia.

Without acting the guide, Mr Isaacs revealed just those kinds of intimate things H was concerned to discover. Nothing about the sights or tourist attractions; Mr Isaacs's way was to relate his own experiences, the faintly droll ones of a person who, disguised as an ordinary citizen and speaking fluent German, stood just sufficiently back from the scene to grasp its special details. Through Mr Isaacs H got to know which restaurants to take Iseult to and which to avoid, and where he could change pound notes to the best advantage. To the middle-aged Jew these people were charming, trivially sensual (Mr Isaacs, H supposed, took sex with Old Testament ceremony), feckless, and unreliable.

'Quite shameless, these young men and women! The other day a girl came into a urinal I was using, squatted down, and peed right beside me.'

Iseult had picked up a companion of her own, Frau Sczeky, an out-of-work violinist who'd fled from Budapest and the Bela Kun regime; it was the second time H had heard this dreaded name; and she had an old German, Herr Hansen, as poor as herself, as protector.

A pale girl with faded, fair hair scraped back into a knot, she spent a lot of time in a small café on the Praterstrasse while Hansen came and went on his black market dealings.

Mr Isaacs was also engaged in dealings, though in a much bigger way, as he confided in H after they'd been meeting at the furriers' café each morning for a week. He was buying diamonds and sending them to England inside cakes, or the back bindings of books. Rings bought for the equivalent of eighty pounds at a jeweller's on the Kärnterstrasse fetched about two hundred, he said, in London, and because of the constantly falling Kronen, these two hundred pounds, by the time he received them, were worth three times his original outlay.

He took H with him on one of his expeditions. Just a stroll up Mariahilfer Strasse and a call at a long, narrow restaurant, like the dining car of a train, on the way. A couple of waiters were folding linen napkins and laying the tables for the midday meal. Mr Isaacs, picking up a menu, showed H the famous name embossed in gold on it, which, to both of them, meant more than Schönbrunn or Belvedere, because about the gilt and plush here there was still a faint warm whiff of the past which would long have evaporated with disuse from the showplaces.

One of the dishes that, as they stood in the narrow passageway between the two rows of tables, Mr Isaacs's finger, moving through the violet, hieroglyphic jungle, paused to indicate was bifteck tartar. But before H could learn what it was, Mr Isaacs, apropos of the nicotine stain on his forefinger, was diverted into recounting something that had happened the evening before. Nothing dramatic, just one of the trivial incidents that H felt as part of the undercurrent of the life going on here that he had need to share in imaginatively.

Mr Isaacs had spread the precious tobacco that was difficult to come by and costly on the black market on a sheet of the *Wiener Neueste Nachrichten* by the open window of his hotel room and, having filled his mouth with water, was damping it with a fine spray, it having become too dry through long storage, when a gust had lifted the fine shreds and blown them into the street.

H was fascinated by this little tale which he was to remember decades later; why, he didn't know, a peak of receptivity was making him take every scrap of news about what was going on here in privacy (the tourist attractions and public performances were of no use to him) and weave them into an unforgettable image of place and time.

Mr Isaacs finished his sensuously detailed account of the tiny misfortune outside a jeweller's a few doors further on. H waited in the street while his companion went to inspect the tray of diamond rings, but Mr Isaacs came out without having bought one.

'He put up the prices as soon as I made my inquiry. Though my German's pretty good it sometimes gives me away.' And H was as disappointed as if he himself had suffered a loss.

When he told Iseult about his new friend she was indignant. Like her mother, who, through Iseult's father, had belonged to the anti-Dreyfus, Boulangist faction in France, she disliked the Jews. H sensed that this hostility was more than just political, especially with Iseult. She lived too much in the mind, by moral or spiritual judgements, not to distrust what he was beginning to see was the Jewish character: humble where she was proud, realist where she relied on abstract principles, revelling in the senses which to her were tiresome. If there was a Jewish idea, which was surely a contradiction, it was a hidden, unheroic, and critical one, a worm that could get into a lot of fine-looking fruit.

One Sunday afternoon Mr Isaacs took H to the Hotel Bristol, Iseult having declined to come, where there was dancing in the basement ballroom. Mr Isaacs wasn't there to dance or drink champagne, but to show H something of the life of the city inexpensively, just as he'd taken him to see the famous restaurant.

They sat at a table by the wall over coffee and cakes and H watched a dark girl in black velvet, as tall as Iseult, and caught the glint of a diamond on a finger of the hand that rested lightly and, it struck him, contemptuously, on the shoulder of her bald elderly partner.

'What a lovely creature!' H exclaimed, not impulsively, which was never his way, but to see what his companion, whose feelings for women, apart from the disapproval he'd shown for certain Viennese girls, he kept to himself, would say.

'You think so, Mr Ruark?'

'Don't you?'

'You forget she could be my daughter.'

Mr Isaacs was not rebuking him (of that, H felt, he was incapable) but was rather intimating, very subtly, that for him the girl's beauty to which H had drawn attention was painful.

'Care to dance with her?' he asked a moment later when H thought the subject had been dropped.

'I can't dance,' H told him, startled by the suggestion.

Mr Isaacs regarded him from under his heavy eyelids, and mentioned a sum of several thousand Kronen. 'That's all it would cost you,' he said. 'About twenty-four shillings in our currency. And of course you don't have to dance.'

H realized that Mr Isaacs had been imparting information rather than making a serious suggestion. His veiled glances had revealed H to him too accurately, at least in this respect, and of course not just the glances, for him not to have realized that H was both too shy and unsure sexually, leaving out the question of Iseult, to be tempted by the proposal.

With Iseult and her new friend Frau Sczeky, H spent a lot of time in a café in the Praterstrasse. Once or twice in the course of the afternoon there appeared a grotesque female dwarf waddling between the tables, selling her papers and exchanging witticisms with the habitués. Frau Sczeky told them that the creature had several wealthy lovers and H sensed Iseult's satisfaction at hearing this as another indication of the basic nastiness of sex. Yet when he saw the sadness on her face at that moment and at other moments in cafés and restaurants, he was troubled. He didn't comment on it, though, even when they were alone, because he was always afraid she'd bring up the subject of their return to Ireland.

Out of the snowy street came in the stocky, fur-collared Hansen with news about the sealskin coat he was negotiating the purchase of for Iseult which he told Frau Sczeky so that she could pass it on in English.

Ah, the long, dark, dreamy, snowy, coffee-scented days of that winter in Vienna that H already knew he'd never quite get over!

In the mornings, after breakfasting with Mr Isaacs, he went to the Diana Bad, a large, ornate building on the Donau Kanal where, as well as Turkish baths and a massage room, there were three swimming pools. One, the smallest, was as warm as a hot bath, another, slightly larger, was temperate, and there was a big unheated pool in a hall whose tiled walls depicted woodland scenes.

Undressing in a cubicle, breathing the steamy air, and catching the sibilant echoes from the steaming walls, the watery apparitions clustered round him. There was the one in the quilted jacket and high boots and the other (both Russian, these) in ballet skirt and square-toed ballet shoes, as well as the hearsay girl who'd squatted down to piss on the floor of the gents' urinal, the young Jewess flashing her diamond ring and, last but not least, the dwarf, all head and torso, with the evening papers under her arm.

10

Magical city of tropic pools still aglow with the fabulous past, of snug cafés with worn plush curtains hanging from shining brass rods across street doors whose glass turns blue in the haunted evening, of succulent dishes of game from nearby forests under battered, crested, silver-plated covers in narrow, opulent shabby restaurants, and of the bifteck tartar that Mr Isaacs had drawn H's attention to but, as was his way, not commented on.

Seeing the alluring name on the menu of a small restaurant in Stefansplatz where he and Iseult were dining, H ordered it. The proprietor, with an intimacy born of his knowledge of English, leaned over their table to explain that the dish, consisting of minced, raw meat, garnished with herbs, might not to be H's taste. The warning, coupled with Iseult's look of faint disgust, made H assure him it was his favourite dish.

By the time the moist red lump hollowed on top to take the egg yolk, was placed before him, H was in an argument with her about his pretending to be familiar with the stuff. He took the wooden spoon, deftly folded the raw meat over the egg, added the capers, red and black pepper, finely chopped onion, and whatever else ringed the damply oozing mass, and forced himself to take a mouthful.

'Well?' she inquired with the familiar disdainful curl of her lips.

H stuffed in a second mouthful so as not to have to answer straightaway. By the time he'd swallowed this he was over his initial nausea and well on the way to appreciating the subtle flavour, tasting almost of nothing but the added spices.

'Marvellous! It really is. Here, dig in your fork and try, Pet.'

H pushed the plate towards her just to see her recoil.

Here they were in this city of subtle sex, *haute cuisine*, and long, sleek cars that looked, parked in the square outside the bright windows of cafés, like boats in a harbour, and all she could do was disapprove!

The almost tasteless taste of the raw meat, the water nymphs on the tiles of the Diana Bad, the creak of the car tyres over the tight, polished snow, entering a warm café in the evening through the heavy curtains and hearing the jingle of the rings, these were exciting him.

It ended by Hansen being asked to have a lookout for a second hand car for them, one in which, as mentioned for Iseult's benefit (to suggest that it might turn out an economy), they could drive to a French port when they went home.

Sums were discussed by H and Iseult; they had been saving money because of the cheapness of everything in terms of their currency. Pounds became hundreds of thousands of Kronen while Hansen listened, and in spite of not understanding a word, sagely nodding his close-cropped head. There was no doubt it could be arranged, Frau Sczeky told them after a consultation with the old man.

But H started studying the second-hand car advertisements in the *Wiener Neueste Nachrichten* on his own, puzzling out the abbreviations. They went by tram to outlying parts of the city where they hadn't been before, and in back sheds and ramshackle garages were shown various vehicles that H lingered longingly over even though they lacked the trim ship-lines of those outside the cafés. Iseult came with him on these expeditions, more for a chance to show off her sealskin coat and cap, he supposed, than because she was interested.

They had a trial run in a little three-wheeler steered by a tiller with an uncovered single cylinder engine over the front wheel, from whose short exhaust smuts were blown into their faces. The price was moderate and, apart from that, the old-fashioned vehicle fascinated H, but he had to admit he didn't see them setting out on the long trip across the continent in it even though it had a hood of sorts. Then there was a long, low, narrow two-seater sports car they were shown in a littered suburban shed that H was even more taken by. Climbing into it (there were no doors) and sitting on a cushion resting on the floorboards, he was already guiding its pointed, red nose along roads beside the Danube, the Rhine, the Moselle.

Afterwards, dining in the cellar in Stefansplatz, or in the big, almost deserted dining room of the Imperial Hotel on the Ring, where a waiter, regarding the hundred Kronen note that H had given him as a tip, remarked that it was the equivalent of no more than tuppence, H would have liked to discuss cars but the look on Iseult's face dissuaded him.

When Mr Isaacs invited them to dinner at his hotel, on the opposite or smarter side of the canal from the Diana Bad, she surprised H by accepting. Not that the meeting was a success. The place was so full (it was a few nights before Christmas) that they were seated at one of several extra tables on a landing outside the dining room where Iseult complained to H that it was draughty and kept her sealskin coat over her shoulders. H was aware of their host hiding his distress while relating the small adventures of his day, the sort of things that H listened to eagerly over their breakfast, but which here, against the background of excited babble and Iseult's disinterest, embarrassed him.

Before H could find a car on his own, Hansen brought the news that he had the very one to suit them. First he took them to a flat overlooking the Volksgarten where he knew someone who'd give them a better rate of exchange for their pounds than the banks did. But the black marketeer, his housekeeper told them, had gone to spend Christmas in the mountains at Semmering.

H was busy observing the room, the ormolu vases of peacock feathers, the plush-and-gilt framed photos, the silk, tasselled lampshades, the double doors to an adjoining apartment, marvelling at having been transported into the middle of a morning in Imperial Vienna and, for this was one of his few real gifts at the time, evoking a moment that no history book could recapture.

From there they accompanied Frau Sczeky to an American soup kitchen at which she had coupons to eat, and where she could play the hostess, while Hansen went to do some of the telephoning that took up so much of his time.

Then back by tram to their home-from-home café in Praterstrasse outside of which a car was standing.

A man, huddled into the fur-lined collar of his short shabby jacket, and with the earflaps of his cap pulled down against the icy wind blowing up the street from the Danube, was sitting in the driving seat. H guessed it was the dreamed-of vehicle by the way the driver turned his head as they got out of the tram and then seemed to retreat further into his well-worn mufflings.

With Frau Sczeky, who whether interpreting or talking directly to Iseult was a chatterer, suddenly silent, they all got in and chugged off, and H could tell there were only two cylinders under the boxlike bonnet. Neither did the owner say a word either to her or Hansen who were in the back with Iseult, driving as if hired to take them to a prearranged destination instead of for a trial run.

From what he caught of the conversation at the back H realized he was the least dismayed of them all about the obvious age of the car; it turned out that it was the first Hansen had seen of it.

They turned near the Prater fairground into a wooded avenue, and under an almost black sky, though the snowy road in front still shimmered in the last daylight, were suddenly out of the city.

H was watching every move of the driver's left hand controlling the gear lever that, with the hand brake, was on his far side. H had decided to buy the car in spite of its age – partly because of it – the two cylinders, and the completely smooth tyres that he'd noticed, tyres being unobtainable in Austria, and to take it out on his own the next day which was Christmas Eve. He asked Hansen to tell the driver to bring it back to the garage and, without returning to the café, the transaction was concluded and the garage proprietor told of the change of ownership.

But on Christmas Eve it was snowing so heavily that H didn't try to take out the car but went for a walk with Iseult. When they returned to their room from a freezing stroll through the old city, having peered into the garage in passing to have a glimpse of the new acquisition, there was a tiny tree, the bright green of its artificial branches asparkle with a shimmering powder, on the table by the window. This had come as a surprise from Frau Sczeky and old Hansen, and Iseult and H took from the chest of drawers the small parcels in which were the presents they'd got each other and placed them beside it.

A minute later they were sitting on one of the beds clinging to each other, overcome by H wasn't sure what unexpected apprehension. Their aloneness here at Christmas? Or an intimation of the pure love that, it seemed to H, was a mixture of precariousness and pain? Her first coming to his stable with Minou in her muff, her running on in front of him blown by the wind along the Grand Canal, his arrival at Euston and not finding her on the station, certain hours in the room in Tottenham Street after she'd made clear to him about her previous lover, Dolores's funeral, these came back to make him feel for her with the old intensity.

'My only love!'

'No, I'm not, darling,' she said. 'I'm the willow on the river bank as I told you long ago, and you're sailing out of sight.'

In the morning they had coffee, crisp rolls, and honey brought them in bed and exchanged their gifts, and then H went to the Diana Bad and had a quick dip in the cold pool before returning to the hotel annexe where she was ready in her sealskin to set out with him for Mass at the Stefansdom.

But as soon as Christmas was over she suggested it was time they went home, and when he was silent her melancholy descended like a cloud that lay over their table in *Weinkellers* and restaurants where orchestras were playing Strauss and couples dancing; her face seemed to get longer and her gaze more abstracted.

H saw she had begun to hate Vienna. The sealskin coat turned out a fake, the fur quickly wearing away at collar and cuffs, she found the car too cold (H promised to get side curtains made) and she had developed a cough which he told her came from her constant smoking.

H was preoccupied with teaching himself to drive. The first time he went to the garage to take out the car he was appalled at its size and look of immobility, as well as at the feel of the cold, stiff controls. After many awkward swingings of the heavy starting handle, with pauses to readjust the throttle and spark lever on the steering wheel, the big, awkward, inert piece of metal suddenly shivered and clattered and, after the first shock of delight, filled him with dread at the prospect of getting it out of the garage and into the street.

No time to get the feel of the pedals, the place was filling with blue smoke and the proprietor was watching from behind his workbench.

Release the handbrake, press down the clutch pedal, move the gear lever into the first slot, keep the engine running briskly, but not too fast, and gently manoeuvre the half-ton or more of vibrating metal down the slight slope, turning sharply into the street.

He was out of the garage and moving in first gear in the direction of Praterstrasse too quickly, without having given himself a breathing space. There was so much to get the knack of all at once; the steering alone was a problem; it was taking him all his time to keep on the right side of the street, and he missed the turn and lost his bearings.

He did not dare take his eyes for more than a moment from the snowy roadway in front of the radiator cap which the prolonged driving in bottom gear was causing to steam. To change to second while in what seemed swift motion with traffic passing, and his attention needed for all the other controls, was at the moment beyond him.

A familiar landmark loomed in front, the statue of the poet-dramatist Nestroy outside the deserted theatre halfway down Praterstrasse. He swung around the monument in an attempt to break the painful trance in which he would have to go on driving desperately forward for as long as the engine kept going, but, instead of stopping by the theatre, drove past it down a side street from which he emerged on a track that skirted some waste ground beyond which was the canal. As usual a strong wind was blowing (city of gales and heavenly beguilements!) from the direction of the river.

Clutching the wheel tightly in one hand, H managed to move the gear lever into neutral, and the Opel Darracq – he had learned the make, though the year of manufacture was never divulged – was halted in its wild-seeming flight, though the speedometer needle had never moved above the twenty kilometres-per-hour mark.

A gust of wind, penetrating under the bonnet, lifted the hinged piece of metal and carried it across the strip of waste land and into the canal. H got out and walked to the edge. The bonnet had sunk beneath the opaque, swiftly flowing water and it was clear there was no getting it out. To have a new one made and fitted would take time and probably cost more than the car was worth.

Far from mourning over its loss, H took the incident as another intimation that it was time to say farewell. He drove back to the garage and from there hurried to the hotel with the good tidings he had for Iseult. But when he told her he was ready to go home, she didn't seem particularly relieved. She said that Hansen had promised to get her two Roller canaries from the Harz mountains to take to her mother and until he'd procured them, which mightn't be for a week or two, she couldn't think of leaving.

11

They arrived back in Dublin a few days before the start of shelling by the army of the newly instituted Free State of the Four Courts, where the Republicans, or Irregulars, had their headquarters, with field guns hastily donated by Churchill.

H's mother-in-law had filled the ground floor of her house with beds and turned it into an emergency hospital for the Republican wounded.

While Iseult was busy helping her mother obtain medical supplies from well-disposed doctors, buying quantities of muslin and lint, as well as giving

64

interviews to American and foreign journalists, writing propaganda articles, some of which Iseult translated into French, H took on some humble tasks allotted him by O'Brien, the medical student in charge. He carried out slop pails with rust-stained swabs afloat in them, brought up the trays from the basement kitchen where Josephine grumbled in her patois at the young women from *Cuman na Mbhan*, and was occasionally let change some of the simpler dressings. From time to time Madame, having donned the white uniform with the small red cross on the front of the cap that she'd worn when working in a hospital at Paris-Plage during the war, took a turn at nursing.

At night in their room H and Iseult talked about the civil war and their enthusiasm for the Republican cause brought them close and gave H a family feeling; there was even a bond with his mother-in-law. H had the unfamiliar sensation of belonging within a community of like-minded people.

But soon H saw that this was a misunderstanding and that for him the civil war was something quite different from how Iseult and the others saw it. Language, and even thought, he felt, were inadequate to the expression of certain intuitions of his about the situation. Analysis was not, in any case, H's strong point. It was an effort to make clear even to himself why he was involved in this war in a way he hadn't been in the struggle for independence.

He had been aware, during the Black-and-Tan war, of the oversimplified emotions in the air that, like all passions that unite a lot of people, coarsen the texture of sensibility and lower the imaginative level. Besides the true idealists, this had been a situation welcomed by mediocre minds that only feel at home in restricted, tight-knit communities where influences from without are the more easily rejected as unpatriotic, irreligious, or, a condemnation that gains popular approval in such situations, treasonable.

The civil war created doubt and confusion, and thus a climate in which the poet could breathe more easily. Instead of uniting in a conformity of outlook that had to appeal to dull-witted idealists as well as those with intelligence, it divided people. And once the process of division had started, H foresaw it continuing, and subdivisions taking place, especially on the Republican side, perhaps creating small enclaves of what he looked on as true revolutionaries whose aim had less to do with Irish independence than in casting doubt on traditional values and judgements.

He was spending a lot of time at the bedside of a Republican officer who'd been wounded in an attempt, with some of his men, to join up with the Four Courts garrison at the start of the fighting. This was because H sensed in him a mode of consciousness closer to his own than that of the few members of the I.R.A. he'd met at his mother-in-law's. Theirs, as hers, he'd had the feeling, was a one-track, political approach to something that for him had other more complex aspects. He realized how little politics could ever concern him with their large-scale impersonal values.

One evening O'Brien remarked: 'You're very friendly with the bold Tom Whelan.'

'Why not?'

'No reason, as long as you know the sort he is: a thug and a gunman who enjoys a scrap for its own sake.'

It was this lack of idealism in Whelan that attracted H. He never commented on the rights and wrongs of the situation, referring to the Free Staters as 'those buggers'. What concerned him was the loss of his weapons when the driver of the car in which he and 'the lads' had penetrated into the city had been hit and the car had crashed on the quays. But he was spontaneous and open to all the other things that H discussed with him. When H solved the problem of keeping the trousers of Whelan's pyjamas from wrinkling up over his knees (he felt cold from loss of blood) by getting him a pair of bicycle clips, his cut lips stretched in a delighted smile that ended in a grimace.

When H shyly explained that he'd like to get to the country and take part in the fighting Whelan told him: 'We could make better use of you than that.'

H's heart fell; he supposed it was a polite rejection of his offer; with his half-awake eyes and long, soft-palmed hands, he knew he didn't look much of a fighter.

But Whelan was asking, 'Would you ever slip over to Belgium and bring us back two or three guns?'

He explained that H was to contact the firm which had been smuggling arms among other cargo on ships from Antwerp to Cork for several years.

'I'll give you a note to the old lad in Bruges, Dupont's the name, and he'll hand over what's required without being paid, that's arranged for, and you'll get your expenses from army funds. You'll travel via Hull and Ostend; at this season you can pass through the customs with the crowd of trippers and your suitcase won't be opened.' H evidently wasn't the first to be sent over when a few guns or some ammunition were needed in a hurry.

When H told Iseult about being entrusted with the mission she was pleased, and he didn't say anything to disillusion her. Instead, she told him about Paris-Plage where she too had nursed wounded *poilus*, one of whom, a Senegalese, had brought from the front the severed head of a German in a cardboard box which was discovered under his bed when it started to stink. But her reminiscences soon turned to the uninhibited lovemaking that had gone on everywhere, also under beds, in the sand dunes, in cupboards, between the Canadian nurses, who formed most of the staff, and the French officers, and of which, as always, she'd been a superiorly detached observer.

12

With the letter on a sheet of paper headed 'Oglaig na Eireann' which one of the young Cuman women had typed and Tom Whelan had signed, a single ticket to Bruges and the rest of the money in his pocket, H set out.

H stayed on deck as the ship steamed down the Humber, watching the busy estuary, struck by a solitary figure in white flannels and yachting cap at the tiller of a small yacht sailing homeward in the August evening, elegant and aloof amid the river traffic.

The image of the lone yachtsman returning up the estuary was to become an abiding one in H's memory. Was this not because it so aptly exteriorized his own still indistinct vision of the poet sailing in solitude up the broad traffic-laden stream of life?

He descended to the second-class saloon for high tea in a state where desires are intensified to the point of producing waking dreams of compelling vividness. Sitting at a long table with holidaying families he failed to hear a woman next to him make a request and was shocked by her remark to a neighbour that some people were too high and mighty to pass the milk jug. He had fallen into these states before, as when he'd imagined his cousin Stella coming to his room at night to initiate him into the sexual mystery, and there was always something crazy and perhaps dangerous about the condition. This time he was obsessed by an imaginary conversation with Mayakovsky whom he met in Moscow, having, instead of stopping at the Belgian town, travelled on to the Soviet Union.

He was only aware of Ostend as a pale opulent glimmer of buildings on the edge of the misty, morning sea. Most of the travellers were going no further and he was alone in the train compartment except for a couple of Americans, mother and daughter.

Something he saw from the window shortly after the train left the station put the idea of presenting himself at the Russian embassy in Brussels, if there was one, and suggesting they send him, a poet bearing greetings from revolutionary Ireland to Mayakovsky, out of his mind. Along cobbled roads running parallel to the railway line he noticed the end walls of the villas were pock-marked. Here were tangible traces of the ravening monster that had lurked at the cloudy, blood-red back of his own private dream during much of his adolescence. He stared in wonder and a kind of nostalgia at the signs left of an already legendary event. If only he'd known what it had really been like! But his acute longings in regard both to Russia and to the war had to be satisfied by taking the American girl's hand when her mother had gone down the corridor.

Once in the arms shop after delivering the letter and examining various weapons he gained some comfort by telling himself that the civil war, insignificant as it might seem, could still add a new dimension to experience, and, branching off at a tangent from the familiar ones, lead to a true revolutionary situation such as he longed for without being able to define clearly.

Among the guns laid on the counter for his inspection was one of the type whose loss had worried Whelan: a long-barrelled Parabellum, with detachable stock, that could be used as an automatic pistol or fired from the shoulder as a sub-machine-gun. H selected two of these, hoping Whelan would let him keep one himself, as well as a shorter gun, easier to conceal, that, in describing to him, Whelan had called a 'Peter the Painter', and also a Colt revolver, that, unlike the others which he imagined being used by anarchists and lone snipers in obscure affrays, had been the standby of British officers all over the world.

Back at the Hotel de la Poste, H wrapped the guns in the shirts he'd brought to stop them rattling in the suitcase and then sat in his room drinking one bottle of Perrier water after another; excitement had given him a raging thirst, not the kind, as in Munich, that delights in beer, but a more nervous one.

Dusk fell and down in the *Place* outside the window the townspeople started to stroll beneath the leaves. Listening to the murmur of the men and women's voices he imagined, in the faint, French intonations, sexual undertones that added to his fever.

Why was his imagination so overwhelming and his irresolution when it came to acting so complete that he had let Iseult take the initiative? Instead of listening to her telling him of the sexual adventures of others, during which he was expected to share her feelings of amused superiority, he should have drawn her with him to where sensual obsession banished objectivity and what she'd seen as ludicrous obscenities were transformed into treasured acts.

How? Not by talk, certainly. She was always one up on him there. Nor by the hesitant-tender approach. He must take over and without wasting time trying to evoke the right mood take her in his stride. The initial shock over, she might even be relieved to be able to let herself go.

During a stroll through Liverpool between trains, he had walked down a street where several shops, like those in Charing Cross Road, sold all manner of intriguing rubber contrivances. He resolved to buy some contraceptives on the return journey and on his arrival home early in the morning, by putting one on before getting into bed with her, set a new tone in their relations.

The idea of the French letters now took possession of him and they seemed at least as important as the guns. On the hot, crowded train that ran through sprawling towns divided only by a few smoke-wreathed fields where blackened sheep were grazing, he was in a fever of desire to get to Liverpool and have the devices safely in his pocket. Leaving the suitcase with the weapons in the luggage office, he hurried to one of the shops whose windows were full of unbearably lovely-looking syringes with long, flexible nozzles, douches with lengths of rubber tubing, as well as books by de Sade, Paul de Cock, and Boccaccio with provocative pictures on their covers.

With the discreet little packet safely stowed away, he retrieved the suitcase and took a taxi to the docks. Following a porter along the quay he saw ahead a bench set up where the cross-channel vessel was berthed at which some passengers were having their luggage examined.

H told the porter he'd changed his mind about embarking and the man turned back without a word, with what H saw as a characteristically English indifference to vagaries that didn't directly inconvenience him, and, after doubling what he'd been going to tip him, H shut himself into a w.c. at the waiting room on the docks.

He managed to fasten the Parabellums in their holsters to a belt around his waist under shirt and trousers, the other two guns he stuffed into pockets. Carrying the suspiciously empty suitcase, and hoping his bulky torso wouldn't attract attention, he went up to the bench where what he now saw were Irish Customs officials were waiting; there was evidently an arrangement between the two governments to prevent arms being shipped to the Republicans.

There was something in H's face and bearing, as he was to become increasingly aware in other tight corners during the years, that when others were being stopped, questioned, searched and, on some occasions, thrust into crowded cells, seemed to allay suspicion and even evoke an approving nod and a wave on from the official watchdogs. And this happened now; he was allowed to embark without more than making a token gesture of opening the suitcase.

In his cabin he unbuckled the belt and laid the guns on the berth. He then took out the envelope and examined one of the pale, rolled, rubber rings webbed over with a semitransparent membrane.

It was difficult to adjust, he got it contrariwise, trying to unroll it in the wrong direction. But once in place he felt it was part of a symbolic regalia, like judge's wig or general's baton, whose donning gave him authority.

So as not to exhaust himself prematurely he stripped off the French letter, covered the guns with a blanket, got into the other bunk and tried to let the fever die down. But he could not sleep, and after a time the sound of rapid breathing, gasping, and an occasional groan from the next cabin suggested somebody suffering from seasickness. But he soon distinguished two separate rhythms in the irregular breathings and moanings and realized that a couple was unlikely to become simultaneously sick on a night of summer calm.

By the time he arrived at his mother-in-law's the house was already abuzz. Iseult was up and dressed and preparing to accompany Madame MacBride to the Phoenix Park for an early appointment with the Papal Nuncio, to protest against the treatment of captured Republicans. Crestfallen, H went to the ward, Whelan, swarthy and bearded – he was waiting till the facial cuts healed to shave – welcomed him with a grin, and at once suggested H take a message from him to leaders of columns operating in his area of the country.

13

There were few traces of the civil war in the countryside through which H travelled. All he saw was a girl at a wayside station set fire to bundles of newspapers that a couple of armed youths pulled out of the guards' van, and some bridges that had been blown up. To reach the town that was his destination he had, with other travellers, to finish the journey by road.

They were halted at the river on the edge of the town where Free State troops had a field gun with which they were shelling a stone building that rose above the clustering roofs below. Thus without having to search for it, H was directed to local Republican headquarters which he managed to reach by a circuitous route.

At first they didn't want to let him into what was a former workhouse. A youth wearing one of the green hats of the 1916 volunteers looked him over from an upper window (the lower ones were barricaded) as a shell burst in some waste ground to one side. But when H called up that he had a dispatch from Commandant Whelan he was directed to a door at the back of the building where he was let in by a man in a trench coat.

He was taken into what must once have been the old men's dormitory and where he at once imagined them lying in rows, the grey, dispirited faces turned to the vaulted ceilings while parasites burrowed in their withered crotches. The incidental fantasies that lurked beneath the surface of events took their tone from his state of mind, now despondent partly because of failing to establish, with the aid of the contraceptives, a normal sex relationship with Iseult, and partly because the captain was bewailing the tragedy of old comrades turning on each other.

70

By the time they were getting ready for bed, H being resigned to having to spend the night there, he recognized in the officer the type who was on the Republican side not because, like H, he saw civil war as a splitting-off of the true revolutionaries from the nationalist elements in the I.R.A., but because he was at heart a conservative who needed the protection of insular traditions for his psychic comfort. H caught on his face the expression of a sad and lofty idealism that was not uncommon these days and which he interpreted as an indication of a clinging to a concept of an Ireland in which the Church and the Gaelic League would be dominant.

Warned in the morning that Free State troops had surrounded the building and that he couldn't now leave, H climbed to an upper floor to have a look for himself. From a window opposite a warehouse there was no sign of the enemy. An opening high in the old stone wall with a pulley above it for hauling up goods from the street would surely have made, with some sand-bagging, an ideal position for a machine-gun. But none was there, and H decided he could safely escape.

Before descending the stone stairs he couldn't resist making a pronouncement from the upper window, in the style of Urbi et Orbi, to the effect that, if captured, he'd be proud to be chained to the Cathedral gates with a placard round his neck informing the respectable citizens that here was one of the Irregulars, found with contraceptives in his possession.

In the guardroom he asked the captain to have the main door unbarred so that he could leave.

'You can't, man, the Staters have it covered.'

'That's my lookout; get it opened up.'

It was clear the captain had made up his mind to let the garrison become immobilized rather than fight. This H did not think was through any lack of courage. Supported by what he believed was a consensus of right-thinking, good-living people, as in the Black-and-Tan days, he'd have fought well enough.

H walked through the hall, having taken the Parabellum which Whelan had allowed him to keep, from its holster. He swung it from his hand (he had never fired a weapon in his life) as he crossed the stone flags and he heard the captain behind him give an order to have the door unbolted.

H edged out when it had been opened a few inches, walked down the stone steps and along the wall of the warehouse towards the town centre. After rounding a couple of corners he met some early shoppers, out, he supposed, in search of such things as bread and flour which he'd heard were short. They passed him without a glance, purposely ignoring the gun which they must have spotted from afar.

He wasn't sure whether to commandeer one of the sidecars outside the station, but decided it was time to put the gun back in the holster inside his trouser leg. He shared a horsedrawn car with a commercial traveller that took them some miles to what was now the end of the railway line, passing on the way a column of troops, headed by an armoured car, in which, his companion told him, was General Michael Collins on his way to dislodge the captain and his men from the warehouse.

After several changes of train and a walk late at night in pitch-darkness along sleepers over a railway bridge, directed by the stationmaster at the last station at which he'd arrived, H reached a road and followed it back to the village where Whelan had told him one of his lieutenants had his headquarters. He knocked at the sandbagged door of the hotel and a head was thrust out of one of the lit windows above from which came the sound of a gramophone, and, after a while, a maid let him in and said that, though they'd the 'lads' in the house, she'd find him a room.

H lay in bed listening to the singing and wasn't sure whether these were the men of Whelan's column or Free State troops. He awoke in the night and heard steps in the passage outside his attic room. He took the Parabellum from under the pillow and stood gripping it in one hand and pulling on his trousers with the other beside the locked door.

He was embarked on a private war which he hoped might cause a few cracks in the walls erected by generations of pious and patriotic Irishmen around the national consciousness. Then perhaps the dawn of the imaginative and undogmatic mood, that he saw as the prerequisite of true revolution, might set in.

He couldn't let himself be captured tamely, not because that would be letting down the Republican cause, which had no great need of him, but because this quite different and less popular one must be loyally served by its few defenders.

Whoever they were outside the door went away, however, and in the morning, having heard from the maid that the 'lads' were preparing to hold up the trains, he returned to the station. Through the window of the ticket office he saw a burly figure at a table and, emboldened by the concept of his role that had occurred to him in the night, knocked on it. The man, a pencil still marking the map he'd been studying, looked up.

'We're closed down.'

'I've a dispatch for Commandant Gorman.'

'You have, eh? For Christsake!'

But when H mentioned Tom Whelan the other rose and let him in.

'How did you know I wasn't the fucking stationmaster?'

H grinned. He knew that this was the man of whom Whelan had told him, the sort of Republican that, apart from Whelan himself, H hadn't yet come across. He watched the gunman as Gorman read the letter and saw the thin but expressive mouth curl at the various items of news.

'Tom was lucky to get off with a few scratches,' he commented.

'It's more than a few scratches.'

Gorman, H guessed, had exact information about the extent of his superior's wounds and only wanted to make sure that H had really come from Whelan and not got hold of the dispatch after its bearer had been taken prisoner.

When H told him of the besieged garrison on which Mick Collins was advancing unhindered, Gorman said, 'Apart from Tom Whelan and a couple more, our fellows have taken to shutting themselves up and brooding on Ireland's bloody wrongs. What did they want to occupy the Four Courts for? Mobility is what counts now, boy. Don't think Collins and Mackeown are worried by us taking over some fucking old forts as long as they can travel about the country at their own sweet will.'

Gorman brought H across fields to a farmhouse where they were given breakfast – hunger, not thirst, was now the effect that tension was having on H – and where, in a hay barn, a Crossley tender, a couple of Ford trucks, and a Vauxhall touring car were standing. But it was to a machine-gun post overlooking the road where it ran close to the railway line that H was finally conducted and there introduced to the other members of the column.

The emplacement had been constructed with railway sleepers, sacks filled with sand from the river and some corrugated iron sheets.

'Give Lieutenant Ruark (had Whelan conferred the rank on him in the dispatch?) a feel of her, Mick,' Gorman told a youth cleaning the Vickers gun.

As H hesitated, Gorman put an arm over his shoulder, gently inclining him towards the gun, and with his free hand pointing to a barricade of sleepers across the road on the far side of the railway.

'Rip into that!'

H grabbed what he thought, yet doubted and didn't want to touch, was the trigger, and simultaneously, but as though unconnected with the act, the fragile-seeming quiet which he'd been conscious of all morning since leaving the hotel was shattered.

The sudden din, the bitter smell, and the way the belt in which the bullets were studded was drawn into the metal maw shocked H out of the feeling of taking part in a countrywide charade. He was excited by the line of bullet holes that he could just make out, a pale pattern etched across the dark beams. And when Gorman told him that they were going to hold up the Wexford train that evening and invited him to take part, H was glad of the chance to test the magic power he'd been aware of as he'd examined the weapons in the shop in Bruges.

H sat on the shallow embankment in the warm dusk that smelled of hay and a whiff of paraffin, between Gorman and a young man in a trench coat called Mills. Then Gorman looked at his watch, tapped H's arm, got up and walked away to join two of his men at a point where the track ran close to the road and where they were to unload the petrol drums from the guard's van.

H and the youth were to stop the train, and H would have liked to take out the Parabellum and lay it across his knees, but Mills was lying casually back on the grass with his hands behind his head staring up at the misty moon that seemed to be growing brighter and, dimming the glow of the lantern, making H shiver as he and his companion grew ever more clearly visible. God Almighty, what was that! He caught a distant rumble borne on the intermittent breeze that was blowing up the track. Though the moon itself was now holding its breath and withdrawing into a deeper haze, Mills didn't move.

'Here it comes!' H said.

'Good enoughski.'

H's nervousness made him resent this silly craze of the moment of tacking a Russian ending on to already hackneyed expressions.

The sound of the train was suddenly penetrating the last recesses of H's composure, and a huge black circular object was rolling towards them, trailing beside it bars of light stencilled against the embankment from which Mills had jumped down at the last moment swinging the lantern.

The hot, hissing engine loomed above H with great grinding wheels and connecting rods clattering to a stop. As instructed by Gorman, H jumped on the step of the first carriage, pulled himself up by the door handle and, gun in hand, peered into the bright compartment.

Any Free State soldiers were to be ordered out and, if they resisted, shot. But there were only some countrywomen in the compartment, one of whom had thrown herself to the floor, and H passed on to the next one on his way to join up with Gorman who, starting at the rear, was also proceeding along the train by way of the outside step, there being no corridor.

H heard Mills talking with the driver and fireman and, from the other end, the men unloading the petrol and others rolling the drums to the road where, covered by the machine-gun post, the tenders he'd seen at the farmhouse were waiting.

Hanging by the handles he swung himself along, looking in at women crossing themselves with the crucifixes of rosaries and the few men sitting silently with eyes on the floor. He opened the door of a compartment where there were only two girls and an elderly man and stepped in. Both girls were looking up at him, wide-eyed and pale, not avoiding his glance.

Was this the moment that they, like him, had been waiting for, when familiar habits and conventions were swept away and nobody was safe who didn't want to be, nothing was disallowed to the daring, and whatever could be imagined could be made come true?

He looked boldly into the face of the younger girl and she smiled at him as her sister exclaimed, 'Up the Republic! Up de Valera!'

H was sobered and brought back to earth from the start of one of his fantasies. He certainly didn't share their enthusiasm for de Valera. De Valera was one of the most reactionary of the leaders on either side. He had an integrity and vision that the Free State lot lacked, but this merely ensured that he wouldn't compromise on the national issue; as a revolutionary leader, in the sense that interested H, he had nothing to offer.

It was with Whelan back in Dublin that H felt he came closest to sharing an outlook on the civil war, though they didn't discuss it. Whelan was not only fearless (as his exploits in the Black-and-Tan war had proved) but was endowed with the scepticism that H saw as the necessary saving grace. Without it one was involved in mass enthusiasms that always ended in complacency and set a limit to the spirit's questing.

Whelan, his head on the pillow, was drawing on an unlit half of a cigarette. He had half-jokingly commended H for his carrying out of the mission entrusted to him and was suggesting that he return with himself and his younger brother, Steve, also a patient in the ward, to the south.

'We'll require transport,' he said.

'Any particular kind of vehicle in mind?' H asked.

Whelan indicated that H should lean closer. Glancing over his shoulder H saw the medical student, O'Brien, at the next bed. He struck a match and bent down to light Whelan's stub for him.

'What we need is an armoured car.'

The humorous curl wasn't quite gone from the corners of Whelan's still raw-looking mouth and H couldn't be sure at first whether this was serious. But it seemed he had heard, among his visitors had been some from the Dublin Brigade, that an armoured car went every evening to Amiens Street Station with a couple of army trucks that took military supplies arriving there by train to one of the barracks occupied by Government troops. Nothing more was said about it then because O'Brien arrived at the bed and H went to look for Iseult who hadn't been at home when he'd arrived.

He found her sitting on the bed in their room playing patience. She put her arms around him and her brown eyes darted over his face in the way he recalled as though looking for something there that she feared to find, or hoped for but failed to: sexual desire in the first instance, a spark of patriotic fervour in the second?

He told her about where he'd been and what he'd seen, and he imagined she was disappointed when he didn't report that the kind of puritan and ultranationalist Republicanism she seemed to favour was sweeping the country.

But, ignoring this, she was soon talking to him about an article in a French Catholic periodical in which Ireland was compared to an ark that could save Europe from the flood of materialism, pausing now and then to place a card on one of the rows laid out on the bedspread.

His fingers closed over the envelope in his pocket but he did not draw it out. It would be easier, when the time came, to take the long-barrelled gun from its holster inside his trouser leg and step out on to the cobbles at the station entrance in front of the armoured car.

Yet if he didn't produce the contraceptives now and get her to undress and go to bed, first sweeping off the cards, he might never have such a chance again to give a new direction to their relationship by substituting a sensual climate for all this idealism. But he hesitated; his resolution failed in the face of what he foresaw would be her lofty scorn.

That night, H, having lightly kissed Iseult, slipped out of the front door into the deserted street, where a curfew was in force and where, beyond the railings of the park, the autumn dusk hung thick and brownish, like dregs in a teacup, among the dry leaves.

He paused in the shadows and threw the little packet of contraceptives over the railings. Then he peed through them, although he'd emptied his bladder before leaving the house. The abandoning of the French letters was probably a milestone that, if he survived, he would recognize as more important than any other events of the night. It marked the failure of his marriage.

Once H had joined Steve Whelan he became calmer. The youth, even younger than H, had the casual fortitude of his brother. As they proceeded towards the Talbot Street rendezvous with members of the Dublin Brigade, Steve remarked: 'Here, better have some of these.'

H held out his hand not sure what to expect, a couple of wafers of the gum that his companion was chewing, and a heavy, egglike object dropped into it. Shocked, H transferred it quickly to his trouser pocket as Steve passed him a couple more Mills grenades. The third bulged in the jacket of the beige-coloured suit he'd bought in the Praterstrasse one snowy morning. O city of steamy nymphs, blue dusks seen from inside warm, coffee-scented cafés!

Four or five figures suddenly stood in front of H and Steve with mock cries of 'Stick them up!' They stood on the pavement talking and joking with Steve after what H imagined a quick glance of surprise at himself in the pale suit with the foreign cut and the thick fringe low over his forehead. Then the leader of the gay little band (H had expected the mood to be desperate and determined) drew them, laying a hand that made him tremble on H's shoulder, into an alleyway under a railway viaduct. In a rather offhand way, between draws at the cigarette cupped in the palm of his hand, he briefed them on their respective tasks, outlining the plan for the benefit of H and Steve, and warning them, and H imagined the instruction especially directed to himself, against tossing a grenade through the windscreen of the armoured car which, he reminded them, had to be captured undamaged.

H's bladder was once again stinging as the youths, their faces hidden under the soft hats in the unlit laneway, discussed the blind spots in the car crew's field of vision.

H kept beside Steve. From him, via the indirect route of his brother, he gained reassurance. He saw the younger Whelan's upper lip recede from his teeth in the same way as Tom's in a smile completely unforced and undaunted.

When they took up their appointed positions, it was Steve and one of the volunteers from the North Dublin Brigade who, placed one on each side of the cobbled approach to the station, were first to engage the car crew.

Beside the ticket windows in the railway station H was posted, covering the exit from the platform, while a couple of the I.R.A. men had gone to deal with sentries guarding the station offices occupied by the Free Staters. The leader of the group was, with a lame companion, like Steve recovering from being wounded in earlier fighting, at the main entrance towards which the armoured car would be proceeding.

From where he was H had much the same view of the inside of the station that, with his hand in Weg's, had excited him long ago. He examined one of the posters. The bullock, the gate, the flustered old gentleman whose cheeks were a lighter tint of the bullock's hide, how nostalgically sweet now looked the picture! He could recall his former delight in the caption 'A little Oxo keeps the doctor away.'

The first shots from inside the station came as a relief. From then on H kept his eyes on the few yards of platform visible through the entrance beyond where he stood. He heard an explosion and machine-gun fire from behind him and the sound reassured him that he wasn't, as he'd almost ended by imagining, holding the fort alone.

He felt a cold, sharp pressure at the back of the neck. Two survivors of the crew of the armoured car had entered the hall without his hearing them.

14

H was marched by a small party of Government troops to a barracks by the canal. In the guardroom a captain in a new green uniform took the Parabellum from the sergeant in charge of the patrol. The grenades had been removed from his pockets by his first captors.

'One in the breach, and a full magazine,' the sergeant remarked, laying the extracted bullets on the deal table.

'Not the spirit of the old days,' the captain agreed.

'Gave himself up, sir.'

So H recalled his original captors, themselves in a galling predicament, telling the sergeant. He himself hadn't said a word, and didn't now. He was cast down; what he was ashamed of was not having once fired a shot from the gun that he'd brought back from Belgium with so much pride and expectation.

He spent the night with a crowd of prisoners in a long barrack building where at first he was eyed doubtfully because, perhaps, of the foreign-looking suit which, however, would surely not be what an informer planted there by the Free Staters would have worn. But he was soon noticed and spoken to by one of a group of captured officers at the end of the building, Noel Lemass, who himself had Continental connections, and who remembered H from visits to the house in St Stephens Green. He offered H a Gaulloise cigarette, after which, on his return to his mattress, his immediate neighbours started talking to him too.

Next day the prisoners were taken to Kingsbridge Station. H was in the last of the three or four lorries and as it turned into South Circular Road the military car that was following dropped behind. H, at the front of the open truck and facing forward, became aware of a movement of those standing beside him and turned to see a couple of prisoners jump from the tailboard, roll over on the roadway, pick themselves up, and disappear down a side street through the strollers in the Sunday afternoon sun.

Lemass, awaiting his turn to jump, gestured to him to make his way to the rear of the truck, but H didn't move. He had seen enough of the civil war to grasp the fact that it hadn't much to do with him after all. Under either De Valera or Griffith, art, religion, and politics would still be run by those who at best used them to give them power, prestige, and a good living, and, at worst, for this to H was more dangerous, as a means towards a sterile, high-toned conformism.

On his next birthday he would be twenty-one and captivity would give him the chance to take a long look at his own position and face the fact that it seemed he'd come to a dead end both in his marriage and as a writer.

Once entrained, they were counted compartment by compartment. Then a man in civilian clothes well known to some of the prisoners from earlier days counted them again. His eyes moved quickly from face to face and those who'd been his former comrades-in-arms he hit across mouth and nose with the butt of his revolver.

As the train at last pulled out they saw the solitary figure of the former intelligence officer standing at the very end of the platform swinging his revolver by its cord and the prisoners took a heartfelt oath, both those like H unscathed and those still pressing bloody handkerchiefs to their mouths that, once free, their first task would be to find and even out matters with him.

H was put in a cell already occupied by two political prisoners from whom he heard that he'd arrived at a time of crisis. Parcels had been stopped for some breach of regulations and the prisoners' commandant, whom they pointed out to H at exercise, handsome, with pale gold hair, eyebrows, and lashes, an I.R.A. general in spite of his youth, had threatened to call a hunger strike.

In the first few days, however, what struck H was the unexpected tranquillity, in which all that occupied him were trivial aspects of prison life that quietly took possession of his thoughts. When at midday he received the can containing, on top, some potatoes boiled in their skins, then green, grey-veined cabbage leaves, and, at the bottom, several slices of meat the colour of old leather, he carefully decanted the layers on to his enamel plate in a steamy aroma, intent on keeping them separate, and ate the meal with peculiar relish on his bunk. The early supper of cocoa and two thick slices of fresh bread he also lingered over lovingly.

Then one afternoon as the door was unlocked for exercise and H had just finished meditatively cleaning his utensils, a whistle was blown, the agreed-on signal, his cellmates told him, to set fire to the prison.

The three of them set about ripping up the mattresses, piled the stuffing in the middle of the scrubbed wooden floor, placed on it fragments from the broken stools, the legs of the deal table, added the contents of a blue packet of sugar, highly inflammable according to the red-bearded prisoner, Murphy. H was pained at the destruction of objects that, by covering them in a finely spun web of the imaginative plasma that certain hostile situations caused him to secrete, he had transformed into part of his inner world.

At a second blowing of the whistle a match was set to the mattress fibre and the prisoners crowded out into the small yard that was soon filled with smoke billowing through the broken glass of the barred windows. Rain slanted down over the high stone wall on to the shining coal heaps outside the basement bunkers, and along a barbed-wire fence across one end of the exercise yard H saw soldiers in uniforms darkened by rain, and blurred by smoke, take up position.

At the first volley of rifle fire the prisoners threw themselves on the muddy ground. After a moment of silence H cautiously raised his head. One prisoner was still standing facing the wire above the prone bodies, a look on his brows that puzzled and thrilled H, and a tuft of white sprouting from amid his dark tousled hair. At the next volley H ducked down again, pressing his cheek to the wet earth.

Silence came rushing back into the fearful vacuum made by the rifle fire and with it, giving it a special emphasis, the moans of the wounded. A cap in which H had a glimpse of some bloody effluvia, that his neighbour assured him was brains, was passed under his nose.

As the stretcher bearers arrived, the prisoners began getting to their feet and after drifting dazedly around for a moment or two, coalescing into tight little knots of curiosity. There were all sorts of conflicting accounts. The troops had fired over the prisoners and some bullets, ricocheting off the wall, had hit a few of them. They had fired directly at the prisoners in the belief that they were making a mass attempt to escape under cover of the smoke and the casualties had been heavy. H counted about a dozen carried away on the stretchers, but whether dead or wounded he couldn't be sure.

It rained steadily, and from time to time during the night H, with five others, three at each side, helped to hold prisoners who'd fainted from shock and exposure above the mud that was soon inches deep, until they could be taken off on stretchers. The rows of barred windows glowed all night, and towards morning H lay down in one of the heaps of coal and slept soundly, waking for a moment or two to hear the muted roar of flames and the low, rhythmic slappings of the cheeks of those who'd collapsed.

He arose in the grey, wet dawn full of an acrid reek, the Praterstrasse suit soaked and coal-stained. All sorts of rumours had arisen in the night and were being discussed. General Mulcahy, the commander of the Government forces, had arrived in an armoured car and was at this moment reprimanding the prison governor for mishandling the situation. He was advising the governor to have the fire hoses turned on the prisoners. He had ordered their immediate release; their transference to another place of detention. They were all about to be confined in the coal cellars on a ration of bread and water. Two Republican columns, one commanded by Tom Whelan, were converging on the prison and having breached the wall with a charge of gelignite, would plug the guards and rescue the lot of them.

The one certainty was that a delegation from a section of the prisoners had

80

gone to the fair-haired commandant, Joe Regan, to ask him to request the governor that they be allowed back into the burnt-out block. Hearing of this, H approached the group in a corner of the yard standing around Regan, one of whom he saw was the young man who'd refused to lie down when the firing had started. H pushed his way towards him rather than to Regan, as he had intended, to protest against any move there might be to return to the cells.

But the youth anticipated him by asking if he played bridge and when, taken aback, H hesitated, he added, 'You look as though you might. My name's Sean Lane.'

H introduced himself and, before answering Lane's question, said he hoped Regan wouldn't listen to what he'd heard the delegation was proposing.

'Oh, those are the cookhouse lads,' Lane said. 'The ones who've had it easiest always crack first.'

He spoke as though it was a matter of indifference to him, and then brought H to Regan and introduced him as the fourth for whom they'd been waiting, and Regan, the raindrops sparkling in his fair hair and eyebrows, started dealing the cards on to an upturned packing case, though H had still not said whether he played or not.

Around midday Regan, after having been called to the governor's office, ordered the prisoners back into the block. Once inside, H was glad of the warmth that radiated from the walls, and the smell of burnt wood that, when mingled with cigarette smoke, turned to a peculiar sour-sweet aroma was to him for a long time, whenever he caught it again, the vivid recollection of that phase of his existence that began as, with the single blanket issued to each prisoner, he climbed the hot iron stairs in search of a new abode; all the doors having been burnt, there was no more sequestration.

Finding an empty cell on the top floor H spread his blanket on the concrete. He was joined by another prisoner in search of a corner of his own who, with a look around the place, exclaimed: 'We can do a bit better than that.'

His new companion, Bluett, was soon threading a length of wire he'd managed to detach from one of the strands that formed a safety screen along the catwalks above the well of the prison through the hems on each side of the blanket. Under his direction, they constructed a hammock with their two blankets and stretched it high from the window bars at one end to the old gas bracket above the door at the other. Climbing into this with the aid of the packing case that H had had the foresight to bring in with him from the yard, they lay feet to feet in comfort and seclusion.

Soon parcels, dispatched by lorry from Dublin by anxious relatives, started arriving, and in each of the first received by H and Bluett, besides the welcome foodstuffs, was the very same thick book in red cloth binding. In the excitement of unpacking, and reading the labels on the jars of jam and potted meat, shrimp, tongue, chicken-and-tongue, salmon, they looked at the title twice and supposed their own book had been handed back by mistake until, after a further exchange, it was still the same: *The Brothers Karamazov*.

They lay reading all day in their hammock, only descending to take in their rations and to go to one of the two lavatories, now doorless, the bowls broken, the floor flooded, at the end of their landing. As for ablutions, H couldn't have recalled on any particular day when he had washed last.

At lights out, when they came to discuss the day's events, which meant those in the novel in which they were involved far more deeply than in the almost imperceptible prison ones, they marvelled together, comparing notes, at the vast range of emotions, whose impact was overwhelming on their impressionable young consciousness, from the most murderous, lecherous, cynical, to those at the inner heart of peace, faith, and holiness.

Though exercise was no longer compulsory, H occasionally went to the yard for a breath of air that was free of the constant smell of damp, charred wood. On the way there he crossed the well of the prison block, flooded at the time of the fire, and now, it struck him, inhabited by those who preferred a kind of slum freedom to the tentative order being restored on the upper floors. It was down there that an army doctor, on a tour of inspection, had entered one of the wet cells, picked up a blanket by its corner and, to the amusement of the occupants, exclaimed, 'By Christ, it's lousy!' And it was at a cell entrance there that H had run into Lane again and been asked to come and play bridge of an evening. But though the idea attracted H, not for the sake of the card game but because of Lane, he couldn't tear himself away from the novel. But after several days of absentminded scratching, he and Bluett discovered with their thumb nails the pearly vermin in the seams of their shirts and underpants, and this ended in their having to take down the hammock and spend a day shivering in coarse prison underwear while their own clothes were fumigated.

Without the hammock the cell was uninhabitable, and H and Bluett were forced to separate and each find himself a place in one where improvements had been carried out with what odds and ends of timber, some surreptitiously prized from the platform in the tailor's shop that had escaped the fire, could be laid hands on.

H returned to his former cell where, perhaps because of the lavish parcels sent him by Iseult, his two former cellmates were ready to welcome him.

To construct a bunk for himself at this late stage when all the available material had been taken wasn't easy. But H had noticed where the portable altar, used by the chaplain on Sundays, was stored near the entrance that joined the burnt-out wing to the rest of the prison. This entrance had been covered by a wire screen and a sentry posted there; the brightly lit passageway leading to it was a kind of no-man's-land.

H walked, neither hurriedly nor with any suggestion of lingering or hanging around, to where the dismantled structure leaned against the wall. He took hold of the wooden top of the altar without a glance at the sentry, hoping by his movements to suggest, as he had to himself, that he was taking it for use in some devotions that had been authorized for that evening.

Once safely out of the passageway, and without telling him what it was, H got his bearded cellmate, Murphy, to help him carry the heavy piece of wood up the circular, iron stairs. With the packing case that he'd brought from the other cell, H had a bunk raised from the floor and comfortably wide if not long enough to lie on without tucking up his legs. A coloured photogravure torn from a magazine, and stuck above his cot with some of the breakfast porridge, completed his new haven. The picture of a London street at night, the Victoria Palace theatre was on the right and the station precincts on the left, though he would have preferred a photo of the Coliseum, with its promise, or if not promise, for he'd not yet begun to long for freedom, reminder, of all that was going on beyond the prison walls, was a link both with the past and the future.

On the evening that H finished reading *The Brothers Karamazov* the theft of the altar top was discovered, and after a search of the cells, H and his cellmate were, on the orders of Regan, shut up in the tailor's shop while their case was being considered. Or as the punishment already decreed, H couldn't be sure which.

After an hour or two of pacing up and down the floor the door was unlocked and Lane appeared. With a prod in the ribs he told Murphy he'd been granted a Royal Pardon and conducted H to Regan's cell, informing him on the way that he'd got him released to make up the fourth, no satisfactory player having yet been found, at cards.

So H, just as he was emerging from his intense Dostoevskian dream, entered a period of orderliness, spending evening after evening in the comfort of Regan's cell, seated on a solid bench at a table covered by a blanket, and served tea by an orderly. It wasn't the cards that interested him (they no longer exerted the spell that they once had over him when he played with Iseult half the day before they had even dressed) but the company of Lane and, to a lesser extent, of Regan. (The fourth player was an elderly man who had been the Provisional Government's representative somewhere or other before the Treaty.)

H was told by his cellmates about an exploit of Lane's during the Black-

and-Tan war, an event that might have become a legend, like that of Kevin Barry, had it not had about it something distasteful to the public whose attitude decided such matters; that H hadn't heard of it was probably due to his having been in Vienna at the time.

As related by Murphy, Lane, with a companion who'd been killed in the course of the operation, had forced his way into a Dublin hospital, dragged from his bed a notorious auxiliary officer recovering from wounds, knelt him on the floor and, with a gun to the top of his skull, split open his head. He had then shot his way out of the building.

The second of H's cellmates added the information that it was then that the lock of Lane's hair had turned white.

Every evening Lane slipped up the three flights of iron stairs from his damp ground-floor abode and, always the last to arrive, padded into Regan's cell in an old pair of bedroom slippers. Win or lose – they played for cigarettes – he was ready to continue far into the night. Mostly he and H were partners and there was natural accord between them, not just in their play but in the conversation that sometimes took the place of the games; they formed the critical, disrupting half of the foursome.

One evening a soldier entered the cell with a note for Regan from the Governor, and the other three waited, cards in hand, while he read it.

'Mick Collins was shot dead today by some of our lads in County Cork,' Regan announced.

H saw his fair, handsome face harden as he added: 'That's bad, you know. Nobody had a right to do that.'

The elderly diplomat, his expression grave, nodded. H remained silent. He hadn't taken part in the fight against the British and it wasn't for him to speak.

'It's not what he did in the past,' Lane said, glancing at H first out of his soft grey eyes, 'that was easy enough, given the guts. A hero was needed and he fitted the part. Mick, the brilliant guerrilla leader with a charmed bloody life. But he wasn't the one to stand up alone and ask, "Fuck the lot of you, are you fighting for a piece of the old bloody pie, or are we baking a new one?"'

'Hey, Sean, have a heart,' Regan protested. 'If it hadn't been for him we'd never have been offered even as much as the Treaty. In signing it in London he did what he believed was best at the moment.'

'All I'm saying is, when the chance came of becoming the honourable ex-gangster and renting the police chief's snug bloody villa and having him and his family in to tea to show there was no ill feeling, he couldn't resist. Mick was too fucking flattered the moment Churchill put a hand on his arm and took him into the study for a private chat.'

84

In the morning Regan blew his whistle and had the prisoners assemble in the yard. Standing in front of the first row, flanked by the diplomat and a leader from the South, he told them the news.

There was a moment's silent shock while the sentries watched from their wooden platforms high on each of the two corners of the wall. Then came a cheer, short, hesitant, and far from general, which H, but probably few others, knew was led by Lane, and in which he joined.

15

Other news from outside seeped in, though they saw only an odd newspaper, and letters were censored.

Noel Lemass's body had been found on a mountainside near Dublin. And, but this news came directly by way of a volley of rifle fire early one morning, prisoners captured with arms were being shot.

A man with a bandaged hand, returned from the hospital wing that overlooked the execution yard, came to Regan one evening during a card game to describe the three youths coming without hats or coats into the rain accompanied by the prison chaplain in a black oilskin and a Free State lieutenant. Two of the young men had rosaries in their hands and the officer a gun. At the wall the little party halted and turned around. The priest blessed the three youths and then walked across the yard. The officer then said something and received a reply from one of the three, before he too turned and walked towards the firing squad.

Rain fell on the three faces, two of which were upturned with closed eyes; the face of the other was inclined downwards, his eyes open but lowered. When the volley was fired this one's hands shot up to his chest and through his wet shirt the blood flowed over them. He fell on to his knees, his head bowed over the boy who had collapsed first and lay, face down, in the mud. The third fell back and was momentarily supported, choking, by the wall with a bloody froth bubbling out of his mouth.

Lane told H of a tunnel that, under the direction of an engineer from the Arigna coal mines, was being dug from a ground-floor cell, the earth being taken at night in sacks and deposited under the wide platform of the tailor's shop. He asked H to volunteer for the day and night shifts, not of digging, but of keeping watch at the window of one of the w.c.s from where the door across the yard from which the guards would emerge to carry out a raid could be kept under observation.

H took his turn standing for four hours every night after the card-playing (he had no day shifts) in the w.c. to which a door had been fixed and kept closed on the pretext of it being out of order. He kept his eyes on the entrance faintly suffused with light reflected from the lamps that shone on to the top of the outer wall.

In the long chill hours beside the broken, seatless lavatory bowl, gazing intently out between the bars until he imagined the hazily illuminated door had opened and shadows were thronging out, H reflected on what becoming a writer meant. He believed it was being able to exteriorize in fiction or poetry the intense but cloudy and otherwise inexpressible intimations and insights that obsessed him.

After the night vigils H slept late, having managed to make himself another plank bed, undisturbed by the vast prison hum that, swelled by confluent streams of sound from each floor, rose from the central well. He awoke in time to empty the contents of the dinner can on to his enamel plate and, with additions from his parcels, as well as more solid food, Iseult sent unnecessary, exotic items like stuffed olives, eat the meal sitting up under the blankets.

Because of his work on the tunnel Lane had to give up the evening card sessions and, instead of going to Regan's cell, H visited him during his rest periods. It was Lane who kept a countercurrent flowing in the prison, not only of opposition to their jailers but also towards much of what H had felt was the conformism of the world outside.

With Lane H discussed the things that were on his mind, such as the news that Iseult had written him about W. B. Yeats being awarded the Nobel Prize.

'I don't know much about the fucker,' Lane said, 'but to me it sounds like a sellout, letting them hang the ribbon with the bloody medal on it round his neck. If he wrote the sort of poetry that told the truth he'd be more likely to have the other kind of noose slipped over it.'

H instinctively accepted what Lane said; at the same time he had to defend Yeats as a poet. Lane lolled on a platform he'd made with some of the planks from the tailor's shop above the perpetually wet floor of his cell and beguiled H with his crude fantasies such as the one about an interview the wife of a newly appointed minister had given a lady reporter.

'You've no worries, Mrs O'Toole, with the big majority I hear your husband has.'

'No, indeed, Ma'am, none at all. Would you believe it when I tell you at the last erection he only just got in!'

'Do you ever feel at a loose end up here in the city, Mrs O'Toole?'

'Oh, I do indeed, Ma'am! But with Jimmy out at the Dail all bloody day, it's often night before I can get my hands on it. And then you can bet, Ma'am, it isn't loose long!'

H admired Lane more than anyone he'd come across, more than gunmen like Whelan or Gorman, more than any of his schoolboy heroes. Lane struck him as bringing to each situation a fresh, pure, critical gaze, unclouded by any of the preconceptions of the time and place.

Though Lane hadn't the gift of the poet, his vision seemed to H a sharp and shining instrument cutting its way towards the treasure buried under the accumulated silt of convention.

'It's only when I'm with you,' H told him, 'that I'm not aware of guilty secrets that I'd better keep to myself. What most people here respect, such as religion, literature, or nationalism, I either despise, or if at first I do seem to share some of their beliefs, like about poetry or the Republican cause in the civil war, it soon turns out that it's for quite different reasons and that we're even further apart than had we disagreed from the start.'

They looked at each other and Lane's dove-grey eyes lit with laughter at H's sudden earnestness. H went on to tell him of his feelings on hearing of the girls chained to the church railings. Lane nodded, his mouth full of bread and onion, apparently not thinking it necessary to make a more explicit comment. H, however, wanted to make sure that Lane understood.

'What's so horrible,' he said, 'is to live by established categories. Then anyone whose behaviour collides with the popular faith of the time and place is automatically condemned. Those girls probably acted from selfish greed, or perhaps just sex, but at least that prevented them from being absorbed into the soul-deadening community of the righteous, and losing their power to grow inwardly either in guilt or innocence.'

A few nights later H, from his post at the window, saw the reflected light on the door he was watching suddenly fade as it opened inwards and, instead of the shadows that sometimes formed and dissolved around it, a detachment of soldiers emerged at the double.

H leaned through the wire screen of the top catwalk, blew his whistle, then went to his cell and got under the blankets. He lay listening to the uprush of noise from below, the clanging open of the gate to the yard, the clatter of studded boots on stone and, finally, two dull explosions that, echoing from wall to wall and reverberating along the metal floors of the catwalks overhanging the prison well, rattled the enamel utensils in the cell.

Murphy, who had had to be let into the secret because of H's late shifts, murmured, 'They've lobbed in a couple of eggs.'

And H imagined Lane, having received the warning too late to crawl out, crouched at the end of the tunnel, wounded by splinters from the grenades. He got up and pulled on his trousers.

'Where do you think you're going?' Murphy asked.

'To have a look. I won't be long.'

'Don't act the bloody idiot; they'll plug anyone they catch sneaking around.'

H put his bare feet into the pair of boots Iseult had sent him. Without trying to lessen the sound of his descent, he started down the spiral iron stairs.

If he'd trusted his own eyes at the first movement of the door and raised the alarm a few seconds sooner, whoever had been working in the tunnel would have had that much more time to get out.

H reached the ground floor – the noise he made being similar to that of the studded boots of the soldiers hadn't called attention to him – and, walking close to the wall on one side where the rainwater that leaked in through the glass roof broken since the fire, collected, made his way towards Lane's cell. When had he had this identical sense of dread? On Iseult's non-appearance on the platform at Euston three years before.

H slipped into the cell and, instead of the empty bunk he'd feared, saw the recumbent form, covered up, head and all. He pulled back a corner of blanket and Lane – had he really slept through the racket and not been near the tunnel at all? – looked up.

'For Christ's sweet sake!' he exclaimed.

H left the cell again without a word, standing for a moment in the shadow close to the wall cast by the first-floor catwalk. But he'd been seen by an officer at the entrance to the cell where the tunnel had been found. The Free Stater called a sergeant who, a colt revolver in his hand, strode across, shouting: 'What the hell do you think you're doing?'

'I heard a noise, Sergeant, and came down to see what it was.'

The sergeant examined H with an astonished gaze while H, conscious of his sad and innocent-looking face, stood meekly before him.

'He says he heard a noise, Sir!' the sergeant called to the captain.

'Take his name!'

'Name!'

'Ruark.'

'Fuck off back to your cell!'

As H turned to go he had a glimpse of Lane wrapped in a blanket (he slept naked) in the doorway of his cell.

16

In late winter half the prisoners, H among them, were moved to an internment camp at the Curragh where they were lodged in corrugated iron
huts with concrete floors whose channelling indicated their former use as
stables.

It was like moving to a drab suburb from the heart of a city. H missed the
teeming, three-tiered prison existence where, on winter evenings, to descend
the spiral stairs, itself as thronged as Jacob's ladder, and stroll around the
prison well and back by one of the lower catwalks had been to become aware
of a teeming activity like that, he imagined, of a besieged town from which
the women have been evacuated and where the shops and offices have been
closed.

This new placee was more exposed to, though shut away from, the outside
world. They watched racehorses exercised in the early mornings beyond the
furze bushes and the comings and goings among the barrack buildings up
on the hill.

The big grassy compound, the breath of outside air blowing in through
the wire, made it hard for H to surround himself with an atmosphere to
replace the sooty, sour cigarette-scented, brightly lit, humming air of the
prison block.

Batch by batch they were allotted huts the evening they arrived, but some
switching about was possible and H managed to end up in the same hut as
Lane, the last but one of the third and outer row. Here, furthest from the
muddy track that ran from the entrance gate between the first row of huts
and the cook and washhouses, seemed a corner they might make their
own.

But it turned out that Lane had chosen it because it was next but one to
the barbed-wire perimeter. The last hut, he explained to H, though handier
for tunnelling from, would come under closer scrutiny by the guards.

Lane and his chosen squad set to work the second night, first moving the
wooden lining of the end wall inwards a couple of feet, an alteration to the
long hut unobservable except by careful measurements, thus creating a space
where the excavated earth could be hidden.

Neither Regan nor the fourth of the bridge players had been transferred
to the camp, and in any case Lane who was directing operations, the mining
engineer having also remained behind, had no time for cards.

H found a companion in Joe Campbell, a stocky, grey-haired poet of
whom he had heard, who marched round and round the compound in riding

breeches and brightly polished boots with H and talked to him about literature.

Although he didn't admire Campbell's parochially native verse and found the talk about books that he hadn't read less than absorbing, H liked the little man with his big porous-looking nose. According to prisoners from the same unit, he could have cleared off at their capture on account of his age but had insisted in climbing into the Free State tender with the rest of them, glad of a respite from his wife and children.

H's thoughts began to turn to the hospital hut of which he'd heard favourable reports and his temperature soon became high enough to gain him admission. There he lay in bed and read whatever was available.

What he asked of a book was that it preoccupy and haunt him. For this the novel needn't have a high literary quality, his taste being still immature, and he was soon absorbed in one by Gilbert Frankau set in the mysterious East in which the hero eats the seeds from a plant in the jungle the natives call the Tree of Life. He then retires with a dusky girl to his room in a ramshackle hotel, and the sentence occurs that transported H far from the drab camp: 'To be under the spell of the drug with the naked woman he loved in the hot, steamy night was to enter a paradise closed to other men.'

H reflected on this and a few other passages that took his fancy as his own peculiar fever ebbed and flowed, always appearing to rise in time for the daily visit of the old army doctor who, in any case, was sympathetically inclined to him. While usually adamant in sending patients back to their huts as soon as he could, his invariable comment after taking H's temperature was 'Hmm ... Another week at least, young man. Then we'll see ...'

H awaited a visit from Lane. Every afternoon he put down his book that, after the Frankau novel, was *Moby-Dick*, sent him in a parcel by Iseult, and when the blankets that screened off the dispensary and the entrance end of the hut parted he hoped to see the tousled, parti-coloured head of Lane come stooping through.

When he did come, the talk, carried on in a low voice, was mostly about the tunnel and the setbacks that had arisen. Water was seeping in and the lighting was bad. Though a cable had been run down from the hut, it was only of use during the hours when the camp current was switched on. For most of the time they were using candles improvised out of mutton fat.

It struck H that away from the card table or the intense atmosphere of the prison, they had little to talk of. What they shared were instincts and, perhaps, an outlook too subterranean to discuss except at rare moments.

Joe Campbell arrived one morning, suffering, he said, from piles, or perhaps as H guessed, lack of a patient listener, with an armful of back numbers of the *New York Times Book Review* which his wife, who got them from her brother, or it might be his, in America, had sent on to him. Luckily for H, neither of the adjoining beds were vacant, and he and the poet were separated by the central passageway with the iron stoves and supporting posts along it.

Campbell lent H the book supplements and he studied this world within a world with surprise and dismay. They reminded him of his glimpses of literary Dublin, of the closed society in which the writers were preoccupied with something called literature that to H was still somewhat of an abstraction and with their own reputations as participants in this mysterious contest. The idea of a weekly paper devoted wholly to literature struck him as peculiar as having religious periodicals. Both seemed to cater for those who liked to indulge their sectarian interests in a closed, self-protective circle with their fellow addicts.

For H, literature was only to be experienced by those who dared pluck it direct from the tree of life, as, he assumed, was also the case with sex. Religion possibly grew on the same Hesperidean branch, but being a fruit he hadn't bitten into he couldn't tell if it had the beautiful wild taste of the other two, or if, as he suspected, its flavour betrayed the confectioner's art.

This weekly review of books had nothing to do with exploring the lonely and dangerous paths that led to the tree where these fruit grew in secret splendour.

He didn't know how to express his reaction to Campbell. Like his other obsessions, his feeling about literature, or poetry as he still thought of it, was very hard to speak of without falsification.

Not that Campbell seemed to expect any pronouncement by H on the subject. He was back to say good-bye the next day, indignant at having been discharged by the doctor while, according to him, his complaint was not yet cured.

'The mills of God grind slow but sure,' he told H, frowning down at him in his role as prophet of retribution; for the doctor? the free Staters? his wife, whom, it seemed, he suspected of infidelity?

H made the best of the days in bed, waking in the spring mornings and kneeling on his cot to watch the first strings from the racing stables cantering in the distance, then, propped on his pillow, having the big plate of porridge plonked on his knees and spooning it up – one of Campbell's complaints had been of having this irreplaceable object, his spoon, stolen – with a sense of the quiet hours in front of him, that, for all the apparent idleness, weren't being wasted.

He thought his mind was becoming less confused as some of the sediment sank to the bottom in these weeks of quietness.

But a day or two later Lane brought the news that the tunnel had reached a point outside the wire and it would shortly be time to fix a moonless and, if possible, overcast night for the escape.

'So you'd better be moving.'

'You're taking me with you, then?'

He knew that only those prisoners it was thought could be useful outside had been chosen, and that some in the hut had been told they'd have to exchange places the night before the attempted breakout with prisoners from others.

'What did you suppose?'

H shook his head. He'd begun to feel out of it again, as not belonging to those courageous few chosen to dig the tunnel nor to the larger group whose importance in the fight, still forlornly being waged, entitled them to the chance to escape. Neither was he a bit of cultural yeast among the prisoners, giving the cause, as Joe Campbell did, an intellectual prestige.

'There's no extra charge for staying a bit longer,' the doctor said when H told him he was feeling in perfect health.

H had difficulty in persuading him to be allowed to return to his hut. The night after he got back there was a breakout from the adjoining camp, Tintown 1 (Gorman, he heard later, had been among the escapees) and next morning, which was that of his twenty-first birthday, the Tintown 2 prisoners were sent into the compound where they remained most of the day while the huts were searched.

As, cold, damp, and getting hungry, he tramped about with the others, it struck him that literature and sex set off in most of those involved manageable, if exciting, reactions quite different from the mostly painful and obsessive hauntings they produced in him.

Talk or writing about them were therefore likely to have a tone as of pleasures to be enjoyed with the barometer set fair. Whereas, he reflected with a gloomy satisfaction, if ever I meet my true love or manage to write a book it will be when the weather is stormy.

'That's good-bye to all our work,' said a prisoner from H's hut standing beside him in the drizzle. H saw where a piece of ground had caved in under soldiers and iron bars some yards beyond the barbed wire and midway between two of the raised sentry posts.

'I'm going to make a protest to the International Red Cross,' Campbell interrupted his march round and round the confined space in which they were herded to tell H. 'It's a flagrant breach of the Geneva Convention to deprive political prisoners of food and shelter for a day.'

'Balls!' exclaimed Lane to the stocky receding back of the poet off on his rounds again, head down into the wet wind that blew off the Curragh plain.

'I'd have gone and talked to them myself but, good Christ, I'd the job on my hands,' Lane told H, 'and you'd have thought there'd be somebody could be trusted to have got it across to the other camp that they'd only to wait another bloody night!

'Do you know where we'd have been by now?' Lane went on. 'In the room above Barney Doyles's at the North Wall having a cleanup and something to eat before going on board the Liverpool boat.'

'The Liverpool boat!'

'We'd have stayed with a couple of motts I know in Scotland Road. If it got too hot in Dublin I was always welcome there, they'd have put us both up and, by the same bloody token, taken time off to keep us company.'

The casual suggestion of an interlude spent with what H took to be two Irish street girls in Liverpool before, presumably, returning to take part in the last stages of the civil war attracted H. Though the plan had miscarried, the idea kept him awake most of the night after they'd finally been let back into the huts, imagining a dockland area full of pubs and warehouses and the drunken girls and upturned, powdered faces in dim, briny alleys and, best of all, being there with Lane without letting Iseult know of his escape.

Next morning a detachment of their guards entered the hut, with its inner wall ripped out and the piled earth disgorged, and waited inside the door while the Free State captain selected a dozen or so prisoners from those standing at the foot of the beds.

These were marched off and lined up outside where they were confronted by soldiers with fixed bayonets and then ordered by the captain to take, alternatively, pick or shovel from a pile in a handcart. The first couple of men stepped out of the rank and up to the cart, with two prisoners from another hut at its shafts, and picked up an implement. When it came to Lane's turn he didn't move. The captain repeated the order and the prisoners, H among them, at the windows held their breath. Not another move towards the cart, neither from the man next in line beyond Lane, nor from anyone further down it to whom the captain, whose mouth they saw open without catching the words, gave the command. Another order and two of the soldiers stepped in front of Lane and levelled their bayonets. The captain opened his mouth once more and H watched Lane's pale face in a kind of agonized adoration, unbowed and unblinking under the dark, damp curls, for it was still drizzling, the white one clearly distinguishable.

H saw one of the soldiers lower his bayonet and, with a forward flick of the wrists, jerk it into Lane's thigh. With a quarter twist the blade came out again before, it seemed to H, there'd been time for it to draw blood.

For a long, long time, on H's inner meter, nobody moved and nothing happened. Then, around the slight tear in the trouser leg, the grey cloth darkened.

Four others refused to start work on the trench that the prisoners were ordered to dig around the camp inside the wire to discourage further tunnelling. Two of these were also bayoneted, and, the three wounded men riding on the handcart with the surplus implements, the five recalcitrant prisoners were taken away, to the military prison on the hill called the Glass House, according to one of those watching with H.

When the remainder of the work party returned, mud-caked and with blistered hands, H's hut and the one between it and the wire were evacuated and the inmates distributed among others.

Anxious not only about the fate of his friend but with a more indefinable fear, H was glad enough of the rowdy company in the new hut. They were an easygoing lot, noisy – setting up a daylong din tapping half-crowns into rings against the bed rails – callous – catching seagulls on baited fish hooks and lines from the windows of an evening – tellers of drab dirty stories that were unleavened by the fantasy of Lane's.

Rumours filtered through from the Glass House. The punishment inflicted by the military police on soldiers for insubordination included stringing up by the wrists for hours at a time. What would be done to the men they'd taken from the camp was being discussed in the corner where H had his bed. It was reported that one of them had had his leg amputated.

'Take out the hook and let that bloody bird go!' H shouted across the hut. He'd been aware of the white frenzied flapping of the gull while listening to the rumours. And the youths opposite, fishermen from Kerry, released the seagull without a word, somewhat to H's surprise.

H took his turn at digging the trench, there was a directive from the prisoners' OC against further refusals, and his companions whose hands were harder than his took his pick when the sentry wasn't patrolling just above them and gave him a respite. But when one morning, after being lined up in a work party, the officer, not the captain who'd superintended the bayoneting, but a young lieutenant with bright, new leather belt, straps, and holster, took a look at the palms of his hands (had he been holding the handle of the shovel gingerly?) and told him to fall out, H shook his head.

'Get back to your hut!' the lieutenant, his face pink, shouted. H didn't move.

'Don't act the fucking idiot!' the prisoner next him whispered.

H, with the pale, sweaty face of Lane, as he'd been wheeled off in the cart, before him, hesitated. Wasn't it rather late, and safe, in the day to make a stand? H took the shovel to the shed where the tools were stored, returned to his hut, and started writing in the exercise books that he'd got Iseult to send him in the food parcels.

H wrote steadily throughout the next days, with the rain, that ran down the windows and kept the prisoners in the hut, falling across the plain and helping keep his thoughts translucent and flowing. The trance from which he worked was preserved by the soft hiss against the corrugated sheets of the roof, magically insulating him with its constant cool, wet whisper from the noise of the hut and from the wood-smoke of the small fires burning at the foot of some of the beds, with black cans suspended over them.

He filled several exercise books without having more than an indistinct idea about what he was writing. Though, with the drowsy inkling with which a dream is half recalled and given a name, on the third or fourth day he turned back and wrote on page one the title: 'Sweat of the Martyrs', misspelling the last word as 'matyrs'.

Paula, the daughter of a wealthy Viennese couple, the Rosenbergs, is forbidden to become engaged to Stefan, a pastry cook employed at Schönbrunn, whom she meets one evening in the Prater in the early days of the war.

Comes defeat, the end of the monarchy, devaluation, and the vanishing of the Rosenberg fortune. These large-scale, exterior events H found hard to weave into the story without tearing the delicate fabric.

Stefan joins the Communist Party and sets up shop on his own. When Paula slips into the café in Praterstrasse one evening, she sees it's too late and that, to have convinced him of her love, she should have disobeyed her parents earlier.

Episode: The café at night. Paula in black sits at a table loaded with Wiener Torte and a cup of Tee mit Himbeersaft, watching Stefan busy serving the customers. He hasn't a moment for her.

Paula leaves home. Herr Rosenberg starts smuggling motor tyres from Switzerland and selling them on the black market. He and his wife are searching the city of cold cafés, empty restaurants, and steamless bathhouses for Paula.

Episode: The Hotel Bristol, Opernring. Herr Rosenberg has returned to one of his former haunts, like everything else, changed out of recognition. Watching the dancers he sees Paula in the arms of one of the *nouveau riche*. His companion, a former clerk in his bank, seeing Herr Rosenberg's interest in the tall girl in black, offers to introduce him to her.

'You know her then, Gregor?'

'Everyone here knows her, Herr Direktor.' He can even tell Herr Rosenberg what it will cost to take her home.

Early one morning, H was awakened by the hut door being unbolted; an officer, followed by a sergeant and two men, marched up the centre aisle to his bed.

'Get up and dress!'

H pulled on his trousers, regarded with sympathetic glances from pillowed heads in neighbouring beds. To be taken away at six-thirty in the morning boded ill. Had another Free State political been shot? Was he one of those selected for reprisal?

The sergeant pulled out H's suitcase from under the bed and took from it the school exercise books which he handed the officer who sat down on H's cot and started to read them with the sergeant taking up his position at the foot and the two soldiers in the background. The young lieutenant, the one who'd dismissed H from the work party, was scanning a page or two of each book before dipping into another.

Finally he rose without a word, left the blue exercise books scattered over the grey prison blanket on the cot and marched out of the hut with his small detachment.

'Thought you were for it, mate,' one of the two Englishmen, deserters from their regiment at the time of the Treaty, whose beds weren't far from H's, told him, while his own compatriots teased him about missing a chance of dying for Ireland; they hadn't got over his reluctance to escape the trench digging.

Herr Rosenberg approaches Paula and asks her to return home with him. She refuses, and they talk in her room at the hotel where she's living in a luxury that convinces her father of the truth of what the former clerk suggested.

Episode: Herr Rosenberg tells her of how, while taking one of his solitary Sunday walks in the Vienna Woods, at the top of a hill he saw, or imagined, a procession approaching from the other side, dragging with them two malefactors, one a notorious murderer and the other a black market speculator.

'In the Christian fable the one I saw as myself would have been the "good" thief.'

'Don't you see, Father,' Paula explains, 'that it's not the lesser sinner who's saved, but the one whose despair is complete!'

'There was no question of who was saved because there were just the two of them, no third figure bowed under His cross.'

By the time of Lane's return to the camp both the eight-foot-deep ditch around its perimeter and H's story had been completed, although he knew by then that it was a failure.

Skirting a group of prisoners in the muddy thoroughfare between the row of huts and the wash sheds, H saw a shaved head at its centre and was struck by a pale spot on it, not a bald patch but what was left of the white tuft at the crown.

They made way for H to be among the first to greet the returned hero, one of them calling, 'Hey, Sean, here's your buddy.'

When the prisoners detailed to fetch a bed and mattress from the stores returned through the wire gate, H indicated the hut to which to bring it and had them set it up beside his own.

Lane didn't talk of what it had been like up at the Glass House. Apart from the leg wound, which had healed, and a dislocated thumb – had they strung him up? H couldn't bring himself to ask – and the shaved head that, though, instead of suggesting a convict, accentuated, as perhaps with the girls chained to the railings, the dove-greyness of the eyes, nothing had happened to him. Nothing, that is, of all the things that at one time or another H had feared.

He had seen the papers and told H about the Republicans giving up the fight, having first dumped their arms in caches, though, and not surrendered them as the Government had insisted on as one of the conditions of a general amnesty.

But that wasn't what concerned them as they talked in whispers after the hut had fallen silent at night. Lane's only comment was, 'Defeat is a bloody sight better for us than the sort of patriotic shit that goes into victory.'

Lane preferred to talk of tales he'd heard in the Glass House of how, when the British were stationed at the Curragh, the sex-starved men of the Black Watch had had intercourse with sheep at night. 'The poor bloody ewes were so harried that the farmers sent a petition to the CO asking him to bring some motts over from Glasgow and open a kip.'

They realized that their voices had risen and that the conversation was being listened to in nearby beds. Lane's concern was that the two deserters might have taken his remarks amiss, but H, who'd got to know them quite well, pointed out that they belonged to an English, not a Scots, regiment.

They also discussed a boxing tournament which Lane suggested organizing on an inter-hut basis, and in which H, foolhardily, agreed to take part.

Lane said he'd heard from the couple of girls in Liverpool. 'One big room with a sink in it and a view to the docks, sea breezes, and Paris perfume, lashings of cold beef and ham, a couple dozen bottles of stout set up on the table, that's how they welcomed me last time, and just the four of us with no call to go out for the whole bloody weekend.'

H had letters too, after a holdup of mail following the discovery of the tunnel, from Iseult, telling him that her mother had moved to a large house in the suburbs where, with the help of a rich woman friend, she was bringing some of the first prisoners to be released to recuperate. Recuperation was suddenly in the air. She also wrote that, as forecast, Yeats had received the Nobel Prize. There were letters from H's mother, too, with news of Weg's death as well as that of her pug dog Snuff, which they'd buried in the garden at Aunt Jenny's. She signed herself in full, as always, Libby Clements.

'Or if you'd wanted they'd have shown us the town, they know Liverpool, inside out, these two; more inside than out!'

'Hey put a sock in it, lads,' a sleepless prisoner called.

17

H was matched at middleweight; in spite of his height he was estimated, in the absence of scales, to belong to that class, with a member of the team from one of the other huts. Lane was fighting a lightweight, and one of the Englishmen was their light-heavyweight representative.

Turner had boxed for his unit behind the lines in France. He took on H's training, while Lane neither bothered to train nor expected H to, regaling him with talk of the war that, only five years away, had for H already a legendary aura, if as yet for hardly anybody else. The memory of the pock-marked walls in Belgium was still a magic one.

'That was before I lost these two fingers,' he told H, 'bringing in a wounded bloke. The poor bugger'd been lying out a couple of days and when we went out the second night to fetch him the bloke I was with got hit. So I had to bring the first wounded bloke in across my shoulder and that's what saved me from worse. He was hit twice.'

It wasn't just because he was a foreigner that H thought hospitality demanded that Turner won his first bout, if not his section of the tournament outright, but because he was going to be sent back to England for court martial having preferred to stay in Ireland rather return with his regiment.

On Lane's behalf, in spite of the casual way he was taking it, H had no anxiety. For himself, he thought he'd last out the three rounds of his preliminary bout. He practised hard, swinging what he imagined were vicious right hooks, while guarding his jaw with his left glove, at the improvised punch-bag Turner had strung from a rafter and anchored to an iron stake in the floor. 'You're winning all your bloody fights but the one that counts,' Lane remarked one evening from where he was stretched on his bed.

And it was true that by the time a ring was roped off in the centre of the hut and the tournament held one afternoon, H had lost some of his zest.

He was gasping for breath halfway through the first round, totally unprepared for the two dangerously glistening leather pistons shooting into his face.

When at last the bell went, H stepped over the single rope and slumped on the bed that served as a corner stool. His jaw was numb and he couldn't close his mouth.

'Here, bite on that,' Turner told him, shoving the handle of a hairbrush into it.

H took deep breaths with Turner applying pressure with a hand on each side of his chest. He couldn't speak till he felt the handle of the brush between he teeth and then he told Turner he didn't think he'd last the second round.

'You're OK, mate,' Turner told him as H imagined him telling his wounded blokes when they were hit a second or third time.

He was ducking and dancing, slipping the leather pistons that flashed at him from all angles. Supposing the timekeeper's watch had run down or he couldn't find the knife with the metal handle to ring out the end of the round with on the bedrail, or the setting sun was standing still, low in the autumn sky above the yellow gorse bushes?

Not a shot fired in the civil war, not a blow landed in the Tintown 2 tournament, nor a French letter worn in a bold sexual bout! He, the caster of doubt on all kinds of things from the Irish Literary Renaissance to Iseult's right to pronounce moral judgements, at least knew what it was like to have doubt cast on himself!

H lost the contest on points, though had it gone another two or three rounds, Turner's view, not H's, he'd have worn the other bloke down.

Lane crouched between gloves held high and tucked-in elbows. Stylish footwork. Lacking condition, he must go for a quick KO. H was still breathing quickly, his face bruised; the soreness would come later. Round Two: Lane hammering away, getting in one in three or four and taking his opponent's blows on gloves and arms. Looking good, if H hadn't seen, in the minute's pause, a snowy pallor spread over his face.

Lane returned to his 'corner' at the end of the round, lay back on the bed, and from his mouth flowed, soundlessly, a bright stream of what Turner said was arterial blood.

Though Lane told H to carry on, Turner, who was to fight next, refused to enter the ring until Lane was safely in hospital.

The prison doctor felt Lane's pulse, had a look at the bloody handkerchief and sent out for a stretcher on which to transfer him to one of the huts in the adjoining camp where, unlike the improvised place in Tintown 2, serious cases were treated.

While they waited, H asked Lane if he'd ever had a haemorrhage before. Yes, he'd woken one morning a year or two ago with the pillow bloody.

'It warned me that my days were numbered.'

'Nonsense. Tuberculosis is no longer hard to cure.'

Lane didn't answer. H's heart was heavy, faced so soon again with its own isolation.

A little later, with Turner, and accompanied by the doctor and a Free State sergeant with the keys of the gates, H helped carry Lane to the other camp and up the wooden steps into the hut raised above the muddy compound.

Short messages came from Lane, and H wrote to Iseult to meet him when he was released and bring him to her mother's until he could be sent to a sanatorium.

Before he had an answer, a hunger strike was called. This took H, who'd been out of touch with camp affairs, by surprise. It was, it seemed, in protest at the delay in starting the release of the thousands of Republican prisoners, although there'd been no fighting for months, and was being embarked on simultaneously in the various internment camps.

Ignoring a directive issued by their doctor advising a gradual tapering-off in their eating, H and the prisoners in his corner finished up what was left of their last parcels in one huge supper shared with the parcel-less Englishmen. Eggs, rashers, sausages, black pudding, and bread were fried in the enormous pan made from the severed bottom of a galvanized bucket on one of the iron stoves along the centre of the hut.

Close on midnight of the day the strike was due to begin, H opened a couple of tins of sardines which, with a packet of sugar, was all that remained of his stores, and these were consumed. After a final mug of tea he pulled out a fish in his fingers, dipped it in sugar and swallowed it, in an extravagant celebration of what he was ready to see as a last supper shared with those who, if for different motives to his, were banded together against the order now firmly established outside the camp.

As the hut commandant announced zero hour, they piled together what remained, which in H's case was only a bottle of Scotts Emulsion his mother had sent him on hearing he was in the hospital hut, and threw the lot out of the window on to the waste ground between their hut and the next. On the sixth or seventh day, when the pangs of hunger were becoming acute, H noticed that the bottle of thick, creamy tonic had disappeared.

After the clamour and bustle, silence and inactivity. The prisoners lay in their beds with mugs of cold water beside them, another of the doctor's recommendations, or of hot water with a little salt in it, which, when a pinch of pepper was added could be taken for weak soup, listening to the rumours which began taking shape of themselves by the spontaneous combustion of hunger and expectation.

Another few days and the gates would be thrown open; there had been a heated debate in the Dail; several prisoners had already suffered heart attacks; two had died; Jim Larkin had held a mass protest meeting, stopping the traffic on O'Connell Bridge.

H's neighbour on the other side from the unoccupied bed, a youth called

Reilly, who slept most of the time, was, in his waking moments, a surprisingly active disseminator of news.

H lay in bed and instead of sex, thought of food, only getting up to straighten the coverings, a task which some days was arduous, each blanket feeling as if lead were sewn into its seams, while on others he felt a mysterious access of energy and could have emptied the five sanitary buckets, which began to stink by evening, single-handed.

What opportunities he'd missed of examining the displays in the food shops of the cities he'd been in! At the Cuisine Bourgeoise in London long ago he'd been too taken up with Iseult, and the enigma of sex, to give serious thought to the menu; in Bruges, too preoccupied by the purchase of arms, and too thirsty; in Liverpool, too taken with the idea of contraceptives; in Dublin, with everything else under the sun.

Only in Vienna, and then intermittently, had he been aware of what could be eaten, and fascinated by the wonderfully subtle soggy flavour of bifteck tartar.

One night H felt his bedclothes twitched and a hand was stretched from the other bed with something in it which crackled when he took it in his own.

'Look out for the crumbs.' Reilly whispered. H drew the biscuit, a cream cracker, under the bedclothes and sniffed it. He held it carefully while deciding what to do with it. He could return it to Reilly, or, he supposed, put it in his pyjama pocket and get rid of the pieces in the morning. He started nibbling.

A biscuit a day keeps the doctor away.

After the first few days prisoners began getting up, dressing, bundling a few belongings into a blanket or a suitcase, and presenting themselves at the gate whence they were taken to a special hut to be housed and fed. Their preparations were watched in silence and even after their departure there were only comments from one or two prisoners, Reilly among them, who expressed the view that they were letting their comrades down.

18

H was driven by one of the Prisoners' Reception Committee members to Deer Park House, arriving one evening when Iseult was sitting with two or three women members of Cuman na Mbhan at the fire – he'd been released shortly before Christmas – in her room in the big, new house. The others disappeared and he and Iseult were alone together after more than a year.

A wave of warmth drowned out their momentary shyness. There were all sorts of things to recount and propose, and, in the offing, was the sensational event that had been looming ever larger for him as the releases were speeded up.

H asked about Lane, who, it turned out, was staying with a young American couple, friends of Madame's, in a country house near Dublin, and who proposed taking him back with them to California.

Other pieces of news: a back street printer was bringing out H's poems, both the early ones and a few he'd sent her from prison. Yeats had read them in proof and told her: 'Your husband who everyone, including his own relations, thought half-witted, shows signs of being our white hope.'

Iseult had only just prevented H's mother, who'd been staying with them, from marrying one of the ex-prisoners recuperating here, a good-for-nothing, Iseult said, ten or twelve years younger than she, out for her money. Iseult had intercepted a letter from a hotel confirming the booking of a room in the name of Mr and Mrs Clements.

H wasn't sure if he approved of these tactics in which, it seemed, his mother-in-law had had a hand, even if his mother's remarriage would cut off their immediate means of livelihood. But Iseult assured him it was to save her from an experience like that with Henry, and H wasn't going, at this crucial moment (he was impatient to be in bed with her) to become involved in an argument about whether loneliness, for there was now not even the pug, was preferable to some weeks of bliss followed by disillusion.

The supper table was crowded and afterwards there was no slipping up to their room with all the talk going on in which H, as the latest to come out of the emptying camps, was expected to take part. When at last they went upstairs, Iseult lingered with her mother and H heard them, through the door he'd left ajar, talking at the other end of the passage. It suddenly struck H that the vital difference between the camp and the world outside was that between the absence and presence of women. This seemed now a matter of life and death. He was overwhelmed by the sudden intensity of his feelings, and in trying to examine them was forced to conclude that the expression 'sex-mad', that he'd heard casually used and had been thoughtlessly ready to accept as a term of opprobrium for a condition outside his ken, was the one that best applied to his present state.

He imagined having kept his release a secret and gone to Liverpool. He would now be sitting down to a supper of beef and ham, with no political talk, and a couple of bottles of Guinness apiece, and then he'd have gone to bed with the girls for a bout of drunken kissing, rowdy laughter, and uninhibited coupling. Iseult returned, lit a cigarette and started telling him of a visit she'd made with her mother to the Papal Nuncio while she slowly undressed. Once in bed there was a painful hiatus as she seemed to realize it was time to break off her story and stub out the cigarette butt. She then lay staring up at the ceiling.

'You know, darling, we don't have to act like everyone else just because you're back and it's our first night together,' she reminded him when he made the first advances.

At first H had a reluctance to go into town, the currents in the streets and shops were so much vaster than what he was used to in the camp. He had to have Iseult with him, even when he went to the barber to whom, unable to bring himself to explain why his hair was so long, it being the sort of establishment frequented by the old ascendancy, he said something about a protracted trip abroad.

She took him to buy clothes in a big, Grafton Street store, persuading him into a heavy, black overcoat, its upper part and sleeves lined with leather which elastic bands drew tight at the cuffs. The ceremoniousness was something he wasn't used to. There had been the trying on of the enormous coat in a glass-screened compartment attended by a clerk attired in black, and at the bank they were conducted to an office where he was ritualistically presented with a cheque and bankbook. The sum of a hundred and fifty pounds had been entered in the latter, the amount that had accumulated, with interest, from a weekly five shillings deposited for him by a Quintillan great-aunt up to her death, and which had become payable at his twenty-first birthday.

But in the afternoon he went alone by tram to a suburb and from there hired a car to take him to the house where Lane was staying. Lane saw him drive up from a window that he was supposed to keep open day and night and came to the door himself, speaking in a whisper that H supposed was to obviate being waylaid by his host or hostess, but which, he soon realized came from the infection having spread to the throat.

'I can do most of the talking and you just write down what you want to say,' H suggested. He'd noticed a pencil and pad beside a packet of menthol cigarettes and a medicine bottle on the bedside table.

'I can talk O.K.,' Lane whispered, 'it's only with the Hardings I make the most of this bloody microbe, especially with his lordship.'

'Harding? That wasn't the name I heard.'

They were Neville G. and Shirley Harding, Lane explained, though Neville, who was a nephew, or grand-nephew, of a former president, had changed his for a time to Gilbert with an idea, his wife had told Lane, of making a career for himself on his own merits, but was now, the career having come to nothing, calling himself Neville G. Harding again.

For Christ's sweet sake, was this what they were wasting the precious time, and Lane's voice, on?

'Iseult said the people, whatever they call themselves, were taking you back with them to California.'

'Have a heart! What would I go to California for?'

'The climate. It'll cure you quicker than Switzerland.'

'Do you see me tagging along behind a couple of rich Yanks on the off-chance of a cure?'

H didn't answer. He had a lot to tell his friend: about the book of poems, about the unexpected sum of money, about the hunger strike, and even about the biscuits, which he hadn't mentioned to Iseult.

'Hunger strikes!' Lane whispered contemptuously, 'appealing to the buggers' humanity.'

'To public opinion.'

'Fuck public opinion! A nice bloody pass when that's what we rely on!'

'If you're not going to America, what will you do?'

'Don't worry about me. Better any day Glasnevin in the rain than a balcony in sunny California!'

A gong sounded for the evening meal and H slipped out without having to meet the Hardings, and walked back the couple of miles to the tram terminus.

The knowledge of how little Lane clung to life, set against his own instinct for self-preservation, yet Lane had passions as urgent as H's, came as a painful revelation.

Some evenings later the young maid opened the door of their room and ushered in an impressive fawn-suited figure with eyes seemingly astigmatic behind his glasses. H knew who it was before Iseult exclaimed, 'Uncle Willie!'

Yeats stopped just inside the door, raised his leonine head (lion, eagle, rabbit – H later imagined, at various times, a likeness to all these in Yeats), and announced with an emphasis that made H momentarily suppose it was what he had come to tell them, 'I didn't ask for Maud. I thought it might be unwise for us to meet.'

The lock of hair falling over the imposing brow and brushed back by a pudgy finger, the full short lips, the black ribbon from the glasses to the lapel of the jacket, the folds of the waistcoat over the slight belly bulge, the mixture of deliberation and absentmindedness, all was being registered by H as manifestations of the first, and possibly only, great writer ever to come his way.

Yeats was telling Iseult that the Royal Irish Academy, a learned society that H had heard of in connection with historical research and, he thought, the preservation of ancient monuments, had selected H's little book of poems, of which she had sent a copy to Yeats, for one of their literary awards.

The successor of Blake and Wordsworth had appeared in their room, stared blindly around him as if in sudden darkness, announced the extraordinary news in a kind of chant, and, head inclined while shoulders remained unbent, soft hands clasped behind him, descended the stairs and was gone again.

H had vacillated between delight and an urge, at once dismissed, to refuse, between words of thanks ('Knowing, of course, from whom this honour comes, bestowed by nobody else would the laurel wreath – Yeats had mentioned the form of ceremonial – become for me the true and treasured crown') and others, equally contrived ('The only eminence left to which a writer can climb without dishonour is some kind of scaffold').

What he'd actually brought out were some awkward sentences of gratitude. What did H really think? His ideas about the poet and the novelist were gradually clarifying. They would be drawn towards ever greater areas of solitude from which they were unlikely to bring back the sort of news that would be greeted with applause.

How correlate these ideas with the facts of Yeats who combined being an outstanding poet and a respected public figure? H had an inkling that his concept was valid for the days that were coming, and that Yeats belonged to the last of the great writers whose vision could still be contained within the moral and cultural structure of their time. Later, there were occasions when it struck H that Yeats was not unaware of this and that, playing with the idea of revolt and disruption, he adopted certain extreme attitudes which weren't spontaneous.

With the money left him by his great-aunt, H bought a car. Its purchase was nothing like the dreamlike, intense transaction planned in the small café and concluded, through an interpreter, in the winter dusk of the Praterstrasse. This time they were taken for a trial run by a salesman from Cork along a familiar Dublin Street – no wide, grey river, no avenue through a forest deep in snow – and, at a question of Iseult's as to how the car climbed hills, up a suburban road that rose in a slight incline.

That afternoon H drove in it to see Lane. Lane, who couldn't go out in the damp, wintry evening, admired the car from his window. His throat was worse and he had to use the pad and pencil to talk to H with. He made a quick sketch of the car, all radiator and big blunt nose, straddled by a naked girl.

'What's this?' asked H, startled.

Lane continued his rapid sketching, depicting two hearts pierced by a single arrow, two figures on a bed, one of them leaning out to spit into a chamber pot, the car again, this time from the back, disappearing in a cloud of dust, and finally a coffin.

In this way Lane was trying to tell him several things: his relationship with

Mrs Harding, his admiration for the car, his non-belief in his recovery, and possibly the final parting.

H experienced one of those jumps forward that was to be his mode of progression, as throughout nature energy is transmitted in bursts of separate quanta and the pear tree blossom opens not in a continuous expansion but, as years later he was to observe just outside his prison bars, in a series of tiny jumps.

He'd reached a point where, at least for a few days while inspired by Lane, he could say something like, 'Give me a cliff, Lord, and I'll climb it as high as I can.'

When Lane had told him, 'Better Glasnevin in the rain than a sunny balcony in California,' that struck him as true love of country compared to which the attitudes of most patriots were hollow. And Lane's relationship with this American girl was equally genuine and painful.

Lane said that when they made love they didn't kiss in order to lessen the risk of infecting her. He showed H a Byronic love poem Mrs Harding had written beginning

> Burning, burning, mouths apart,
> Burning, burning, heart to heart,
> Burning to the bitter end.

'I chanced my arm at a few lines myself. In an attempt to get away from the Celtic twilight ditties I may have overdone the speak-out-and-be-buggered style,' Lane whispered, giving H a slip from the writing pad on which was scrawled

> Grey is the hair of the granny
> And thin in the breeze it blows,
> But my mott's exciting fanny
> Is fresh and pink as the rose.

At supper that evening his mother-in-law congratulated him on the book of poems, ungrudgingly praising those 'To a Dancer', and on the award that Iseult had told her about. But she hoped that H, in his speech of thanks, wouldn't call Yeats 'Senator'.

The ceremony had for H the mixture of the serious and the ludicrous, the innocence and falsity, that he came to associate with Yeats. He made a speech about art and Ireland, coming around to the prizewinners, of whom there were a couple in other branches of literature, and finally intoning some generous remarks about H, as he held open the amateurishly produced booklet. 'When I came on these two little poems of Luke Ruark's they so disturbed my imagination that they kept me from my sleep.'

At a whispered word from an usher, H stepped on to the dais and knelt down while Yeats, enveloped in one of the clouds that seemed occasionally blown across his path, was groping around for the laurel wreath that, with the others was lying on the table in full view of everyone else.

When it was all over, Iseult walked down the street with Yeats and a Major somebody, both in top hats and frock coats, leaving H, retreated into his black leather-lined carapace, alone with the huge figure of G. K. Chesterton, the reason for whose presence at the prize-giving H had no idea of. He was afraid his companion might, out of his overflowing friendliness, try to make him share in his enjoyment of what H imagined Chesterton – he was as usual underestimating someone whose ways were alien – calling God's great world. How much more reassuring was Yeats's keen and wary glance, even at those moments when it seemed to go out of focus!

At Deer Park House, H, and to some extent Iseult, were becoming restless. From their window they saw the hills, the same to which H had sometimes lifted his eyes from the camp, till now darkly defined and opaque, grow insubstantial and begin to hover like clouds about the far horizon.

Spring was in the air, and they went for long drives in the car to get away from the atmosphere of being at a perpetual public meeting that, outside their room, pervaded the house. On one of these expeditions, when they visited Joe Campbell, he showed them a cottage to let a few miles up the mountain valley from his.

With his memories of the other glen, H was hesitant, but this place turned out to be quite different to the narrow boulder-clogged valley, sunless and echoing with donkey brays and waterfalls, where they'd spent the first hectic weeks of their marriage.

From the pale, gritty road which sparkled with fragments of mica where H had stopped the car, they looked down to the red, iron roof of the long, whitewashed cottage and across a moss-grown yard into a plot enclosed by walls of loose granite stones that Iseult immediately envisaged as a tiny, flowering oasis in the mountain wilderness. After they'd rented it for seven-and-six a week, Iseult, in an unusual bout of activity, looked for secondhand furniture in the shops along the quays to add to the few antiques in her room, bargains she'd picked up long ago in London.

There were plans about Lane living in an open-ended chalet in their as yet undug garden and Shirley Harding coming to stay with them from time to time, about his going to Switzerland where the girl would join him later, and other projects which Lane listened to with an expression inattentive and impatient, having, H thought, made up his mind about what was actually in store for him.

19

Three rooms, three windows all facing the yard and the enclosed plot beyond, the only bit of level ground for miles, and a tiny square of glass let into the thick back wall that looked directly on to the mossy bank of the excavation in the hillside on which the cottage stood.

A cattle byre which H swept and garnished to receive the car, a stable with, at one end, a roughly hewn lavatory seat through which if he bent low he could squint down the steep slope that dropped to the oak wood in the valley floor.

Iseult set to work to lay out her garden with a bay tree in the centre, while H dug beds around the low, loose wall, pausing to lean on his spade and, with his back to the mountains, contemplated the valley, a shallow, gilded bowl tilted towards the morning sun.

At dusk H coaxed the logs to blaze on the hearth and placed the screen so as to shut out the draught from the wind that blew down the glen. Then, as he waited, muscles aching pleasantly from the day's work, sniffing the mingled scents of woodsmoke and paraffin cooker in the small end room from which Iseult would soon emerge with the tea tray, it did seem to him that they were at the start of a more hopeful time. But at the back of his hesitant optimism was the thought of Lane.

One day they went to Dublin and, after leaving Iseult at her mother's, H drove to the Hardings and the door was opened by Shirley's husband, Neville.

The type, darkly, handsomely, wealthily neurotic, though new to H, was grasped by him imaginatively right away. He realized that there was a bond, of background, taste, weak and sheltered nerves, even, in spite of the chamber pot, of habits of hygiene, between him and his wife that Lane could never break.

With a hand on his shoulder, Neville, but Shirley addressed him as Gilbert – had there been another change? – brought H to his wife in the sitting-room.

'Oh, Luke,' she said, holding out both hands to him, her honey-coloured eyes wet and wide, 'You've heard about Sean? He had a haemorrhage and we've sent him to a sanatorium.'

Back at Deer Park House H found Iseult in the garden with her mother taking cuttings to transplant in her mountain plot. He explained that he wanted to go to the sanatorium straight away, from where they could drive home across the mountains without having to return to Dublin. Then he went and waited in the car.

But of course she didn't come. She seemed hardly to have taken in what he'd told her and had immediately afterwards gone on discussing plants with her mother.

H drove off, the old feeling of noncommunication between them strong again. At the sanatorium he was taken to one of the huts.

The place was like a Tintown tidied up with white paint, white sheets, bedside tables, neat lawns, but in the air was a greater threat than any that had hung over the camp.

Lane was propped against pillows in his cot and the greeting that H had begun to murmur faded out as he took in the deathly mask he was addressing. There was pad and pencil beside him as before as well as a white delft mug with a lid.

H was going to give him the writing materials but Lane shook his head.

'There's no need for that any more.'

'How do you mean?'

'No need for anything but the box and the shovel,' Lane whispered.

The remark made impossible the kind of sickbed talk that H had been ready for and he resented it.

All the same he made the suggestion he had in mind.

'You could come and live in a hut in the garden of our cottage.'

'Take a look at me, Luke. I've been in prisons and camps and the Glass House, but they were picnics. It's the real thing this time. Here you have to pronounce your own sentence to yourself at certain grim hours of the day and night, and it doesn't provide for any parole.'

H recalled Lane as he'd first seen him standing erect when the other prisoners had thrown themselves to the muddy ground of the compound.

'Until I grasp what you're telling me I'll never be the sort of writer I hope to become.'

Lane didn't try to reply. From a drawer in the bedside table, he took a cutting and showed it to H. It was a short newspaper account of the Royal Irish Academy prize-giving.

'I've always told you everything,' H said, 'and I was going to tell you that too. But it's far more important to hear about you.'

What did the slight headshake mean? That Lane wasn't criticizing H for accepting the award, but, on the contrary, had proudly been preserving the newspaper clipping? Or was it in contradiction to H's saying that it was he, Lane, they should talk about?

Silence descended and, in desperation, H rose.

'I'll come back tomorrow.'

Why tomorrow? Why not express today all that was in his heart? His heart? What could it contain that wasn't shabby in the clear luminosity of Lane's?

Lane regarded him from his dove grey eyes and gave no sign. At the slightest of indications H would have stayed.

He drove home across the mountains, approaching Glenmaroon from above, instead of at the eastern, down-tilted lip of the saucer, as when coming from Dublin, catching sight of the splinter of red roof in the desolation of slate and stormy blues, rock and cloud greys, bracken browns, and various melancholy, evening-faded greens.

The Chinese figures on the screen that he drew around his chair in the empty cottage, the brown pot of tea, the white china jar of 'Gentleman's Relish', with its Latin inscription, that he'd placed on the table couldn't prevent sub-thoughts from the older, deeper strata cancelling the more conscious ones.

Next morning H stayed in bed, at first intending to get up within the hour but, as the day dragged on with the wind breaking over the roof of the cottage, postponing doing so. What obsessed him was the thought that no matter how long he waited no word would come to him from either Lane or Iseult. There was no telephone to ring and the postman, who called thrice a week, could bring no telegram nor letter; Lane did not even know the address. Nor would Iseult taking in, at long last, what he'd told her in the garden, decide to return and walk out the six or seven miles from the bus terminus. If she did, all would have been possible between them, but that, he believed, was something that she wouldn't be capable of, that wouldn't even occur to her.

He turned his face first to the window through which he could see the last line of fir trees along the mountain ridge, black and bleak against the ragged, rushing clouds, and then to the wall.

The following day H drove to the sanatorium. Lane's bed had screens placed around it and the nurse moved one of them to let him in. Lane opened his eyes for a moment when H sat down by the bed and spoke to him, but afterwards, when H laid his hand on Lane's, there was no response. Sitting at the bedside H felt the immense distance between Lane's grey lips with a smear of blood at a corner and his own that could no longer speak to each other.

He tried to feel he was keeping silent, peaceful vigil by his friend, but he couldn't pretend that such was really the case. He was no more capable of being beside Lane in these last days and hours than he'd been in the prison yard or outside the hut confronting the soldiers.

On the homeward drive he had a glimpse of the red roof from the pass at the top of the glen before losing it again as he let the car drop down the whitish track with engine switched off. When the cottage came momentarily into view once more he watched the space between the loose, low garden wall

110

for a sign. And one came, as a negative, in the couple of pigeons that rose from the newly dug earth.

After he'd made himself a meal, the first for two days, he sat by the window in the now clear evening. As it began to grow dusk in the shadow of the mountains, he saw a figure, too far away to recognize, but that lightened his heart, coming up the road. He recognized her visually as, after vanishing, she reappeared around a bend, and hurried to meet her, running the last few yards.

They clung together on the roadway without speaking before H led her by the hand up the hill to the cottage.

'Moura said you looked ill when you came out to the garden the day before yesterday and when you didn't return I was worried.' Sickening for syphilis? But this was not the moment for holding a grudge against her mother.

He didn't mention his visit to the sanatorium to her because he didn't want anything to overshadow, or even perhaps give her an excuse for postponing, what he foresaw soon taking place between them in celebration of her return. This seemed an act so sensationally direct and brazen, when suddenly recalled like this after an absence from his thoughts of several days, that he could hardly wait patiently while Iseult prepared the evening meal, and the awareness of Lane's impending death was driven from his mind.

H lit the open fire while she made tea on the paraffin cooker, the sounds from the next room coming to him as a reassurance that she was really there and that he would soon cancel out with her the misery and silence of the last day or two.

Afterwards she put on a gramophone record of Maria Jaritza, the Italian prima donna, and they lay in the firelight on the rug, Iseult preferring to make love with something else going on, a cushion stuffed into the recess of the small back window that overlooked the hearth. With the last high note repeated over and over as the needle revolved in the final groove, she kept H pressed tightly to her, making their simple contraceptive measure impossible.

After Lane's death – the funeral was not at Glasnevin but at a cemetery near the sanatorium, on a sunny morning – H took to serious reading again. There were two bookcases of Iseult's in the sitting room and, as before at his aunt's, he came to what, without precisely knowing it, he was seeking: the lives of certain artists.

There was the story of Keats receiving a letter from Fanny at his lodgings in the Piazza di Spagna in Rome in the winter of 1792 and handing it unopened to Severn to place beside him in the coffin. There was Dostoevsky as he waited his turn at the stake in Semyenovsky Square, Petersburg, on a winter morning in 1849; van Gogh sitting in a hired carriage taking him from the asylum at Saint Rémy on a farewell visit to a girl in a brothel at Arles on a summer afternoon in 1889.

What attracted him were the lives of those writers and painters he admired. He read everything about them he could lay his hands on with feverish intensity and a kind of impatience as though looking for a particular message. And in several cases he came on what he'd subconsciously expected, experiencing an almost unbearable excitement, and believing himself on the verge of a vital revelation that he was not yet quite ripe for.

From these he turned to the mystics, of which Iseult had a wide range. Soon he was absorbed by states of mind that appealed to him first because they ran counter to the familiar ones. He began to put his whole heart into trying to share this kind of consciousness, quite strange, in which intense emotion was joined to a daring imagination that seemed natural to him, though it was rare in contemporary literature.

It became clear to H that to study these accounts profitably wasn't an academic exercise. He had to expose himself to them, and this involved a turning from other activities and preoccupations.

As always when, as it seemed to him, a widening of his horizon was concerned, all worked together to make it easy. One afternoon when they'd climbed the mountain at the back of the cottage and entered a thick plantation of pine trees where in the dim stillness under the black branches, surrounded by flocks of midges, though it was winter, they'd disturbed, H imagined for a moment that she'd brought him here to make love. But, standing in the utter silence, Iseult told him she was pregnant.

He sensed that she had brought him to this place to make the announcement because she related her condition to the secret life she had apart from him and even her mother, perhaps also to her memory of Dolores, and in which her austere love of nature had a vital part.

Leaving Iseult to her now more comforting thoughts, he spent a lot of time in the spiritual company of the women mystics. There was Blessed Angela, whom the Holy Spirit had told God loved more than anyone else in the Vale of Foligno, Juliana who lived, with a maid, who fetched her daily bath water, in an anchorage built on to the wall of Norwich Cathedral, St Catherine of Siena, whom a young malefactor told the scaffold was holy because she was accompanying him to it, and St Rose of Lima who spent her days in contemplation in a hut in her parents' garden.

Early one spring morning H placed a tub, of the type known as a hip bath, on the square of lawn at the centre of the partially cultivated garden and filled it from the rainwater barrel. The dip in the icy water was a kind of baptism into what he looked on as a new phase of existence. And when he saw a portable hut advertised in the paper, he bought it to erect in the garden.

Once shut up in it, like Rose and Juliana in their hermitages, he felt he had opted out of the world (the phrase, not yet coined, expressed his mood exactly) to study, irrespective of their sex, mystics who were only names to him: Jacob Boehme, the Silesian shoemaker, Jalala Djin, a Persian contemplative, William Blake and William Law, Richard Rolle of Hampole, St Mechtilde of Magdeburg, St Bernard of Clairvaux, Madame Guyon.

The hut was delivered in seven sections, including the two sides of the tarred-felt roof, and, with the help of a handyman, bolted together and set up under a granite rock that overhung a corner of the walled plot.

When all was ready H brought Iseult out to inspect it. 'I'll sleep and spend part of the day here,' he told her, 'reading, making notes, and, if I've any gift for it, reflecting on what I've read.'

'You'll have to learn to pray, darling, before you can make any headway.'

He felt the old antagonism, although he couldn't deny her right to speak on the subject. Not only had she read these books long before he had, but seemed, compared to his intense but cloudy impressions, to have a clear idea of what they were about.

'Find a priest and be guided by him,' she was saying. 'Learn humility, and don't imagine that by indulging in extravagances and going to extremes you'll solve your problems, Luke.'

This suggestion irritated him. He would keep his newly discovered world to himself and had no intention of inviting inspection from outside.

Equally unwelcome was the news she sprung on him that a French cousin and girlhood companion, Claude Conseil, a niece of Iseult's father, was coming to stay with them.

'Well, darling, if you don't like the idea of a priest, and want, as usual, to go your own sweet way,' she told him, 'you might try reading the Gospels.'

So on their next trip to Dublin H bought a copy of the New Testament; Iseult's was in French and he no longer had his school Bible. They also brought back a dachshund puppy, a present from her mother to keep Iseult company alone at night.

He rose early next morning when the sun was a wet glistening silver coin that had just been fished out of the sea beyond the eastern, open end of the glen, and settled down with the Gospels to get some idea of the sort of person who was, as Iseult had said, the source of all Western mysticism.

It soon struck H that here was somebody in the grip of new kinds of perception and emotion, preoccupied with the experience of an extreme sort of relationship, which he still called love. His obsession seemed to be to find and keep a few friends who were capable of sharing this new intensity. Having failed, predictably enough, he made a last desperate attempt at arousing the extreme response he seemed to need by offering himself in an unheard of consummation.

From the first an air of disrepute and coming disaster had clung to him. The socially integrated sensed it and avoided him. Those who were normal and sound, firmly established, happily married, honoured, justified, appeared to wound him by their very presence. He never got over the general indifference to his all-or-nothing approaches.

H reported his impressions one morning at breakfast when he first noticed Iseult's belly beginning to bulge: 'His was a very private kind of message that could only be communicated in parables, there not yet being available the kind of subjective, imaginative style that certain modern writers have forged. Furthermore, there's no record, in what I've read so far, of his having any great regard for the family. He seems to have avoided family gatherings as being part of the kind of security he hoped to disrupt, except for a wedding reception on one occasion. He'd have felt more at home with the two Liverpool motts (H forgot that she didn't know who he was talking about) than a happily married couple, and in general sought out isolated individuals with, at most, a sister or a lover or two in the background.'

H saw her forehead darken and her liquid brown eyes narrow in distaste. She seemed to become annoyed and anxious, to wish him to stop talking and, at the same time, to be curious to hear what he'd say next. But for the moment he had no more to say.

The Gospels began to obsess him. As Iseult, in a flash of insight, had once told him, 'Whatever you don't react against violently, you come under the spell of. There's nothing between, no detachment, no balance, nor perspective.'

The spring and summer were turning into one of those rare ones, as hot and cloudless as when Dolores had died. A lizard came from between the loose stones of the wall just beyond the hut windows to sun itself, and the roof of the cottage, when he climbed on the bank at the road end to try, was by afternoon too hot to touch. The golden, sun-drenched glen, with distant squares of green patched on to the rust-coloured slopes where a few small fields had been laboriously cleared of bracken and boulders by boys from the reformatory, and an occasional cottage wall shimmering pale, became for H the hot landscape of Judaea.

In the warm evenings, after he'd been several times by the mossy path to the mountain stream that flowed under the road beyond their garden wall, and while Iseult was using the buckets he'd filled to water her young plants, H at the open window of the hut, played a Gregorian chant on the gramophone.

How far were these sounds echoing through the undisturbed silence of centuries from a medieval abbey choir from Maria Jaritza's high notes issuing out of the same small horn as an accompaniment to his organistic crescendo! The austere exaltation of the Kyrie Eleison helped evoke past times and places when the outward scene had been the embodiment of spiritual beatitude. The glen grew insubstantial and trembled, a misty gleam from below reflecting into his semi-trance the sea of Galilee.

This blessed aura must have been what Juliana, Rose, Angela, and the others had retired to their anchorages, cells, and huts to steep themselves in.

But he wasn't left long in tranquil enjoyment of these fantasies. Meeting Claude at the mail boat one evening, H was shocked by her breath-taking prettiness. The oval-faced, full-lipped, dimpled, black-lashed, Paris-perfumed girl, with smouldering grey eyes and a French accent, might, in the light of the kind of consciousness in which he was trying to enter, have come to tempt him.

It took resolution to remain most of the following morning in the hut with Juliana's *Revelations of Divine Love*, instead of crossing the corner of the garden and yard to see if Claude, who'd had breakfast in bed, was up yet.

Not that this English anchorite who kept herself spotlessly fresh in body as well as spirit – her daily ablutions were to H, though himself not greatly concerned with hygiene, an added appeal – had nothing to set against the attractions of the visitor. Indeed, quite the opposite, for she promised a felicity that just then seemed more compelling that the sexual one. Obsessed by a love that had no earthly outlet, she was drawn to that mysterious magnet of so much medieval passion, the Jesus of the Gospels, who in turn responded a hundredfold, centuries earlier, time's flow being reversed by new sensibilities of love.

Reflecting on each of His separate agonies suffered for her, Juliana, in her nest under the cathedral eaves, evoked images that haunted H no matter how strong the pull in the opposite direction.

For instance, on the crown of thorns: 'and in the coming out the drops were brown-red, for the blood was thick; and in the spreading abroad they were light-red; and when they came to the brows, then they vanished . . . the plenteousness is like the drops of water that fall off the eaves after a great shower of rain . . . and for roundness they were like the scale of herring, in the spreading on the forehead.'

In the afternoon H joined the two girls who were listening to a Tchaikovsky record and drinking vermouth from a bottle that Claude had brought with her. The bittersweet tang of the aperitif seemed to him part of the mellifluous stridency of the music and also – though almost tone-deaf, music had suddenly entered his awareness – of Claude's way of sitting upright, shoulders straight, dimpled chin slightly raised, as she listened.

Iseult, during one of her accounts of what to her was the childish folly of sex, had told him that when she and Claude with their respective mothers, had been staying at an Alpine resort, Claude had confided in her that a man there, a consumptive who'd become her lover, had always made love to her on a chair.

When they came near the end of the bottle H said he'd drive to Dublin to fetch another; he wouldn't be long, not much more than an hour, and meanwhile they could play more records and finish what was left, though if Claude suggested accompanying him, better still.

Though he sensed she would have liked to come, she didn't (out of consideration for Iseult?) say so, and H drove alone by the shortcut across the mountains, instead of via the lower valley and then by the bus route. He went to a wine shop in St Stephen's Green that he recalled from the days of his mother-in-law's house there, and bought two green bottles of what had become for him an elixir, glinting pale in one, dark in the other, behind elaborately engraved and coloured labels reminding him of notes of huge denominations in a debased and foreign currency.

Hardly taking in the city, he headed back for the mountains, having to stop near the end of the long climb and, after the steam had ceased to hiss out, unscrew the radiator cap from the clouded, hot expanse of chromium on the front of the car's bonnet to let the water cool.

When he reached the cottage the mood there had changed. Iseult and Claude had just come back from a walk down to the wood at the bottom of the glen with the dachshund puppy, Blossom, and were about to prepare supper. The gramophone had been put away, the glasses rinsed, and H did not even take the bottles in their corrugated cardboard cones out of the car, the women seeming hardly to recall where he'd been or on what errand.

But next day when Iseult brought him a cup of coffee out to the hut at midmorning, she told him: 'When we were undressing last night Claude said to me, "I've got that boy of yours in my blood"; it's a French expression. And, do you know, darling, what I should have done if I wasn't such an old dog-in-the-manger? Called you over, which I knew was what you wanted too, and told you both, "There you are, children; you've my blessing." '

'And let me sleep with her?'

'Claude's always been like a little sister and I thought I wouldn't be jealous. But when it came to it I couldn't.'

Though he usually came to himself with a start when he heard Iseult ring the bell, H went to the cottage before it was quite time for lunch. As he crossed the yard he heard Chopin's *Polonaise* and at the open door sniffed the Paris scent.

'Where's the booze, chéri? C'est l'heure de l'apéritif.' And there he was back again in the tense, expectant atmosphere of the day before.

In the afternoon Iseult said she had promised to have tea with the Campbells and couldn't disappoint Mrs Campbell who wanted to pour out her heart to her; she was making up her mind to leave the stocky little poet.

Iseult was going to walk to the Campbell's cottage and back, but, by reminding her how breathless she became even on the way up from the oak wood, he persuaded her to let him come with the car to fetch her. He knew that her pride was forcing her to leave him and Claude alone; she couldn't bear what she thought had been her failure to take a detached and superior attitude to their attraction for each other.

Once alone with Claude, H became nervous. He thought that both he himself and the whole place must strike her as uncivilized. He'd noticed that morning that she'd dropped several of the newspaper pieces they used for toilet tissue down the earth closet in an attempt to cover by one of them the evidence of her use of it.

With her breath of the boulevards, her sophisticated lovers, her daily change of dresses (however many had she with her?) she seemed hardly touchable, and it was only her remark about him reported by Iseult that gave H the courage to sit beside her on the divan.

Even then it was with the excuse of pointing out to her whereabouts in the valley the Campbells had their cottage. Claude sat with shoulders straight, chin tilted, lips slightly parted, without bothering to turn her head, and he realized with a shock that she was waiting impatiently to be embraced.

It was the first time H had kissed another woman, apart from his despairing embrace of Polenskaya in Prague, and the impact of a strange mouth, smell, skin texture, made him afraid.

It was always Iseult who made the final moves, a habit that had remained from the days of his utter ignorance, and it was hard for him to take the initiative.

H had been influenced by Iseult's way of keeping the sexual act from impinging too clearly on everyday consciousness. For her it was a weakness, an aberration, best confined to night and darkness, or disguised by musical accompaniment, never indulged in too deliberately but, if possible, slipped into by chance and quickly forgotten.

He sensed that Claude expected him to pass quickly beyond mere kissing; 'the French don't waste time flirting,' he recalled Iseult telling him. But he didn't know how to begin, what to loosen or undo, her clothes or his; didn't dare slide his hand – up or down? – under her fashionable dress, was afraid that long before he'd got into the right position his nerve would have failed.

When they met Iseult, Claude having come with him in the car, H saw that

117

she was trying to guess from their faces what had happened in her absence. Probably failing to come to any conclusion she put what was meant to be a casual inquiry as how they had spent the afternoon.

'We flirted like Billy-o,' Claude told her. Like many foreigners who speak some English, she used colloquialisms that were out of date, 'but that was damn all!'

H lay in bed in his hut in the hot night beset by alternating fantasies about the holy quiet of hermitages and medieval abbeys in their deep woods, having been fascinated by pictures of Clairvaux, and about Claude.

Aroused by a knock on the wooden wall of the hut, he jumped out of bed, his pyjamas clinging to his damp flesh, and, still in his own warm, sensual aroma, opened the door.

Claude stood there in her nightdress holding Blossom.

'She's been kicking up such a row with us – did you hear her? – we can't go to sleep, and Iseult thinks she might settle down with you.'

So Iseult had finally sent her 'little sister' to him!

H held out his arms – for the dog? for the girl? – and, her cool perfume mingling in the still air with his hot boyish odour, Claude gave him the dachshund, hesitated, and then returned to the cottage.

20

A few days after they'd seen Claude off, H running down the pier to keep abreast of her as she stood waving at the rail and Iseult following more slowly, Iseult suggested he accompany her to the chapel at the head of the glen on Sundays.

'Not just Sundays, Pet, I'll walk there to Mass every morning!' He resolved to make up for his backsliding.

'That's you all over, Luke, forever going to extremes.'

He admired her for the way she had tried to live up to her ideals during her cousin's visit and it inspired him to a more dedicated pursual of *his*; the trouble was he was still not sure in what these really consisted.

He started attending daily Mass, trudging the four or five miles up the mountain road and back, with the newly assimilated concept that the Mass stood in some sort of numinous relation to the Last Supper and Crucifixion as recorded in the Gospels sinking into his mind.

The idea was one that fitted easily enough into his kind of imagination. The psychology of the hours on the cross he recognized as belonging to the deepest experience. This was a familiar nightmare, the longing of exposed, tormented beings, stripped of their protective aura, for the coming of darkness. How often, for no conscious reason, had he experienced the shadow of terror in the part of him – the neurons and chromosomes? – he shared with the brute creation? He grasped instinctively the trapped beast's hope for some slight respite when darkness falls.

With His gift for taking in nuances, Christ wasn't likely to have missed a single wagging head or the spleen of the remarks of those below, solemnly reproving, contemptuous, or, especially in those addressed directly to Him, facetious: 'Give us a tip, O King of the Prophets, for Sunday's chariot race at Antioch.'

Let darkness fall. That of the time before the fiat: let there be light. This would engulf Him, his pain and humiliation, if the disaster was complete. This was the darkness that had been at the fringe of all His prayer and which He'd tried to find a path through. He had tried to shatter the treasured image that men had of themselves, of their moral judgement particularly. His presence had raised some doubt about their cherished thought processes. Now that they had Him up there, any unease and mental discomfort remaining could be erased by an orgy of righteous indignation.

Christ had held the most forward position of His time for several hours. And it would fall to the condemned, the sick-unto-death and perhaps a handful of unregarded artists to defend these areas of consciousness in the coming days as best they could.

Not that these reflections reconciled H to what he saw and heard of the functioning of the local church, and of the average priest with his stomachful of indigestible dogmatics and a half-starved mind, self-poisoned by the complementary toxins of love of authority and fear of its loss.

'Why, I'd have done it better myself, Pet!' he remarked to Iseult during an argument. 'If I was asked to compile a further instalment of the life of Jesus I'd at least have tried to follow Him in the direction he'd been going. I'd have kept his spontaneity and directness, His delight in concrete realities, and certainly wouldn't have had Him suddenly pronouncing all kind of abstract and irrelevant dogmas like His Mother's bodily Assumption into Heaven. And I'll tell you another thing, now that we're on the subject, I'd have made Him reconsider His plan to rise from the dead which, as I see it, has been the cause of all the trouble. I'd have Him forgo the Resurrection, though it would mean the loss of those wonderful incidents of recognition such as Mary Magdalen at the empty tomb, the realization, after He'd gone, that came to the two men at the inn at Emmaus as to who had been with them, and – isn't it the most touching of all reunions? – being seen and, after some doubt, recognized early one morning grilling a few fish on a fire He'd lit beside His beloved lake.

'You see, Pet, without the Resurrection there'd be no bandwagon, no grocer's scheme of reward and punishment! Just the haunting Jesus disaster to illuminate our lesser disasters.'

'No, that's too much! Some little Jew without moral values or spiritual authority; take away His teaching, His miracles, and His mother (H hadn't said anything of this sort), and that is what's left. Don't you realize it's through the Blessed Virgin that the simple and humble come to Him? When I pray it's her I see, not her face or figure, but a deep blue calm expanse like the sky just before night falls and, right across it, in even darker blue, a huge M.'

H returned to the hut leaving her sitting on the unmade bed, weighed down by her belly, surrounded by patience cards and cigarette butts, bewildered and hurt.

When an invitation came from Mrs Yeats asking them to spend a few days at the Yeats house in Dublin, seeing Iseult's face brighten at the chance of some intelligent company, H didn't voice his own disinclination to have his seclusion broken again so soon.

They were given, and H was conscious of the honour, Yeats's bedroom in the tall Georgian house on Merrion Square, with reproductions of Blake's wraithlike figures on the walls: a mother and her little ones floating, upright and elegant, down the River of Life; an angel leaning precariously from her heavenly steed to gather in her arms a whimpering babe. On the outside of the door Georgie Yeats had pinned a note: 'Willie, this is now the Ruarks' room.'

'Otherwise you'd have him wandering in at any hour of the day or night,' she told them.

On the very first evening at dinner H saw that if he was to contribute to the conversation, as the poet evidently expected him to, he'd have to emerge from his own preoccupations and think up the sort of things that would interest Yeats.

As for Iseult, she was quite at home in the intellectual discussion; perhaps she should have married Yeats, but he'd have got on her nerves with his formal and deliberate ways, while H himself, idle and uncivilized, with his quiet and deceptive delinquency, still attracted her.

Yeats was talking about the newly constituted state of which he was a Senator. The whole setup hadn't come up to his expectations; he'd have liked, H saw, a role such as d'Annunzio was playing in relation to the new Mussolini government.

'Would the people you fought for have made better rulers?' he asked H, turning on him his keen glance across the table, and then unfocusing him again and dropping his head as though awaiting some revealing words.

Should H say that he hadn't fought for anybody or anything, but in pursuit of an obscure impulse of his own which had become somewhat clearer after he'd met and talked with Lane? Could he explain Lane to Yeats?

'If you mean: would they also have imposed a censorship and forbidden divorce, I'm sure they would.'

H caught Mrs Yeats's eye, glowing green below her coppery hair, her bracelets jingling as she raised her long-stemmed wineglass, and it struck him that she was the one who guessed some of his real feelings.

H didn't share the sense of outrage of Yeats and his fellow intellectuals at the censorship law. It was a matter of indifference to him. The Irish censorship would catch the smaller fish but if a really big one was to swim into view it would be set on by far more ferocious foes than any Irish ones.

'If somebody somewhere writes a book which is so radical and original,' H announced, not looking at anyone in particular, 'that it would burst the present literary setup wide open, that writer will be treated with a polite contempt by the critical and academic authorities that will discourage further mention of him. He'll raise deeper, more subconscious hostility than sectarian ones and he'll be destroyed far more effectively by enlightened neglect than anything we would do to him here.'

Yeats had lifted his head and was regarding H intently.

'You believe that the artist is bound to be rejected? You equate him with the prophet?'

It was costing H a lot of nervous energy to formulate concepts for Yeats to take hold of. And, apart from that, he mustn't forget he was a nobody in the literary world addressing a Nobel Prizewinner.

'A poet may escape persecution because his vision is veiled from the literary arbiters, but the novelist who speaks more plainly is bound to scandalize them.'

H caught what he thought was an appreciative smile on Georgie Yeats's barbaric-looking, vivid, russet-tinged face in recognition of his adroit slipping out of the dilemma.

H could only contribute to this kind of talk by allowing himself to get into a state of nervous fever in which his power of invention and improvisation came to his aid.

That night, quite exhausted, he went to bed under the Samurai sword that hung over it, his thoughts madly racing. He lay awake, being anyhow miles away from sleep, and prepared some largely imaginary anecdotes embodying unexpected and original-sounding comments on the kind of things that interested Yeats.

It ended by his being carried away by his own flights of fancy and pursuing them late into the night beyond the point where they could be used in conversation to his host, quite apart from the fact that Iseult, who clung to

121

the factual, would be sure to interrupt with, 'But, Luke, darling, whenever did all this happen?'

Example of one of these night reveries in the form of a conversation between himself and a chance acquaintance in a café in Paris, where H had never yet been:

'A votre santé, M'sieur. Ahhh! Ce n'est pas mauvais, ce "rot" ici.'

Establish the locale, provide a touch of authenticity, that would compel Yeats's interest right away. 'If I were to stop a passerby out there' – H and his imaginary acquaintance were on a café terrace – 'introduce myself as an Irishman compiling a work on France and ask him who was the keeper of the French conscience, what do you suppose he'd say?'

'Depends on his political affiliations. He might well direct you to the Elysée Palace and there, after a wait, it's possible you'd be issued, Monsieur, with an answer typed on official paper, on which you'd be charged the stamp duty.'

The reference to stamped paper which H recalled having heard from Iseult was used for all official documents, he'd put in to add what he thought of as 'density'.

'And what would it say?'

'I'm not Monsieur le Président, but if you want me to hazard a guess, something to the effect that it is guarded in the works of the great writers of France, past and present.'

That would have to suffice for his little contribution to tomorrow's conversation, which he'd have to get in when Iseult wasn't there. But by now, well past midnight, it wasn't just the idea of impressing Yeats that was impelling H, but his own feverish exhaustion that made him imagine new stories to recount. He was soon involved in other even more fantastic incidents.

He saw himself in New York or San Francisco in conversation with a young woman whose husband, a university extension lecturer, whom H had been sent to interview on a subject of vital interest to Yeats, which was yet to be thought up, was unfortunately not at home. That very morning he'd taken the Studebaker and gone to summer school in a place called (just a minute) the Silver Barricades. What make of car had she said? The name, that he made her repeat, moved her lips into seductive shapes, purely American, that fascinated H.

Yeats was forgotten; he was indulging his own unprofitable night fantasies.

Yes, well, where were we? Up in the Silver Somethings with the professor of English? No, nothing to beguile himself with there. Listening to his young wife order an oven-ready chicken on the phone; then call from across the hall that she was having a quick shower but wouldn't be more than a couple of minutes. With one ear on sounds from the bathroom, H had started half-heartedly to leaf through a critical work by the professor when his hostess called again she'd be with him in a moment. She was just giving herself a rubdown with some special lotion.

'It's called Deodonus, Gift of God. Cute, isn't it? You see, we don't have air conditioning in an old place like this and the humidity clogs the skin with particles of city detritus.'

This open-fronted living, as well as the hygiene was, in H's evocation of the American scene, part of the social code and, to have left him in the dark as to what she was doing while out of his sight he imagined would have been a breach of hospitality.

What was so exhausting was that not only had H to present vividly imagined milieux of which he'd no direct knowledge, but also to remember that it all had to lead up to the significant sentence or two that, repeated across the dinner table, would come as the sort of revelation that Yeats seemed to expect of him. Not that in this particular case he wasn't being carried far beyond any such possibility, but he couldn't free himself.

There came a humming from the all-electric kitchen. Had she pressed the wrong button and, instead of turning on the infra-red roaster, shot the chicken down the outward-delivery chute, and, with the metal tag (Solidonus, Gift of the Sun) still round its leg, was it already on its way back to the department store?

In the morning H awoke red-eyed and jaded. The visit was too much for him. He tried to spend an hour or so whenever he could alone in their room with, as a respite from his imaginary American hostess, the Blessed Juliana and her 'dearworthy Lord'. But it had begun to strike him that these charming women like herself, Rose, and Angela had had rather too pleasant a time of it in their hermitages.

On one of the last evenings H came up with a view of the writer's situation that he'd been keeping in store.

'It's that he must be doubly involved.'

'Doubly involved?'

The eagle glance, the quick withdrawal, the moment of charged silence with leonine mane pushed back.

'It's the writer who's one with his work, and doesn't create it as a thing apart, as a beautiful artifice outside himself, as, say, Synge does, who says the things that now matter most.'

Had he struck a spark? The sea-green eyes, autumn colouring, and Roman nose of Georgie Yeats were in the background like an ikon. Was this the vulnerable spot? Not only had the poet failed to merge his life and his art (the classic intellectual situation, perhaps) but the style of his living was so formal and unspontaneous that it was in constant opposition to the increasingly disreputable spirit that was inspiring much of his later poetry.

21

During the last weeks of Iseult's pregnancy she went to stay at her mother's. H remained at the cottage which, with the addition to the family not only of a baby but of H's mother, who'd suggested she come and help Iseult when it was born, was going to be small. After talking it over they decided the best solution was to have an extra room built, but first they had to buy the place; her mother, Iseult thought, would give them the money.

Their landlord came in answer to a message H had sent him by one of his children who brought the milk, an old little sheep farmer in a battered bowler hat, his shylock's face framed in whiskers, wheezy and asthmatic, stumping down the road on a stick.

It was soon clear that he wasn't going to sell them the cottage and plot, or if he did, only at a price they wouldn't expect Madame to provide. But it was hard for the old fellow to be final, forgoing the sum, which they never even came to naming, within his reach, and he kept talking and wheezing, wheezing and talking, the best part of the evening. In the end he was back at what he'd said at the beginning about keeping the place for his eldest son.

Before he left the old man recounted an incident he'd read in the paper about a busload of people from a provincial town on a pilgrimage to a popular shrine who, when the brakes had failed on a hill, had escaped death by a miracle.

H knew that his landlord told him this in the belief that, as a devout Catholic who was seen walking to Mass morning after morning, it would appeal to him, whereas it set the seal on the depression the fruitless conversation with the old man produced in H.

The story afforded H another depressing glimpse into the kind of religiosity in which many of these people seemed to find all they needed in the way of an image of God. It struck him that their central pulses, whose vibrancy determines the depth of men's responses, had a mechanical tick. Set to a parochial clock, they went tick-tock, piously recording the do's and don'ts for each day of the week, while around the cosmos the lingering echo of the original upheaval was merging with the first rumblings of the final bang.

It seemed they would have to move, and the prospect disturbed H. At least he had the hut to set up wherever they went. His obsession with the mystics was coming to an end, but until setting out on a new inner journey he didn't like the idea of emerging from it.

He hadn't slept with Iseult all these months, since soon after she had conceived. But he knew, not only from the Claude episode, that that problem had been bypassed but not resolved.

When Iseult returned with the baby boy, whom they'd christened Ian, accompanied by H's mother, though H remained in the hut, he was drawn to spend more time in the cottage. He was unexpectedly delighted with the baby and proud of how it responded to him.

Ian was robust and demanding, indulging in paroxysms of crying that were quite different from Dolores's whimpering in the night. Only H could quieten him, taking him in his arms and sinking into an inner repose that enveloped the baby too as he walked with it slowly up and down the room.

After he and Iseult had talked it over, H and his mother went by train, the car being no longer serviceable, to look at a house that was for sale in a remote glen.

It turned out to be an ancient blockhouse, surrounded by a high wall, one of a series built by the British in the mountains after the rebellion of 1798. Somebody had made an attempt to disguise its origin by turning it into a castle with a turret and crenellations along the front of the roof.

H hadn't a clear idea of what they were looking for. He was too confused, the future too undefined, for him to have formed a norm by which to measure and judge what they were shown. And so Dineen Castle with its granite walls and fake battlements struck him as just the place in which to start a new unpredictable phase of their lives.

Circumstances conspired to support this supposition. They had hardly moved in, camping in the bare rooms, only corners of which could be furnished, when Iseult announced that her mother, after providing the purchase price, had given her the balance of a larger sum she'd owed her. It turned out – if H had ever heard of this, he'd soon forgotten – that the villa in Normandy had been a gift to Iseult from her father, but when they'd sold it on leaving France her mother had used the money to buy the house in Dublin. Now, having realized some capital, or certain investments having matured, for the financial jargon stuck in H's mind without his being sure of the meaning, she found herself with money in the bank and was repaying Iseult.

Never before had H had a say in the disposal, as he'd heard it called, of so much money. And just when it was needed most. Or did its possession create needs previously absent?

Iseult suggested they turn a small ground-floor room into a bathroom, where the baby could be bathed and nappies washed, and put a sink in the kitchen on the other side of the wall to the bathtub, thus saving extensive plumbing. Another of prosperity's principles: the more money wisely spent the more saved.

Realizing that they weren't going to live the simple life of the cottage, H decided to invest – another of the solid-sounding terms he was picking up – what was left over in some project to bring in the extra income they were going to need.

He discussed the possibilities with Iseult, who, however, he soon saw wasn't going to contribute any worthwhile suggestions. But H discovered in himself a practical capacity, inherited from his hard-headed Ulster forebears who had gone to Australia and made fortunes in sheep farming, all except his father who'd drunk himself to death too soon, that he'd always been half aware of.

After buying and studying various agricultural journals, as well as a number of books on pigs, hens, and market gardening, H decided that what the few acres of mountain, inside and outside the wall, was best suited for was poultry farming.

He embarked on a bout of buying that seemed to have no end. He ordered a dozen portable laying sheds, each accommodating twenty birds, on small iron wheels, and then bought a car, a slightly reduced demonstration model of the then new Peugeot 201 saloon, capable of towing them to positions on the hillside so that all the land could be put to use.

Before the sheds were delivered, and while he was speculating as to whether the main flock should consist of Speckled Leghorns or White Wyandottes, Iseult received a letter from a London solicitor telling her that an aunt who'd died there recently had left her five hundred pounds.

Money breeds money. Had H heard this proverb or invented it in the fever of the moment? He arranged with the contractors, still at work on the sanitation, to repair and convert the huge, old outbuildings, used as stabling by the British garrison, into laying houses, and had a local carpenter construct tiers of pigeonholes with which to line the whitewashed stone walls. These nests H designed, from instructions in his *Poultry Encyclopaedia*, with trap doors resting on notches, which, when pushed up by an entering hen, fell shut. Then, on his hourly rounds, he would note down the numbers on the metal rings clamped to the scaly legs of the birds before releasing them, and thus have a register of the most prolific layers from which to breed.

With the outhouses ready, and what particularly pleased him were the skylights let into the thick old slates that shed from the unexpected angle a flood of limpid light through the ancient shadows, he bought an extra hundred White Leghorn pullets and laid in a store of Sussex-ground oats, bran, fish meal, maize meal, oats and barley. He sent to Holland for a dozen

Welsummer hens and a cockerel; a new breed that, according to the advertisement in *The Poultry Farmer*, produced eggs of a darker brown than those laid by Barnevelders, which held the record for depth of colour up to then.

He had an urge to compete and excel. He began keeping the very darkest of the eggs to exhibit at the Spring Show in Dublin and among the imported fowl was already picking those whose feathers glowed deepest with the smouldering ember of Flemish farmyard paintings.

While assembling the sectional sheds and dragging them behind the Peugeot to sites on the heathery slopes, H had lost sight of his own hut which he came on one morning, erected by the contractor and his mate against the back door, to serve, Iseult explained, as a place to eat in order to save meals being carried down the long stone passage from the kitchen to the dining room.

H had only time for a passing regret. He had no inclination to consider whether his new preoccupation was likely to give him what his spirit yearned for. Indeed, at the moment, the desire he was conscious of was for a high egg yield and a prize at the show. Juliana and St Catherine of Siena were far away and long ago, whispers in the clamour of chirping, crowing, rustling, pecking, to say nothing of the flushing, cascading, gurgling that he could set off at the pull of a chain or turn of a tap.

Planning to have a second flock coming into lay when the first started to moult in early summer, H bought a paraffin-burning incubator and some hoovers for rearing chicks. He also decided to go to a farm in Lancashire in answer to an advertisement and collect both chicks and eggs in person; of a dozen eggs he'd had sent and put under a broody hen, only four had hatched out, for which he blamed the jolting in the post.

Travelling via Holyhead and Liverpool with the big, padlocked, yellow-varnished eggbox, H arrived in Manchester at breakfast time and, by local train, at his destination an hour later. A longish trudge with the eggbox, twice directed by passersby with the kindly concern that he recalled from his time in England. The place was smaller, shabbier than he'd imagined it. But Mrs Wright turned out a tawny-haired girl, with an accent that increased her exciting strangeness, in breeches and gum boots.

'You *are* an early bird, Mr Ruark. I don't suppose I can make up four dozen eggs right away. We'll have a look, and if not, you won't mind waiting a bit, will you? There's always a few hens that don't lay till early afternoon; but there are plenty of chicks, we've only to put them into boxes.'

'I brought you a present of some hatching eggs from a special dark-egg strain.'

'That's very kind of you. Look, you may as well stay now that you're here till we can make up the four dozen. It's a long tramp to the village and back and you won't get much of a lunch there.'

She was leading him around the side of the house before he could decide whether to accept what appeared to be an invitation to the midday meal. No word of a husband, no sign of young children. It was the realization of the imagined visit to the American professor's wife.

She showed him around the crowded, odorous sheds. It was a poultry slum compared to the rural luxury in which his own fowl lived.

'Much plagued by B.W.D?' she asked.

'What's that?'

'Bacillary white diarrhoea. Have you never come out of a morning and spent the first half-hour collecting stiff and flattened chick corpses for the incinerator?'

H recalled a section of his encyclopaedia devoted to the disease, but so far he'd had no call to study it.

'Don't tell me you've no red mite either.'

He pretended that this was a pest he wasn't entirely free of in case she began to suspect something strange about him, that he was no more a bona fide poultry farmer than he suspected he appeared.

'Ever tried painting the perches with nicotine preparation?' she asked. 'You've got to be careful, though; a drop on their beaks and, wham! they topple over like that!' She turned, looked up into H's excited face and slapped her thigh.

During lunch which they ate with Mrs Wright's mother, who'd evidently prepared the meal of sausage-and-mash followed by custard, there was a sense of restraint at the table. Mother and daughter hardly spoke, the girl keeping her face lowered like a punished child, but once alone with him in the smelly little office at the end of one of the laying sheds, she bubbled over.

H watched her out of the corner of his eye.

'God, don't you ever get tired,' she asked, 'of this eternal racket, and long for the silence of a South Sea island with nothing but a warm lagoon and a silvery beach?'

'Well, no, that's not exactly what I dream of.'

Her face came closer as she asked: 'What *do* you dream of then?' He realized that it wasn't his innermost thoughts she was inquiring about. She couldn't have indicated more clearly what she wanted of him, and if he didn't act on it he would return home one degree nearer the all-around defeat that all the outer activity couldn't disguise. More serious than his failure as a hermit was the fact that he'd stopped writing, hadn't tried to revise the Viennese novel and send it to a publisher. Was he about to be released from his fantasy world of inodorous, indecorous, but never startlingly sexy, wraiths? Would he be immersed with this most normal of girls, whose common English accent intensified her desirability, in the great mainstream of sex which with Iseult he'd never managed to reach? What a wonder it would be to slip into the real world by the back door and be welcomed to its sensual heart!

H leaned towards Mrs Wright and kissed her. All was easy; she slipped from the table on which she'd been sitting into his arms and showed him that with kisses, as with poultry diseases, there were varieties he was unaware of.

Breaking off, she said, 'What time did you say you wanted to get a local train? Supposing we have a last look for the hatching eggs and then you pack the chicks while I go and change. I'll drive you to Manchester and tell Mum I went to the pictures after leaving you at the station to account for any delay in my getting back. What about that?'

'Wonderful,' he said, 'simply marvellous!'

He was shocked, excited, aghast.

Mrs Wright showed him the cartons for the day-old chicks and, hardly knowing what he was doing, he started taking the yellow balls of down from under the hoover, losing the tally, and having to count them all over again in the boxes.

She reappeared in what seemed no time, wearing a dress with a string of Ciro pearls, whose name he knew from his brief but concentrated examination of the windows of jewellers' shops at the time of selling the necklace, and got out a Ford station wagon that, once seated in it beside her, smelled of fish and bone meal.

On the drive she started telling him a dirty story.

'Solly comes home unexpectedly from a business trip one night and, before turning in, goes to have a peep at his young wife. Her room is dark and the night is hot and his little Myra has pushed off the bedclothes and Solly can just get a glimpse of her breasts. This bloody light always turns red just as you reach it! "There, there my turtle dove," he murmurs. She's breathing so quick he thinks she's having a nightmare. He puts out a hand to soothe her and instead of a nice big bazoom guess what he touches?'

As they waited at the traffic lights H heard the chirping from the perforated cardboard containers and thought: For the sweet sake of our dearworthy Lord don't make it more explicit!

'His neighbour Izzy's arse.'

Mrs Wright stopped the car at an off-licence sign at the outskirts of the city and told H to buy a bottle of whisky for a Mrs Cullen to whose house it appeared they were going.

'A compatriot of yours, as a matter of fact. Not that I'll introduce you, of course, but we'll have to have a drink with her.'

They spent a few minutes with the proprietress in the office of the shabby hotel and then she led them to a room upstairs where, though it was broad daylight, she drew the plush curtains and switched on a red-shaded lamp.

H deposited the heavy eggbox, and the girl the cartons of chicks, on the worn carpet, and then took another look at the door that Mrs Cullen, another name that was to stick in his mind, had just shut after her to make sure, as he'd thought at first glance, that it had neither bolt nor key. He didn't remark on this nor did the girl. It was the final indication that the miracle wasn't going to happen, however he liked to imagine it, whether in purely sensual terms or psychologically, as the current from his highly charged system flashing into hers.

He lay on the bed with her to the chirping of the chicks and the sour, chemical scents (poultry manure had a high sulphate – or was it potassium? – content) that seemed still to cling to her; having changed without washing? Through neglecting to wear a head scarf at work? When she, in her turn, chirped in the query, 'Happy now?' the debacle was complete.

22

By early summer, the second since their move to Dineen, the eighth since H's release and the death of Lane, the poultry farm was bringing in some return for what he'd spent on it. H had come to an arrangement with a deceptively small and unimposing-looking greengrocer's in Dublin, a place that women from the fashionable districts imagined as an obscure little shop they'd discovered where they could get fresh country supplies at reasonable prices, to deliver eggs to the old woman who kept it at an all-the-year price of two-and-two a dozen, guaranteed laid the same morning, the shells sealed with butter while still warm, and brought to town by a milk lorry.

Whenever there was a pause in the busy day, however, or at certain hours of the night, the messages flashing to his mind from less practically occupied centres whose signals he registered without always deciphering, grew more and more urgent. Whatever these nerve cells, subconscious, subliminal, or unused concentrations of mental energy, they kept sending out intimations of their discontent.

When the business had reached this point, Iseult told him that her mother, who'd been suffering from rheumatism, was going to a spa in France and that she had promised to accompany her.

'Couldn't you join us, darling, towards the end of the cure, and we'd go off somewhere on our own while Moura spent a week or two in the Pyrenees?

The doctors always prescribe a short holiday to recuperate after the dieting and baths.'

Yes, if all continued to go so well, apart from what was going so ill, and if he found a suitable assistant in time to take over, he certainly would. He was secretly surprised at the suggestion.

Answering some advertisements in the *Feathered World* and another trade journal, he considered asking for a photograph but refrained, partly because it struck him as an impertinence, and partly because since the Mrs Wright fiasco they were no longer urgent sex messages that seemed to pass up and down his spinal chord but ones that related to a different obsession.

As a step towards heeding these he began to read again, especially books by modern writers, to find out whether they had more to say that concerned him than the mystics finally had. He joined the Dublin branch of the Times Lending Library and brought home novels that he'd either read about or was guided to select by what he believed were inner signals of the same origin as those that had brought him there.

Reading late into the night, for he hadn't a free moment by day, H devoured the *Forsyte Saga* in just over a week. Nothing! Not a reflection of a shadow to match his own vivid shadow show. What he'd yet no inkling of was that ninety-nine per cent of seriously considered English novels were social commentaries of one kind or another without any pretensions to communication on the level where he was listening.

H, who needed a lot of sleep, postponed further reading till Linda Burnett arrived from Liverpool, as she did one morning and met Iseult and him, as arranged, in a café that opened early. As she breakfasted, H put on his casual air behind which to study her, while Iseult, after asking a few polite questions lapsed into semi-oblivion, blowing cigarette smoke across the girl's eggs and bacon.

Miss Burnett soon struck him as suitable to leave in charge. She wouldn't cause the highly strung pullets to panic by a sudden clatter of buckets, as he'd seen Mrs Wright do, she was neat and alert; accustomed to Iseult's untidiness and blindnesses, these seemed valuable virtues to H.

On the drive down alone with the girl – Iseult was spending a few days with her mother – she asked no questions, though H guessed it was a relief to her to find his mother, the child, and the maid at the old fort in the wilderness.

Soon she had taken over most of the routine work, leaving H to give his leisurely attention to selecting six pullets for the Department of Agriculture's laying competition, the choosing and matching for exhibition at the coming Horse Show of half-a-dozen of the darkest Welsummer eggs, and, above all, in novel reading.

He started on *Ulysses*. From the first page he felt the new impact, though it wasn't till Bloom appeared at his morning chores that H experienced a similar shift in his angle of vision to that which had taken place when he'd filled the tub from the mountain stream and had a baptismal bath.

No writer, as far as he knew, had ever before stooped low enough through the portal of sense in order to register the tangible feel of life. At the other end of the scale, Dostoevsky kept his characters at the highest levels of consciousness, constantly in a spiritual crisis, while existing in a kind of vacuum, sketchily housed and inadequately fed and clothed, without earning a living, washing, shopping, or making love.

Not that H found in *Ulysses* what he was seeking. Joyce's central nerve was a marvellous compound of the physical and intellectual, but in its pulsations H didn't find what he was listening for. What was that? To ask was to realize the difficulty of an intelligible answer. Let's say: certain waves of disturbance travelling through outer space and echoing in the psyche, such as, at one point in the history, the Gospels had seemed to record.

Joyce had a beautifully flexible style forged, in the first place no doubt, as his own interior communication system, with which to explore familiar but (till then) largely unrecorded areas of consciousness. But, however much H admired him, they were not the areas to which H's own inner nerve responded with the kind of excited beat that he craved to have set in motion.

The selection, from among hundreds of pullets coming into lay, of the six most likely to produce a high egg yield during the autumn and winter months of the competition was proving beyond him, and he called in the county poultry instructress to help.

A dark, pale-faced girl appeared one morning in a white coat, which she'd put on when she got out of her car, standing there after he'd opened the door, arms hanging as though weights were attached to them, slim, yet heavy, and seeming to droop. All this struck H in the two or three seconds it took her to introduce herself as Mary Doyle.

It was Miss Burnett's day off and she'd gone to Dublin by bus, he not having offered her the loan of the car as he knew she'd hoped, and he and the girl rounded up the birds from the mountain into one of the stone stables.

H felt the heaviness of her arms as she lifted them to drive the pullets towards the back gate in the castle wall sharpening his imagination to a blade held against a sheaf drooping with ripeness.

This air of passivity and slight languor she managed to preserve while catching a pullet, grasping its legs in one hand and measuring the space between its pelvic bones with the fingers of her other, her pallor seeming to increase with her exertions, whereas his chest was sticky beneath his open shirt.

132

After running a hand down a pullet's feathers, to determine, perhaps, the degree of silkiness, testing the texture of its wattles between thumb and finger, looking it in the eye with dreamy-seeming glance, she let the average birds flutter from her hands. The rare ones whose hidden promise she'd discovered she handed to H to let through to the adjoining house.

(Joyce fascinated and repelled H. He felt that at the heart of Joyce was a pool of acidity in which certain fragile treasures, prized by H for their very insubstantiality, were completely destroyed.)

After she'd culled the flock, he brought the instructress through the somewhat gimcrack addition to the old house where the back door and the door of his former hermitage now faced each other under a new strip of roofing, down stone steps and through a room that housed the pump, to the bathroom to wash her hands.

While he waited in the passage and heard Iseult giving Ian his midday meal, he tried to elucidate the nature of his infatuation.

What did he want of her? Something impossible like entering into her mind and feelings? An interlocking, in fact, of their neurological organisms? Or something much more simple: slipping, after the blissful initial pressure, into the secret heart of her feminine passivity? Or did it all boil down to a dream tryst and his reading her a love poem?

He was, incidentally, beginning to realize that the sweet shock of sex was in proportion to the incongruity of its introduction into a non-sexual context. For those in a brothel, sex was no doubt something of a bore. Whereas the unexpected recollection of it in the middle of a day busy and preoccupied with the poultry came as a delight.

What he really wanted, in regard to the instructress, was both specific and less than a complete sexual encounter: to open the bathroom door, that he hadn't heard her lock, and stay with her while she attended to her ablutions and still more private needs.

When she emerged, he led her along the stone passage to the hall door without taking her to the kitchen to introduce her to Iseult who would be sure to resent the intrusion.

As he walked with the girl down the avenue between the rhododendrons to her Austin Seven that she'd left at the bottom of the hill, she told him she'd just returned from a holiday in Brighton.

'It rained a lot, but it was fun; we enjoyed it no end.'

Brighton! That added new undertones to his image of her. And who made up the 'we'? God Almighty, what was he missing? Would he never emerge from what seemed his impoverished situation, both sexually and at other levels?

23

H shared a cabin with a middle-aged Englishman on a southbound liner to La Rochelle. Slipping past holiday beaches – Birkenhead? Blackpool? he wasn't sure of the topography – to a summer night and a long day of sea that from one side of the ship was deep matt blue, from the other colourless bright with at times black blobs of porpoise amid the sparkle; of raven-haired, olive-tinted faces of South American women in the first class café above, and, higher still, the slow pendulation of mast-tips across a blanched sky, and, finally, slithering and lurching through the watery green evening, startlingly small trawlers.

H and his companion dined on the train from La Rochelle; where it went beyond Dax, H wasn't sure; the Englishman had mentioned Bordeaux, but he'd also talked of going to Marseilles, and afterwards drank a glass of Armagnac.

It was the first alcohol, apart from the vermouth drunk during Claude's visit, to Tchaikovsky – or had it been Ravel's? – music on the gramophone, that had ever gone to H's head, after that is, his companion had ordered another round.

The mysterious, foreign landscape opened out beyond the white cloth, radiating from it on the geometrical as well as the mental plane, with the walls of farmhouses and barns moving in arcs of varying diameters and at varying speeds, between the front frame of the wide window and the rear one, at the circumference of circles whose centre was his glass.

A steward was short-stepping down the dining car, flicking a cloth across the tables that had been cleared, and, at passing those still occupied, saying something that H didn't want to catch.

'We're coming to Dax,' his conscientious companion told him.

A minute or two in which to make up his mind about a problem that had only arisen a moment before. Should he ask the waiter, who was already returning along the car, for another couple of Armagnacs, or return to his compartment for his suitcase?

Who could advise him? He knew what Lane would have said, 'For our sweet Christ's sake, aren't there motts in Marseilles, or bloody Nice?' Bloom would have weighed up the pros and cons and being *au fond* a family man, would, with a fatherly smile, have come down for H getting off as planned. Mr Isaacs? He'd met Iseult at least once and they hadn't taken to each other. Besides, he lived in more chaotic times and, unlike Bloom, was a gambler and smuggler, in diamonds, possibly in furs, almost certainly in *Devisen*, and might well have thought that in letting the train take him on to its destination, from where H could telegraph to his wife, no great harm could result.

H returned to the compartment, and out on to the platform, and had his suitcase handed down to him by his staid fellow traveller who, in his concern about H getting off in time, hadn't even noticed his reluctance.

A taxi took H past gardens full of pale roses glowing in the dusk, across a bridge over the Adour – he'd been studying a map at home – where geese waddled homeward in single file along a bank of dry mud, to a long, yellow hotel by the river. At the reception desk he was directed to the grounds at the back where the two ladies, he was told, were expecting him. He walked through the warm, twilit garden where hot green water bubbled up among porous rocks and the rheumatic sufferers were sitting at café tables; were they drinking apéritifs? after-dinner *fines*? He'd lost track of the hour.

He heard his mother-in-law call to him, before he saw them, in her vibrant voice. When he reached their table she greeted him with the enthusiasm that he distrusted as he kissed Iseult on the cheek.

They told him he'd have time for a bath before dinner and he didn't say he'd already eaten, and then Iseult accompanied him back to the hotel. They were awkward and shy with each other, but H, letting his thoughts as usual carry him away, imagined: She knows I don't want a bath at this unearthly hour – all was unearthly here – and she's taking me to our room so that we can make a propitious start to our holiday.

Having conducted him upstairs, instead of stopping at one of the numbered doors, she led him further down a passage and handed him over to a woman with bare red legs who showed him into what appeared to be a bathroom, turned on the water and then draped the inside of the tub with towels.

As she carried out the peculiar ceremonial in the strange-looking room with its floor of wooden laths laid an inch or so apart, H was reminded of the crone in the chapel during their wedding.

Did whisperers of the eternal 'No' in the shape of the most humble of mortal women come to haunt him, as had his witches Macbeth, at hours of destiny? Or was he inflating his sense of disappointment into psychic proportions?

While pulling off his trousers, several of the franc pieces he'd received in change on the train slipped from a pocket and disappeared between the laths, but nothing would have made him pull the bell cord and ask the old woman if there was a way of retrieving them.

Divested of his shirt, he wiped the big mirror which, like the coffinlike draperies hung over the bath to protect the rheumatic sufferers from the cold porcelain, H supposed had a purpose connected with the cure. Regarding his body with the same new eye that had seen the landscape from the train, the roses in the dusk, the file of ghostly geese, it too fascinated him.

H saw it, through the mist re-forming on the wet glass, as an outmoded, handmade machine, with its big polished, old-fashioned-looking indicator at 'go', something forlorn and discarded, tuned for an operation for which, however, a vital part was missing.

In the morning he went into the town with Iseult while her mother took a mud bath and drank the water from the hot springs. She who had once inspired Yeats's love poetry now only asked for some amelioration of the aches in her joints.

He dragged after Iseult around the cathedral of which he decided to take no note, and then looked on while she purchased the rucksacks she said they'd need for their walk. And next morning, after another night alone in his hotel room, and after a slow train had taken them a few stations south-wards, they set out along straight sunny roads whose green verges were regularly stencilled with black tree-shadows towards the low, blue, insub-stantial wall of the Pyrenees.

Iseult slunk alone with the slight forward stoop of the natural tramp, while H never quite managed the right way to balance the weight on his back nor to slip into the proper long-distance gait. It irked him to be going to Lourdes – she had sprung it on him the previous evening – whose choice seemed to bode ill for his hopes. Pausing while one of the fairly infrequent small French cars, Citroëns, Renaults, and an occasional blue Peugeot 201 like his own, whizzed by, Iseult regarded H as though seeing him again after a long time. After the intent appraisal, her large eyes melted in a soft liquid glow and her upper lip drew back in a smile that disconcerted him by its innocence. He saw that for her the walk was a pilgrimage.

The wayfarers, passing a hostelry towards evening, by then one of them was limping painfully, inquired for a night's lodging and, having been told there was a closet available, requested the innkeeper to prepare them a repast. While awaiting it they retired to the upstairs chamber assigned them and the female servant of God, having undone the thongs of her sandals and the servitor, somewhat inconvenienced by his pilgrim's staff, which he didn't care to relinquish, gave themselves over to contemplation of the unincarnate Platonic Light.

The servitor, however, not far advanced in the Purgative Way, and finding the achievement of inner quietude beyond him, hobbled over to the servant of God's corner and, under the spell of the Old Adam, suggested that the time might be passed in more amorous exercises.

Repulsing his advances with distaste, she exhorted him to use the hour or two that remained before the meal was ready in advancing in the virtue of patience.

At supper they were served a dish of bear meat that, the innkeeper explained, was a special recipe in those parts and had been buried for a time before being dressed with bay leaves and simmered in wine.

After sitting for a while in the taproom where the servant of God answered inquiries from the inn's habitués, the servitor having only a partial knowledge of the tongue, about the news they had gathered on their journeying, they retired to their chamber.

The servitor, first stripped, waited until the servant of God had slipped on the loose kirtel in which she slept, standing with bruised feet and pilgrim's staff, from which he never parted, midway between the two cots.

The servant of God, after rising from her knees, said, 'Come, in the name of St Sebastian and all the holy martyrs,' and stretched herself crosswise on the pallet.

The next morning was thundery, and they only walked the few kilometres to the next station, where they sat in a whitewashed waiting room discussing the future in the light of the previous night. What was worrying Iseult was the idea of sex in their daily life at home. As long as it could be kept from impinging on her withdrawn kind of existence centred around the baby, the flower garden and her endless patience-playing – but he was probably wide of the mark in listing her preoccupations – she didn't mind indulging in it occasionally.

But he wasn't prepared for her extraordinary suggestion: 'Suppose we only have it outside the walls?'

'What walls, for God's sake? Oh, you mean the castle walls. And what about the winter?'

Her face fell. In her desperation she'd hit on what she hoped was a fair compromise.

They got out of the train at the station before Lourdes and reached the town on foot. H suspected that each thought the other wanted to keep up their pilgrim guise. Walking through streets in which almost every house was a hotel or pension named after a saint, H breathed again a familiar aroma of outward pieties and inward worldliness.

Iseult booked them separate rooms at a hotel towards the centre of the town, remarking, in an aside slipped in and overtaken by mention of other matters before he could question it, something about 'keeping to the spirit of the place while we're here'.

Too footsore to visit the grotto that evening, H bought a booklet on Blessed Bernadette Soubirous at the hotel bookstall and retired with it to his room. He became absorbed in the story that was told in that limpid tone that recalled to H the pure, near-manic clarity that accompanies states of possession experienced by poets, mystics, and madmen, and which he himself responded to obsessively. For him it was the song of the hidden psyche, inaudible to well-balanced, normally functioning brains, announcing its kinship to angels or demons as in the poem of Emily Brontë's:

> He comes with Western winds, with evening's wandering airs
> With that clear dusk of heaven that brings the thickest stars;
> Winds take a pensive tone and stars a tender fire,
> And visions rise, and change, that kill me with desire.

There were passages in the Gospels with these peculiar, limpid notes of the psyche's secret song, like the description of the disciples coming from the lake in the evening and slowly recognizing the risen Jesus tending a fire on the shore.

What this child here had seen, H reflected, was her own hidden or 'risen' self that she called in turn 'a white girl' and 'the Blessed Virgin'.

Bernadette had interpreted her vision according to images available to her. What fascinated H was the fact that, in spite of first impressions, whether because of a genetic variation, an abnormality in the structure of her brain cells or some other breach in the defensive thought-mechanism, signals had been received from that area of the subconscious with which there is all too rare communication.

Bernadette, with a couple of other children, was gathering firewood along the bank of the Gave when:

> I lifted my eyes and saw a mass of branches and brambles tossed and waving this way and that under the opening in the grotto though nothing stirred around. Behind these branches, in the opening, I saw immediately afterwards a white girl, no bigger than I ... I saw the girl smiling at me *avec beaucoup de grace*.

Standing before the grotto next morning with Iseult, on the wide expanse of wet concrete, for it was raining heavily again, with the candle flames blackening the cave in the rock of Massabielle and the rather grimy statue in the opening above, he was far from immune from the tremor of excitement that, with the whiff of hot wax, was in the air.

Iseult was the one to criticize. 'Ugh,' she exclaimed, 'how tawdry!'

That evening at the hotel a tall, sallow-faced man, having evidently overheard H and Iseult conversing in English, asked them, as they were leaving the dining room, to have coffee with him. Iseult had promised her mother to put through a call to her at the Pyrenean village where she was staying, and H sat down alone with the stranger who introduced himself as assistant head of the Medical Faculty of Lourdes.

Up to a few years ago, Dr Sherry told H, he'd had a lucrative Harley Street practice, earning two thousand a year, then becoming tubercular, he'd come here on a visit, recovered, though he'd now only one lung, and returned to live in Lourdes and attend the sick and crippled pilgrims in the asile.

The doctor spoke impersonally about himself as of an acquaintance with whom he wasn't vitally concerned. Only when he mentioned the Blessed Virgin did a note that H, an expert in these matters, recognized as the hopelessly obsessive, in distinction to the merely pietistic, appear.

The daughter of the proprietor entered the dining room with a message for one of the guests and the doctor called her over to drink a *fine*, causing H to postpone mentioning what was on his mind.

'With a dowry and looks like hers she could have any of the local young men she fancied, eh, Dominique?' Dr Sherry said in French, after introducing H to her.

She laughed and her black eyes lit with a mixture of southern warmth and business acumen, and H, who had a way of interiorly illustrating anything that caught his fancy, first saw her married to the son of the Prefect of Police – orange bloom on petit point – and then kneeling beside H himself at the grotto, her dusky face blurred by her intense gaze at the rock that he too felt was hallowed.

The doctor, startling H by seeming to read his mind, was asking her, 'If Mr Ruark was single would you marry him?'

By this question, inappropriate and irrelevant, the doctor seemed to H to prove he was so immersed in another world that he mismanaged the polite conversation of this one.

'You can't really enter into the spirit of Lourdes while you keep one foot outside it,' he told H when the girl had returned to the reception desk.

'That's just what I don't intend to do, Doctor; amuse myself while I'm here. I'd like to work as a brancardier, but I don't know if that's possible for somebody who isn't here on an organized pilgrimage.'

As H had hoped, Dr Sherry promised to arrange it, but, he warned H, about whom he seemed to have some lingering doubts – he didn't know about the separate rooms – that he'd have to be down at the asile every morning at six to help get the patients into the wheelchairs or into the trolley stretchers.

24

When H arrived at the hospital by the river well before the appointed hour – all his life he was punctual – he was assigned another dark girl, but thinner and without either the southern glow or shrewd eyes, to take care of. As he stood by her chair before the start of early Mass at the grotto, she introduced herself as Maggie Bradley and told him she lived in London, and when he asked whereabouts, having a liking for details, she said within sight of the Crystal Palace.

After Mass he wheeled her to the baths, leaving her in the care of a couple of blue-eyed colleens belonging to a Dublin Diocesan pilgrimage who told him, in an aside that ignored the English girl, that the water was so cold that only the paralysed didn't gasp or cry out when lowered into it. But it was with the Crystal Palace girl, as she was briefly for H, before he started calling her Maggie, that he felt an affinity rather than with them.

'Where do we go now?' he asked her when he called for her again.

She had memorized, from the card given the patients at the asile, the round of Masses, communal prayers, processions, and benedictions.

She was neither pretty, nor specially intelligent, nor had she the marks of illness observable on many of the faces of the invalids.

'You've a lot of patience wheeling us about, getting up so early, and hanging around with us all day,' she said when they'd taken their place in the semicircle of wheelchairs and stretchers on the barracklike square before the Basilica.

'My wife says it's a stunt.'

'A stunt? She isn't taken with Lourdes, then?'

'Not very much.'

'My parents weren't taken with the idea of Lourdes either,' she told him. 'It was through another girl at the switchboard I got to hear of it. I work as a telephonist; I used to type but it tired me too much.'

It was not the crippled telephonist who attracted H but the girl's hidden psyche that Lourdes had released, as it had whatever in him roughly fitted such a description; it could also be called a mania for intense new perceptions. He felt he had a companion in her, though they expressed their obsessions differently.

They were hushed into silence by a brancardier beside them as the priest, followed, behind the acolytes, by a couple of dark-suited, solemn-faced doctors, of whom one was Dr Sherry, approached around the inside of the half-circle bearing the Blessed Sacrament in the ciborium.

She liked to be at the sooty rock face in front of the blue and white statue. But best of all she liked the huge representation of the Virgin in ermine cloak, stooping forward in an attitude accentuated by the outward curve of the wall towards the vaulted roof of the Church of the Rosary with outstretched arms. She had H take her into the Basilica when there was nothing going on just to gaze at it. H thought she saw in the long-mouthed face in the mosaic an image of that part of herself that had emerged and was communicating with, and being talked to, by H.

As he wheeled her from the church to the grotto, to the square in front of the Basilica of the Rosary or to the Piscines where the sick were bathed, H talked to her as he hadn't to anyone since Lane, with whom he'd also shared certain deep-rooted instincts.

It started by his trying to explain, in answer to a question of hers, his attitude to Lourdes. She had wanted to know what he did while he waited beside her.

'Do you pray?'

'No.'

'But you believe in Lourdes?'

'It's all new to me, Maggie. I'm trying to understand it, to see what's real and what isn't.'

'That sounds as if you doubted the apparitions.'

'I think that reality can express itself as well in fiction as in fact. Some fictions are completely true and some facts are not true except on the most superficial level.'

'That's beyond me.'

'No, it isn't, Maggie. Listen, let's take the Gospels. What we want to know is do they reflect reality, which is a better way of putting it than asking, are they true? Because the right question is the one that involves not just the upper mental surfaces in the answer. The worthwhile answers are in tune with the deeper emotional and imaginative pulsations. Reasoning can't distinguish true from false except on fairly extraneous levels. Do you never feel inside you, Maggie, a series of nerve cells, some sort of fine chain, linking you with reality? I think, if we haven't broken it, we're aware of something like that, each link a little more substantial as it comes closer to consciousness, transforming the vibrations into what can just, at the last link, enter the mind as thought. What I'm getting at is that the Gospels, transmitted to us by this route, do have the impact of reality.

'As for this place and Bernadette, I don't yet know. What she said she saw she certainly didn't invent. But whether it can be part of reality for me is another matter.'

Another time he told her that reality was what involved one most.

'Death does that, at least in some cases, completely. Then, as nobody knows better than you, Maggie, there's illness. You have to come to terms in your thoughts with the pain in your body. And there's love. That involves both the conscious and subconscious pretty thoroughly.'

She seemed to listen to him with much the same absorbed attention as that with which she gazed at the statue in the opening in the rock face or at the huge mosaic in the Basilica.

When Iseult suggested leaving and joining her mother in the mountains, he said he'd like to stay on till the end of the week when Maggie would be returning to England.

'She's used to having me to wheel her about and would hate somebody new for the last few days.'

'You wouldn't like it either, leaving her before you have to.'

It astonished him how much his thoughts were occupied with the sick girl. Wasn't their mutual attraction also largely a misunderstanding?

He thought Iseult liked to be with him when no demands were made on her, even if it was only at dinner and afterwards sitting on the balcony of her room, as he was mostly too tired to go for a walk with her.

H held her hand that was resting on the picture postcards in her lap to which she'd been affixing the foreign stamps after licking them with a tongue stained by the red wine they'd drunk at dinner, the glimpse of which re-kindled the old longings.

They sat in silence, on the verge of the illusive understanding they so often seemed about to reach, only to have to realize, which to Iseult came each time as a surprise, that the things that should have bound them, nationalism, religion, literature were stumbling blocks between them.

H woke before the alarm clock rang at five. Though he'd be ready too soon, he couldn't linger in bed. When he was dressed he sat for a few minutes by the window from which, unlike that from Iseult's, there was only a view of roofs rising towards the hill at the centre of the old town, forcing himself not to hurry.

He arrived at the asile in a kind of fever that abated when Maggie was wheeled out of the women's ward and left in the passage until, after helping to dress the men patients, he was ready to take her to the grotto.

Did he fear her stretcher might have been taken by another brancardier? What on earth made him rush like this to the hospital? Of what was the expectation that burned in him like heartache? Surely not for the first morning sight of Maggie. The part of him that responded to certain extremes of apparently non-sensual passion in poems or in some of the mystics' canticles celebrating their spiritual marriage, drew him to the crippled girl.

On the last morning H rose at four and went to the grotto while it was still dark. Two or three pilgrims were already there and some of the longer candles that had been burning all night were still lit, and there was what had become for him the magic smell of melting wax in the warm air. From beside the slab on the pavement that marked the spot where Bernadette had knelt at the time of the first apparition, he could just make out the statue, a pale, slight, fragile shimmer like a shrouded, waning moon. The poplars at the river rustled behind him and he shut his eyes to listen to what he supposed was the nearest sound to what Bernadette said she'd heard just before seeing her white girl.

After returning to the hotel for breakfast, he went, with other brancardiers, on one of the buses taking the departing English pilgrims to the station.

The stretchers were lifted on to the train through the windows, cracking several of the glass flagons of Lourdes water in their wicker cases tied to them. After giving a hand with these, H helped Maggie into her compartment and stayed with her there while water dripped from the luggage rack and her travelling companions, faced with the long painful journey home and, he imagined, suffering from the letdown at the end of all the devotional intensity, huddled, packed together in their seats.

In spite of the assurances he was giving Maggie, H foresaw that the intervals would increase, either one or both would not return next year, the memory would cease to haunt and then, quite soon, even to be more than rarely evoked. Others had been, more than Maggie, his all, and where were they? Where was Weg? Of the rest only the thought of Lane was still painfully acute.

That afternoon H and Iseult took a bus that climbed from Argeles up the valley to the village of Arrens where Madame was staying at the farmhouse at which she, Iseult and Helen Molony had spent a holiday fifteen years earlier, at the start of the war. At eighteen, he reckoned, Iseult hadn't been very different from what she was now.

They were given a room panelled in a local timber – Madame mentioned walnut – and furnished with an oak press and one big bed with a carved head of another kind of unvarnished wood.

In these pieces of furniture he noticed patterns formed by the grain in the heart of the wood. And, as though a new preoccupation had been seeking some means to enter his mind, there flashed into it with the urgency of a revelation: 'Like that must be the process that records a writer's inner growth in the spiral-like pattern of his work.'

Iseult paused in her unpacking to press her hand into the feather mattress and remarked that she recalled sleeping on such a one that other time. Surely during one of her telephone calls from Lourdes to her mother she had asked for them to be given a room with a double bed, otherwise she would have shown some surprise at the arrangement.

Before dinner, which they were to have at the hotel in the village, Iseult led him up the path along the rocky bed of the almost dry torrent apparently used by herds of shaggy goats, some of which they met being driven down from the high pastures.

H was puzzled by her taking him on this expedition before she had spent more than half an hour or so with her mother. The sun had set behind great grey crags that seemed to reach higher into the sky than he'd imagined the natural laws allowed. And the view was a wilder one than any H had seen, with the tilt of the planes more extreme, the contours more violent than in their honeymoon glen; just above them rose the deserted monastery that she had said something about wanting to show him and, adjoining it, the pale, newer walls of a building that also appeared abandoned.

She led the way through the partly boarded-up entrance, through the hallway, where the herds of goats had sheltered, and up the wide stone stairway to a long corridor from which opened doorways where doors had never been hung. She was telling him that the place had been built as a sanatorium by a Jewish deputy for the Hautes Pyrénées in order to assure himself votes, when the outbreak of war prevented its being finished.

She led him to one of the rooms in which the mountain silence was intensified. H still wasn't clear about why there was this urgency to explore the big deserted building, smelling of damp plaster and whose floors were covered in dust and grey wood shavings.

She was suddenly leaning against one of the bare plaster walls as if overcome by exhaustion. He couldn't make it out, but was conscious of a growing excitement at their being all alone together in the big building, added to which was the realization that the self-imposed discipline at Lourdes was no longer in force.

Could she possibly be affected in the same way? He stood in front of her and put an arm around her which could, he thought, though she showed no sign of needing one, be interpreted as a support to prevent her back slipping further down the wall and her legs sprawling apart on the floor like a rag doll's.

She leaned forward and pressed her mouth to his, thus providing the impetus for him to loosen his trousers with his free hand which, in turn, as, he imagined, a series of impulses are set up along a line of wagons by an impact at one end, impelled her to pull up her dress.

When they entered the hotel dining room where her mother was waiting dinner for them, Iseult told her without apology: 'I took Luke up to the old monastery and we had a look at the Rothschild sanatorium. It's just as they'd left it when we were here.'

That night in the farmhouse when H made a tentative advance, his wife, deep in the feathers, drew him on to her in a fervid embrace. So the earlier episode hadn't been a momentary aberration induced by the circumstances, nor an unaccountable flash in the pan!

During the day she spent much of the time with him, showing him the sights, the red and yellow pumpkins stored on the wooden balconies, the slopes of autumn crocus, the old village church with its ancient oak statues; had she one day been intending they make love behind one of them when someone had come in?

Only after they'd left and were on the journey home did it dawn on H that their seeming at last to have achieved a sensual bond was in reality the latest and most hopeless in their series of misunderstandings. She had been leaving nothing to chance, doing everything possible to make conceiving most likely.

Not that she hadn't been carried away by the sensuality of prospective pregnancy, otherwise he'd have grasped the situation sooner. Oh, she had entered into her plan body and soul! Far from seeing it as a deception, H admired her resolution in breaking out of her deep inhibition in order to return home with her longing fulfilled.

They had dinner next evening, before catching the train to Dieppe, in the Paris hotel where Madame was spending a few days. While she was selecting hors d'oeuvres from a trolley wheeled over the soft carpet to their table, Iseult whispered to him – it was one of the first opportunities she had in a day spent drudging through the Louvre and various churches – that she'd longed the previous night to be sharing a wagon-lit with him instead of with her mother.

As an initiate of the secret cult, H too was now entering into this kingdom towards which he'd been groping since his early youth by such clumsy means as the mattress he dragged in his boyhood dream to an attic and, undressing, hugged on the dusty floor.

Here in the hotel restaurant all was hushed and dimmed, draped, shaded, and perfumed in preparation of body and imagination for the coming night when, all over Paris, in the sanctum of hotel and private rooms, attics, parked cars, the Bois, in any corner where it was possible, the miracle would be performed according to its various rites and accompanied with all kinds of private incantations. H whispered to Iseult a few words of an introductory canticle and she responded by suggesting they take a cabin on the boat.

The only one available, however, turned out to be a stateroom that cost more than, with the little money they had left, they could afford.

25

At home again, H started filling blue copybooks, while sitting on the side of the bed, so that the maid had to wait till midday before making it, rapidly in pencil. In her room at the other end of the top floor of the old house Iseult also perched on an unmade bed, was smoking and playing patience, and, he guessed, anxiously awaiting an indication that she was going to have a baby. He began to see it as a race between them as to which would first attain what their hearts were set on.

But one day, seeing her pale and dejected, H went after lunch to her room and she told him she was having her 'time'.

'I'm losing so much blood that it must be a miscarriage.'

Her resolute and beautifully carried out plan all for nothing! H took her in his arms, moved, since he didn't know how long, by something approaching pure compassion.

Now, as well as working on the novel – glories, miseries, pitfalls! – he spent more time with her. After lunch, when Miss Burnett finished reading the paper and went back to the poultry, they played cards or backgammon by the fire in the big sitting room. He pottered about the garden while she weeded or planted the cuttings of flowering shrubs whose names he never managed to memorize. And sometimes he came at night to the big, white-distempered room where Ian was asleep in his cot and Iseult in bed with a book, which, though, she wasn't reading but using to play a favourite game that consisted in counting the number of times certain letters appeared as the initial ones of words on a given page and noting the result on the margin.

She had relapsed again into apathy and a kind of disgust with life that he could only guess at. His efforts to comfort her came to nothing because, perhaps, he hadn't the necessary imagination and resolution. They made love in what he saw was, on her part, dispirited indifference, and it was on one of these comparatively rare occasions that she once more conceived.

With Iseult safely pregnant, H gave himself up to his novel. He'd write away quickly, fabricating what seemed something real and durable out of the stormy flashes that he took for inspiration. But in the ensuing sobriety he'd see how insubstantial and forced, or, less often, stale and commonplace, was what he'd written.

In order to enter the level of consciousness from where he knew a novel must come, he looked up old notebooks in which he'd put down phrases that had, by evoking deep responses, produced a semi-trance in him in which the surface mind was stilled: 'His calling isolates the artist, as does his crime the criminal.'

Even when he was no longer sure how he had interpreted some of these quotations at the time, they still had an effect on him. What had he meant by copying this passage long ago in prison from the Book of Jeremiah? 'Then I said, I will not make mention of Him, nor speak any more in His name, but His word was in my heart as a burning fire shut up in my bones, and I was weary with fore-bearing and I could not stay.'

In prison, and in the company of his friend, he had heard his spirit singing its own sweet song but now, it seemed, he had become distracted, pre-occupied.

He became idle, lay for hours on his bed doing nothing. Then suddenly one morning he restarted writing, haunted again by imagined situations of isolation and disaster for his two protagonists, finished the book in feverish haste and sent it to a publisher.

Days of anxious waiting when he feared the parcel had been lost in the post, followed by worse fears that what he'd written was incomprehensible rubbish, and, at last, a letter of acceptance.

He travelled to London and, with the money for the advance, went on to Paris.

26

H's room at the Hotel Terminus, Gare St Lazare, in spite of its nearness to the station, was peculiarly quiet. This silence induced by the heavy curtains, the double door and the dumb electric clock on the wall opposite the bed, was not what he'd expected. He lay stretched on the bed high above the deeply carpeted floor – like the door, was the mattress duplicated? – while the consciousness of where he was seeped into his mind. Paris was like a sun rising from a new point of his interior compass, casting beams into dim corners; it was like Bernadette's apparition, uncovering hidden springs of new delight and expectation. Rising from the bed he went in search of the barber's shop mentioned in a notice on the wall of the room, in order to emerge into what awaited him gradually.

While having his hair cut he was enveloped by a current of warm, perfumed air issuing from the adjoining ladies' salon, an aroma full of promise, inexpressible in words, that he inhaled while the clipper buzzed at his ears. Drugged and trimmed, he set out for Montparnasse.

Cities were always to obsess him. The familiar names of streets that evoked a quality and intensity of life, sensual and imaginative, were painful for him to read at their corners. The private ecstasies of the flesh and spirit that had never been shared above these small shops and cafés could never be shared with him, they must remain forever beyond him to make his own in memory.

Entering what seemed a newer addition to the famous café Dôme, H ordered a drink from the American barman, and the tall glass, with the ice cubes stained pink by the vermouth poured over them before the soda, had hardly been placed on its saucer in front of him when there was some sort of commotion further along the counter.

H saw everything now as part of the legend of Paris, and when the girl, whom the barman rescued from a drunken fellow countryman of his and directed to the empty stool beside H's, smiled at him, it became part of it to get into halting talk with her.

Because she was sixteen and had only been in Paris a short time, she told H, Monsieur Garry took care of her. But it was a few minutes, until she'd asked his petit-nom and told him hers, before she was revealed to him in all her – if not glory, though, in a sense, that too – accessibility as a street girl.

But for that night H had had all the sensation he could bear. He needed to call a halt and try to absorb it. Inventing an appointment, he arranged to meet Lisette at the same place the following evening, and left the café. Crossing the boulevard to the Vavin station and being unable to concentrate on the métro chart, he took the first train going in his general direction. From where he decided to get out it was a long walk up the whole length of the rue de Rivoli, and beyond, to his hotel.

He was glad of the space and time in which to reflect on his good fortune. The only other occasion when he'd had a rendezvous in a strange city, with Polenskaya under the Propylaeon in Munich, he'd experienced this same dizzy lightness of heart.

Next evening when, after arriving in Montparnasse far too early and hanging around out of sight of the Dôme, H entered the café, she was there at the right-hand end of the bar, furthest from the wall with the large mirror; these details were important to him. She introduced a companion beside her as Danielle, as fair as Lisette but with, instead of the younger girl's longish face with contours soft and unset, a round and dimpled Paris countenance reminding him, though it wasn't so pretty, of Claude's.

What a relief to know that nothing mattered here as long as there was money to spend! He didn't have to give an account of himself; the girls enjoyed whatever he enjoyed, drinking at the bar, till – at midnight, or two, or four in the morning – he returned to his hotel.

As he felt the first slight onset of intoxication he asked for another Pernod for himself; the girls were still sipping their bière cassis. His desire to get drunk might be another of his last-minute evasions, but again it might not. He was not going to risk a letdown after the violent, excessive expectations.

He awoke in his room at the hotel with the silent clock in its gilt frame recording the hour of ten and a desire to get up and go to a café for a long cool draught of iced orangeade.

He spent most of his waking hours with Lisette and Danielle, either in the American bar or the older part of the Dôme. On their advice – they pointed out the economy, resenting the money not spent in their company – he moved to the hotel in the rue de la Gaîté where they were living, and when he woke in the early afternoon they were sitting on the foot of his bed, silk wraps over their nightdresses. Then they would breakfast with him and chatter and laugh until it was time to get up, by when it was dusk and the red-shaded lamp, beside the litre bottle of Chianti in its wicker container, was burning on the bedside table.

For weeks H never saw Paris by daylight, leaving the Dôme, they told him, around three or four of a morning and making his short way to the hotel in a drunken trance, always stopping en route, without being able to recall doing so, to buy Italian wine at a shop in the rue Delambre that stayed open all night.

Drunkenness had a retrospective effect, casting its shadow back over some of the earlier hours of the evening, so that only certain memories remained clear amid the strange, crowded, dissolving impressions. One of these was of Lisette coming back from the 'Ladies' in the old Dôme and, opening her handbag under cover of the marble top of the table at which they were sitting, showing him a scrap of bloody cotton wool. Why? To convince him that she couldn't sleep with him that night? But surely he hadn't asked her to. He even thought she'd pointed out that Danielle was free of the disability. Accompanying the girls up an alleyway to buy a poodle puppy for Danielle, kissing Lisette in a taxi taking them to a bar in the rue Danou on one of their rare expeditions to another part of Paris and her saying, 'Pas comme ça, comme ci, chéri.'

While he dressed, H would finish what was left of the Chianti, he and the girls having been drinking it while they sat on his bed, and then stroll along the wall of the cimetière Montparnasse, which was the dark side of the street, making a detour for the sake of the only fresh air he breathed those days on his way back to the Dôme where Lisette soon joined him. Danielle came later. She had a friend in whose American car, she told him, she spent the earlier evening driving with him about Paris on business that, like all else here, had never to be explained precisely.

The late afternoons, before l'heure d'apéritif, was one of the best times, with the café almost empty. While he might be pondering on a title for the novel (Gollancz considered 'I Won't Be Wearing Shamrock on St Patrick's Day' too long), Lisette played dice with Garry the barman, filed and polished her nails, or read *Paris-Soir*. When, during one such quiet session, the hour of compline in contemplative orders, the thought came to him from another world, a Russian woman, drinking with a couple of young Frenchmen further up the bar, pulled down her black dress to expose a big, pallid breast. Garry reproved her with a shake of his head and Lisette whispered that the girl showed no regard for le bon ton.

H's money was getting low and still he couldn't drag himself away. He asked Iseult to send him five pounds, and a few days later was awakened by the postman coming to his room and asking him to sign for the registered letter.

He opened the envelope, counted the notes, glanced at what Iseult had written and went to sleep again. Later, after breakfasting with the girls and before dressing, he read the letter more carefully and, on taking out the notes, found only three.

The theft shocked H, but only fleetingly. To the girls, as Lisette had suggested without waiting for an answer, one evening when, having stayed later in bed, he'd gone to her room at the hotel to take her to dinner before going to the Dôme, he was a rich landowner in Ireland; otherwise why spend money on them gratuitously?

He hadn't said anything one way or the other. Instead, as he sat on her bed over which were fastened photographs of sleek, flashy-looking men, while, behind the pleated, pink silk screen on a bamboo frame she washed herself at the basin, he started to tell her about his father.

What with the noise from the busy rue de la Gaîté; none of the opulent silence here of the previous hostelry; the intermittent running of taps and gurgle of waste water, as well as the inadequacy of his French, it was hard to convey to Lisette the circumstances, not entirely clear to himself, in which his father had died.

All the red wine, vermouth, Pernod, and Chianti he'd drunk in the previous couple of weeks had, it seemed, polluted the normal channels of communication with the outside world and opened up other subterranean ones unused since his boyhood fevers and fantasies.

When he walked to the Dôme of an evening, having just got up and in what he thought of as the state of third-degree intoxication produced by the Chianti drunk while still in bed to quench his hangover thirst, he entered into touch with entities in his subconscious and in the past, or at the insection of these where, when he managed to reach that distant spot, he met his father.

The signals that he was registering he believed were those emanating from chromosomes near the base of his being which gave it its linkage to the past, the inherited intimations that usually never reached his mind. He felt that only a slight prolonged succession of these would give him profound and possibly unbearable insights at the price of permanently damaging its normal functioning. Even as it was, it was possible that the utterances echoing within him with the resonance of revelation would turn out to be feverish babbling once he emerged from the toxic trance.

As he walked in the shadow of the cemetery wall the first of these utterances that he could interpret clearly was a cry of thirst. He was back where he'd been at waking an hour before with a parched and, he imagined, swollen tongue. He had emerged from what seemed an unchartered sea of oblivion and in order to try to get his bearings he had, as on other mornings, sought for and clung to the last recollection of the night or early mornings. This was always the same. At a certain point in his drinking Danielle slipped her cool fingers, tipped with pink shells – this was his impression at that moment – inside his sleeve, and his last contact with the outside world was her light grip on his arm.

Thirst! That was something his father had plumbed the detailed and normally unimaginable recesses of. So had Lane, unable to swallow more than a few drops. H had been present without being capable of sharing in his agony. Now he could do so. And Christ on the Cross had suffered more from thirst than anything else, at one phase of the three hours, an arbitrary timing of the timeless.

'I want nothing, no posthumous rehabilitation even in your thoughts. I deny and abolish everything that happened to me in my life and don't wish you to think that it, even less my death, had any point at all.'

Whose despair was he receiving intimations of? His father's? Lane's? Christ's?

The sap in the cells had dried up and they were beginning to disintegrate into shapes like those of the minute, shrivelled deep-sea organisms left on the beach at high tide. The imagination had escaped momentarily and was refreshing itself at the cool deep wells of Galilee. Not for long. It hadn't a quiet, darkened room for its fantasies, but was exposed to the vindictive glee of some of the crowd.

'How are you doing up there, Mr Big Head?'

Approaching their final disaster, did these beings indulge in escape into lost possibilities, catching perhaps from the kitchen the small reassuring sounds of a companion preparing the evening or morning meal, pouring the coffee, unstoppering the wine jar. Or did they scorn such weaknesses?

(Once safely at the Dôme H would drink quantities of bière cassis.)

Other remarks that Christ may have heard passed through H's mind as he waited for one of the girls to arrive: 'A little fellow with big notions.'

'Yes, but time catches up with people like that.'

In the end he managed to slake his hangover thirst, but there was a sense in which he could only refresh himself and emerge from the nightmare by means of the girls' femininity. Not by sexual contact, but by a more subtle, imaginative merging which he couldn't define. Like the Chianti on his parched tongue on waking in the afternoon, their presence was a balm. Sometimes he took Danielle's hand, cupped it in his, and licked the palm to banish the lingering deathly taste from his mouth.

Another initiate into the hell of thirst: the wild animal caught in the trap, waiting in agony for dusk to fall and perhaps catch a drop of dew in its tongue. What did he know of those raging fires of delirium tremens and of the other deliriums? And of the terrible ache in the innermost part of the brain as the sap in the cells and neurons is polluted and poisoned?

In spite of the linguistic difficulties, though in some degree helped by them too, he thought he managed to tell Danielle one evening some of what was on his mind. She called him over and he watched as she finished rinsing out the bowl of the washbasin of the grey suds; like a child she seemed to pick up dust and grime and city scents. Beside her within the small enclosure made by the screen, and with the light above the washbasin mirror gleaming on her wet arms, she lifted her long still childlike face that was serious and devoid of make-up and said: 'C'est ne faire rien, chéri, there are plenty like you, born that way. Maybe you'll get out of it, some do; if not, you're sure to make some nice friends of your own sort.'

27

Katherine was born and H's novel appeared. Rereading it in one of his presentation copies he realized that it would take him a lifetime of increasing obsessions and intensifying hauntings, as well as the lucky avoidance of false repute, to become a true novelist.

The book appeared in America and was given headlines in the Sunday magazine section of the *New York Times*, one of the literary papers Joe Campbell had dumped on H's bed in the hospital hut in Tintown. Among cuttings his publisher sent him was one to the effect that a Brooklyn pastor was taking the theme of *I Won't Be Wearing Shamrock on St Patrick's Day*, H having failed to find a shorter title, as a text on the following Sunday!

Every week in the ledger in which he kept the poultry-farm accounts there was a balance of several pounds to the good, and the novel earned him over three hundred. The baby girl, darker than Ian, had also a more placid nature and was less in need of H's tranquillizing effect.

In spite of all this, things were going from bad, or from moderate, to worse.

The dust, when he ran a finger along a windowsill, lay thick, cigarette butts sprouted in clammy clusters from the undersides of tables, and when he couldn't help taking a look under the bathtub it depressed him to see the various discarded bits of filth Iseult had kicked out of the way. These he recognized as signs of the apathy that was growing within.

Retreating from the domestic shambles, H started a new novel, abandoned it and began studying the racing page of the newspaper.

Iseult adopted her superior air, telling him that if he had nothing better to do he should occupy himself more with the children.

On his return from Paris, when he'd given her a very sketchy account of how he'd spent his time there, she'd remarked, 'How very boring!'

Browsing through a Dublin newsagent's H came on the thick, squat, buff-coloured, paperbound publication called *Racing-up-to-Date.* As soon as he saw it he knew it was what he was looking for, as years earlier he'd been drawn in an out-of-the-way corner of a bookshop to a life of St Rose of Lima, Juliana's *Revelations of Divine Love*, and *The Ascent of Mount Carmel*, by St John of the Cross.

The book contained a record of the previous season's flat racing, and at home in his room he was soon familiar with the new symbols and hierogly-phics, the secret language, not of mysticism this time, but the abbreviated racing jargon in small and crowded print. After the tensions built up by the novel, the torments of uncertainty where there was nothing to test the validity of the signals coming in from distant areas of imagination but the almost indetectable contraction or expansion of a nerve centre situated on the fringe of consciousness, the comparatively simple ciphers of the Form Book, with their reference to events of the most tangible kind, came as a refreshment.

With the buff volume, its thick top edge already thumb-stained by constant opening, as guide, H studied the runners in a big spring handicap about to take place at Hurst Park. It was, he believed, a matter of close and detailed weighing of the previous performances of one horse against another, tracing form lines through a third, even a fourth. He learned to translate distances between horses at the winning posts into pounds, three pounds equalling one length at five to seven furlongs, then examined the weights allotted in the race he was analysing.

After several mornings spent in this close scrutiny of the brown paper-covered book he felt arid and drained. He was overconcentrating and, as a result, what he'd unearthed as the probable winner hadn't the hard-to-perceive gleam of true treasure trove.

This was a five-year-old called Jarvis, a name that, even when he came to have trouble recalling that of the crippled girl at Lourdes, he never forgot, to be ridden by Freddie Fox, and that he'd finally worked out had four or five pounds advantage over its most favourably weighted rivals and should thus win by, say, between one and two lengths. The odds against it were quoted in the antepost bookmaker's lists at 100–8.

Aware that something, though not in his calculation, was lacking, an indication of another sort, he all the same felt too involved in time and nervous energy spent to draw back. Taking a cheque for ten pounds with him to cash at his bank, as he was still awaiting the dollars from his American publishers, he went to Dublin the day of the race.

After stopping to buy the morning papers and the midday racing edition of an evening one, H parked the car in St Stephen's Green, on to whose greenery the window of the room in which he'd spent the first magic after-noons with Iseult in her blue, tasselled dress, over tea with hunks of Josephine's crusty bread and pear jam, had looked. Walking towards the tea shop in Grafton Street where he meant to read what the racing journalists had to say about the race – he'd yet to realize that this was pointless – he saw an imposing figure in a fawn spring suit; spring was in the air, in the park, on the distant English racecourse; coming towards him, head bowed, hands clasped behind curiously straight back.

It was too late for H to avoid Yeats, the last person he wanted to have to talk to at that moment, whose glance, in spite of its seeming blindness to what was near at hand, fastened on him with an upwards jerk of the head at the last moment.

The poet, without preliminary greeting, announced, 'George Shaw and I want you to become a founder member of the Irish Academy of Letters, an association we are establishing to oppose the censorship introduced by these nonentities of ours in their effort to establish a safe parochialism here.'

Freddie Fox he knew, Brownie Carslake, Joe Childs, but who for God's sake was George Shaw? Then he recalled that this was how Yeats always referred to Bernard Shaw.

'We are inviting Liam O'Flaherty to join us,' Yeats was saying; 'I believe he's a friend of yours.'

O'Flaherty was the only writer with whom H had had any contact, having been introduced to him in a Dublin pub shortly after his return from Paris, where he had been drinking, though more circumspectly than during the long nights at the Dôme. He'd been struck by his handsome brown face and keen gull's eye.

H's instinct was to keep clear of literary circles. When he thought about the literary situation it seemed to him that with Joyce they'd reached a

154

parting of the ways. *Ulysses*, far from being a novel to end the novel, as some claimed, was a revelation of the form's possibilities. Post-Joycean fiction had had two paths to choose between and it seemed to be taking the old, well-tried one, with its practitioners producing novels and stories easily recognizable as realistic portrayals of local character and situation. No great risks were being taken, the pitfalls were being safely avoided, no imagination had been set alight by Joyce's smoky torch. A few tricks had been learned from him, but his obsessive kind of writing was not inspiring any of H's contemporaries to delve deeper into themselves. And so there was little to haunt, disturb, offend, or affect in any significant way.

H thanked Yeats, ashamed at not declining there and then, but unable to partly because his resolution was weakened by the wavering of his attention between what he'd just been told and the race, and partly because of a reluctance to appear disrespectful.

Ready to discover oracles everywhere, H, on leaving the poet, took the meeting as a bad omen.

In the teashop: open the first of the papers at the page of vital news, though not yet the piece with the fatal finality of the few somewhat indistinctly printed words in the late news column of the early evening edition. Scrutinize carefully the list of runners for any last-minute withdrawal, change of jockey, etc. Take a sip of the coffee that has been placed unnoticed on the table, simulating the air of an unobsessed midmorning customer. Regard the list again, this time with the intuitive eye that effortlessly, if all was functioning properly, registers on the inner retina the shimmer of coming triumph that is already mysteriously cast around one of the names.

H read what the racing correspondents said about the contest with rather more seriousness than what had been written about his novel, though the New York pastor's evident misconception had intrigued him, grasping more about the inadequacy of most reviewers than he yet did in regard to these other experts whom he credited with considerable insight and with some vital information of which he wasn't in possession.

When he found a favourable mention of Jarvis, he read the sentence or two over again, memorizing it, according it a disproportionate weight. At the same time, he was unable to shake off the feeling that he'd misread the signs and portents and that it would now be wiser to get back into the car and drive home.

Instead of which he placed his bet with a bookmaker, it being before the opening of betting shops in Dublin, in an upstairs office where such business could be transacted.

In the Grafton Street cinema where he went to wait till the evening papers were on sale, the shadows that passed over the illuminated screen had

155

nothing to do with the centre of reality that had been transferred across the sea to the greensward of Hurst Park.

When at last he caught behind the piano music that accompanied the silent pictures the faint shouts of the newsboys from the street, H got up and made his way from the semidarkness into the threatening glare of the spring afternoon.

At the corner of St Stephen's Green he bought a paper which he waited to open at the late news till he was in the park.

This was the first of many such dread moments when, in parks, doorways, at street corners, the city (Dublin or London) was suddenly drawn away to the fringes of consciousness while on some sparse grey print in an almost blank column his whole attention concentrated. The three names, placed one above the other, were registered by other more vulnerable nerves at the same time as by the optic one. And had some passerby asked him, as occasionally occurred, what had won the big race, he would have found it hard to answer intelligibly. H recalled some lines of Yeats's: 'What portion in the world can the artist have/Who has awakened from the common dream,/But dissipation and despair?'

Surely Yeats had never been much immersed in the 'common dream'. But he was not sure if he understood the poem correctly. The dream, common or uncommon, needed dreaming with exhaustive intensity and in agonizing detail if a writer was to have something worthwhile to report. No important book was ever produced by trying; it came about as the by-product of an all-obsessive and perilous inward journey.

His betting losses, which he didn't hide from her, annoyed Iseult.

'Look at the rags I have to wear while you fritter the money on horses. What did you get me in Paris? A few needles and some sewing cotton from Woolworth!'

Not Woolworth, as she should have known. Prixuni, or was it Uniprix? But she was right. It did strike him as mean, the little embroidered case of mending materials. And she didn't even know about the poodle pup he'd given Danielle! Yet it had been an effort to leave the Dôme that last evening and walk along the broad pavement to buy her even that miserable gift.

H took a room in an apartment house in Dublin for the four days of Royal Ascot. He had the papers brought him on his breakfast tray and spent the morning in bed making an intensive study of one of the day's two-year-old races.

In the small room at the top of the house his heart lightened. For the first time it was a relief simply not to be at home. He didn't try to analyse the reasons, in which a sense of guilt had a part, but was content to be able to run his finger under the edge of the table by the corner window without dislodging shrivelled cigarette ends.

H had progressed in the subtle, if trivial, as Iseult tried to make clear to him, art of comparing the speed and staying power of horses, one against the other, since the spring. Though, at first, this was more evident in the bets that, through discipline and foresight, he avoided putting on, rather than in actual gain.

It was on the third day of the royal meeting that in his pursuit of the painful excitement of taking the paper from the newsboy and looking for the three slightly smudgy names, he saw that the top one was the embodiment in print of that which had been all afternoon in his mind. To postpone the fatal moment he had taken the sheet, without opening it, to a nearby pub, and it was there at the corner that he saw that his choice had won at 100–8.

Hearing his name called in the tone used, he imagined, to announce those of distinguished guests at formal receptions, H looked around to meet Liam O'Flaherty's keen blue glance as he inquired, in the same jubilant tone, 'What's your particular brand of poison?'

'You need to get out of this dreary, provincial town,' he was telling H, 'with its petty secret obsessions (had he an inkling why H was here?) and meet some civilized people. If you're interested in cuties – excuse me, if I'm obtruding on delicate ground – I'll call up a bevy tomorrow evening.'

O'Flaherty was inviting him, H began to realize, to come to London and stay with him in a flat he'd taken there.

'I take it, Luke, you enjoy intelligent talk – which you won't find much of here – and you'll meet Harold Stroud, who'll sit up all night discussing anything from dialectic materialism to the test matches.'

O'Flaherty started mimicking this friend of his, putting a finger inside his collar, stretching and turning his neck and announcing in a cockney drawl, 'In the last analysis, Liam ...'

28

As soon as O'Flaherty had unlocked the door of the flat, H was aware of a hum that filled the three small rooms, the passage from the sitting room to bedroom at the back and, particularly, the bathroom whose tiled walls magnified it. He had never before noticed this throbbing of the great city, perhaps because the volume of traffic had grown in the ten years or so since he'd lived here with Iseult or because here in one of the narrow streets in the riverward-sloping district between the Strand and the Embankment he was nearer its heart.

It became the just audible accompaniment to these days and nights. Even when he awoke in the early hours to stumble to the bathroom – all the ale drunk in pubs, together with the nervous stimulation, like long ago in Munich, was affecting his bladder – it was still echoing from the gleaming walls.

H overheard O'Flaherty leaving a telephone message at a place called 'The Plough' for Harold Stroud, asking him to call round for a game of chess. Chess! Was that what was to come of all the promises?

'Is that where he lives?' H inquired, altogether at sea.

'It's the pub where he spends most of his evenings, run by George Jefcote who serves the best Mild and Bitter, not to mention jellied eels, in town, very knowledgeable about horses too, as is Harold if it comes to that, though with him it's the same theoretic approach he brings to Marxism.'

H was trying to keep up, registering the un-Irish details that were part of the new atmosphere.

'And I've asked Honor Maxwell to have dinner with us at Stulick's. When I met her first time she told me, "I'm feeling so relieved because we just had a letter from my father saying he's been given permission to keep Angora rabbits."

'Ha! So that's the game, I said to myself: Mystification! But it wasn't. You see, she thought I knew that her dad was Lord Dynant, the old boy who got five years for issuing a misleading company report and swindling shareholders. I told her we were all ex-jailbirds in Ireland and that my friend, Luke Ruark, did two years for capturing an armoured car and shooting the crew! I lent her your novel, and she said just now she'd adore to meet you.'

Dinner at the Tour Eiffel, the red glow from whose table lamps H had seen when he leaned at night from the window of his room at the other end of Charlotte Street the time he'd sold the pearls and stayed on and met Polenskaya. The jailed magnate's daughter whose eyelids drooped and whose long pale mouth, seemingly devoid of make-up, turned down at the corners as she uttered certain phrases, in a language that H hadn't yet the hang of, seemed to ignore him in favour of O'Flaherty.

Afterwards O'Flaherty asked her back to the flat and when her car, a small Standard, nothing showy, H noted, wouldn't start, H lifted the bonnet and struck a light to depress the needle and see if the carburettor was flooding properly. Ignited by the match, the surplus petrol from the float-chamber burned with a blue flame that H, quite unperturbed by the danger of the car catching fire, saw as one of those signs that, though perfectly explicable on a natural level, he took as signalling the imminence of happenings of special significance.

O'Flaherty inserted a gas nozzle under the coals in the grate, as the summer night was chill, and lit a fire in his sitting room where, saying he was going to bed to read, he then left them.

As though she'd only been waiting till they were alone together to talk about what was on her mind, the girl began to tell him how sympathetic 'everyone' had been to her mother, and that Queen Mary had come the other afternoon and stayed to tea.

H listened, nodding occasionally as though the situation was one he was familiar with and then with an ease and lack of self-consciousness that surprised him, started kissing what he thought of as her sophisticatedly naked, London mouth. After momentarily responding, she withdrew it, turned it down, flickered her eyelids shut and said, 'I'm sorry, but I have the curse.'

H still wasn't sure what she was talking about. When it dawned on him, he sensed from her apologetic tone, though he was still far from grasping her ways, that she hadn't intended the announcement purely negatively.

'Never mind,' he said, which remark, because he guessed that that was what she hoped he'd say, wasn't so bold as it sounded, 'that needn't stop us getting into bed.'

She got up, undressed without a word and lay down naked, except for the small hygienic device she'd warned him of, on the bed that O'Flaherty (with the adroitness of the ex-seaman) had made up earlier when he and H had arrived. H lay down beside her, pulling the bedclothes over them, shutting himself in with the long, alabasterlike, recently-washed body. Her extreme cleanliness struck him and increased her strangeness, but the fact that he wasn't expected to make love to her helped him overcome his nervousness. He was reassured by the pale shell of her ear beside his mouth; it was an orifice he could touch with his tongue and not feel the anxiety that contact with moist, exclusively feminine organs would arouse. He felt freed by the presence of the neat little obstruction at the vital part from having to try to direct the lightly rippling wavelets of feeling towards that well-defined and custom-hallowed goal.

He couldn't hide from her his lack-lustre kind of desire, but, far from resenting it, she seemed to apologize and then ask, 'You don't mind being in bed with me, Stephen?'

'My name's Luke.'

'I know it is, my sweet, but I'm going to call you Stephen.'

Let her call him what he bloody well liked as long as she let him explore this situation, that he'd evaded so long, in his own sweet time and way.

'But you do like kissing my ear, don't you?' she was murmuring in a tone of gratitude.

It began to dawn on H that she was as anxious that he respond to her in it didn't matter how slight a degree as was he himself.

'You see,' he told her, 'you're the first woman I've been to bed with except

159

my wife.' He didn't think it necessary to mention the abortive business with Mrs Wright.

'She spoiled it for you with anyone else?'

'That's not quite it,' H said, 'not in the way you mean.'

Honor was somebody to whom, as well as not having to make love straight off, he didn't have to explain things which he himself wasn't sure about. He saw with relief that she, too, was in the dark, for all her assurance and sophistication on other levels, in these matters.

She told him how on her wedding night – she'd married a wealthy young aristocrat – she'd got up, dressed, and gone out to walk the streets of Westminster. She had wandered as far as the Army and Navy stores which she had circled two or three times. Within a week she was back at her parents' town house in Half Moon street and was now in the process of obtaining an annulment.

'But I don't suppose you're a virgin.'

When all looked so promising that would have come as a setback.

'No. But only just not. Mother took me to Capri where we'd a Russian manservant and I let him make love to me one hot afternoon in the garden to help me over my fear that nobody'd ever want me. But he was a brute and it really proved nothing.'

His tongue explored her ear with more abandon.

'Shall I turn over, Stephen, so that you can kiss the other one?'

Was she going to put her arms around him? No, she was evidently too uncertain and too vulnerable to risk anything more at the moment.

They rose and dressed in the firelight, Honor not bothering to put on her flimsy underclothes (she wasn't wearing stockings), but stuffing them into her handbag; later he found her brassière on the bed. After she'd driven away, H stood in the narrow, sloping street beneath the black city sky with its clouds stained pink, and listened to the sound of the car fade away and merge into the general throbbing.

When H was in the bath next morning O'Flaherty called him, and, wrapped in a big bath towel, more luxurious than anything they had at home, he talked to Honor on the telephone beside the bed in which his friend was reading the *Telegraph* and, prompted by him, asked her to meet them for lunch.

Left to himself H might not have invited her, partly out of want of experience in these ways and partly because, as he hadn't been in Paris, he had become somewhat money-conscious. He had what he'd won on the race at Ascot, but this had to last till the payment through his London publishers, who acted as his agent in the U.S.A., of the American dollars. Besides all this, there was another reason for economizing. He had formed a daring though still tentative plan which, if he gave it a chance, might loom large in the late summer and for which an initial outlay would be needed.

'You can't expect the girl to come here and share a tin of sardines with you,' O'Flaherty told him.

O'Flaherty was enjoying a successful phase. He'd shown H the proof of an advertisement his publisher – who was also H's – was putting in one of the papers that devoted several pages to literature the coming Sunday. It consisted of a good half-column of carefully selected quotations from reviews, and was headed: 'Triumph for a great Novelist'. Although O'Flaherty's novels struck H as stark and gloomy, he respected the untamable spirit both in them and his friend, and rejoiced in his increasing renown, whose tangible fruits were lavish entertaining.

They were back at Stulick's, as H was now familiarly thinking of the restaurant in Charlotte Street with all its period greenery, red plush, and mahogany. This time they were joined by a second woman, one with black, prominent eyes under heavy Jewish lids, O'Flaherty's girl, H supposed, who insisted on paying for them all.

After lunch, the pubs being shut, O'Flaherty took them, though it was Enid who seemed to know the place and had them admitted, to a club up the street where, in a couple of big, drab rooms furnished with little else than fruit machines, they could drink during the proscribed hours.

Not that alcohol was what H was after; the nightly oblivion in Paris had served its purpose in opening channels between the conscious and sub-conscious, one reality and another. While the gambling machines were whirring away with the coins that O'Flaherty and his girl kept putting in them, H took Honor to a dusty corner and, with the untasted glasses in their hands, asked her to marry him.

'That is, providing I can get a divorce.'

Honor turned her face to him, eyes closed, pale mouth stretched out, for once not depressed at the corners, and said, 'I'll get you a town suit for our wedding, my sweet.'

'What's wrong with this one?'

'Nothing, Stephen. Only I'd like to have one made for you at my father's tailor.'

One of the fruit machines disgorged a jangling stream of shillings and half-crowns in front of O'Flaherty and Enid. H wanted Honor to return with him to the flat, of which he had a key, leaving the other couple counting their winnings and drinking brandies. But she said she'd an appointment (with the queen? at her dressmaker's? to visit her father in Wormwood Scrubs?) that she couldn't get out of keeping.

After accompanying her to her car, H hadn't time, nor inclination, on the short walk back along Charlotte Street, which as the Praterstrasse had been, was, it seemed, at the moment his street of destiny, to consider his brushing

161

aside of his deep and mostly painful involvement with Iseult. But as soon as he was back in the club he couldn't help telling O'Flaherty and the nervy Jewess with her staring black eyes, scarlet mouth and sober-hued silk summer dress, that he'd asked Honor Maxwell to marry him. How would it strike them? As fantastic as it already seemed to him?

'Splendid!' O'Flaherty exclaimed. 'I told him I knew just the girl for him,' he went on to Enid. 'His wife's been trying to make a monk of him for years.'

H had to laugh at O'Flaherty's intuitive interpretation of the situation, unfactual in detail though it might be. He wouldn't get any conservative advice from his friend, that was clear. But unexpectedly – yet hadn't there been a Jewish boy at Rugby, a Mrs Abrahams, a Mr Isaacs to come to his help in new or critical circumstances? – Enid asked him whether, if his mind was made up, he'd like to consult a reliable solicitor.

One of his minds was not only made up but beset by fears of the possible setbacks that could come between him and Honor. In his other mind there was a temporary cessation of normal functioning.

With this girl, and with nobody else, he could enter the magic realm of sex that, except for a few days in the Pyrenees, had always been barred against him. He was now in the grip of an obsession that was obliterating wife and children as well as his writing.

That evening O'Flaherty introduced H to the person he'd heard so much about, seen mimicked and affectionately mocked, and received an impression of as the seat of all humanist, liberal wisdom.

Stroud rose from a wet table in the saloon bar of the Plough in Museum Street – 'The Plough Tavern,' O'Flaherty had told the taxi driver, investing it for H with a special aura – a long thin figure in a navy blue suit with gentle grey eyes that gave H a shy glance from the sheltering glint of his glasses.

This was the first of many evenings H spent there, consuming quantities of 'bitter' at fourpence-ha'penny a glass, with O'Flaherty, Stroud, an occasional bookie or a bookseller, an Irish doctor from the East End and, like Stroud himself, one or two others of apparently independent means.

Almost the only woman who sat with them at the table was O'Flaherty's latest love – Enid, it turned out had been more in the nature of a boon companion than an inspirer of passion – who, at first sight, struck H by her ugliness, though later he got used to it and even ceased to think of it as such.

He was also struck by her name, Ankaret, and, perhaps too, by O'Flaherty announcing, in her presence, that she belonged to a very old and inbred family of which most of the members were out of their minds.

Settled behind their usual table on which stood the four or five glasses of ale, replenished by each of them in turn, though when the bookie was present or one of the occasional Irish doctors and it came to their turn, it was whiskies

162

all around, the secret recollection of Honor turned the gathering into a happy symposium. The disturbing passion that he had begun to doubt ever being able to exteriorize, he had now, against all probability, a partner to share. What he'd feared were hallucinatory images fashioned by him to suit his peculiar temperament had miraculously become flesh and he couldn't get over it.

He never ceased to wonder at Honor's eagerness to come to the flat at any odd hour when she could manage it, and if possible when O'Flaherty was with Ankaret at her house in Chiswick, peeling off her black dress and going straight to bed with him. No delays, no pretence at conversation while waiting for him to take the initiative.

They accomplished easily and harmoniously what each had feared might be a difficult achievement and one that was not for them. They were a wonderful reassurance to each other in that secret and vulnerable centre where, in different ways, they had suffered defeat.

They were content to leave the question of marriage in abeyance, though it was understood that H would see if there was any chance of the divorce he'd lightly mentioned that first afternoon at the Charlotte Street club. Honor's annulment was in any case far from being settled.

The present was so full that it was easy not to worry. Once, discussing with Honor H's eventual return to Ireland and her going with her mother to their house in the country, Honor said to him: 'I'll have hunting as a cure for what you've made me long for, Stephen. At least three days a week I'll be too tired to want it.'

Enid came one morning to take H to her solicitor, as she'd promised, and also, he guessed, in the hope of meeting O'Flaherty and making an appointment with him for later in the day. But O'Flaherty when he heard she was coming, had exclaimed, 'Tell the crazy bitch I've gone back to Ireland!'

Enid, arriving half an hour before they were due at Mr Davis's office off the Strand, didn't ask for O'Flaherty, but her black prominent eyes kept darting down the passage in the direction of his room.

To escape her anxiety, H went to the kitchenette and made coffee, also hoping, by laying the tray with only two cups, to indicate, without having to deliver the message, that his friend wasn't here. H guessed what O'Flaherty meant to her: a disorderly, daring, unpredictable, endlessly entertaining, and gifted spirit, belonging to a world that her banker friends and family, the house in Hill Street, with its lift, its leather gadget on the hall table, where in an aperture against the embossed name of each of the Phillipsons, a printed card was turned either to 'In' or 'Out', had given her no inkling of.

Yet here she was discussing with him his own affairs in her hoarse staccato voice, wondering if Iseult would consent to divorce him, which H, regarding the situation soberly, was sure she would not, and, having heard, from O'Flaherty, presumably, that he hadn't been quite eighteen on his wedding day, suggested that this could be grounds for having the marriage annulled.

Annulments were in the air! H pictured himself telling Iseult, 'A Jewish solicitor considers that, in the legal sense, we've never been man and wife.'

Mr Davis, youngish but evidently overworked – even his fair hair looked faded – was considering, he told Enid, emigration to South Africa where the future was rosy. He then apologized for the dust he blew off his table where he'd been going through old documents with the previous client, and composed himself to listen to what they'd come to consult him about.

Jews struck H as having an admirably skilful way of handling the messy, jagged-edged, broken mechanics of life, piecing together and straightening out what they could and making the best of what they couldn't. Concepts of perfection and abstract ideals were things they didn't indulge in, which was partly what made them reliable critics both of society and art, and at times, original artists themselves.

Mr Davis pondered the question of a divorce, an annulment, and also other matters, H thought, which he hadn't been consulted on specifically, such as H's character and the financial situation of the parties concerned; he asked where, if it was a matter of remarriage, as he supposed, H's intended new wife was domiciled and if there was anything else in regard to her that H might consider relevant.

At the mention of Lord Dynant he smiled very slightly, his faded blue eyes on the table where the dust had resettled and in which H half expected to see him write with a finger.

29

Stroud gently asserted his philosophy of the freeing of the mind by reason from the bonds of illusion of all sorts in which most of middle-class society was shackled. 'You and Liam,' he said, 'waste time and energy running after women who, in the final analysis, Luke, have nothing more to give you than the ones you can pick up (with a twist of his long neck and a nod in the direction of the British Museum) out there.'

'For those of us whose needs are complex and unspecifiable in purely functional terms what's the point in spending money on a girl who can't satisfy them?' H demanded.

He had a knack of edging Stroud out of his rational vantage point and arrogating it to himself by assuming a more comprehensive view and the use of a kind of impersonal, textbook jargon. It was at such moments he liked to recall how, just a few hours ago he'd let Honor into the sitting room, which opened direct on the dark landing, of the little flat, how she'd stood in her evening dress, under which she was naked, with her back to the window, whose curtains he hastily drew, closed her eyes and said, 'Stephen, my sweet, I simply couldn't imagine living without you.'

Stroud also, H knew, had his own means of liberating himself from outward existence and gaining another level of consciousness. This was his Marxism and it was partly because he was afraid of hurting H's social or political susceptibilities, which he couldn't know didn't exist, and partly because of the seriousness of the subject, that he almost never mentioned it.

There was talk of racing, in which Jefcote, having a glass of ale with them – one of the few publicans in London who joined his customers in a drink without coming around to their side of the bar, Stroud commented – sometimes took part. Stroud's knowledge of and absorption in racing H saw, with alcohol, as another of his means of escape. He had a memory for the past performances of the outstanding horses of that season, recalling just where they'd finished in Guineas, Derby, and Oaks. When flatly contradicted by O'Flaherty who grew impatient at statistics, he'd appeal to Jefcote across the bar.

There was, more rarely, talk of books. Stroud admired Joyce and also a French writer, Céline, of whom H hadn't heard and whose deceptively girlish name, as well as the evocative title, almost as long as his own, of his novel *Voyage au bout de la nuit*, he took as an indication that he might be the 'prophet' who H believed must soon arise.

Why he felt this he didn't know unless because without an intimation from a profound imaginative source that, notwithstanding indications to the contrary, all was not yet lost, the outlook was too dark to bear.

Not that he asked Stroud to lend him the novel, then only available in French. In fact it was many years before H read and was disappointed by it, because by then the human situation, and H's consciousness of it, had moved into a more extreme and complicated phase.

Calling one afternoon to see his publisher, Victor Gollancz, in a windowless office at the back of premises in Covent Garden, H let him suppose that he was well into another book. This was partly so that it would be easier to ask for an advance on it before it was delivered should the project he had in mind make this necessary. And partly he didn't want his publisher to suppose he'd just the one book in him, which he anyhow knew was not so.

Gollancz was wearing a dark-blue shirt and button-down collar, of a kind called, H thought, aerotex, just like the one he himself had on and which neither crumpled nor showed the dirt, and this, rather than anything the publisher had to say to him, was the beginning, for H, not for Gollancz who probably hadn't noticed, of the forming between them of a tenuous sort of bond that lasted a long time and survived several crises.

If H had known Gollancz better, and himself been fully articulate, he'd have told him: '*I Won't be Wearing Shamrock on St Patrick's Day* burst out of me as a shriek does from, say, a lone starling with a damaged wing left behind by the flock, or as the howl from a trapped wolf. But, Mr G, being neither bird nor simple beast of prey, I've a long way to go before my spirit opens beak or maw a second time, impelled by what must be a more conscious urge.'

Actually H was tongue-tied and wondering whether Gollancz would offer him a brandy as both O'Flaherty and a popular young woman novelist called Barbara Smith, a friend of Enid Phillipson's, had told him they were invariably treated to when they called at his office. When he didn't, H left feeling that, in spite of Gollancz's words of encouragement, the publisher's confidence in him and his future was accompanied by certain reserves.

At this period what concerned H vitally wasn't a publisher. He had at last a mistress (wonder of wonders!), had, reversing the original process, broken into a secluded, scentless, sensual paradise. What he needed now to pursue the dream to its end – what dream? what end? – was a small but shrewd trainer to buy cheaply a yearling for him at the coming Dublin sales and prepare it, at a reasonable charge, for next season's two-year-old races.

Before moving away, probably for good, from the subject of his first published novel, he reflected on the fact that it had evidently been very easy to misinterpret. Among several letters he'd received from strangers, one, written on grey paper embossed with a discreet-looking pair of red wings and headed by the address of the R.A.F. Club in Piccadilly, had come from a wing commander who wrote that the book expressed, 'in no uncertain terms', his own beliefs as an Empire Royalist. Hardly was H over his astonishment at this communication when one from a girl in America arrived, in which she enclosed two coloured photographs of herself ('Ginette gay and Ginette sad') inviting him to come and stay for as long as he liked at her parents' sumptuous mansion on Long Island, a photo of which was also enclosed, where he'd have his own private bathroom. Another final reflection: in spite of what O'Flaherty had told him, Honor hadn't read his book. Later she'd asked him should she read it and he'd said no.

'You'll tell me when to read what you write, won't you, Stephen?'

But H couldn't think of his writing in relation to Honor. To whom could he relate it, if it came to that? Iseult had admired his early poems, especially

166

those to Polenskaya, and had praised the poetic parts of his novel, but these were what he had to get rid of, or transmute, before he found his own tone.

One morning, after an evening when a doctor friend of O'Flaherty's from Stepney had insisted on buying several rounds of whiskey at the Plough, H was mixing himself a glass of Eno's, a poor substitute for the Chianti of Paris days, when, summoned by a ring, he found Honor at the door.

'What's up?' he asked as soon as she was inside it. The hangover was making him jumpy, abrupt. He hadn't yet pulled the curtains from across the window and, with the light on, she was standing as usual with her back to it; there was nowhere else to stand, except by the couch, in the small room. Through the ache at the back of his eyes he glanced down at her legs and saw that she wasn't wearing stockings. That meant no underclothes, so all must be well, all manner of things must be well.

Not this morning they weren't, not bloody likely on a day when his resistance was undermined.

'What time is it?'

He hadn't wound O'Flaherty's travelling clock but he thought it must be early which meant that her appearance could only be due to one of two disasters: either 'the curse' was overdue, or it was to tell him that . . .

'Stephen, I can't marry you.'

'Why not?' What he'd almost asked was, as about the suit, 'what's wrong with me?'

'It wouldn't work, my sweet.' Who had supposed it would, except in bed? And who had cared to reflect beyond that?

H heard the tap, at which he'd been filling a glass, running, went to the bathroom, still echoing the suddenly less promising city hum, to turn it off, leaned over the basin to see if he wanted to be sick, found that he didn't, splashed his face with cold water, spat a couple of times, and returned to the little sitting room where Honor had switched out the light, drawn back the curtain and was getting out of her dress.

After they'd made love – O'Flaherty had spent the night with Ankaret – H said, 'It'll take a lot of hunting to make up for this!'

Was he stunned? Had a treasure his imagination had been poring over been withdrawn and locked away? Well, no. It was a rejection, but of something that had never been quite real. As long as he could still lie in bed with her, making love or, like this, in the aftermath that came with a sense of a great subterranean cave-in that shifted his neurological setup from its too firm and tightly constructed base, all was still well.

All the same, the idea of her sharing with somebody else, who wore town suits, their sensual trances, was an image to be let gingerly into his mind where it immediately seared and shrivelled all other thoughts.

But, again, by the time O'Flaherty returned, H could tell him the news, and, what's more, observe himself doing so with a wry smile.

'Good Lord, what a setback!' his friend exclaimed, but in an exuberant tone that expressed his own delight in the risks of these great games, as he looked on them, in his ugly duckling and in the knowledge that the world was at his feet.

A few days later, at a party given by Enid, spoiled for her by O'Flaherty's not turning up, H met a girl because of whom he put off his return home. Iseult in her letters was growing impatient at what he'd explained initially as a business trip to see his publisher's being so prolonged.

No clouds hovered over the fair, doll's face of Julia Jenners; she later showed H a cutting she kept in the tattered first edition of *Vanity Fair* that had pride of place on the mantelpiece of her room in Hertford Street in which a well-known drama critic – she was an actress – compared her to a piece of Dresden china.

Here was a girl from another world that he had hardly known the existence of. It repelled and fascinated him, and he wanted, as well as dreaded, further shocks that would penetrate some of the still-closed areas of his consciousness.

Not that she was going to be as inexpensive as Honor, that was clear. When he asked her to lunch the next day it had to be at the Berkeley. She scintillated at the table by the window, which in an unaccustomed excess of forethought he'd booked in advance, entertaining him with imitations of notabilities who attended first nights, but the bill which he paid with an air of indifference, not interrupting her in her miming act to place the notes on the slip and push the plate towards the table edge, appalled him.

She invited him back to her flat which, she told H, June, a magic name in London just then, had sublet to her furnished, consisting, as far as he could see, of one large dim boudoir with walls of old gold, a tarnished gilt-framed mirror in which the buff-coloured spread of the divan was reflected, a couple of armchairs covered in beige brocade and, on the limed-oak mantelpiece, nothing but the first-edition copy of *Vanity Fair*, held upright between two Victorian paper-weights, whose worn leather binding gave a pseudo-sophisticated touch to the overripe effect of the place's décor.

Julia had heard about his being a writer, and on this first visit to her flat told him that the brother of the novelist Aldous Huxley was a friend of hers who came around to her dressing room at whatever theatre she happened to be acting when he was in town. She was keen on literature and literary people, and used them to create a more sophisticated aura around her than her parts in light comedies and as principal girl in Christmas pantomimes would have evoked.

H had to promise to give her a copy of *I Won't Be Wearing Shamrock* which, he guessed, she would 'simply love'.

He had still to find out whether he was now capable of sex with a woman who was 'normal' and who obviously felt completely assured of her desirability. He wanted to put his fears and self-consciousness behind him. So, in the midst of the literary chatter, he put his arm around Julia and kissed her.

She responded, but not too fervently, and then went on to show him a signed copy of a book by her scientist-friend's famous brother.

H didn't withdraw his arm from around her waist, and, after a few more not-too-promising kisses, thought that if he didn't soon take the plunge he'd be beset by the old neurosis, and asked her to come to bed, though apart from anything else, it seemed a lot to expect her to spoil the whole effect of the room by disarranging the coverlet, and its evidently carefully thought-out reflection in the mirror, of the divan, from which a cream telephone apparatus would also have to be removed.

Julia closed the novel, put it back on the shelf at the head of the divan and left the room.

Had he offended her by his abrupt interruption of her showing him her treasure? In his panic, for such a failure now might put him back in the weird no-man's-land he'd been in before meeting Honor, he began to wonder if she'd left the flat. He concluded, however, that the door that he'd heard shut must have been the one from the tiny hallway to the bathroom, which he'd noticed coming in, and not that on to the landing.

After ten minutes she still hadn't returned, and H was beginning to think of slipping away when she reappeared in what seemed a voluminous nightdress.

'You can hang your things in there, Luke,' she told him.

In the narrow entrance hall, the door of which she closed on him, H put his clothes on a spare hanger he discovered among her array of coats. It reminded him of undressing in one of the cubicles of the bathhouse in Vienna.

Once under the covers of the divan he found that, beneath the nightdress, her breasts were swathed in some gauzy material. Very different was all this from Honor's quick stripping. He caught a chemical whiff that seemed to come from the muffled up and apparently untouchable part of her. Rather than pretend he'd noticed nothing unusual and ready, in order to lessen his own disconcertion, to discover, in the hospital scent, a trance of briny ozone, he remarked, 'You smell like the sea.'

At that moment the telephone rang and she stretched out an arm to answer it. The interruption, while she chattered away, wasn't conducive to his entering the sexual trance. When, despite the various diversions, he made love to her, she struck him – here his intuition was acute – as being uninvolved in the act. Not that, as with Iseult, there were any signs of it being distasteful to her, but that her participation in it was part of a role she was playing.

Before H left, Julia said she'd have a ticket kept for him at the box office of the theatre where a new play she was in was opening in a couple of days.

'Put on a dinner jacket,' she told him.

Before seeing about hiring evening attire, H wondered whether he shouldn't return home. There were moments when he felt like it, though he foresaw continued tensions between himself and Iseult. The tone of the whole day was set at the moment when, coming into the dining-room hut late for breakfast, he caught sight of the torn hem of her nightdress that she hadn't bothered to mend under the coat she'd hurriedly slipped over it. Depressed, irritated, and debilitated by a sense of guilt, he seldom managed to halt the decline that continued till evening.

What did he expect to gain from Julie Jenners? If, as Honor had rightly foreseen, their relationship wouldn't 'have worked', how much more was this true with the little porcelain pseudo-shepherdess!

But she'd explode certain of his habits of thought and widen his world for him by the series of minor shocks he experienced in her company. The opposite polarity of her mode of thought and reflexes to Iseult's fascinated him and gave him a glimpse of the extent of possible relations.

It ended by his turning up in the rented dinner jacket in Julia's dressing room before the performance where he was met and given a glass of sherry by Mrs Jenners. Julia's mother was dealing with all the last-minute details, putting a quick stitch in a costume, while Julia's dresser was busy behind the curtain that divided the room, deciphering the name on a card attached to one of the bouquets and, at the same time, apropos of one of the well-wishing telegrams, telling H that, though her daughter, as was inevitable, had a number of admirers among rich socialites, she was a serious and solitary sort of girl.

'She's always loved books, Mr Ruark.'

Ill at ease in the stiff shirt and hard collar, which, with the cuff links he'd had to buy, he was half sorry he'd come and half touched by this strange appeal by Mrs Jenners on behalf of her daughter, who, against all likelihood, seemed to be taken with him.

As he was leaving the dressing room he had a glimpse, through a gap between curtain and door, of an elderly woman leaning over Julia seated before the mirrors, binding up a huge bluish white breast, the bandagelike material already hid the other.

H was back again at the end of the comedy, which made no impact on him one way or the other, met at the door of the now crowded room by Mrs

Jenners and taken under her wing while Julia was getting into a wrap behind the curtain. She asked him had he recognized this or that celebrity among the first-night audience, people whom, apart from Hugh Walpole, H had never heard of, mentioning with special satisfaction that General Gombös, the Hungarian prime minister, at present in England for crucial talks, had been in the second row of the stalls.

Back at Julia's flat, whence her mother didn't accompany them, there were the same ritualistic and secret preparations. H, after Julia returned from the bathroom, robed like a priestess of some ancient cult, was shut up again in the narrow hallway where he struggled out of his crackling garments. And into them half an hour later, for she had to get to sleep before midnight.

30

H told Julia about his wife and children, but this didn't diminish her efforts to arrange as much as he let her of his life; she soon suggested they have a meal together in a pub in Shepherd's Market, near where she lived, every evening before she went to the theatre. And, in order to economize, for she quickly realized that H hadn't much money, she would have sent her mother to O'Flaherty's flat with a cold lunch for him, if he hadn't dissuaded her.

The relationship was often irksome and he was at times on the verge of deciding to break it off. One of the things that fascinated him was her energy, even though it was a constant threat to him. When she took him to see a house that was being converted into mews flats, just becoming fashionable, he played with the idea of living in one of them with her. He guessed she was Jewish, though neither she nor her mother ever referred to the fact, by several signs, one of which was her readiness to gamble by trying to add him to the other prizes she'd determined, by making the best of her limited gifts, to wrest from life. She seemed to believe that, after writing several novels, he'd become admired, at least by a limited, discerning circle.

The thought of what he might be heading for stimulated as well as made him uneasy. The possibility of an even more unsuitable second marriage than the first, remote though it was, did something positive to his psyche that thrived on the threat of disaster, though this was not the sort that he was subconsciously seeking.

H was letting Mr Davis continue his investigations into the possibility of divorce or annulment without telling him that it was now another woman whom, if free, he was thinking of marrying.

What worried H more than anything else at the moment was the effect that a prolonged relationship with Julia would have on that other risk he was planning, the one that involved buying and putting into training a yearling at the August bloodstock sales in Dublin.

His fears on this score increased when Julia told him that a jeweller she knew – a member of her race? – had shown her a ruby ring that he was willing to let her have for ten pounds, the sum that it had cost him wholesale.

H reluctantly wrote out the cheque. A day or two later she was wearing the ring and suggesting that they ask a few people to lunch at a restaurant in Jermyn Street whose proprietor she'd spoken to, and who'd agreed to supply the food free and to charge H only for the drinks.

'Who did you think of having?'

She mentioned Julian Huxley, the brother of the novelist, and his wife (but they couldn't come), another couple whom H hadn't heard of, and said she thought they should invite the Turkish ambassador who, with a mutual acquaintance, had come to her dressing room on the first night.

'What about General Gömbös?'

'Who, Luke?'

'The Hungarian prime minister. Your mother said he was also at the theatre.' H took a delight in contriving an even more fantastic situation. But, Julia, seeing it neither as comedy nor extravaganza, shook her head.

A couple of evenings after the lunch party, at which the talk beside him had been of Deauville and Trouville and the merits of various kinds of mustard, Stroud showed him a paragraph in the gossip column of a mass circulation picture paper: 'At lunch at the Ilex where Miss Julia Jenners and the young Irish novelist, Luke Ruark, were entertaining a few close friends, I noticed Julie was wearing a ruby engagement ring.'

'You've a good chance of getting damages for libel out of the filthy rag,' Stroud told him.

After the Julia fantasy which, charadelike, he went through with between the dimly faded, over-mirrored atmosphere of her sitting room and the bright, functional one of her dressing room, the Plough was a haven of simple sense. He went there most evenings, even when he had to leave before closing time and put on a dinner jacket, now hired by the week, before calling at the theatre, and accompany Julia to one of the parties where he was introduced to Hugh Walpole, Princess Troubetzkoy, George Robey, whose Falstaff Julia enthused over, and Queen Marie of somewhere or other.

He didn't tell Stroud, what he himself had only just grasped, that the ring, the lunch at the Ilex, and the presence of the gossip columnist had been arranged to coincide by Julia and her mother. He knew how Stroud would slowly have pivoted his long neck and, turning a quizzical, concerned glance on him, say in this cockney drawl, 'You realize, Luke, what you're letting yourself in for? She's evidently set her heart on marrying you.'

Speaking from his own uncomplicated Marxist logic he would tell H that, in the last analysis, any one of the several women sitting at that moment at a table across the saloon bar from theirs could give him anything Julia Jenners had to offer while leaving him his freedom.

'Why take everything so bloody seriously, Harold,' O'Flaherty exclaimed. 'If Luke likes to invite this Turk to meet his cutie at a smart eating place that's hot news, isn't it? It's what the mass of readers want to hear about, ambassadors and actresses, and not what bloody Trotsky had to say.'

He knew that O'Flaherty took his part because of sharing the same obscure and apparently self-destructive impulses. In O'Flaherty these expressed themselves in many ways, including at times excessive drinking and spending and, particularly, in a belligerent attitude towards these critics and other writers who could have been of help.

The morning after this discussion Honor Maxwell turned up at the flat, saying she could only stay a minute, that she was on her way to meet her mother – and the queen? (she had on stockings and a big hat) – at a flower show, and suggesting that she and H spend the weekend at a country hotel. Had she read the piece in the paper and did she want to see if she could still get H back, temporarily, for herself?

When she'd left H wasn't sure if she'd mentioned Maidenhead or Maidstone. Maidstone, he thought, was a jail, possibly where Lord Dynant and his pet rabbits were, and it might be that Honor planned to combine a visit to her father and a weekend with himself.

In other respects, too, the complications were increasing. That evening Mrs Jenners had asked him to dine with her, and he kept the appointment with apprehension. Yet she was more easygoing, less dominant than her daughter. Although everything she did was determined by her devotion to Julia, she only mentioned her briefly, to tell him that she suffered from glandular trouble that caused a swelling of the fingers, no mention of the breasts, which was being kept in check by drugs, but which, after the play had had its run, might have to be treated surgically.

She also mentioned seeing Huxley, the novelist, that morning on a bus and watching him spend the journey scribbling shortsightedly in a notebook.

'Always industrious, never a moment wasted, that's the sort of person he is.'

'Not like me, Mrs Jenners, a layabout bent on nothing profitable.'

She smiled and ordered him another 'Pimm's Special'. Whether or not she approved her daughter's choice, and H felt she didn't disapprove of it so actively as his mother-in-law did of Iseult's, she would do all she could to further the relationship, to please Julia.

They talked over coffee. He'd refused brandy, guessing that Mrs Jenners wasn't well off; though Julia was now earning twenty pounds a week, there were periods when she hadn't any work. And H lost his initial nervousness. She was open and humble; with what he'd learned was the Jewish feeling for family, she told him about her own marriage and early widowhood, her small flat in an unfashionable suburb, the job she had taken to help Julia through drama school and, reverting briefly to her treasure, that her daughter had never made it easier for herself by responding to the advances of agents or producers.

'She's a good girl, Mr Ruark.'

Luke nodded. Yes, she was, though it wasn't necessary to believe that she'd always rejected the advances of the sort of theatrical people who could advance her career.

When Honor appeared briefly next morning to say that, after all, she couldn't manage the weekend, H was relieved.

His talk with Mrs Jenners gave him an inkling that Julia was more deeply involved with him than he'd thought. It wasn't an act for her, as, in a sense, almost everything was for him: his mystical studies, the civil war, Lourdes, horse racing. No, that wasn't quite right, he reflected. If they were acts they were also preparations for something that would be his reality.

Then there was this glandular complaint of hers which, he had an idea, wasn't going to be so easily dealt with as Mrs Jenners seemed to think. The longer things went on as they were, the harder it was going to be to find a way out. It looked as if Julia had less reserves, was less capable of a quick recovery from shock, or, as the break might gain the proportions of, if it came first to living together, with the prospect of eventual marriage, disaster.

Not that he had any idea of how gradually to loosen up the relationship. Julia wanted them to see more of each other, not liking to leave him so much of the day to himself, and suggested they get a set of chessmen, Mrs Jenners having unearthed an old draught board, and that he come in the afternoons for them to have a game or two together.

She didn't approve of his friendship for O'Flaherty, whom H was in no hurry for her to meet, but even less, he knew, would she approve of Stroud. Nor did she care for his spending his evenings at the Plough while she was at the theatre.

H knew she'd have liked him to spend the morning writing a new novel, eat the bread and cheese, or cold meat, with a cup of coffee, that her mother would have gladly brought him for lunch, spend the afternoon with her playing chess, talking – lovemaking being kept for after the performance –

then, after taking her to supper at the pub, accompany her to the theatre and, at least some nights during the week, hang around between her dressing room and the stalls; she could always arrange a free seat, for the place was never full.

The chess-playing never came to anything because, having said one evening that she'd have a look next day for a set, he hadn't offered her the money, not that she grudged buying it herself but she probably sensed his lack of interest.

H received a cheque from Gollancz for the amount of the American advances on his novel; it had been long in, but Gollancz only made up accounts half-yearly, in January and July. This gave H's thoughts an added impulse in the direction of the August bloodstock sales. He found he could buy copies of the *Irish Field* at the *Irish Times* office in Fleet Street and in it study the Irish racing scene. What, among other things, he was looking for was a not-too-successful trainer who would consider it worth his while to choose a cheap yearling to train for H.

Going through the entries for coming races H occasionally came on the name M. Deasey in brackets after the name of a horse entered at one of the minor meetings. Deasey was evidently in a small way of business, but whether because of ineptitude at his calling or just through the throw of the dice, an expression of O'Flaherty's, H had no way of knowing. He realized that the whole plan was, on any discernible level, so far from practical and so fraught with possibilities of failure, that this was only one risk among many.

H discussed the matter with O'Flaherty; there was nobody else to whom he could have mentioned it without head-shaking and long faces. His friend instinctively grasped what drove H to apparent follies.

'Deasey!' he exclaimed, 'a Cork man by the sound of it. Still, he could come from County Limerick, which wouldn't be so bad.'

He set great store by where a person came from, and had strong local loyalties which he never thought of hiding and which was the cause of endless arguments with Stroud.

H let things drift till the end of July. When at last he told Julia he had to return to Ireland she didn't seem to take it badly. But that evening a fellow actress in the play, the wife of the producer, asked them to a party and when H had to refuse, Julia explained that he was going home to talk things over with his wife and see if she'd consent to a divorce.

He'd once mentioned having consulted Enid's solicitor, and, in answer to a question of Julia's, said he didn't know whether Iseult would agree to divorce him or not. But that had been weeks ago and he'd supposed that from his subsequent silence she'd guessed that the idea had come to nothing.

H returned to Ireland after a kind of inner shift. The experience of Honor and Julia had caused an upheaval that left him both flexible and apprehensive.

The racehorse idea was an attempt to plunge into an adventure that was a substitute for the one he either wasn't ready or hadn't the resolution to embark on. Without being able to define this precisely he knew it concerned his writing on the one hand and a grappling with the problem of his marriage on the other.

31

Getting into bed the first night, breathing the warm, familiar forgotten smell from the paraffin lamp and recognizing the shape of the stain on the opposite wall below the false turret, where the portrait of St Catherine of Siena still hung, H was surprised at the sense of relief that flooded into him at having no longer to adapt part of himself to Julia and her ways. He felt as if recovered from an illness that while the fever lasted he had acquiesced in for reasons that now, that he had the temporarily forgotten standard of health as a measure, seemed perverse.

How relaxed he felt putting on his old clothes again in the morning and breakfasting with Ian and Miss Burnett; Iseult was always late and his mother gave the baby her porridge in the kitchen. The little boy, for whom H had brought back a magic lantern, was impatient for him to put on a show in the sitting room while Miss Burnett was giving him news of the poultry; the fertility rate of the eggs delivered weekly to a big nearby farm to be hatched in a huge incubator that looked like a battleship was keeping high; a few drops of iodine in the drinking water had brought down the mortality rate of the chicks.

A satisfactory report; pleasant, straightforward news. No more struggling into a stiff bloody shirt to attend parties at which Julia hoped to show him off – did she imagine her obscure lion would impress them? – to semi-celebrities and smiling happily while she told third-rate writers about their semi-engagement.

There was no sign of Deasey when H arrived at the sales ring one August morning. As usual he was early, just as Iseult was always late, and he saw by the number in the frame that the first of the two or three yearlings that Deasey had marked on an advance copy of the catalogue he had sent was thirty or forty lots further on.

He sat down in one of the first rows of the little amphitheatre to take in what was going on, and was soon nervously following the transactions. These young horses led around the arena were the hot-blooded, ammonia-scented, sleek-skinned actuality behind the sparse, greyish print in the late-news columns. Passing from one to the other produced the shock of reality that progression from erotic fantasies to women's naked bodies did.

H studied the pedigrees where the names of famous racehorses that had become myths – Gainsborough, Ard Patrick, Persimmon, Pharos, Spion Kop – increased his excitement at watching these quite unmythical-looking animals excreting bright yellow droppings on to the sanded ring.

The staccato chant of the auctioneer from his rostrum: 'Two hundred I'm bid, any advance on two hundred for the Sansovino colt? It's against you on my right. Thank you; two hundred and ten guineas, two twenty, two thirty, two hundred and thirty guineas for this half-brother to three winners . . .' was a music as potent as had been, at different times, that of Tchaikovsky, the Gregorian records, or the last high notes of the Maria Jaritza arias.

What in the name of God was keeping Deasey? The colt by Hurstwood, third in the Derby of 1924, the year after his release and that of Lane's death, was only a dozen lots away. Should he bid for it himself if Deasey who'd said something about getting a lift up from the Curragh – evidently no car and wanted to save the train fare – hadn't arrived? If it went below the sum up to which H could go – what, for God's sake, was forty pounds? They were nearly all being put in at a hundred! – mightn't that be because of some serious defect of conformation that his unskilled eye had failed to spot?

But just before the eagerly awaited yearling appeared, the little trainer, who'd at one time been a jockey in the north of England, tapped H on the shoulder from the gangway and signed to him to come up to the passage behind the top row of seats. 'You get a better look at them from here, Mr Ruark,' he said with a deprecatory smile that seemed to be apologizing to H for his own superior knowledge.

When the colt was led in, H was watching Deasey who was regarding the yearling meditatively from under the turned-down brim of his hat.

Failing to get a bid of a hundred, or even fifty, the auctioneer put it in at twenty-five guineas. Without H catching a movement anywhere, there came the cry from the rostrum of 'Thirty I'm bid.' H saw Deasey make a surreptitious-seeming sign with his catalogue, as though removing the drop from the end of his nose, and the auctioneer, stabbing out a finger in their direction, called, 'Thirty-five, thirty-five on my left.' For a few seconds H was the owner of the bay son of Hurstwood out of a mare that Deasey had ridden in the days before having had, as H concluded from something the trainer had said, for he was never explicit, his jockey's licence withdrawn. Other bids followed quickly, Deasey lowered his head and dropped out, smiling his humble, patient smile under his long, pointed nose.

The next lot whose number the trainer had ringed with a pencil in the catalogue was a filly by Sonning whose dam Deasey had trained; his interest in horses seemed always personal. And though H had expected to hear that she had been a good race mare, all that Deasey had said about her was: 'She had a bit of character, Mr Ruark. Oh yes, a lady with a mind of her own,' and he'd chuckled to himself. Deasey, H soon saw, lived in a very private world, shared only by his two brothers – whom H didn't yet know – from which he seldom emerged, or for that matter, let the horses in his care do so either.

The filly looked disappointingly small to H, but he saw Deasey, who had appeared, after one glance, to take no further notice, nod his head, or rather, by moving it almost imperceptibly, cause the brim of his hat to dip a further couple of inches, a signal that the staring, fanatic's eyes from the rostrum didn't miss.

The Sonning filly was knocked down to them for forty guineas. That Deasey had secured it for the sum that H had set as the limit, seemed to him to bode well for the enterprise. After giving his name to the auctioneer's assistant, he followed the trainer out of the amphitheatre to examine their purchase.

While a stableman held the yearling by the bridle, Deasey walked slowly around it, stopping fore and aft, in front to run his hand down the forelegs from knee to fetlock; on what the meditative glance rested a couple of moments as he stood behind the animal, H didn't know.

Whatever he thought of the filly Deasey kept to himself, nor did H try to find out his opinion. Now that the step had been taken, he could be endlessly patient.

H went to find Iseult as soon as he got home that afternoon. She was washing her hair.

'What's that, darling?' Sluicing her head and stooped over the bathtub, she hadn't heard properly.

'I bought a yearling at the Horse Show.'

She turned off the taps and grabbed a towel to keep the soap out of her eyes while she lifted her head.

'You've bought what?'

'A racehorse. It's in the nature of an investment.'

'Are you out of your mind? What about all the bills? And me putting off getting the things the children need so desperately till the sales. As for your wife, she's simply nothing to wear, all her clothes are literally such rags that I'm ashamed to be seen out in them. I kept my mouth shut when you went to London and spent the American money giving lunch parties and buying some tart a ruby ring, but this is the bloody limit!'

H guessed which of their neighbours had come running to show her the piece in the paper: one of the genteel, lace-curtain country women.

Not that he didn't realize that Iseult was perfectly justified, but he felt no urge to admit this and confirm her even more in what he thought of as her sense of moral superiority. Instead, he shut himself up in his room and started writing a new novel, the theme for which had suddenly come to him.

A young man, H (alias X), who works on a biweekly paper in a provincial town, on his way home in the early hours of a Sunday morning, is passing the largest of the sixteen churches, the presence of one or more of which in every street sets the pious, self-laudatory tone and causes a prolification of the complacent tapping of fingers crosswise on foreheads and chests by the passersby.

Always afraid of coming on some tortured animal in a sack or hung from a shop window grille on his twice-weekly late-night walk (the frustrated seek an outlet in the meanest cruelties), X pauses to investigate what sounded less than a groan. He finds a couple of girls standing by the church railings and at first doesn't take in the fact of the placards, the shaven heads, and the chained wrists. The girls try to hide their plight for fear, as they later tell him, of offering a late-homing clerk or pioneer publican a safe chance of dipping his fingers into something more exciting than a holy water stoop.

The girls catch a breath of his own soul-souring loathing of the town which he has never had a way of expressing till now and confess they are dying of thirst. Ten minutes and he'll be back with a thermos flask of hot, sweet tea. A slight hiatus in the confiding flow of communication which he at once detects; is it a hesitation to let him go, or have they another urgent piece of personal information to impart?

Because he's involved with them, body and spirit, the less embarrassed, or more trusting of the two, Maureen (the other is Peggy) tells him not only are they dying of thirst but – yes, that's it – they are dying for a pee but are afraid of leaving twin rivulets across the broad pavement which would not have dried by the dread hour of dawn and early Mass.

If they can hold out the quarter-hour it'll take him to get home, brew the tea, find a suitable container and be back, he'll take care of that too, gladly and with his whole heart.

All is accomplished, though Pegeen admits later that she didn't believe he'd come back.

'Not come back?'

He was astonished that she hadn't seen into his (to him) crystal-clear psyche and grasped just what crimes it could and could not commit.

'Eight of any ten of the leading statesmen you like to name I'd be happy to assassinate if I could get away with it, on the grounds that anyone

179

responsible for maintaining an army, to say nothing of other legitimized instruments of murderous intent, deserves a taste of unlegitimized murder himself.

'There are quite a few other less public acts generally accepted as highly criminal that I wouldn't mind having a try at if the circumstances were propitious, because they wouldn't generate images to haunt me afterwards. Whereas, if I hadn't come back here I'd have been plunged into a nightmare of such imaginative proportions that my life wouldn't have been bearable.'

He was chatting away in this somewhat egocentric fashion to help them over the awkwardness of having him take down their knickers. He'd asked them which of the two needs should have precedence in being relieved, and they'd simultaneously done a little dance to indicate the urgency of peeing.

He'd brought a couple of empty gallon-size paint tins from the builder's yard at the back of the house where he rented his two rooms. These he held between the girls' legs (they were so closely chained to the railings they couldn't squat down) and, as if two taps had been simultaneously turned on full blast, he had to tense his wrists against the gush into the cans.

Glancing into their shadowy faces he caught a look of dreamy bliss that both thrilled and filled him with foreboding at the thought of the coming confrontation with the expressions of the first daylight passersby and early Mass-goers.

Church, family, nation: the magic, threefold sign signifying the cherished distinguishing mark of the tribe, moral rectitude, branded on the Sunday morning faces, that's what they'd be exposed to.

Would the streams never stop? Was there a hint of competitive eagerness between the girls to see which would flow the longest?

X was registering currents of physical awareness between them and himself. Not surprising in the circumstances which were not of the purely clinical or neutralized hospital kind, for, despite their plight, the girls were perfectly healthy and functioning normally.

Having emptied the cans into the gutter he left them outside a shop further along the street. He then held a mug of tea to Maureen's mouth which she sucked in in blissful gulps, murmuring ah! as she paused from swallowing to get her breath. Peggy's turn next, and a second shudder of delight that, combining with the other relief still spreading through tensed-up muscles and nerves, produced a rapturous sense of physical reverberations of well-being passed from them to him as in the act of love itself.

Pee, piss, pock (the sound of the last winning drop into the can) chimed the town clock: 3 a.m.

He and Iseult were on speaking terms again, following several days of ignoring each other after the quarrel, and she even agreed to come with him to the Curragh to see the filly.

On the drive over the mountains she told H she regretted his having given up poetry for fiction. Not that this was news to him; he knew that she disapproved not just of what he'd have tried to alter had they been in accord in other ways, his selfishness and irresponsibility, but of what seemed to her the fatal course his imagination was set on.

At the small training establishment to which they were directed H inquired of a stableman for Mr Deasey.

'Which Deasey is that?'

'Mr Michael Deasey.'

'*I'm* Mick Deasey.'

'I thought the trainer was Mr M. Deasey.'

The man regarded H with the patient expression one adopts when speaking to a backward child.

'It's my brother that's in charge, but the establishment is in my name on account of the jockey's licence being in Tom's.'

'Then it's Mr Tom Deasey I'm looking for.'

'I think the man you're after will be my brother Matt.'

He disappeared through the back door of the big dilapidated house and his voice echoed through what sounded like endless empty rooms.

Iseult had got out of the car and was regarding with surprised distaste, as if this was the last thing she'd expected, the heads of the horses that were thrust out over the lower half of several of the stable doors.

'Which is yours?'

How, in God's name, should he know? He bent to speak to the little boy without answering.

The trainer came out followed by the third brother, Tom, if H had got the names right at last. He smiled his apologetic smile, raised his hat, which he'd emerged from the house wearing, wiped a drop from the end of his long nose and shook hands with them while Tom remained in the background. Mick had entered a loose box and was murmuring to one of the horses.

'Would you care to see the animals?' Deasey asked.

What did he suppose they'd come for? No mention of the filly. Had she contracted an equine disease and died and was Deasey putting off breaking the news?

Tom opened a door and went into the enclosure in which there loomed through the dimness a huge equine shape which, at a slap on the steep flank, pivoted around to a rustle of straw and presented a long flat front of bony forehead narrowing and flaring out again in huge red nostrils, above a glistening, black, down-twisted muzzle, the whole angular structure topped by a flash of white in a startled, staring eye.

Was this the filly? He didn't dare commit himself and hoped that Iseult wouldn't disgrace them by inquiring.

181

'A regular lazybones, aren't you, eh?' Deasey said, stepping up to the horse and letting it push its wet muzzle under the brim of his hat. 'Don't mind him, Mrs Ruark, the old fellow's as gentle as a lamb.'

Each time a door was opened H was tensely expectant till the trainer or his brother made a remark.

'Belongs to Mr Kelly (Hey, back there! Where's your manners) the book-maker,' Deasey was saying. 'Do you know what he named him, Mrs Ruark? Tea Leaf. Isn't that a shame now, a grand honest fellow like that!'

Iseult tilted her face away from the hot whiff of horse piss in the box, while Deasey explained to her that, in rhyming slang, the name meant thief.

Frightened by the horses, Ian had turned his attention to a pet cock that had perched on the shoulder of the other Deasey and was pecking oats from his hand.

Turning around, H saw Tom Deasey standing in the middle of the yard with the hollow-backed animal he recognized at once.

'Our little filly,' he exclaimed, partly out of delight and partly to stop Iseult should she be about to make some embarrassing, ignorant remark.

Deasey asked H what he was going to call her. This was something that he'd been giving a lot of thought to, jotting down names and hoping to catch any counter-flowing reverberations emanating from whichever of them was destined to gather lustre as top of the three in one of the races in the results columns.

The name he'd settled on was Sunnymova, largely because this had already a public sound, echoing that of a famous film star, Nazimova, while being based, for the sake of continuity, on the Sire, Sonning.

But he pretended not to have considered the matter. He didn't want to pronounce the name, on which so much depended, then and there and risk Iseult asking, in her superior tone, 'Why ever that, darling? What on earth does it mean?'

32

H attended a dinner of the literary association that W. B. Yeats had lately founded. Among his fellow members were one or two who were what was called making a name for themselves in literary circles outside the country, especially in America, by presenting a view of Ireland that didn't conflict with the one already accepted there among the better-read, but at the same time that added some unexpected, but never disturbing, sidelights.

One of these writers H got on with well enough, though he seemed to have a small wireless broadcasting apparatus secreted on his person from which was repeated at intervals during whatever conversation was being carried on: 'Yes, you are in the presence of X Y, whom the distinguished poet Z compared to the famous Russian writer B and who, in the authoritative literary periodical C, was hailed as . . .' and so on.

He left early, thankful to be back in his mountain obscurity. As he entered the house by way of the back passage he caught something that Iseult was telling Ian as she bathed him. In answer, evidently, to one of the little boy's anxious questions, H, as he was passing the bathroom door, heard her say, 'You're more than anyone in the world to me.'

It was all very well for H to explain his wincing by telling himself that it was this emotional preying on the child that was making him even more nervy than he was already, but there was another more painful pang for him in what he'd overheard.

H went to his room and lay on his bed to review the situation. It was then he had the first indications of a new sensation in regard to his wife. Up to now when he thought of her while she wasn't actually present, it had been in the light of their beginnings and of the time when they'd been alone together in the cottage, even if it was to feel appalled by how much she, and he, had altered since then. But tonight he felt for her the beginning of what he didn't dare at once recognize as dislike.

Not that he didn't see clearly what she had to suffer from him. When he wasn't concocting his imaginary tales, he was deep in plans about the racehorse or else off to Dublin or London to meet his, in her eyes, dissolute friends. All she had was her patience cards and her cigarettes.

Only when she went for a walk up the mountain road and returned with a bunch of bogland weeds, tiny wild flowers, and feathery long-stemmed grasses that she'd found by the rock stream, did her face have the vivified look that he'd seen on it occasionally when he knew her first, in particular on the night she'd run along the canal and through the windy streets.

He sometimes thought of suggesting they get a suitable book and press the flora in it. But he didn't, and later he'd find the little bunch abandoned.

Instead, he took her to race meetings at which – it was a chilly autumn – her fingers, as he saw when she took off her gloves to half-heartedly mark her race card, turned bluish. Once, on the other side of the mountains, he lost his way and later she told him that she'd known when he'd taken the wrong road but said nothing so that they wouldn't, as usual, arrive too early. They missed the first race.

He spent much of his time in his room with his two fictional darlings for whom he had X rent a ramshackle bungalow in the sandhills. They had jobs in the kitchen of a seaside hotel and X often spent the nights with them. There was an Auxiliary from the camp further down the coast who also visited them and brought drink and cigarettes.

Summer night festivals à quatre with the girls slipping, via the sink, for a quick wash (what H wrote was 'sluice out' because he felt precision should balance the immediately following passages) from one to the other of the two beds in the room the four of them shared.

Their hands, winged by the memory of chains, played over his flesh till, like children unaware to what threshold their game has led them, they seemed to hesitate just before reaching the spot where they could arouse the most response, intensifying the expectation. Then the fingers descended with an utter unfamiliarity of touch, a coolness that might have come from the other side of the moon.

For X, existence had always only been separated from a state of nearly insupportable sensation by the fragile but tightly knit fabric of the material world. Wherever this wore thin he felt in danger of being exposed to one of the varying degrees of horror that it normally veiled. But there were areas behind the physical curtain where the exposure was to rapture, and the way to the commonest of these was between the couple of loose, stretchable stitches that had been left in that part of the fabric that constituted the body of a woman.

H's fiction tried to reflect the world in which ecstasy was never far from nightmare. X, standing beside the girls as the first Mass-goers arrived at the church, had heard an acquaintance mutter something about 'acting bloody Christ between the two thieves.' Now, holding one or other of them in his arms, he caught the dreamy bliss that softened her face and felt the laugh that rose from her belly as the Auxiliary murmured to his partner in the other bed, 'You sexy cunt!'

H began to think more and more of a room in Paris or Vienna, an attic, say, that he'd keep neat and clean, perhaps in the Praterstrasse or the rue Delambre, not far from the Diana Bad, or alternatively, the Dôme.

Let the filly, after they'd backed her, for the prize money itself wouldn't be enough, win a race in the spring, or let the novel have some success, and he'd be able to leave Iseult with the allowance from his mother plus what the poultry farm was making, while he would be having enough to settle in a foreign city and live there, say, a year, by when he could have written another novel.

H spoke of his longings to Kay, but not to Ian, who was already too aware of his parents' dissensions, on his walks with her while the little boy was at school, and, as a matter of course, she promised to pray for the success of his plan.

Reconciliations no longer came easily, nor did they bring with them the sweet, aching, humble forgiving sense of relief that they once had. They also lacked the healing, sensual balm. There were days on end when they didn't speak to each other and a dismal pall descended on the uncared for barracks of a house, casting its shadow on the children and especially Ian. As for Iseult, she went about the place in seeming oblivion, averting his glance when they met in the passages or on the stairs.

Driving along the road out of the glen after one of their rows, H was aware of nerves he hadn't managed to pull up and take with him whose ends were still in touch with, and registering the familiar vibrations of, all he was leaving behind. He depressed the accelerator and shot the car forward up the incline in his effort to break away. He had a premonition that all this – the wrench, the pain, the anger, the flight – was a foretaste of what was coming in an irreversible form. He drove fast, his face set and stony, his heart torn between past and future.

He'd sold the Peugeot and bought a six-cylinder Buick tourer, complete with side curtains, which, during the trial run, the owner had had to admit couldn't be coaxed above forty, a fault that H, listening to the exhaust, had privately diagnosed as a stoppage in the silencer and, getting the car cheap, had soon put right.

On this wet autumn evening the busy city reassured him and effaced some of the forebodings. He parked the car by the pavement and ran alongside the railings of St Stephen's Green and on to which the dark overhanging trees were dripping, sitting in it a minute or two, hearing an occasional larger drop splash on the hood, before banishing the impulse to drive straight home again.

H crossed the roadway to brightly lit Grafton Street. There was just time to buy, before Woolworth's closed, a card of safety pins, one of which he'd use to fasten a loose braces strap to his trousers, Iseult having neglected to sew the button on.

Having made the adjustment in the lavatory of the back part of a fashionable restaurant where meals were served at the bar, he climbed on a stool, with the evening paper, and ordered an underdone steak, the nearest thing he could get in Dublin to bifteck tartar.

He also asked for a Jameson, not that he set any store by a particular brand of whiskey but because the pronouncing of the name was part of the ritual, like his studying of the racing page as the white-jacketed barman placed the steak and pommes frites before him with the touch of deference that increased the illusion that he'd put his neurological imbalance, with its wild hopes, intenser than the factual kind of reality, feverish dreads, and ambiguities, behind him, and escaped, for a breathing space, into a secure, well-ordered world.

In spite of which he would have liked to be back in the room at the Hotel de Royal Bretagne watching the grey suds, while sniffing the soap scent, drain away in Lisette's wash-basin behind the pink, pleated silk, bamboo-framed screen and waiting for the long Paris evening to begin.

In the hotel on the Green to which H strolled after eating he recognized a dark girl sitting alone at a table in the lounge with a drink in front of her. She was an orphan brought up by two uncles, rich merchants, one of whom owned racehorses, and her Christian name, not the Irish one which he'd failed to register, but her once telling him Call me Molly, and finally her family one, O'Dea, came back to him.

'How is she bred?' Molly asked when he had made the, to him, dramatic announcement about his ownership of the filly, taking it, just as he'd hoped, as a matter of real interest.

'Matt Deasey trained her dam, a potentially fast mare who never quite came right at the proper time and place.'

Molly nodded into her whiskey glass.

'A first foal?'

'That's right.' He wouldn't admit that he didn't know.

'It's mares that, for one reason or other, never produce the brilliance they show at home on the racecourse that often breed really good offspring. As Uncle Rory says: "What's only realized in private in one generation often makes the public breakthrough in the next."'

These were the sort of considerations that, sent flowing through a consciousness strained by trying to assimilate too many ambiguities, threatening or stimulating messages, relaxed the tension.

What would be winter favourite for the Derby? H was glad to be beguiled by promises of a future rich with prizes snatched in the last few strides, by the golden glasses of smoky elixir, by Molly's pale, blurred face and eyes of the faded blue of a hot summer afternoon. He suggested Mahmoud, who'd finished third at Royal Ascot to the Bossover colt, later named Wyndham, that H had backed that memorable June day when he'd met Liam O'Flaherty in a pub just after reading the result.

Reassuring were the promptly appearing drinks, the talk of great races whose results were known and verifiable and, above all, Molly's robust body beside him, in which the final factual prize of the night was already promised.

When her Uncle Rory, who never read any but the sporting pages of the papers, heard that Mussolini had taken both Harrar and Addis Abbaba, that old worthy, who still kept polished brass spittoons in his study, had commented, 'Good for him, whoever the bugger is! It's time somebody besides the Aga Khan got hold of a few promising yearlings.'

H went with Molly in a taxi the short drive to her uncle's flat, continuing their talk of racehorses between the kisses which it seemed to him they exchanged as a further assurance that all was going smoothly, sweetly, promisingly, deliriously. After they got out, and as he turned from paying the driver, he saw she'd fallen flat on the pavement.

This seemed to him perfectly natural, being in that state that is isolated from normal standards to which to refer what happens, and he helped her up without comment.

While she got out her key she asked him to come up to the flat to undo for her the brooch that fastened her blouse at the throat.

'Isn't your uncle there?'

'He sleeps like a log. It's an awkward clasp and I'd bloody well prick myself.'

Take a good look at it, H thought with the seeming common sense in the midst of excess that was part of such drunken states. It appeared to have a diamond at the centre and a couple of rubies, at least the size of the one in poor Julia's ring that the Turkish ambassador had had to admire, at each side.

Inside the hall she paused to say, 'These lights will go off before there's time to get to the second floor if we don't look sharp.'

If you fall a couple of times on the way up, no doubt they will, he reflected, with satisfaction at the idea of an interlude with her on the stairs rather than having to risk waking her uncle, but they reached the door of the flat before they were plunged into darkness.

Once in her room, where he noticed a row of buff-coloured form books on a cream shelf, she sat on the bed and took off her shoes.

'It's these fucking high heels,' she said, 'that cause the bloody trouble.'

Later H recalled taking one of the shoes into his hand and pretending to examine it in order to hold on to something concrete against the pull of waves of oblivion that were now washing over him.

He had no recollection of unfastening the brooch nor of leaving the house. When consciousness returned he was gripping the starting handle and standing in front of the big, blunt nose of the Buick.

Whatever had taken place between him and Molly was gone in the mists of drunkenness. He paused, holding the starting handle, and made an effort to recall some detail that might then drag up with it from oblivion the rest of the precious moments. Because, if the memory of the time he'd spent in her room was lost, then all the reassurance the night had started by giving him was annulled too and he was back where he'd been when he'd left home the previous evening.

33

H took a break from his novel and spent a few days with Aunt Jenny. He knew that his visit both pleased and disturbed her. He brought a dangerous, unknown element with him into her careful existence. She asked him what she tried to make appear casual questions about himself, his writing, the children and, above all, the filly, which was what seemed to both excite and cause her the most misgivings.

And H was offhand with her. 'Oh,' he said, in answer to a question about the trainer's honest opinion of the yearling, 'he doesn't know a thing about her. It'll be spring before we'll be any wiser.'

This airy tone was very far from what H really felt. It was partly just because he shared some of his aunt's northern caution that he assumed it, repudiating, as it were, those tendencies in both of them he liked least.

At supper she didn't offer him any of the whiskey he knew she had locked in the big mahogany sideboard, one of the many antiques with which she'd filled the house, and even regarded him anxiously while he filled up his glass from the flagon of Australian burgundy on the table.

She was watching for an indication that he might be taking after his father. What irritated him was her tendency to fear only the obvious; her mind moved along narrow, predictable channels, whereas H knew that what he might have inherited wouldn't manifest itself primarily in alcoholic excesses.

He woke in his room at the back of the house to the sounds from the yard, the creaking of the handle of the pump, the cackling of the farmyard hens, as Aunt Jenny clanked the bright-scoured much-dented tin basin of mash on the cobbles, her voice, as she called them, rising to a peculiarly high, emotional pitch.

At breakfast H sensed that his aunt had something on her mind that had nothing to do with her avid but veiled curiosity about him and his doings. He thought he could read the not very varied moods that passed across her leathery, mannish face, the lower part covered with a yellow fuzz, and he knew she was making up her mind to some daring suggestion.

'It's not often you come to see me these days, Harry, and as there's racing over at Proudstown Park this afternoon I thought you might drive us there in your car and hang the expense!'

He was ready to go, although a nerve in him began to pulse with an uncomfortable throb as soon as he agreed. He knew that in racing, especially in buying the filly, he was seeking a substitute for the more vital risks that he didn't yet know how to take, even if he had the courage to.

He'd guessed for some time now that it was only through surviving perilous situations, such as his father, Lane and the others hadn't survived, that he'd gain the insights he needed to reach whatever degree of psychic and imaginative depths he was capable of, and be able to communicate these in his fiction.

The excitements and risks of racing, however minor, appalled him because of what he imagined them as a foretaste of.

Inside the enclosure his aunt's movements were painful to him in their slow deliberation. On the way to the parade ring she stopped to take out her spectacle case and then had to feel in both pockets of her tweed jacket before finding her race card. Once moving again, she stumped along energetically enough, but her short legs seemed hardly to be getting her anywhere.

For H the time between races wasn't long enough for all he had to attend to. After studying the race card, memorizing the colours of certain horses to be able to follow them in running as well as the names of their jockeys – matters still unfamiliar to him – noting the sires and dams, and other incidental information such as the owners and trainers, he had to decide whether or not to risk a bet. And all had to be gone into calmly and thoroughly against a background of increasing tension. When, with a sudden movement through the throng in front of the bookies, a last-minute move was made for one of the horses, with his aunt in tow he wasn't quickly enough on the spot. Not being in time to note the previous odds, he couldn't tell which of the new ones being chalked up had been shortened.

His aunt met acquaintances, neighbouring farmers, and men in the cattle trade, whom she stopped with a tug on their sleeves, though H may have been exaggerating her behaviour, to get tips from. Then, with further delay and an air of sharing a piece of valuable information, she'd impart to him what Mr X, or old Y, types whom H saw at once had neither the intelligence nor flair for successful betting, had told her.

The next part of the charade was the very deliberate extraction from her purse of a ten-shilling note which she smoothed out (had she crumpled it beforehand to delay the parting with it?) while telling H, with a reckless gleam in the upward glance she shot at him: 'I suppose I'm a fool, but I'm going to risk my maximum.'

H believed that before most races there were certain signs and intimations pointing towards one or two of the horses, and it was these that he tried to perceive and distinguish from the obvious indications such as short-priced odds, a tip such as his aunt had just had, the newspaper selection, that inclined him towards a popular fancy. When, for instance, during his study of the racing results, he'd noted, weeks or months previously, that a certain horse, though evidently not meant to win, had finished strongly, and later, at a meeting where this animal was a runner, he thought he saw signs of its being more seriously fancied, though still far from being favourite, H believed in betting on it. But if he failed to find these pointers, either because, as now, he wasn't given a chance of attuning himself to them, or because they seemed contradictory, it was then a matter of patience, self-discipline and forgoing a bet.

Having seen the horse his aunt had backed well beaten he was reassured, with that special racecourse satisfaction that comes from avoiding disasters taking place around one. But in racing, as on the deeper level whose inter-penetration H never lost the sense of, complacency brings its retribution.

Concluding that it wasn't an afternoon to try to win money, H relaxed and began to enjoy the peculiar pleasure – all racecourse pleasures are peculiar to that restricted white-railed world, as are its miseries – of being able to detach himself from the intense activities and anxieties in which he'd been on the point of becoming involved.

At one moment: peace of mind, self-congratulation, leisure in which to invite his aunt to have a drink, and perfect ease in which, in their slow stroll to the bar, to look out over the misty distant fields and even recall some lines of, he thought, Wordsworth:

> The holy time is quiet as a Nun
> Breathless with adoration, the broad sun
> Is sinking down in its tranquillity.

The next: running into Molly O'Dea and her Uncle Martin, not Rory, of whom he'd heard. Introductions, drinks, and, above all, the untimely distraction of sex. Sex was a counter-obsession to that of racing and, H thought, was as out of place on a racecourse as in a monastery.

Instead of the sherry H had meant to sip, it was whiskies all around ordered by Mr O'Dea who was wearing a pork-pie hat on whose silk lining when he placed it crown down before him, after the barman had quickly wiped the counter, H read the name of a hatter in Bond Street.

There was talk of horses, not just the academic reflection such as he and Molly had spent an evening over, but a disturbing discussion about what was going to win the next race, or run well, be in the shake-up, give an account of himself, beat more than beat him, trouble the favourite, for Mr O'Dea, like most regulars, avoided the bald statement. H could have still managed to dissociate himself from all this hadn't it been for a blow to his serenity from an unexpected direction.

While Aunt Jenny was deep in conversation with Mr O'Dea – a racehorse owner of substance and solidity, he was just the sort of person to impress her – Molly asked H, 'Did you make love to me after you saw me home that night?'

190

'I don't know.'

'We were both pissed!'

Where had the girl picked up these expressions of hers?

'Why do you ask?'

'I'm a bloody sight overdue and I've been racking my brains to remember when I'd taken any chances.'

His aunt turned to H to repeat something she'd just heard with a certain malicious glee: 'Mr O'Dea tells me the man you sent your filly to lost his jockey's licence in England some years ago.'

She was enjoying talking to somebody she looked on as an authority whose opinion of the Deasey brothers she was neither surprised nor, H imagined, sorry to find unreassuring.

After the two large whiskies, which he hadn't wanted, and with this worry of Molly's sprung on him, to say nothing of what old O'Dea might be telling his aunt about the Deaseys, though H had of course already imagined various ways in which, if so inclined, they could swindle him, H stood in front of the row of bookies with no trace of his recent calm.

How regain his carefree state? His feeling that a time of troubles and grief was setting in, for he was prone to seeing omens in all that happened on a racecourse, could be proved superstitious if he now had a substantial win.

If luck, as he supposed, was not at the moment on his side, it would be safest to back the favourite here, providing that other things besides the short price pointed to it. Not that he wasn't aware that, once nervously come to the conclusion that the favourite is going to win, and everything points to it through a defensive mechanism that dulls all but confirmatory perception in the mind's search for assurance.

He had the five pounds which he'd brought with him to his aunt's. After some vacillation, drawing back after actually stepping up to a bookie offering five-to-four against his choice, already evens on some boards, with the notes in his hand and replacing one of them in his pocketbook, H bet four pounds on the horse, a three-year-old called Captive Knight, another of the names he'd recall when far more illustrious ones had faded, to win five.

As soon as he'd had the bet, H wandered off on his own, not wishing to join the others till shortly before the race. He studied the clouds to see if the light rain was likely to turn to a sudden downpour, not that that could appreciably affect the going, nor did he know what kind of surface the horse he'd backed preferred, but with forebodings of future hazards added to the immediate ones. What was risked wasn't just the money. The sum, though in itself not inconsiderable in his present situation, was a means by which he probed both the near and further future. It was the lead the sailor swings to gauge the depth, or the sample bore a prospector takes from a mine. With the bet lost, crises not yet arisen or even divined would lose at least a fraction of their chance of a happy issue.

He met the others on the stand when the horses were already at the start and by the expression on his aunt's face, set and secretive – like his own? – he guessed she'd risked another ten shillings on the strength of some private information from Mr O'Dea.

He didn't ask her what she'd backed, not wanting to expose himself to the possible shock of hearing another horse preferred to his as he waited for the tapes to go up and to express his temporary relief by joining in the cry 'They're off!'

He turned to Molly, towards whom, unlike his aunt, he didn't feel on the defensive and, without a word, she offered him her binoculars. But he preferred his own sharp eye to the framed, foreshortened image he'd seen through the glasses.

H was to bet on the outcome of many races, long and short, great and small, English, French, and Irish Derbys, at Epsom, Ostende, Chantilly, Maisons Lafitte, Baden-Baden, Hoppegarten, Newmarket, the Curragh, and other courses, and there was always this revelation that unfolded in three stages.

First, the phase immediately after the start, distant and relaxed, which could still be viewed with comparative calmness. Then the second and intermediate unfolding when the pattern of shadowy horses and bright riders, against a background of woods, parked cars or wide plain, was still nebulously woven. In the third phase, lasting, say, from ten to thirty seconds according to the length of the race, the final picture formed with terrifying speed in its irreversible form.

Molly divined his loss, while he saw by his aunt's face, excitedly flushed a yellowish pink, that the other two had had the winner. He heard Molly accepting his aunt's invitation to come over to supper – her uncle's house was no more than half-an-hour's drive away – and the moment they were alone together she promised: 'Don't worry. I'll come over this evening and we'll sneak off somewhere so you can bloody forget about this even if we have to make do in the car.'

Sitting at supper between his canny, virgin aunt and the reckless young woman in the white silk blouse, with the brooch at the neck and pleated skirt, changed into from the tweeds she'd worn on the course, H was conscious of secret channels of communication between him and Molly, and delighted in the element of disruption she had brought into the orderly little house.

After supper they moved to the sitting room across the hall where Aunt Jenny, after what H saw was some hesitation, asked Molly if she'd care for a whiskey. Molly, who was standing with her back to the fire, for the dining

room had been chilly, accepted with alacrity, they having emptied the bottle
of Australian Burgundy at the supper table, and exclaimed, 'Uncle Rory
always told me:

> Never drink with your back to the fire,
> Never fight with your face to the sun,
> And always sit with your legs crossed.'

'By the hokey, that's a good one!' Aunt Jenny exclaimed. What evidently
made it acceptable was it being supposed to come from one of the O'Deas
whose praises she'd been singing all the way home in the car.

Tea was brought in and his aunt had H open the window at the top, close
the shutters over it and them draw the curtains while she made up the fire.

'Give Miss O'Dea some more whiskey, Harry,' she told him after he'd
completed the autumn evening ritual at the window.

He refilled Molly's glass and poured himself a smaller drink, aware of the
close watch being kept on the bottle by Aunt Jenny.

Molly entertained them with the reminiscences of her uncles, Martin and
Rory. These two elderly bachelors lived a life of old-fashioned luxury that
was peculiarly Irish, Martin with his horses, his trips to foreign spas, his
entertaining his trainer and parish priest to oysters and champagne; Rory
playing bridge and drinking brandy with his Dublin cronies and occasionally
travelling to Rome, with a stop at Paris and in Switzerland, to attend a
meeting of some confraternity (the Knights of Malta?) of which he was a
member.

When Molly had to retire, it was H she inquired from as to the whereabouts of the lavatory. As it was situated outside the back door in a small
yard to itself, he said he'd show her. On the way down the dark kitchen
passage she fell, toppling silently over with no fuss, and he helped her quickly
up without a word that his aunt might catch.

H waited to conduct the drunken girl safely back to the sitting room,
leaning with his back to the yard wall for what seemed a surprisingly
long time. He was about to call to ask her if she was all right, in case
she'd fallen again in there, when he heard her exclaim, 'The curse of Christ
on it!'

He waited, reflecting on the expletive rather than on what might have given
rise to it, a sign of some degree of intoxication in himself. The curse of Christ,
he recalled, was that pronounced on the fig tree that was barren. What on
earth was keeping her? And why had she taken her handbag with her? Had
it really been in case his aunt might have a look into it and discover a packet
of contraceptives? He wondered was she too far gone to keep her promise.

When at last she emerged the first thing H noticed was that the brooch was no longer at her throat. Not that she left him long in doubt about the delay, brimming, as she was, with good news. And, in his own highly charged state, the ancient annunciation struck him as rich with joyful accrustations gathered from ages. Women had been hurrying to their lovers, jumping out of stage coaches, emerging from privies of café toilets, bedrooms or public conveniences, with the good tidings for centuries.

He kept his arm around her on the way back to the sitting room, his own disappointment at their now not being able to snatch a few minutes together in the back of their car after she'd taken leave of his aunt being balanced by his sharing in her relief.

34

He spent much of the time he wasn't writing in reading the English and American novels he got from a Dublin library, looking for a writer who thought and felt differently from his fellows, but he didn't find one.

Part of his concern was because he saw his failure in his own novel to deal in any but the old currency, even if polished up a bit. He longed to take in his hand a bright new coin with a strange design on it.

Was there no contemporary writer of the kind of Baudelaire, Poe, Keats, Melville, Emily Brontë, Dostoevsky, Proust, or Kafka, to name a few, who because of alcoholism, sexual excess, tuberculosis, venereal disease, rejected love, condemnation, and banishment, as well as even more extreme isolation factors unnamed and unknown, acting on ultra-responsive neurological systems, had been driven beyond the place where the old assumptions are still acceptable? Nobody whose imagination had been so extended by personal disaster of one kind or another to glimpse beyond the present limits of awareness?

Ah, what a dreary waste of comment on prevailing social and psychological patterns! Accomplished angling of mirrors held up to the familiar faces to reveal new facets that the sophisticated reader could pride himself on recognizing.

The few celebrated forays were along trails carefully cleared for the reader in advance.

Joyce, although too much of a meticulous little filing clerk, had, Christ knows, had a kind of daring, largely technical it's true, but he'd taken risks that not one of his admiring fellow countrymen would dream of.

Hemingway had an attractive glitter, but his responses and sensibilities, or those of his characters, were woefully restricted. Eliot seemed to H to be weaving a fine web in which to catch gnats. The Spenders and Audens were innovators who knew just how far to go. Only Lawrence, who was some years dead, might have what H was looking for but, ironically, he hadn't yet got the hang of him.

At least there were hints of a running down, a coming to a stop. It was near the end of this long wet day and in the muggy twilight its decaying ideas were left sticking like sewage when the flood water falls to the underside of everything.

At last he finished the novel, wrapped the typescript in brown paper, sealed the parcel and took it, not to the small local office, but to Dublin where he watched it crossed with blue pencil, date-stamped, and safely put into the receptacle for registered packets.

It had become the focus of all his hopes, even the filly was forgotten, and he didn't rest till he heard of its safe receipt.

Then, mysteriously, his doubts about it, his endeavours to see it in a detached manner, disappeared, and it became easy to think of it as what he'd looked for and failed to find among the novels he'd been reading.

In sudden lightness of heart he scrubbed out his room, moving about the furniture, but later he saw that the release of energy and delight, as when he'd taken the baptismal bath at Glenmaroon, came from some purely subjective source and was not a sign that the novel was any good.

'A heavenly book,' Gollancz wrote. It was some years before H realized that this was Gollancz's way of saying that the novel had a quality of its own even though it wasn't strictly, successful, and wouldn't appeal either to most reviewers nor to any but a very few readers.

Iseult shared some of his delight, not grudging him the praise, though she disapproved of the tone of the book and remarked that 'heavenly' was the last word to describe it.

In his freedom, with time on hand, H wrote several letters and, in reply, got one from Liam O'Flaherty in London telling him of evenings at the Plough and mentioning an Irish steeplechaser called Royal Danieli that, all being well, would win the Grand National the following March. There was also one from Julia in which expressions of a hope that she would see him soon were mixed with theatrical gossip. H decided to go to London after Christmas on the half of the advance from Gollancz; the second half would be paid on publication.

But when the lamps were lit in the dark of the early morning and he saw the tree standing in the sitting room, into which the children weren't allowed till after Mass, in the shadowy expectant hush, H felt what it would be like to be safely and sweetly within a united family, the family in turn encompassed by the Church.

After Christmas, with winter pressing in from the mountains and intensifying the sense of familiar seclusion inside the house, the children got flu and Iseult moved into H's more easily warmed room with them, and he slept in theirs.

One evening when they were all gathered there, Miss Burnett having gone off somewhere with her doctor friend, while his mother had been reading out, and it came to the good-nights, Ian suggested H move back, asking whether, with the four beds arranged in the firelit room, 'It wouldn't be very homely, Daddy.'

Iseult agreed; it was just what she would have liked, the domestic non-sensual intimacy. H hesitated, tempted to carry back his bed and erect it with its head to the wall close to where Iseult had hung an old stone holy water font, from the Pyrenees, above Kay's, with Blossom's dark coat ashine in the glow from the coals, the lamp turned low, the wind in the fir trees along the steep drive.

But something made it impossible. If he was ever to have experience, in his ordained degree, of what he thought of as the nature of reality, he had to be in the exposed place where such could reach him. Those enjoying sheltered existences received comforting intimations about the relevance of their beliefs which, for their continuing peace of mind, they had fiercely to defend. For him, all cherished faiths were suspect; an inner fluidity and refusal to attitudinize was the only valid mode.

The night before H was going to London they were again gathered in his former room, the children, nearly recovered, propped up in their beds.

His mother was reading to them in her habitual tone of voice that never attuned itself to the changing sense of the words, whose very monotony, however, for H at least, conditioned to it from his own childhood, gave a peculiar strong atmosphere to the story. This one, called 'The Last Lodge' was about an old beaver, the last of the colony to leave the cunningly constructed home by the wide river at the approach of the lumber men.

Coals shifted and revealed glowing caverns beneath the bars, the two china dogs, brown and white, shimmered at each end of the mantelpiece in the yellow lamplight, and the fair child-faces were rapt.

H was engrossed too by the wide stream flowing through the silence where nothing had ever changed but the seasons, with the coming and going of the salmon, modulations in the tone of the wind, until the first sound of the axe was blown on the breeze.

The old beaver was alone as the first of the lumberjacks came around the bend in the river with their gear of destruction.

H experienced an agony of doubt. The old ambiguities were present again, confusing his thoughts. Was there a poison in the sap in his cells that prevented him accepting the natural and humble task of staying with Iseult and, if not loving her with the love that was itself an inner revelation, trying to reassure her?

35

If Iseult had asked him that evening not to go to London, if she'd said something like, 'Let's complete our journey hand in hand,' he'd have taken her in his arms, he believed, and promised to turn over a new leaf in her regard. But partly because of her natural haughtiness and partly through the emotional channels between them having become blocked, she couldn't, he knew, do so.

The following evening, reflecting on these old and melancholy matters, H stepped over the brassbound lintel into the first-class smoking saloon and saw Molly at one of the anchored tables with an elderly gentleman – the uncle he didn't know.

In answer to Mr O'Dea's invitation he said he'd have a bottle of stout.

'Take a brandy, lad, it settles the stomach.'

'They've put up the shutters,' Molly added in way of confirmation.

Whose stomach? What shutters? He was thinking that whatever Iseult might have said wouldn't have availed in the end, because the shared emotions that had cemented their marriage were already falling, like the vital mortise from a fatally cracked building, from his memory.

They were going to London, Mr O'Dea was telling H, for 'the little lady' to do some shopping and see a few shows.

'We're putting up at the Berkeley; what about you?'

'Mr Ruark is a well-known writer, Uncle, and has a whole lot of friends over there with whom he can stay.'

Mr O'Dea nodded, but H sensed he'd gone down a degree or two in the old fellow's estimation.

After a couple more brandies Mr O'Dea retired to his cabin.

'Let's get out of this bloody place,' said Molly 'and breathe some air.'

They opened the heavy door on to the deck and it clanged shut as they lurched up the sudden wooden incline that rose before them. Molly, who lost her balance so easily when drunk, was now the sure-footed one and took H's arm to guide him along to the front of the ship.

H told her about having finished his novel.

'Are you pleased with it?'

'Oh, in one way I'm enchanted with it. But, all the same, I know that I'm not yet capable of uncalculated risk.'

'What's that?' The wind was making it hard for them to talk.

'I don't yet know how to risk all I have to give.'

This girl who seldom read a book would know instinctively what he was trying to say. It was something he wasn't sure if even Yeats would grasp.

She and her uncle were travelling first class on the train so H parted from them when they disembarked at Holyhead, having arranged to ring up Molly at her hotel.

He was glad he wasn't with them on arrival at Euston where the first figure he saw in the lit murk of the platform was Julia, looking chic, with no sign of oversize breasts in her winter attire. Though he'd written to say he was coming, her appearance at such an hour was unexpected.

Associating this winter morning with the one years before – sixteen? seventeen? – when Iseult had failed to meet him, he couldn't but feel the falling off in the quality of the experience.

But kissing her and smelling her scent again, with the medicinal whiff in it he'd once likened to ozone, there came the thought that there was no more desirable spot than under the beige cover of her big divan.

'Had a rough crossing, darling? You look quite green,' Julia told him as they went to look for a taxi. Evidently meaning: 'It doesn't suit you at home.'

Instead of her address in Hertford Street where he'd hoped they were going, after which there was time enough for him to find a place to stay, she gave the driver the name of a hotel.

'It's an inexpensive little place I found for you not far from me in Mayfair.'

This wasn't at all what he'd had in mind. At this exhausted hour of the morning, he reflected, sick people die and lovers experience the longest, sharpest orgasms. After the train journey, full of steamy vapours and harsh clangings, surrounded by indifferent strangers in the mechanically vibrating compartment, the background had been so far away from the sensual that it now came flooding back with a shock.

Julia chattered on, her eyes sparkling, china-doll face tilted at the slightly upward inclination that came, he thought, from playing to the dress circle, and vivacious, though he was never sure how far the vivacity was also a theatre trick. He didn't touch or kiss her again, not wanting her to guess how nervously impatient he was; all must wait till she was safely in bed and he emerged from undressing in the narrow hallway.

She didn't ask him about the divorce, which, from his letters, she'd probably guessed wasn't going to come to anything, but mentioned a mews house that she'd seen and hoped to move into (with him?) after the panto-mime finished its run.

H left his suitcase in a modest looking room in the little hotel, whose name was the same as a famous one not far off, which was something that would weigh with her, while Julia talked with the proprietress with whom she seemed on good terms.

The taxi had been paid off on her instructions. H would have sooner driven to the flat than waste more precious time in walking the remaining distance, however short.

Through the hall where the porter didn't stop his vacuum cleaning to greet them – he wouldn't, H guessed, get lavish tips from Julia – up in the mirrored lift and, at last, into the room with its big couch, which he saw with a sinking heart she had made and neatly spread with its gold-embroidered coverlet before setting out to meet him, and the off-white table lamp, matching the bookshelf and just a shade off that of the telephone, which she'd left switched on.

H waited till she'd taken off her coat, hung it in the hall, and was sitting in the big armchair, before saying, while trying to keep the desperate urgency out of his voice, 'Come to bed, Julia.'

'Let's wait till tonight, shall we, darling?'

In his anxiety her refusal came as a defeat, although his reason told him her disinclination was only for the trouble of undressing, swathing herself in garments she wore at night, at least in his company, and afterwards the going through it in reverse plus having to make her face up again. He knew by now that sex in itself meant little to her one way or the other; she looked on it as a means of keeping happy those who, for other reasons, she needed.

Then what, for God's sake, have we hurried here for? H wondered despondently.

He could have breakfasted with the O'Deas in their suite at the Berkeley. Or, better, on his own at the Lyons at the corner of Tottenham Court Road that was open all night, while gradually absorbing the feel of being in London again, which because of the other preoccupation he hadn't had time for.

It appeared she'd plugged in the electric ring in the bathroom on which she boiled the kettle when she'd gone to hang up her coat; and she said the tea and rolls would be ready in a few minutes. After which she suggested he go and rest in his room at the hotel till she called for him at lunchtime; she was taking charge right away. But H was far too worked up to be able to spend this first morning in London which, though not, as Vienna, a magic winter city of bluish snow with coupled-together tram cars circling the Ringstrasse with their exciting articulated movement over unfrozen tracks to the clang of bells, offered secret excitements below its teeming, savage surface, in resting.

He took a bus to Chelsea and found his friend, Liam, in his room at the address in Sydney Street just getting into the jacket of the dark blue suit, with the paler blue stripe, that H always admired as suited to the lithe figure that had the air of having a coiled spring secreted in it just between the shoulders. And as if the springiness extended to its extremities, O'Flaherty was having difficulty in brushing smooth his fair hair, remarking that it never lay flat till late in the day.

Knowing that his friend worked every morning, starting punctually at nine, no matter how late he'd been up the night before, H explained he'd only come to announce his arrival.

'What about your girl? Haven't you been to see her?'

Though H had never taken Julia to meet O'Flaherty, aware that they wouldn't have got on, he quickly surmised such things.

'Oh yes, she was at Euston to meet me and we had breakfast together.'

'Good God, Luke, then you rushed off and left her! What's the game? How come?'

H couldn't have explained what made him adapt to Julia's alien ways when all would have been easier with Molly. It was no use telling O'Flaherty, who was impatient of anything savouring of mystification, that what he wanted wasn't an easy relationship of shared instincts. As far as it was clear to himself, he wasn't for the present seeking a comfortable sexual or emotional integration with a woman. And the constant shocks and collisions with almost incomprehensible attitudes that he experienced with Julia were what his psyche needed.

He asked about Stroud and the other habitués of the Plough. O'Flaherty made a grimace.

'Harold has surrounded himself with a lot of refugees from Germany, *canaille* for the most part.'

Up to now H had only the vaguest idea of what was happening in Europe, of what was happening anywhere outside his own intense world.

Before leaving H got an address of a lodging house just across King's Road where a room might be vacant, O'Flaherty himself having moved out after some objections to his late-night entertaining.

H took a bus to Charing Cross Road whose black, glistening, traffic-polished, petrol-vaporous expanse of roadway, with its extension, Tottenham Court Road, still evoked in him his sense of London more than any other street, because of the associations: the night when Iseult had told him about her relationship with Ezra Pound and he'd hung around the late-night cafés, the evening he'd strolled with Polenskaya from the Coliseum to Trafalgar Square.

He called at a small shop he remembered off Cambridge Circus to have his hair cut, and as the clipper buzzed at the back of his neck the barber repeated one of the current Hitler jests.

In the crowded semidarkness H approached the row of bookmakers. When he was near enough to see that the price against Ferryboat had shortened to five-to-two, and couldn't immediately calculate what he stood to win at these odds, surreptitiously feeling in his pocketbook again, he added another five-pound note to those in his hand.

In the few moments between wagering half the sum he'd received that morning and the traps flying open, he'd hoped that the tension would fleetingly expand the frontiers of his thought so that certain things about himself and his work, and especially its direction, that no amount of quiet meditation could illuminate, might become clear. This had semiconsciously been what had finally induced him to make the bet.

The race itself was a crude affair compared to the three subtly distinct phases of a horse race. The dogs streaking out of the traps after the hare rattling and sparking on its electric rail was a blow in the solar plexus. He was just getting back his breath when the fawn, stripe-jacketed dog bounded into the lead along the back stretch. Coming to the last bend a red-coated, brindled greyhound edged in between H's dog and the rails, and his stomach muscles contracted in an effort to propel his dog from afar.

He was hollow in the middle, sick and exhausted, when it was over and the last glimmer of hope extinguished; it was his bladder, as usual, that took the first shock. He was on his way to relieve it when he met the others coming from the bar. Without appearing to scrutinize him, her eyes lowered, her pale face perfectly composed, Molly asked: 'What won that bloody race? No, don't tell me, let's concentrate on the next.'

H touched her arm, detaining her while the others pushed their way on through the crowd.

'Wait for a minute.'

He led her to a spot by the wall near the entrance to the 'Gents' where she'd be out of the way. While he urinated, mingled with the physical relief was the deeper one of having her there just around the corner to return to.

That's better, he thought, everything's already better and soon all will be well and all manner of things will be well. He'd have to return here in a few minutes, though; his bladder quickly filled again during these nervous states.

He walked with Molly away from the crowds between the main stands and the track where they could stroll undisturbed. But whether it was H or Molly who turned their steps in that direction, they were soon back in front of the bookmakers. This was the race in which Brady's bitch was running but Molly said she'd no intention of backing it.

They were one in their rejection of Brady and all his works. By now H knew he was going to try to recoup his loss, but he was determined to persevere on his own. He couldn't imagine things ending well for both Brady and

As H sat in the white sheet at the barber's, he felt like someone who, as the doors are being shut and the curtains drawn, is left outside. Fleetingly he was reminded of the sense of apprehension mixed with the conviction that he was where he had to be that he'd experienced when he'd stood, as X in his fiction, beside the girls that Sunday morning.

That evening Julia took him to the Windsor Dive in the courtyard of Victoria Station to eat before going to the theatre just across the street, and had him order steak and kidney pie, with a cooked oyster on top, and a half-pint each of ale served in metal mugs.

'What about your novel, Luke? What does Victor Gollancz think of it?'

'He doesn't know what to think, so he says something nice about it. He has an idea that if he's patient, and meanwhile doesn't actually lose money on me, I'll once write something that could add to the prestige of the firm.'

'So you will. I'm sure of that, darling.'

Like his publisher, she had the Jewish instinct for picking winners, but H was afraid he might let them both down.

He saw the pantomime from a seat beside Mrs Jenners in one of the front rows of stalls. The curtain rose on a village street of crazy-looking, gaudily painted houses, where richly apparelled revellers were strolling inside pools of gold and silver spotlights.

The orchestra, its leader a big, handsome, tough Norwegian-Canadian to whom Julia introduced H in her dressing room one night and whom H supposed had been her lover, struck up a popular tune of the time, and Julia came tripping out, girlish, petite, coy, accompanied by the boldly strutting principal boy, whose calves and bottom bulged in tights below the short, bespangled cloak. Throwing a shapely arm over Julia's white-powdered shoulder, the Prince whispered to her a résumé of the plot while Julia stood on tiptoe, tilted up her face and gazed, her eyes alight with Belladonna or some such sparkler, towards the upper circles.

'A damn pretty girl,' a military-looking gentleman beside H remarked.

Later Julia sang a song in front of a drop curtain of a formal garden, while the main scene underwent one of the frequent transformations, with the comic lead, a fat schoolboy in an Eton collar. Her pseudo innocence and his greedy precocity formed a welcome and titivating interlude for the middle-aged fathers with their offspring.

> The ghost of the turkey
> Goes on gob-gob-gobbling,

he sang. And then, as the fat boy made a grab at her, she danced out of reach to the refrain of:

I know what you are thinking,
And what is on your mind.

'I was afraid these knickers were too short,' Mrs Jenners commented, 'I'll bring another pair tomorrow,' more to herself than to H.

Was a glimpse of bare thigh above the top of Julia's stockings when her short skirt twirled high as she pirouetted not an accepted part of the sly allusions to sex, all the cruder and more exciting for being pseudo-accidentally glimpsed in the course of the childish fairy tale, H wondered?

36

H went to the show the following night and home with Julia afterwards, getting up again and fumbling into his clothes in the cubicle of a hall and trudging the short way, with a 'Good night, officer' to a policeman he passed (to reassure himself that all was well?), to his hotel.

A letter from Gollancz was on his breakfast tray with a cheque for the first half of the advance of his novel. Its receipt so soon after his arrival gave him a sense of contact with the busy daytime life of the great city from which, as a stranger, he'd felt excluded. Now he walked through the congested, fumey streets around Covent Garden where Gollancz had his office, and the W.C.1 on the street nameplates reminded him that here in the magic heart of the City he also had legitimate business.

From the post office in Bedford Street he rang up Molly and made an appointment to go with her to the dog races at the White City that evening. The idea of trying to double or treble the amount of the cheque he'd just gone with a secretary from the office to his publisher's bank to cash now pre-occupied him. He was conscious of unfamiliar energies released in him that he might well put to use. Coming fresh to the dog races inspired by the sense of monetary success, he believed he was capable, while the rather precarious state of heightened perception lasted, of picking a winner.

At the track Molly met an Irish couple she knew, a man who had a greyhound running and his girl friend.

'Don't worry about the first couple of races,' Brady told them. 'It's the third my bitch is in.' He took a roll of notes out of a trouser pocket, abstracted one and gave it to the girl, pointing to a name on the first page of his race card.

'What are you backing?' Molly asked when the girl had gone to queue in front of the totalizator windows.

'That's just to keep Eddie occupied. She gets worked up when I've something going.'

A youth slipped up to Brady from behind and whispered over his shoulder. 'Be back in a jiffy,' he told them, 'wait here for me.'

'Where's Dan?' Eddie (Edwiga? Edwina?), who came back a moment later, was asking.

When Molly told her of his sudden disappearance, she made a grimace and said: 'That means he's gone to have a bet after all. It's bad enough when he has a lot of money on a dog of his own without risking it on one of the duds a buddy tells him clocked a fast time at a trial.'

Brady reappeared after the first race and insisted on buying them drinks, though from the look of him H couldn't tell if he'd won or lost. His pale, narrow face had the repressed, tight-lipped expression H had noticed on the bowed faces of young men coming back down the aisle after receiving Holy Communion in churches at home.

Telling Molly, who in the most unlikely situations, he'd noted, managed to look Madonna-like, he was going to have a look around and slipping into the crowd before she could suggest coming with him, H made his way through one of the tunnels that emerged on the strip of concrete in front of the track. The bookies, electric bulbs clipped to the tops of their boards, were chalking the prices against the names of the six dogs in the second race.

Having spent most of the afternoon with an evening paper going through the fifty or so greyhounds engaged in the eight races, comparing their previous recorded times, weights, ages, and manner of racing – quick or slow trappers, wide-runners, or tending to hug the rails – he had finally, out of the mass of unaccustomed details and measurements, been drawn to a dog called 'Ferryboat'. Almost all the hidden signs he had laboriously and lovingly deciphered, contradictory and confusing in respect of the others, had pointed to this one. Drawn No. 6, that is to say in the outside trap and wearing the striped jacket, Ferryboat was in this coming race and had a 'three' beside its name on the illuminated blackboards. What it came to was this: A] Was he to risk seeing his possibly unique inkling, plus intimations he'd had that he was at the start of a financially lucky period, wasted? B] A success in this entirely new sphere would give him the resolution he was soon going to need to take certain decisive steps. C] A win would cancel the sense of guilt at spending money here in London that Iseult needed at home, quite apart from what he would soon require for the monthly training bill for the filly.

But the impulse that finally made him take out his pocketbook, withdraw the envelope from the inner compartment and slit it open with the end of the pencil he was using to mark his race card, was an obscure one, and more compelling than any of the other reasons.

himself, he had the feeling that their paths wouldn't run parallel even for one evening.

In spite of his distrust of favourites, H decided to back a dog called 'Glittering Dew' whose price had just come in to six-to-four. He took the envelope from his pocket and extracted the remaining twenty-five pounds under Molly's eyes with none of the furtiveness with which he'd made the previous wager. There was a difference between that one and this. In making the first bet he'd been conscious of some extravagance, now he was already halfway to the gambler's painful sense of having no alternative.

He handed up the five five-pound notes and received a ticket in exchange, after which the bookmaker rubbed out the 6–4 and substituted 5–4. Molly made no comment, either then or up to the moment the race started, beyond murmuring, 'Trap No. 2' as she studied her card when they'd climbed into the stand.

H was calmer than before the previous race. This wasn't only because of having Molly beside him but because he was now facing the possibility (probability?) of a complete debacle.

As soon as the dogs flew out of the traps Molly kept up a running commentary which was partly obscured to him in the last seconds by the shouting of the crowd: a belly roar directed at various dogs by their backers.

'Come on No. 2! My sweet Jesus don't let that fellow through on the rails. There goes my lovely blue boy . . . nip in now on the bend, Jesus, Jesus, Jesus, it's a fucking beauty! Christ, the darling!'

A quick calculation: twenty-five at six-to-four is thirty plus the twenty-five stake is fifty, odd, fifty-what less twenty-five lost is – let's see, which, for the love of God, left him down on the fifty he'd had in the envelope to begin with! But not much, or perhaps not at all, for he was mixed up. With Molly beside him sharing in what is always the sweetest of triumphs, that snatched from the shadow of disaster, twelve five-pound notes and a few single ones were counted into his hand, relieving him of the need for any further mental arithmetic.

On their way to the bar, where they met the disconsolate Bradys, though the young man's face had still the look of a communicant, H regarded the moon. While all else had been moving at high velocity, the greyhounds, whizzing around, his heart beating at a terrific speed, his thoughts racing, the old silver snail had crawled no more than an inch nearer the roof of the opposite stand. What, if anything, he asked himself, was the relevance of this realization? The relativity of all timing devices, psychological, clockwork, lunar, cosmic?

37

Julia suggested they spend a weekend in the country; was she hoping they'd make another appearance in the gossip columns?

H called for her after the show on Saturday night and they caught the last train from Paddington. There was no hotel car to meet them, a failure to see to which on his part upset Julia, not, he thought, because of the walk from the station, but because arriving on foot and apparently unexpected, having to wait outside till somebody came down and let them in, wasn't how the sort of weekends that got into the popular papers started.

The place was as he'd expected: panelled walls, oak beams, burnished brass and copper; their room chintzy, with a lamp in the form of a galleon on the commode beside the double divan, cream-coloured radiator under the leaded windowpanes.

Julia, over her annoyance, was enchanted, but hadn't she been here with the others before? She kicked off her shoes and padded about on the carpet, preparatory to retiring to the bathroom across the passage with towels and a silk, zipped bag containing, he supposed, bath salts, cosmetic removers, and her medicaments and bandages. When she reappeared in a scented aroma and a pink nightdress, she thrust the bottle of bath salts into his hand so that, late as it was and disinclined as he felt, he had to go through his part of the ritual.

Later, the lovemaking came as an obligatory part of the observances as, after breakfast on Sunday, did a cross-country tramp.

Julia started to talk about the world crisis which H, after seeing her read the leading article in one of the 'quality' papers at breakfast, supposed comment on at this time of a Sunday morning was the next part of the canon.

'Are you still a Fascist, darling?'

'A Fascist?'

'Remember what you wrote in my copy of your novel?'

Ah! What on earth was that?

'In commemoration of the day when General Franco reached the Mediterranean?'

Had he had a purpose in adding something like that after inscribing the book to her? Considering the incident seriously, he supposed he had meant to suggest that the only side to take was always the one considered most unpardonable by the circle in which he found himself, in this case that of most intellectuals with a sprinkling of enlightened politicians. There was the further suggestion, hidden, he was ready to concede, from anyone but himself, that the collapse of all these commendable attitudes and faiths, including the cherished ones of those present, was a precondition of imagining, let alone starting to construct, the altogether different kind of society, nearer his largely subconscious dream.

'I suppose at the time I thought it was funny.'

Julia didn't answer and H knew quite well that his own position – whatever it was, and that was only slowly becoming clear to him – was beyond her; though she was by no means stupid or unperceptive.

'We didn't come here to discuss the international situation.' She laughed and turned her wet, porcelain face towards him.

'One must keep informed,' she said. 'Do you know who came round after the show last night? Donald McLaren, the Scots M.P.'

Had she come across these people, including the Turkish ambassador and General Gombōs, at the country houses where she'd formerly spent weekends?

'What about turning back?' H, who disliked walks, suggested. Julia glanced at her watch.

'We can circle round and come home by the old millpond (she'd studied the map in the lounge before setting out) which is all that's left of the original village.'

She had it timed so as to arrive at the hotel at the correct hour to appear in the bar for a leisurely half pint of ale in pewter tankards.

After lunch it was comme il faut for them to retire to their room, pull the chintz curtains and, after she'd been to the bathroom, lie down together on the bed.

She seemed happy to be here in his arms in the smart hotel, and when he kissed her Dresden-shepherdess face it was not just an automatic sexual response. He looked on her as a rather conventionally minded, adaptable girl who, against all likelihood, had set her heart on him. And because they had nothing in common the efforts she made to achieve contact touched him.

When they came downstairs to tea and muffins in the lounge Julia got hold of the Sunday literary supplements and read out to H items she thought of interest.

'You know, Julie, literature would be better served if there was an interdict on all mention of it in the papers.'

She gave her tinkle of a laugh, ready, he saw, to find his remarks amusing in the manner, say, of Oscar Wilde's epigrams, if he gave her a chance.

'But your novel got quite a lot of attention in one or two Sunday supplements, Luke.'

'All the worse for it! What attracts respect are the novels that either help to hide what contradicts the prevailing assurance or those that by delving a precalculated way below the surface provide a few safe thrills.'

He talked on to show her he was serious, and her round face with its china-blue eyes and dimpled chin became attentive. He thought it was her Jewish flexibility that enabled her to listen to what must seem outrageously silly attitudes with good humour.

Up in their room that night when she came from the bathroom she said, after switching out all but the lit sails of the model galleon, and taking off her pink peignoir, 'It's been the nicest weekend I've ever spent.'

Unused to hearing anything but dismal remarks from Iseult on any of the outings they'd undertaken together, he was pleasantly surprised. He clasped her in a hug that came nearest to ending in a shared orgasm they'd yet achieved, careful not to crush her breasts.

38

Deasey agreed to give the filly an early run and her name among the list of entries in the *Irish Racing Calendar*, where it appeared some weeks before the race was due to take place, seemed of greater moment than his own at the head of a review of his newly published novel.

Not that the notices didn't interest him, but, as he'd told Julia, there was something self-defeating in the system. As soon as a book was placed, alone or with others, in the space reserved for reviews it became an exposed and, in proportion to the degree of its quality, slightly ridiculous object.

A communication from an underexplored area of consciousness, reached partly by accident and partly because of earlier traumatic experiences, addressed to anyone who might be somewhere in the same neighbourhood, telling of the exciting shifts that take place there in familiar perspectives, such a piece of imaginative fiction, though with its own inherent consistency, wasn't meant to stand up to a public examination by literary accountants.

Meanwhile a caller had come to Dineen, introduced himself as Herr Scheffler, and invited H to go to Germany to give readings from his novels under the auspices of a body called Die Deutsche Akademie. Iseult approved. 'It'll get you right away from your stale old friends and surroundings, including me,' she remarked.

Now that there looked like being a respite in the life of friction between them, it seemed that what patience Iseult had had ran out and she couldn't refrain from showing her disapproval more openly. And H, while waiting to hear from Scheffler again and for the filly's first racecourse appearance, spent much of the time in his room reading.

A book that he bought secondhand on the quays in Dublin by a writer he'd never heard of came at this critical moment, as he sensed it would turn out, to his help. It was a collection of recollections, musings, and aphorisms called *Solitaria* by a Russian writer, Rozanov, first published in 1912. Glancing through it he saw that it had been suppressed by the Tsarist censor as 'too outspoken in matters of sex and Christianity' and, at once, though short of money, paid the four-and-six (reduced from fifteen shillings) that it cost.

H found that Rozanov had always dissociated himself from the attitudes of his time that 'everybody of importance', his fellow writers in particular, shared. And this wasn't just pride or perversity, although there might have been a touch of these too. Rozanov had an instinct, only partly conscious, the demonic spirit being half asleep in him, that only a response to new situations and events which was unforgivable by his associates would have any final relevance.

All his life, Rozanov wrote, a mysterious attention, not quite his own, controlled him and drew him towards things that surprised him and were often contradictory.

Rozanov had married Paulina Suslova who had been Dostoevsky's mistress and the prototype of the 'proud' girls in his novels. This marriage hadn't lasted long, but it wasn't Rozanov's complicated personal relationships that interested H so much as his complex and flexible psyche that, far from being one of simple opposition, was drawn in conflicting directions. Taken to a meeting of the newly constructed Soviet Parliament, he had shouted on entering the crowded hall, 'This is extremely interesting. Show me Lenin and Trotsky; I am Rozanov, the monarchist.' But the monarchists were alienated by his unorthodox reflections on Christianity, as well as by the attraction he felt and expressed for certain Jewish customs.

The tension between H and Iseult was growing, and it shed a shadow over the whole house. He would have telephoned Scheffler about speeding up the arrangements for his German tour had he not determined to wait to see the filly run at the Phoenix Park. Then Miss Burnett on her afternoon off brought her fiancé to tea and the young doctor, refusing the drink that H offered him, explained that he'd given up alcohol, having just returned from a monastery where he'd gone for a cure. He told them frankly about his stay there, and hearing that anyone was welcome at the guest house (there was no charge; it was left to visitors to give what they could on leaving) H decided to go there himself for a week.

39

As soon as, after a long, solitary drive in the Buick, H entered the big house, formerly the residence of the owners of the estate, he was struck by the emptiness and silence. But for some overcoats hanging in the bare stone hall the place could have been deserted. There was a smell of last year's wet leaves and an aroma of coal smoke that became for H, with a whiff of incense from the church, the pervading breath in which the memory of his stay there was preserved.

The white-robed monk took him upstairs to an uncarpeted room with two beds, two chairs, and two old-fashioned washstands, on one of which was a toothbrush and tin of tooth powder. On the table in the middle of the bare boards lay a book bound in black which H noted was St Teresa's meditations on the *Pater Noster*.

The retreatants rose before dawn and crossed to the monastery church to attend the chanting of Lauds with the monks in their choir and returned there for the other offices at intervals during the day. There were silent hours in the guesthouse parlour before a coal fire where H read *Solitaria*, while the others perused their books of devotion, and the black-suited young man with whom H shared a bedroom and who had for a time, he told H, been a novice in another order, was bent shortsightedly over his St Teresa.

What pleased H in Rozanov was that he could write, 'I love peace so much... and the sunset, and the quiet pealing of bells.' This clinging to the old tranquillities while being drawn into a vortex of painful experience was a neurological condition that he understood very well.

On the third or fourth morning, as they dressed in the semidark without switching on the light, H asked Delaney the question that was on his mind.

'As soon as the last of the early offices has been said,' his roommate told him, 'one of the monks will come from the choir and wait in a confessional until Mass in the public part of the church is over. That happens like clockwork every morning of the year, whether or not a penitent presents himself.'

It was exactly as Delaney had said. As Mass began, the door in the grille separating the monks' choir from the public church opened and one of the community appeared, cowled and grey-bearded, arms folded and hands thrust into the wide sleeves, bowed from the waist towards the altar, and entered one of the confessionals.

H waited. None of his fellow retreatants, nor any of the small group from the women's guest house outside the grounds, made a move.

Had not Delaney who was kneeling beside him nudged him, H's nerve might have failed and prevented him getting up and following the monk into the confessional.

Once inside with the grille opened, he announced the number of years since his last confession, but then broke off to say that there were obstacles to his presenting himself there as a penitent in the ordinary ritual. The monk told him to go on, and for the first time H felt he could express himself about his rather obscure ideas of religion to somebody who presumably had a fairly deep knowledge of the subject.

'Like, I suppose, many others who come to you, I'm aware of being alone in the haunted room of my mind,' H whispered. 'That's why the promise of Jesus to come and dwell with those who love Him has always had such an appeal. It fascinated me for a time and I made a study of the mystics to find out if the promise had ever actually been kept. I see now that that was too academic a way of going about it. I'm not temperamentally a sceptic, Father, my mind isn't analytical and is open about the nature of reality, including the possibility of a kind of super-spirit crossing the otherwise barred threshold of the combined wonderland and cesspool of my consciousness. And for a time the account of Jesus' extraordinary end, from the Last Supper to the Crucifixion, seemed to me to suggest that He indeed might be such a spirit. Of course there have been others who experienced even more extended periods of horror, but there are no reports of anybody with a neurological make-up so receptive and vulnerable who seems to have gone deliberately as far into the depths with the expressed purpose of gaining admission into other minds and hearts. And even if this is looked on as a myth, for me, as a writer who believes in the truth of certain fictions, that is irrelevant.'

He paused in the recitation and the monk said: 'Tell me something about your personal problems.'

'That's what I'm trying to do, Father.'

'You're saying that you've lost your faith?'

'No, that's not exactly what I intended. The promise may have been fulfilled in the past, or even today amongst contemplatives living as you and the monks here do. But for me if anyone could share, even for a couple of minutes, my consciousness with me it wouldn't be the Catholic Jesus. My psyche is beyond the sort of sweeping-out and simplifying that would make it a possible place for such a meeting. This is partly because of the extent and complexity of its pollution, but it is also because of the way His official interpreters present him. What I need, Father, isn't the Christ at present preached by the Church but intimations of a spirit more (at least imaginatively and potentially) perverse than myself, one that has had the experiences

I can only guess and tremble at, who bears not only the signs of the stigmata but of the most terrible traumata as well. I shall always need, and to that extent believe in, the possibility of the companionship of such a spirit, but if there is such now and in the future, it will be, for those like me, an occasional great artist.'

'What you're saying is that you do not lack faith completely?'

'Perhaps not, Father, though the stressing of faith rather than need puzzles me.'

'Tell me one sin for which you feel shame and repentance.'

H was silent for some moments. Had the old monk grasped anything at all of what he'd said? Though it required a painful effort, H frankly described, if not in any detail, his indifference at the time of Dolores's death to his wife's suffering and that of the baby.

'Perhaps I should add, Father, in case I'm here under false pretences, that I do not usually attend Mass or receive the Sacraments.'

'One question. Are you trying to enlighten or reprove us, or are you asking for absolution?'

'Not to enlighten or reprove, that's the last thing in my mind. I'm going away soon, I'm leaving home for a time, and I had an idea of getting things into some sort of order in my mind before what may be a new phase of my life.'

'You're leaving your wife?'

'We've already left each other in all essentials.'

'Have you another woman?'

'No. Though when I was in London recently, I took up with a girl who came to look up to and believe in me. Although we'd nothing in common I let her think the reverse. Then, when I supposed I'd come to the end of what she could give me, I cleared off.'

'Not because you wanted to put an end to the adultery you were committing?'

'That aspect of the affair had no relevance for me, Father.'

Somewhat to his surprise H heard the monk pronounce, not his expulsion from the confessional, but the words of Absolution.

A short interlude of tranquillity, the last for many years: rising in the dim bare room at five-thirty with the terse text (Eternity is long, life on earth but a moment) not quite decipherable on the wall, the green-bound Rozanov on the deal table beside the black volume of St Teresa's essay on mystical prayer, the short walk across the gravel and wet leaves in the pre-dawn dusk to the choir of the abbey church, the pale, hooded shadows, in the dimly lit stalls, the chanting of the psalms and the long (to H) periods of silent prayer, the shallower silence of mealtimes in the guesthouse, the huge roasts of beef and ham, the wire net ladle of glistening, freshly boiled eggs.

Each morning after receiving Holy Communion H knelt by one of the grey stone columns tentatively and uncertainly repeating, 'My Lord and my God.' It was not so much a prayer as the uttering of a sound with which to try to plumb the vastness and possible emptiness of the space into which it dropped.

If all religions, H reflected, should be myths, does that invalidate the experience of this moment? The whole cannot be less than its parts. Reality is nothing if not our most intense imaginative concepts of it.

But these ideas quickly faded and what remained was a new awareness, especially in the dim mornings and shadowy evenings in guesthouse and choir, moments like jewels gleaming, while the psalms were being chanted, the Salve Regina sung, he read a passage in *Solitaria*, or silently ate supper with the others.

40

Time was running out, it seemed to H, not only in the outer world, but everywhere he turned, in the silence of his room at home, in the imagined speed at which the days were passing before his trip abroad; he even came on the same sense of the tempo accelerating before the end in what he was reading.

This was a biography of Keats, and H could trace the process there as having begun with the publication, almost completely ignored, of the poet's second volume of poems, followed by his plans to become a surgeon on board an East Indiaman, which, of course, had come to nothing; another haemorrhage, the booking of passages to Italy on a sailing barque by Severn; farewell to Fanny, and the composition of the 'Bright Star' sonnet, all within the space of weeks: the swift intensification of a short life transforming itself into legend.

On the purely practical level change was also in the air.

'You'll have to get another assistant when Miss Burnett leaves next month,' his mother told him. She knew more about the girl's plans than either he or Iseult.

'Is she getting married, then?'

His mother nodded with compressed lips and a glance at him that he knew meant that Miss Burnett was marrying her doctor in spite of the fact that he was on the booze again.

'I'll probably get rid of the poultry,' he told her. The idea had suddenly occurred to him.

'Get rid of them!'

His mother's mouth remained open as if he had announced the end of the world.

Several possibilities were running through his head. The money he'd get for the laying and breeding stock, the huts and appliances, would keep the filly in training while he was away and until well into the summer by which time if she hadn't won a race, war hadn't broken out, or he hadn't found a suitable means of supporting himself elsewhere so that Iseult could keep what his novels were now earning, he'd sell the filly too and get a job anywhere he could away from home. The money he was being paid for the readings couldn't be taken out of Germany.

When Iseult asked him hopefully about the monastery and it seemed they might be going to communicate with each other for a change, it soon became clear that they were as many miles apart as ever.

They were soon discussing the Church's attitude to sex which Iseult defended by arguing that Christ had shown the same wariness towards it.

'What would the average priest have made of the girl who "didn't cease from kissing", dropping her tears on, and wrapping her soft hair around, His feet?' H asked.

Iseult screwed up her eyes and averted her face, as much, he thought, against him and his ideas as against the smoke from her cigarette.

'If the Church had had its way,' he went on 'instead of slipping out of the sepulchre in the dark to keep the extraordinary tryst with this same woman, He'd have waited until a more reasonable hour to give their Eminences time to breakfast and get there, headed by the Archbishop of Dublin, in full regalia to receive Him and introduce Him to those of the faithful worthy to be presented to the Founder of their Club.'

Far from giving him any satisfaction, these jibes of his, however effective, emanated a sourness and inner dissatisfaction. For however he rebelled against what generally passed as the acceptable norm, as he'd told the monk, his was not an unbelieving psyche. What it needed, he thought, was a concept of reality deep enough to lose itself in.

It was simply that he wasn't impressed by any of the contemporary ideologies or institutions, religious, national, or social, and there were few of his acquaintances he looked up to. In this connection, however, he recalled an afternoon a couple of years ago when walking along the Strand he'd met a fair young man with glasses called Hilliard, the son of a clergyman from the north of Ireland, whom he'd been in the same room with at one or two Dublin parties without really taking in. Meeting a compatriot, and moreover one from his own corner of the island, he had stopped and asked Hilliard to have a drink in a pub near where they were standing.

Certain things were still clear, the rest completely shrouded over by time. H knew the exact location of the pub where he'd never been before nor since, but nothing of its interior. Hilliard had asked for a Guinness – that was also impressed forever on his memory because of what happened subsequently – and had had no money to offer H a drink in return. He told H he'd left the Belfast slum where he'd been engaged on some kind of missionary work and, against the wishes of his family, was on his way to Spain to fight in the International Brigade.

They had left the pub and had walked a few yards down the street when Hilliard stepped aside, bent over the gutter and vomited a black stream into it.

He'd made a light-hearted apology, something about drink on an empty stomach, and they'd parted. Later H had heard that Hilliard had been killed in the battle of the Ebro, much later still he was to hear from somebody in Berlin of how Hilliard had died in his arms.

Hilliard had been killed on the Ebro, and H honoured and admired him, but that wasn't where H should have been killed, supposing such a sacrifice hadn't been beyond him, because the Ebro wasn't his destiny, wasn't, that is, the place where the risk and hardship were of the kind that he needed for his imaginative growth.

On the day of the filly's first race H drove to Dublin in the morning and stopped at one of the garages on the outskirts to ask if they'd buy the Buick while Iseult waited in it. The mechanic came out with him, took a look at the car and said:

'We'll give you a fiver.'

'All right.'

Having pictured being paid for the car and enjoyed in advance the sensation of putting the extra notes into his pocketbook alongside the few already there, H found it hard to refuse. His sense of money wasn't abstract or mathematical. He'd never have made a businessman who deals with figures in ledgers. H had to have something tangible in his hands to know where he was.

'Oh, no. It's worth far more than that,' Iseult exclaimed. 'Why, we've just driven up from the country in it and it runs like a dream.'

The mechanic shrugged his shoulders and H drove on. At the next garage he was offered four pounds which, without waiting for Iseult's reaction, he accepted.

On the tram that brought them the rest of the way into town, H saw that Iseult had taken what seemed to her his giving away of the Buick as another affront.

She had on her oblivious face, as if wrapped away in a realm where neither he nor others could impinge. And as he expected, she soon expressed an anxiety to see her mother, though it had been arranged she and H were to have lunch in town together and then go to the Phoenix Park where the race meeting was taking place.

'You don't mind, Luke, if I spend the afternoon with Moura? I'll meet you at the bus this evening.'

'No, of course not, Pet. I was only taking you to see the fruit of eight months' severe financial strain and much nervous tension. It is naturally of no consequence compared to hearing your mother in her tragedy-queen getup, deep in the dark of her woodowhid (after the Keats biography he'd been rereading *Ulysses*) hold forth on Hitler versus the British Empire.' Not that he actually gave expression to any of this.

'Any luck so far, Mr Ruark? Mick heard a whisper about the last winner, a pity I didn't see you a little sooner,' H was greeted with by one of the Deaseys on the course.

The brothers had the same deprecatory laugh and the way of talking about anything except the matter in hand.

H wanted to ask: 'Where's the filly for Christ's sweet sake? Has she arrived safe and sound and ready to run for her life? And what about your brother? I've got to see him before he goes in to change.' H had registered his colours as Ruark Tartan, gold cap.

But all he did was remark as casually as he could, 'Everything O.K.?'

'The little filly, is it? (as if H had been referring to the moon). Mick's over in the stables with her.'

In excitement that was internally self-combustive and not liable to being switched off by any of the Deasey brothers, least of all the somewhat slow-witted Tom, H made his way through the crowd to the bookmakers' broads.

The figure on all of them against the filly's name was twenty. Not a single hundred-to-six to be seen, no indication that her (by H) long-awaited and dreamed-of appearance was causing the faintest stir.

H had an impulse to approach a bookie he knew, hand up the four pounds from the sale of the car and say, with an offhand nod of greeting, 'Eighty-to-four Sunnymova.'

He wanted to see the filly's price cut all along the row, and then he wouldn't be sure that the hundred-to-six or perhaps even hundred-to-seven was entirely due to his bet, and not the result of a whispered word from Mick to a friend.

Plenty of time, he told himself, though his inner ear caught a muffled sound from his own inner recesses like a stopwatch ticking away, or, an instrument being ground, first one side, then flip, the other against a stone.

He waited at the parade ring till the filly was led in, last but one of the fifteen runners, the actual last into the ring was the favourite, and at the very first glance he saw how much condition she carried. Still somewhat concave on top, her belly seemed to bulge.

It dawned on H – what he should have realized at the time of the trainer's quick acquiescence in his suggestion to give her an early outing – that Deasey would in no way hurry her preparation, and had brought her here to humour him.

He waited till the jockeys appeared, filing through the gap in the white railings and gathering in the centre of the ring where the owners and their wives stood chatting with their trainers. He no longer hoped for a word of encouragement from Matt Deasey, but he wasn't going to let him stand alone out there in the too new looking tartan blouse and with a drop on the end of his long nose under the peak of the bright yellow cap; most of the other colours were faded and in washed-out shades.

'Mr Ruark,' Matt said, touching the cap with his whip and smiling his deprecatory smile.

'She looks a bit backward,' was all that H ventured.

While Mick held the filly, Tom gave Matt a leg up, and H watched as she was ridden towards the gate to the course. The view from behind of her sleek quarters, where the lack of fitness showed least, undulating to the delicate lift of her hooves, and, above, the dark greens and blues of the silk rippling across the jockey's back, caused him an aching soreness as if the sound of honing he'd heard had actually been that of a blade sharpened against his chest. He had looked on the race at what seemed to him the end of his youth as a token of what was in store. To see the filly fall back after two or three furlongs and trail in at the end of the field was a failure and defeat and an intimation of further ones.

'I didn't knock her about,' Deasey said as he passed, carrying his saddle into the weigh room, where H was waiting, half-hoping to hear something in the way of an explanation for the sorry display, though he'd known none could be expected.

The setback started H asking himself some vital questions: Who, and where, was that person, faithful and true, who might act as supreme and ruthless arbiter in distinguishing the real from the hallucinatory? He imagined a sallow-skinned figure in a forage cap (instead of halo?) wearing a long military overcoat (in place of seamless robe?) and mittens. If a leader, not of a Party, if secretary-general, not of any Praesidium, even less of an Arts Council. H saw himself flanked by two sponsors (Lane and Hilliard?) as he was brought before the tribunal.

'What does he want?'

'The painful truth, Little Father.'

41

H called in at the Plough Tavern the first of his couple of nights in London en route for Munich, and found Stroud at the table where, with him, O'Flaherty, and others, H had spent many magic evenings.

It was a sign of the changed times that those with whom Stroud was sitting had foreign ways and expressions and H, after greeting his friend, went and sat alone at the bar. Soon Stroud came and joined him, thrusting his bony wrist from the sleeve of his navy blue double-breasted jacket, that for H also belonged to those halcyon nights, laying his hand on H's shoulder and regarding him affectionately and shyly from behind the strong lenses of his glasses.

H didn't want to slip into the old ways with Stroud on false pretences; before, that is, he'd got out what he'd come here to tell him, after which it would be harder. So he said straight off, 'I'm on my way to Germany to give readings at universities there.'

There was a short silence while Stroud stuck a forefinger inside the collar of his shirt and twisted his long neck this way and that. 'You, as a writer, Luke,' he then said in his slow cockney, 'have a special responsibility to your fellows who are being persecuted and having their books burnt.'

H didn't reply. It was hard to explain that his first responsibility, though he wouldn't have chosen the word, was not towards the victims of organized injustice, who had more effective champions, but, as he'd tried to explain in his novel about the girls tied to the railings, in defence of the indefensible and in questioning the unquestionable. When H didn't answer at once, Stroud uttered the fatal word with a wry grimace of his long thin mouth.

H felt a shudder that ran down his spine. There had always been certain names that branded and singled out those over whom they were pronounced, varying from age to age: Heretic, Terrorist, Traitor, Jew. New anathemas were being added: Fascist, Nazi.

'What you, with your confused feelings don't realize,' Stroud was saying, 'is that anybody who seems to condone the German regime even by going there to give talks at universities shares to some extent in the guilt.'

H hadn't eaten all day and on another level to that of the conversation was preoccupied by the thought of a moist lump of fine-minced raw meat with an egg yolk on top, and surrounded by piquant condiments, that was making his mouth water; he was waiting for a suitable moment to suggest they go to Schmid's in Charlotte Street.

'*Are* my feelings confused? I think they're clear enough, although hard to express because they're out of keeping with the prevailing ones.'

When it came to his turn to buy the drinks, H asked for whiskey. If they drank something stronger it might help to lessen the gulf that discussion couldn't bridge, and also relieve in him the pressure that his failure to explain himself to Stroud had built up.

This, though, was dangerous. As long as he was alone with Stroud, his friend's natural gentleness would restrain him from provoking a row. But if a stranger joined them, one of the refugees with their perfectly natural delight in everything English, he might come out with aggressive remarks.

However, perhaps through Stroud heading off anyone who showed signs of coming to join them at the counter, they remained alone, H getting drunk and waiting until he could slip off to Schmid's, while Stroud's only sign of intoxication was that his neck seemed to grow longer and his glasses, which he was polishing ever more often on a very white handkerchief – he told H he bought a new one every morning at Woolworth's – more misted.

Waking next morning in his cubicle of a room at the Hotel Royal (9/6 bed and breakfast, 'Our best intent is all for your delight' – Shakespeare – in Gothic script on the oak panelling of the foyer) H was glad not to recall anything 'bad' having happened.

After getting through each of the items on the menu that were not alternative choices – porridge, kipper, bacon and eggs, toast and marmalade, milk and coffee in lidded, metal, heat-misted pots – the hangover taking the familiar guise of early-morning well-being that would later leave him high and dry, he rang up Julia.

There was no reply from the Hertford Street flat and he tried Mrs Jenners who told him that Julia was in the London Clinic where she'd had, or was yet to have, H never got the details of what he was told on a telephone straight, an operation to correct the malfunctioning of some gland.

'What about visitors?'

'Pardon?'

He knew his voice, taken in Ireland as English and here as Irish, came indistinctly out of the phone.

'Can she see people?'

'Just myself and a few close friends. Others can leave flowers and messages.'

Ha! thought H, one in the eye for me! Mrs J who, having had to humiliate herself for her daughter's sake while Julia was hoping to marry me, can now show what she thinks of Paddy Whack.

He refrained from asking how to get to the hospital, which he did at the desk in the hall where there was also a flower stall where he bought some roses; having purchased his ticket to Munich in Dublin he had now only to pay his hotel bill, forgo lunch and possibly supper, with luck keeping a few shillings for a light refreshment on the train.

After a wait while a porter made inquiries, H was taken to Julia's room on an upper floor. Sitting up in bed supported by an adjustable backrest, in a pale fleecy bed jacket, her fair hair burnished and bound by a ribbon, eyes sparkling, china cheeks flushed, she looked as radiant as she had on the Victoria Palace stage; no grudges nor resentment.

H laid the superfluous flowers, the room being full of them, on the table and, as she flung out her arms in the little theatrical gesture that brought back everything about her, he stooped and kissed her, much as he'd done every night before leaving her flat in what seemed those far-off days.

When he said he was going to Germany she didn't show surprise or disapproval and her only reaction was to ask if he thought there'd be a war.

'I doubt it. All they'll do here is make protests and let things slide.'

'Don't get caught there if there is one, darling.'

Queer that Julia should casually mention a possibility that had just begun to preoccupy him.

'If you were well I'd take you with me.'

Her laugh tinkled out and she gestured towards one of the bunches of flowers and a bowl of fruit.

'There's someone who'd have something to say about that.'

What H first felt was a slightly unpleasant shock, and only a second later relief at the sick girl having found another lover, perhaps a real fiancé this time, in spite of the ruby ring still on her finger. Had she sold it back to her Jewish jeweller and got her new admirer to buy it from him again?

'We wouldn't have asked him, Julie.'

She tilted her fragile doll's face to him from the white hospital bed, disconcertingly unfamiliar after her broad, brocaded couch, and he saw, or thought he saw, that what she was intimating was that no new fiancé, no matter how distinguished – for that's what attracted her: some kind of distinction, not wealth – could have stopped her saying yes. And making of the German trip an extended version of the weekend they'd spent together.

When he'd left Julia he'd broken the last London links and was on the verge of something new, with his face turned to the dangerously unknown. He paid his hotel bill, left his suitcase at Victoria and spent the time before the boat train left in the vicinity of the station having his hair cut. At the barber's he was told a 'dirty' joke about Hitler's moustache and some itching powder that Goering had sprinkled on his girl friend's pubic hair before entrusting her for an evening to the Führer.

After the night and day in the train, H read the placard 'München Hauptbahnhof' which, like all such signs at the end of foreign journeys, immediately became a magic incantation opening a door to an unknown realm, got out of the train with his suitcase and a folded copy of *The Times*, as prearranged, and was greeted by a handsome young man who introduced himself as Dr Hofner.

42

As their taxi crossed Karlsplatz, H caught a glimpse of the plane trees around the foundation. Sitting beside the director of the Deutsche Akademie, he recognized from the legendary past the sacred grove where he'd come in the mythical-seeming days of his youth, his thoughts full of poetry, the Russian dancer, and Iseult.

H awaited anxiously the moment when the German would count the foreign notes on to the hotel bed where he was sitting , so that from the only armchair, for he was in the unaccustomed position of the one being honoured, H could stretch a hand and have them safely in his pocketbook. His last square meal had been breakfast at the Hotel Royal and he was still obsessed by the thought of the bifteck tartar, not having persuaded Stroud, who it appeared was boycotting the place, to come to Schmid's with him.

Even more anxiously was he awaiting an indication that he'd been invited here because someone in authority (Dr Hofner himself?) had recognized in his novels elements too unusual to be welcome in the traditionalist milieu of English writing, in spite of being aware of the probability that he'd been asked because of the lack of others willing to come.

But what Dr Hofner was showing interest in was life in the English countryside, talking of summer holidays he'd spent there with friends.

'We'd like to live in a cottage in Somerset, my wife and I.' Good Christ, Somerset! But at least, if he was apt to cling to hopes that had become obviously untenable, of which a recent example had been considering backing the filly despite the evidence of his eyes, he was quick at readjusting himself at the last moment.

Dr Hofner asked H if he'd any photos of his home and family and H showed him a snapshot of Dineen castle with its sham fortifications and another of Kay, shy and barefoot on the lawn, holding up with both hands at breast level a tin plate on which was a small unrecognizable object. The German studied the two photographs, his handsome, ascetic face grave and intent. Then, after returning them, he produced a bundle of spotless hundred-mark notes, secured by a rubber band, as well as a slip on which he'd jotted down the payments for the readings already arranged in Munich, Berlin, Cologne, and Bonn.

All the crisp, strangely tinted notes in his pocketbook – at home four or five pounds had been a lot of money to have on him – gave him a sense of freedom. He could go where he liked and do what he wished, with only the three or four dates to keep. He wouldn't delay here after his talk in this Munich where, while the sham Florentine palaces needed redecorating and the façade of the big hotel where Polenskaya had stayed was peeling, big barracklike buildings in what he supposed was the 'clean', Nordic-graeco style had arisen.

It was Berlin that attracted him; the old Europe where he'd lived through his private intensities had largely vanished and he must turn his back on that background to his dream and see where he'd find a new one. Nor did the audience at one of the palaces where he gave his reading strike him as having come to hear about the opening of other thought channels through imaginative fiction. On the contrary, judging by those he met at the reception afterwards, including a well-known woman novelist, the creator, he was told, of charming child characters, they were there in the expectation of a reassuring message that all remained secure and well with the world of English letters, and to hear it in the authentic accents that they revered as those of an unchanging order.

The excerpts he'd selected from his novels, though listened to politely, didn't go down, especially the long one about the ménage à quatre in the seaside shack and the two girls with their shaved heads. Had he really imagined the attitude to accepted principles, as expressed in these scenes, might find a response among what he had supposed were some kind of social revolutionaries?

Not that they weren't delighted to shake hands and exchange a few words with him in English in the tapestried room, with painted ceiling and mirror-bright parquet where coffee and rich pastries, eaten with spoons, were served. Only Dr Hofner's wife, another tall attractive girl – but where had he seen one already? Ah, in his evocation of the vanished past, at the Hotel Bristol, Vienna – spoke to him with understanding.

'You weren't prepared for all these anglophiles?'

'Well, no! I half-believed in a fantasy about a small group of advanced young German writers having suggested inviting me as somebody with something of his own to say.'

'Oh, nothing like that,' she laughed. 'I'm quite sure nobody bothered to read your books. Novels aren't of much account here just now.'

'What about you, Frau Hofner? How do you get on here?'

'I just keep quiet and let them say, "She may not be bright but she's beautiful."'

Who were 'they'? The people in the room? More likely her husband's colleagues at the Deutsche Akademie. H hadn't yet got the hang of the setup.

H walked with the Hofners, and a couple of their friends who'd been at the reading, through the streets, and they showed him the newer sights or 'signs of the times' as Brigit Hofner called them. One of these was the Ewige Licht, the perpetual flame that burnt on the colonnade of a public building in front of which some of Hitler's first followers had been killed marching with him in his abortive Putsch towards the government troops in the square at the end of the street. There was always a guard of honour at the spot, posted day and night, Brigit told him, and as they passed the helmeted sentry with the SS insignia at his shoulder the others flung up their right arms, hand extended as if releasing a dove, in the first 'Heil Hitler' salute that H had witnessed.

H took the Berlin express next morning and as dusk fell it cast a further veil over the unfamiliar landscape through which he'd been passing for much of the day. A stretch of almost total forest darkness was drawn back to reveal a twilit plain where an airplane was standing, its blunt nose tilted eagerly, sniffing the evening sky.

Just as he was beginning to catch signs of the approach of the unknown city, the compartment lights went out leaving only a blue bulb burning on the arched ceiling, and an official passed down the corridor saying something that, slowly and distinctly repeated to him by one of his fellow travellers, H understood to be the announcement of a trial blackout.

A foreign darkness shrouded the platform at which the train drew up, and there would be no question of looking for the assistant director of the Humboldt Klub whom Dr Hofner had said would be at the Anhalter Bahnhof to meet him. H followed the dim figures in front, expecting to emerge into the subdued glow of the city, having had an idea that air raid precautions meant no more than the extinguishing of advertising signs and, at most, of alternate street lamps.

But the only difference in the darkness outside was that it was decorated at what seemed a great height with small violet spots like Christmas tree ornaments sparkling in the upper air while, at ground level, pinpoints of light pricked the blackness beyond the station steps. After a while he saw that the lamps of cars, fitted with shades in which were narrow slits, were indenting the night with these moving scratches.

After groping his way once around the square in front of the station, H found what he thought must be the entrance he was looking for, and fumbling his way through the blackout curtain inside the door was told at the dazzling bright reception desk that it was indeed the Habsburger Hof. A room with private bath had been engaged for him and he switched on all the lights, turned on the taps, and, surrounded by the bright mist, lay in the hot water and looked into himself. He tried to determine by the quality and content of the fantasies evoked by his coming here, which was his way of judging the state of his psyche at any given period, what he was seeking. Was it an acclaim that he failed to achieve at home? In this context he imagined being called for in the morning and driven in a black Mercedes with the crooked cross flying from its front mudguard to the Chancellery.

The Furore – H adopted a system that he believed was phonetic for difficult German words – cap visor pulled low, hands clasped in front of him, as in the newsreels, announced:

'My patience being exhausted by the timidity and conformism of our writers in the Reich, and Thomas Mann having at first had the courage to take himself off like a man to Switzerland, but now degrading his calling by hailing Roosevelt as his saviour, I asked my advisers at the Kulturministerium...'

The long wail signalling the all clear, or Entwarnung, brought him back to the bright, steamy bathroom. Was there anything in this preposterous little fiction that gave him some secret satisfaction? Could he swear before the highest tribunal, the one he evoked at moments of truth, the last time being that evening at the Park races, that this particular fantasy and any others of the kind he looked on was pure farce?

Suddenly, still in the bath, he had an intimation that it was not his innocence or guilt in this respect that was going to matter one way or the other. If he had to experience certain extremes of isolation and exposure the question as to whether his future judges were right or mistaken would be largely irrelevant. He had a foreboding that where he was going was towards a situation in which he'd be distinguished not by acclaim but by the brand of dishonour he and Lane had discussed long ago, and the final finding, pronounced by the terrifyingly faithful and true Arbiter would depend on his acceptance.

As he was dressing, Herr Eberstadt, of the Humboldt Klub, rang up and, in a cultivated English accent, inquired as to H's safe arrival and suggested a short sightseeing tour of the city.

'Though there's not much here of architectural interest. Nor can I take you to any counterpart of Soho or Montparnasse, but there is a café in Kurfürstendamm, where we might have a coffee, that has a rather amusing decor and some quite charming candelabra.'

Good Christ! murmured H.

He declined, on the pretext of having urgent letters to write, arranged to be at the Humboldt Klub in good time for the reading the following evening, and sitting at the big desk that was part of the room's ponderous style of furnishing, studied a map of Berlin he'd bought at the reception counter. He then set out on foot, not trusting himself to the buses nor wishing to get involved with a German taxi driver and the complications when it came to the fare, for the famous Kurfürstendamm.

Although it wasn't on his way, H turned down Zimmerstrasse shortly after leaving the hotel in order to take a closer look at a boarded-up front a few doors along it. The name above was one that, although German, struck him as having a further distinctive character, and as he walked on he saw several more broken and barricaded windows in a street that by now he knew had been a Jewish business quarter.

H, who could best deal in particulars rather than generalities, tried to imagine what he would feel had the names over the damaged shops been Isaacs, Gollancz, and Mogadori (his school-boy hero), those of people who had been his friends. Was his being here a betrayal of them?

The message that reached his conscience from his deepest nature, from what he felt were the genes on which his being was constructed, suggested that he had to experience, in his own probably small degree, some of what they suffered, and, on one level, even more, because he could not claim their innocence. He had long suspected that his destiny bound him to them in a manner more obscure than that of their present defenders such as Stroud. He also realized that he would go to certain lengths in association with their persecutors, in violent reaction against the mores of home, thus ensuring that his condemnation would not, unlike theirs, arouse any sympathy.

The detour brought him back to not far from where he'd started, and, setting off again, he came at last by various streets, many of whose names were to come to have close associations for him of one kind or another, to the boulevard with the narrow strip of lawn down its centre (for the squat trams), its wide pavements dotted with showcases, fragile bubbles of even brighter light in the general dazzle, outposts of the shining shop windows deeper back from the street.

H once recalled his first sight of this busy, luminous thoroughfare when picking his way through the dangerous littered laneway of a later year, and wondered if somebody less preoccupied with his own immediate concerns might have felt a chill at nightmare glimpses from the future.

He did not take in details, not wanting to have to use his outward eye or do anything, apart from glancing over the lit menus displayed by café and restaurant doors in search of his favourite dish, that would distract him from his dreamlike investigation of the city.

During the walk back to the hotel he wandered off down a long street that led into a less prosperous district and, as it started to rain, his sleepy glance, deceptively so in some respects, genuinely unalert in others, lit on a photo in a shop window at a corner where the street, grown darker at this end, seemed to terminate in an iron bridge over a canal or river.

The picture of the girl's torso in the shadowy window, unlit except from the street, with its twin dynamos of sexuality, suddenly connected him with the sensual world from which he'd been shut off and distracted. Standing in the drizzle half-turned from the window, he let the shock through his thoughts as though for the first time; after a period of counter-preoccupation, the fact of sex always struck him as almost incredible. He was realizing once again in astonishment that under their public clothes and behind their seemly façade women are constructed for the most unseemly and sensational act imaginable.

He then turned to take another look at the photograph, short-circuiting reflection with an inrush of direct sensation.

Arriving back at the Habsburger Hof tired, damp, and hungry, but with his private well-being restored – apart from sensual deprivation he'd been living too publicly recently – he entered the hotel restaurant and sat down at a table by a heavy curtain drawn across the room to screen off the part unused at this late hour.

The first item that caught his eye on the printed card was the dish he'd been hankering after in three cities.

43

H bought a dictionary and phrase book. Woefully inept at speaking foreign languages, he began memorizing a few colloquialisms. This he did by ignoring the complicated phonetics of the phrase book and transcribing the greetings, inquiries, and comments into his simplified system of pronunciation.

On meeting friend or acquaintance: 'V gates?' If the other got in with it first, the appropriate comeback: 'S good.' A slightly more formal greeting: 'V gate s een n?' On parting: 'Alice good.' And so on.

This meant he'd never come to think in German, but that was the last thing, as a writer, he wished to do.

H arrived early, as always, at the Humboldt Klub, a building situated in the wooded park that divided the city in two called, though H saw no animals, the Tiergarten.

He was shown into Eberstadt's office where, of course, he'd no need of his painfully learned alternative greetings, for the tall blond young man (how come he wasn't like everyone else here with any pretensions to education, apart from the 'Furore' whose simple Herr was a kind of special distinction, a Doktor?) spoke a cultured English. H knew none to compare with it, for

Iseult's accent was still French, his mother's peculiarly her own, O'Flaherty's West End accent had a Gaelic tinge, Julia's a Kensington mew, Stroud's a refined cockney, and his other friends a more or less Irish intonation.

Eberstadt surprised H by taking from an antique, glass-fronted bookcase the little volume of privately printed poems that had won him the laurel wreath which he'd been crowned with by Yeats.

For this German, he was the Irish poet instead of the English novelist that Dr Hofner had recognized him as, and that was how H was introduced to the audience in the lecture room among which he noticed a couple of uniforms, one, if he wasn't mistaken, that of a general.

The unexpected presence of this high-ranking member of the Wehrmacht disconcerted H. However, he started on his introductory talk as planned, mentioning his long walk around the city that had ended at the shop window in which the photo of the woman's torso had brought him back to the private world of his novels.

He was trying to intimate that the true purpose of fiction was the moving in on unoccupied areas by the imagination and their incorporation into small new aspects of reality. His only concession to the presence of the general was the military imagery.

He passed quickly to the reading proper, starting with *I Won't be Wearing Shamrock on St Patrick's Day*, and introducing sixteen-year-old Siobhan, his heroine. She is one of those rare and unfortunate creatures whose neurological make-up does not adhere strictly to the pattern. A lacuna in, say, some series of nerve cells had let outside signals into the closed circle of normal consciousness. She developed reactions to her particular environment that deeply disturbed her family. When they spoke to her of 'the Faith' and tried to teach her the catechism she substituted, apparently in all seriousness, for the hallowed incantations, blasphemies such as 'I believe in the one True Cat.' This was not pig-headedness, but an instinct to elevate the humble and innocent. She had an affection for animals that, by Irish rural standards, was itself a symptom of weak-mindedness. She endures all sorts of the more gentle, and peculiarly Irish, forms of persecution and is finally confined to a mental home in the midlands where her story, as told by H, really starts.

While reading a passage where the girl and another patient, a young man, Nick Peters, who is there because of a collection of pigtails, pony tails, and other tresses, braided and loose, found in his room after a series of nighttime scissor assaults, and who is writing a novel, keep their first forbidden tryst, H caught a movement in one of the first rows and, out of the corner of his eye, saw the general get up and depart.

It looked as if his kind of writing wasn't going to have much appeal here, neither among the Nazis nor the anglophiles. And he guessed that most of the students present had come to hear English pronounced by a native speaker and note certain grammatical usages.

Afterwards, when the inevitable coffee and cakes were served, though what H would have liked was a bottle of wine, he was placed at a table beside a man in the pale khaki S.A. rig-out, and a reporter from the *Völkischer Beobachter*.

Hans Kolbinsky, the S.A. man, turned out to belong to the English faculty at the university, having lately returned, as the war clouds gathered, from teaching German in a Yorkshire one.

'You know, Mr Ruark, the theme of your novel, as expressed in the extracts you read us, is not one which everyone here can approve of. But you needn't let the fact that old General-Lieutenant Kalbhausen walked out upset you. Though they burned Kafka's books for less, ha! ha! that was because of his race as much as for what he wrote.'

'You don't share the official view of Kafka?'

'Ah, Kafka,' said Kolbinsky with his slyly intelligent (it struck H) smile, 'as a matter of fact I was partly responsible for having him translated.'

Into English? H was uncertain and confused. To him the cause of Kafka, roughly that of all imaginative writers, including himself, wasn't to be furthered by conforming to say, no matter how morally justified, public and national attitudes, but by casting doubt on them all. He was aware, of course, that this was a perilous position, not just because such a writer was somebody neither side could tolerate. There was also the question, never to be completely resolved, of the ambiguity of such an attitude. How far could he go in reaction to the more tolerant outlooks with which he was intimately familiar in seeming to associate himself with the forcibly imposed ones here? As Thomas Mann, the most apparently respectable of writers, had understood, there was an element of what could be considered criminality in the intensely imaginative mind. But the artist's guilt or innocence could never be strictly determined, not by himself and certainly not by those in authority. Perhaps the quality of his work was the only real test of the state of a writer's psyche.

'You see,' Kolbinsky was saying, 'writers like you fall between all the stools. (Is that a permissible use of the old adage?) Being an Irishman, and not a Jew, Czech, or American, you won't be looked on as an example of international decadence, but as some sort of friendly visiting crank. To those here who are ready to admire any writer in English as standing for the sort of freedom they have lost, you'll be rather a disappointment, you know. But they'd be delighted to have you as a lecturer at our university.'

'Do you really think so?'

'If you agree I'll speak to the director of the Englische Seminar.'

All that H now wanted was to be back in time to enjoy his favourite repast in the hotel restaurant where he hadn't felt like eating before setting out, and afterwards to lie in the bathtub, haloed in bright steam, and examine the new design beginning to emerge.

As soon as he could do so without offence – these Germans, he saw, were sticklers for social observance – he said his auf Wiedersehen, to Herr Eberstadt and Dr Kolbinsky, tried an Alice good on the rest of the company and was about to clasp the hand of a blonde girl next to him, whom he'd hardly spoken with, in farewell – handshaking on all occasions seemed the rule – when she told him she was going too, her taxi was at the door and he could share it with her.

Inside it she snuggled down beside him and told him she'd studied for a year at Trinity College, Dublin, where her father, General von Ackermann – oh no, he hadn't been at the reading, he was with his unit in the Protectorate – had sent her in preference to an English university.

'Shall we go to a café in Unter den Linden?' she suggested, 'or would you like to see Alexanderplatz, which is less smart and where there's more going on?'

H made an excuse about having to get off an important letter home; he might indeed write to Iseult tonight with news of the job he'd been offered. Whatever was going on in Alexanderplatz or the even greater excitements of the taxi ride there with this Fräulein, he'd forgo until he'd deciphered the urgent messages reaching the fringes of his mind.

After leaving home Fräulein von Ackermann, who smelt of a skin well washed with Czechoslovakian soap, sent her no doubt by her father if the kind available here was no better than at the hotel, H read the meter and tried to calculate what would be clocked up by the time they reached the Habsburger Hof. He reached his destination clutching a bundle of the strange notes in one hand and coins in the other.

After another late dinner of bifteck tartar and a bottle of Rhine wine – he'd have preferred red but that seemed all to be French and more expensive – he retired to his room to compose the letter home. But instead he wrote to Julia, wishing her a quick recovery and, though it was hard to hit on the right expressions, a happy wedding day, if that was soon to follow. While he wrote, the refrain of a song she had sung, as a duet with the principal boy, in the pantomime was going through his head:

> You may not be an angel
> For angels are so few,
> But if you really want me
> I'll string along with you.

Next morning H was up early and, after breakfasting on coffee and rolls, the spout of the coffee pot, he noted, being pierced to prevent dripping, he started walking. What made him set off on the long trek circling quite a considerable part of the city was partly a need for freedom of movement and exercise after days cooped-up in trains, taxis, hotels, and lecture halls. But he had also a feeling that if, as seemed probable, he was going to be here a long time, that meant becoming involved in unforeseeable events and relationships. These must already have certain associations in the way of streets, parks, buildings, doorways, windows, cafés, which, if not discernible in the conscious mind might shed prophetic gleams into the somnambulant spirit's dreaming.

Leaving the hotel while the vacuum cleaners were being operated in the hall, H passed by the Anhalter station where he'd arrived and keeping on up the busy street came to an openwork iron structure above a waterway, whether canal or river he didn't know. A river was what he was hoping to come on as helping him determine both the shape of the city and its particular aura. But Berlin, he soon saw, had to be explored without any watery guidance.

The iron stairs led to a station of the railway that, supported on girders, ran above. Resisting an impulse to climb it and take one of the elevated S-Bahn trains from which he'd have a better view of the city, he continued his walk which was not, after all, the exploration of a tourist but in the nature of a pre-pilgrimage to places, at present unhallowed, which might become as haunted for him as, say, certain corners of Dublin or the row of iron huts on the Curragh plain. How little he foresaw that nothing from the past had prepared him for what was to come!

He was now looking for a turn to the right, following what he hoped was an intuition of the direction of the residential districts where, if he was to live here for a time, whatever experiences were in store would probably take place. But he was skirting on that side a complex of railway lines, sidings, and sheds too wide for a street to cross and he was taken out of his way before he came to a footbridge spanning the series of tracks. From a street on the other side he emerged into a broad boulevard whose name he noted and above the centre of which the S-Bahn ran.

Bülowstrasse; would those now rather tongue-twisting syllables have gathered in years to come the power to evoke in him intense memories? Continuing along it to Nollendorfplatz, a pleasant square somewhat over-shadowed by another of the superstructures supporting a station of the overhead railway, he turned left into Motzstrasse. Some way along it H reached a residential square called Viktoria-Luise-Platz.

Pausing by a café at one of its corners, he took a look up at the tall, balconied houses, one a pension, he noticed, but nothing pointed with a fingertip of future light to the ornate facade. He pushed on, crossed Prager Platz without pausing in his loping stride and reached a busy cross-thoroughfare divided in the middle by a grass strip where the yellow-and-red tramcars ran. He was growing weary as he turned right into Kaiser Allee and considered boarding one of those whose destination was the Bahnhof Zoo, which he knew from his first excursion was close to Kurfürstendamm. But instead he trudged on because the feeling increased, the more tired his legs grew, that he might be entering the very district that he would always associate with some of the most painful and precious moments of the legend of H.

Coming to a triangular piece of greenery on the left, sign-posted as Meier-Otto-Park, with shrubs, trees, benches, a fountain, and a column topped by a stone hand with upward-pointing index finger, H came to a halt.

As far as he could orientate himself, this was the furthest point in his circular itinerary, the part of the city most distant from the hotel. Perhaps that was the only reason he stood looking around him, and later, recalling this first sight of the monument, though he'd passed more imposing ones with hardly a glance, he may have mistakenly back-dated the special significance it came to have for him later as a memorial, though he never discovered what it actually commemorated, to much pain and some revelations of delight.

44

H introduced his next reading, which was in the university of Bonn, with trepidation, having taken his previous experience and Kolbinsky's warning to heart. He started by telling them what he thought his novels were about. Were the predominantly girl faces glazing over with bewilderment or, worse, inattention?

Although soon in deep water, he didn't dare break off and plunged on into irrelevant praise of some of his favourite writers, dragging in Rozanov (for the sake of crucified Christ!) who, like his own fictional protagonists, was certainly persona non grata with those few of his audience who had ever heard of him.

Sweating, H opened his first novel at the bookmarker and, abandoning his ill-advised excursion, started abruptly to read out. He had chosen an extract from the clandestine meeting between the two mental patients, Siobhan and Nicholas Peters.

'She was looking less than ravishing (after a year in the crowded asylum ward), her face (where once cool and lovely shadows had gathered and settled) stripped of its veil, thin and yet puffy, her hair lack-lustre, red rims to her eyes.

'How did Nicky see her as she entered the shed? (His eyes were rolling slightly in his swarthy Saracen's face). As the young girl cycling home at dusk along the deserted suburban road while he lurked at the corner with his scissors (he'd no scissors now)? Or was she the morning star in whose gentle ray he might be healed?

"They've been sneaking to my bed at night and photographing me," Nick told her. "I was woken when the flash bulb went off."

'She didn't laugh though she knew "persecution mania" had been pencilled into his case history by Dr Barnes's assistant.

' "They want to make an effigy of me to put on public show."

' "Oh, if they had ways of looking into our hearts, yours and mine, Nicky, and a means of recording what they found there in journalese, they'd have articles on us, with photos, in the papers, and perhaps put us into a waxworks exhibition (you in sports jacket and flannel trousers, me in my old navy blue convent school uniform) beside the Malahide triple-murderer, but as it is, Nick, they can ill-treat us but they'll never know anything about us." '

This wasn't the most suitable stuff for the time and place! If he'd been a German, *I Won't be Wearing Shamrock on St Patrick's Day* would have long ago gone up in flames. But, in that case, he'd have had the satisfaction of being welcomed by his native literary circles, not to mention Stroud at the Plough Tavern.

Afterwards H was invited home by one of the members of the English faculty who lived in Bad Godesberg, up the Rhine from Bonn: a name that evoked in H memories of Chamberlain in newsreels with his black-browed sheep's face, his Adam's apple, baaing out banalities.

H was introduced by Dr Linser to a Prince von Kurland who drove them there in his Auto-Union sports car at a terrific pace along a road lined with poplars between whose pale flashing trunks H had glimpses of the dark, fabled stream.

He was greeted by Frau Linser and several small children and taken to the living room where the table was laid, cakes piled on plates, and the coffee already made and being kept hot on a little metal stand above a candle flame.

A picture of the Furore on one wall, as well as the prince having taken a hand from the wheel and raised it in the Hitler salutation as they passed a camion of soldiers drawn up at the side of the road, turned H's thoughts to the German dictator. H was revising his original surmise about him as a blind and infuriated Samson about to pull down the whole pretentious edifice. Hitler had not the stature of Stalin who, like nearly all those dubbed as monsters by enlightened opinion, exerted a certain spell on H as, at least, the antithesis of the mediocrities in the public eye at home. There was a photo of Stalin, one big peasant hand shading his brow, in which his face had a contemplative repose of which Hitler's was incapable. The German leader had an old woman's sucked-in mouth and a way of clasping his pudgy hands in front of him as if he wanted to tuck them under an apron.

Like Rozanov, H's judgements depended to some degree on the physical impression which he believed reflected, for those who could interpret it, the psyche.

After the Kaffeestunde Dr Linser took H up to his study, leaving the prince happily entertaining the children while Frau Linser cleared the table.

'I thought you'd be interested in meeting Prince Biron,' Dr Linser was saying as they climbed the stairs, 'he's one of our young National Socialists, full of optimism and with a genuine feeling of belonging in a pioneer society. It would be hard to find a greater contrast to your Nicholas Peters or the hero of your second novel, don't you agree?'

H was too taken aback to reply immediately. Here was somebody who had not only read his books but had an inkling of what they dealt in. He waited till they were at the top of the stairs.

'Well, yes, I suppose you could say so.'

They entered the study and, sure enough, Dr Linser showed H, on the top shelf of the bookcase beside his desk, copies of his two novels side by side.

'Your Nick Peters, or the girl whose name I can't pronounce...'

'Sheevaun,' H said, having recourse to his phonetics.

'I have an idea,' Dr Linser went on, seating H in an armchair and himself at the desk, 'If either of them had come here it would have been because they'd have felt an attraction to any national or social movement that might disrupt the sort of ethos under which they lived.'

H smiled at the thought of Nicky with his long dark locks, that he'd made such a fuss about having washed and cut that Dr Barnes had had to intervene and postpone the operation, coming here with his two suitcases of old newspaper clippings on such subjects as forgotten film stars, heavy-weight boxers, and law cases, principally those concerning divorce court proceedings and trials for indecent assault and rape.

'If they had that kind of grasp of events outside their very private lives,' H said, 'revolutionary Russia might have made more appeal.'

The doctor had read his novels and evidently understood them, at least up to a point, and, therefore, in a sense and up to a point, knew more about H than he did himself. H felt he had to be somewhat wary because he, on the other hand, knew very little of Dr Linser and his outlook.

'I'd imagine,' said Dr Linser, 'that even two innocents, criminal innocents or innocent criminals like your hero and heroine, would have heard at least some rumours that the situation under the "Little Father" wouldn't offer them more freedom than where they were.'

H, abandoning his caution, began explaining himself, or at least his fictional characters, more fully.

'It's not exactly freedom they're looking for. They've an unconscious urge to do what they can to disperse any gathering mass or consensus of thought. That's what both, in their different ways, had suffered through. It's all the same whether it happens to be liberal or authoritarian, because they sense that even a liberal doctrine held in common tends to produce that sort of assured moral attitude which is fatal to them. Such psyches only thrive in periods of mental doubt and upheaval.'

'If I follow you, Mr Ruark, you're saying that your protagonists are nihilists.'

'No, I don't think so, Doktor. They're not politically enough aware to be anything so definable. They're not involved in social or moral issues at all. It's simply that they fear all communal concepts which increase their own isolation. Of course, what I as their creator know and they don't, is that it is only in isolation, and under pressure from outside, that imagination, their truly redeeming element, reaches its peak.'

'What you seem to be saying is that your heroes fear any established idea or ideal, yet it is the pressure they suffer from these that helps them develop their original gifts, or, if they are writers, like your Nicholas, become good ones.'

'Oh yes, that's more or less it,' said H, laughing. He'd been taken by surprise at the insight of this German professor, or Dozent, as he thought his correct university title was, into matters he hadn't discussed with anyone, not even Yeats, since his talks, on a less philosophical level, with Sean Lane.

'What's the prince doing here,' he asked, changing the conversation, 'he's not at the university surely?'

'Prince Biron?' Dr Linser seemed reluctant to be drawn back to everyday chitchat. 'He's stationed here with the Luftwaffe. If you get up early and go out on your hotel balcony you might see him skimming over the bridges as he pilots a J.U. up and down the river.'

H had been given a room in an annexe across the street, when he'd booked in at the hotel, that had neither balcony nor view of the Rhine, but he let it pass because he was wondering what this German with the larger-than-necessary portrait of Hitler in his living room, though there was none in the study, and his permanently cigar-scented breath, or clothes, really cared about. He was too responsive to the inner life of the characters in H's novels, too aware of the very personal and subjective states of consciousness that H himself was much of the time immersed in, and that are fatal to a sharing in any public faiths or attitudes, to be either a supporter of the German Furore or, like the Hofners and Eberstadt, an anglophile.

'Have you read Rozanov?' H asked. Rozanov was on his mind again lately. Dr Linser nodded.

'There was someone who reacted violently against the acceptable attitudes of his associates, as when he tried to justify in a newspaper article Tolstoy's excommunication by the Orthodox Synod.'

'And that to you, Mr Ruark, makes him a more sympathetic person than his great fellow countryman?'

'Tolstoy, who took morality so very seriously, is one of the Communist showpieces,' H said, 'but Rozanov, like Kafka here, has been put in the cellar.'

Dr Linser switched on a table lamp and let down the shutter, that reminded H of the rolltop to his desk at Rugby, over the window in whose two big panes the light had turned to what H thought of as deep Rhine evening blue.

Now they sheered off from the dangerous problems they'd been discussing to other things.

Such enthusiasts, Dr Linser said, evidently meaning the prince, were often lovers of children, sharing with them the simple, extrovert energies that they called unspoiled. But wasn't there another side to children that they didn't catch? Their moral ambiguity and indifference, their untamed imagination?

'What can the prince have made of Nick in my novel?'

'Nothing. He can ignore the implications because he was told by some Parteigenosse in Berlin to take you around in his car while you were here. So to him you are an acceptable visitor.

'There's a banker in Cologne,' Dr Linser went on, 'under whose wing you've been more officially put. He'll get in touch with you when you go there. But don't let it worry you, he's a very busy old man, and what it amounts to is he'll put one of his cars and a chauffeur at your disposal and not bother you, apart from giving a dinner in your honour at a smart restaurant.'

'If so I hope you'll come to it.'

'Oh no, I won't be asked.'

When he was being driven back to Bonn, H asked Prince Biron about their host. 'He's a man struggling with old prejudices and attitudes,' the prince said, as into the shining funnel of the headlamp beam were poured the row of chestnut trees – were these what H had mistaken for poplars on the outward drive? – 'but his wife is one of us; it's a pity she doesn't speak English so you could have had a talk with her.'

45

During the several days H spent in Cologne, he had a Porsche and driver at his disposal and, a further gesture of hospitality unpredicted by Dr Linser, a girl student to show him around. This precluded such solitary explorations as he'd undertaken in Berlin and meant some of the sightseeing he'd have let slip left to himself.

Having been conducted around the cathedral and the galleries, he sat beside Fräulein Hilde Brandes at the back of the big black vehicle and was driven over the long Rhine bridge along autobahns to ultramodern wayside cafés where, declining the inevitable coffee in pots with dripless spouts, he drank Bowle, a mixture, the Fräulein told him, of white wine, champagne, and fruit juice.

This girl was thin, pretty in a rather severe style, and odourless; H was sensitive to subtle personal aromas. She told him that she lived with her mother in a two-roomed flat that at least had a view on a couple of trees in a square, and seemed to set great store by nature. Not getting far on this topic, she switched to literature and said that Charles Morgan was her favourite English novelist.

'They don't much care for him in his own country,' H told her, 'perhaps because he's not sufficiently concerned with the provincial scene. Nor with the social problems of the middle classes. In fact, the fare he offers is not the insular dish that English novelists, apart from Lawrence, have been feasting their readers on.'

'Death, poetry, and love, those are the three complimentary themes of his novels, according to our professor whom you met after your lecture the other evening.'

H was out of his depths, as often happened when the talk took an academic-abstract turn. Whereas he was sure Fräulein Brandes, if only repeating what she'd learned, could have talked intelligently about the interconnection of love and death in the work of Charles Morgan till the cows came home.

Though the fact of Morgan's rejection by literary circles prejudiced H in his favour, he didn't encourage her. After two glasses of Bowle, served in shallow, open glasses, he wanted to be driven on, if only to another white café indistinguishable from the one where they were sitting.

He was restless and somewhat drunk. Through the faintly golden elixir, with the slice of out-of-season peach afloat in the ice green glass, did he feel he was restoring the balance between his inward-turned attention and the outward activities he'd been lately engaged on?

'Where does the Herr Doktor wish to go now?' the banker's chauffeur would ask the Fräulein who would look at H, and he, after the third or fourth deceptively innocuous-seeming drink, would exclaim, 'Bitte, weiterfahren!' (recalling Dmitri Karamazov's injunction to the peasant on the drive to Mokroe, 'Whip up the horses, Andrei!') in a phrase he'd memorized and phoneticized from his phrase book.

As the lights were coming on in the wide river, H by then completely intoxicated and gripping the girl's hand, but otherwise not touching her, was driven back to the Hotel Dom.

There he'd lie on the bed in his well-appointed room regaining interior consciousness, however clouded, after too many outward impressions, too many people, too much talk.

At the dinner given for him in a corner of the hotel restaurant curtained off by the same kind of heavy drapery as in the dining room of the Habsburger Hof, but now H was on its inner or private side, there were several more people, beside his host and Fräulein Brandes. But the banker, fat, bald, affable, and speaking little English, put H at ease and the talk at their end of the table was kept subservient to the meal, giving H time to savour the Rhine wine, the venison, red cabbage, and sweetish sauce, and also the white, white bosom of the woman next to him that evoked magical associations. With his Fräulein he never managed to sink into semi-sensual silence at the back of the car without her springing nature or poetry, love and death, on him.

The banker was asking Fräulein Brandes whether she and H had had much fun together – when he wasn't himself being addressed H could grasp quite a bit of German – and she answered with a laugh, 'Oh no, we've behaved very soberly indeed.'

'So!' said their host, regarding H out of small bright eyes that, H sensed, had an insight into other things besides the vaults of banks.

'You don't look like one of Ribbentrop's young foreign protégés,' he said. H saw that the little banker wondered what he was doing here if he was neither just out for a spree nor on the make politically as, presumably, had been the other visiting foreigners he'd been asked to entertain.

H would have gladly enlightened him, but apart from having to get the Fräulein to translate he wasn't sure how to put it. He could hardly have mentioned his idea of an imaginative revolution, of a sudden jerk forward of consciousness, especially as expressed in poetry and fiction, which he began to sense might only take place after a new political or social cataclysm. Perhaps if he'd been able to talk to him direct, H would have confided to him the situation at home from which he was escaping, for he sensed that this was something his host would readily understand.

Next morning H made the short train journey to Bonn and, after picking up a couple of letters that had come for him to the hotel there, one from Iseult addressed in pencil and the other in Julia's big scrawl, went to see Dr Linser in his small room at the university full of bluish cigar smoke.

H felt a peculiar gratitude to Dr Linser, similar to that which, in his novel, Nick Peters felt for the asylum director, Dr Barnes, who'd intervened with the house physician and some of the nurses on his behalf.

Dr Linser started to discuss H's second novel, which he said he was holding a seminar on. He had explained to his class the hero's sympathy for the girls chained to the railings as the result of a hereditary trait or childhood trauma.

'You see, Mr Ruark, I have to be cautious. I'm not free to express my own convictions, but at least I can take work that I admire to discuss with my students.

'The first part of the novel is quite clear to me. It's where the girls are exchanged in the night between the hero and the member of the armed forces of the occupying power that I have some difficulty in following where the theme is leading, or your purpose.'

'I don't know that I had a purpose beyond exploring certain situations to see if my hero could adapt himself to them without a sense of shame. That's the only way I know for a writer to find out for himself how far he can go in imaginative freedom without damage to his psyche. The saying of one of the Karamazovs that all is allowable is only true if there's no God.'

'Am I right in thinking that you came here "to explore a situation", as you put it?'

'That's too solemn,' H answered. 'I came here for all sorts of reasons, something like that among them, though less deliberately than you make it sound, Doktor. And, of course, there was a certain amount of vanity mixed up in it,' he made himself add.

'For you it's either some kind of divine myth or chaos? You don't believe in the possibility of a humanitarian future?' H had to laugh. Nobody had even bothered to interrogate him so seriously before. He respected Dr Linser for his insights more than any German he'd come across so far, or any of his own lot he'd talked of such things to for ages, for that matter. But he couldn't make things any clearer than he had in the novel itself. All he wanted now was, having fetched his suitcase by taxi from the station, to board one of the white paddle-steamers at the pier and sail away up the Rhine as he'd planned, disembarking where the fancy took him.

The trip up the river was as leisurely and peaceful as he'd foreseen. He went down to the saloon – the landscape was not yet the fabled Rhineland one – and, at a table by a window through which he could watch the flattish banks glide past, he ordered a bottle of Rhine wine and read the two letters, first

238

Iseult's which he felt sure would contain something to irritate him, then Julia's.

Iseult wrote in faint pencil in her strangely slovenly script, but the sight of it on an envelope lying on the hall table at his aunt's one Christmas had transfused the dark old house in the North – made darker with wreaths of ivy draped over the frame of sporting prints – with the illumination of youthful love.

He glanced quickly through the couple of pages torn from a copybook. Nothing more than usual seemed to be wrong. Kay was ill and asking for him in her fever; Miss Burnett, who'd agreed to stay on till H's return, had disappeared with her drunken doctor; a portion of the ancient wall had collapsed one stormy night; Blossom hadn't given birth to the expected puppies; and, of course, she was worried to death about Ian who, on holiday from school, was begging not to be sent back; to say nothing of the bills that were piling up. No, she wouldn't burden him while he was no doubt having a high old time by reminding him of her constant struggle to make ends meet. At the very end she expressed some mild satisfaction at the news of his appointment, to take effect in the autumn, as lecturer at Berlin university.

H took a draught of the wine

> ...... that hath been
> Cooled a long age in the deep-delvéd earth,
> Tasting of Flora and the country green,
> Dance, and Provençal song and sunburnt mirth.

Halcyon times of which Keats had known as little as did he himself, and opened the letter from Julia.

She addressed him as 'darling' and told him she was soon leaving hospital cured of her mysterious ailment, not that she called it that. He refilled his wineglass and imagined her no longer having to swathe her breasts in gauze and muslin but delight in having them fondled by her lover from the B.B.C. Whereas all he had now was the photo in a Berlin shop.

Next morning when, having disembarked at Coblenz instead of remaining on board till Bingen which Dr Linser had recommended as a charming old village, he woke up in his hotel room with a taste of unedible substances, such as ancient green, oxidized silver coins dug out of cemetery soil, in his mouth. His skull had become the metal sound-box of a bell whose clapper reverberated against it in a dolorous tolling.

He was tempted to press a finger into one of the side hollows in his belly to see if his flesh had turned spongy, as long ago in the school sickroom, but resisted. Spongy, or firm, elastic or flabby, there was, in any case, now no Weg to come to his rescue in her sister's yellow Hotchkiss.

He rose, dragged trousers and jacket over pyjamas, and went out to buy what he'd need if, as he foresaw, he was to be marooned for a time in the hotel room. The main thing was sufficient quantities of a liquid that would both slake his raging thirst and, unlike tap water, wouldn't accentuate the taste of dissolution in his mouth.

After finding what he wanted at a big Woolworth's – half a dozen bottles of an unfermented apple juice called Apfelsaft, aspirins, oranges, corkscrew, and several large handkerchiefs for undefined emergencies – he hung about to give the maid time to make up his room before he returned.

Coblenz wasn't a bad place to get ill in. A smaller picturesque town where little happened and his movements, or lack of any, might have been re-marked, would have been worse. So would Cologne or Bonn where someone, the prince, the banker, Dr Linser, the Fräulein, would have been sure to ring up or call. Nobody, not even his family at home, knew where he was. He could sink into the anonymity and obscurity of illness, sweat, ache, shiver, drink the cool Saft – had Keats's tubercular fever inspired the lines that had already been haunting H the day before? – and give himself to the hallucina-tions he felt were on the way.

Sure enough, when he was back in bed with the covers over his face and two of the opened bottles, one half-emptied, beside him on the floor, he received a startling image of the wet black lips of the filly, curling back from strong teeth, as she tried to nip him while he was saddling her. On her other side he recognized, with an even greater thrill, Maslova with her slight squint and small energetic hands. She was wearing the high boots, short fur cloak, and head scarf for the long march, fifteen to twenty miles a day, he recalled, with one day's rest after two of marching.

'There now! And I cried when I was sentenced. Instead of thanking God for it all the days of my life,' Katusha was telling him, speaking across the filly's hollow back.

He himself had not yet been sentenced. It depended on the outcome of the race. If the filly won he would be allowed to walk beside the girl prisoner all the way from Perm to their final destination. Was the bestowal of such a blessing dependent on the chance result of a race? But had not he sometimes had an intimation, on the racecourse, and at other moments, that what he was risking was merely a token of what was really at stake?

His pyjamas were wet through, but he couldn't interrupt the fantasy in order to change them. He was reminded of the state he'd been in when they'd stayed with the Yeatses and he'd lain awake at night while what had started as stories with which to interest the great poet had turned into semi-hallucinations that absorbed him on their own account.

'Yes, Lubka (another diminutive of her name that he astonishingly recalled), you have the resolution to turn pain to good account. Show me how I can do so, too. It's something I can learn from spirits such as yours.'

There followed an animated discussion in which Maslova tried to impart to him some of her simple faith, and afterwards H had scarcely the strength to lift the bottle of Apfelsaft from the floor to his parched mouth. Later (in the night? after dropping to sleep for only a few minutes?) H was standing with her in Deasey's yard while one of the brothers, whom H did not dare ask how she had run, was sponging down the filly that was in a lather of sweat.

H managed to drag himself out in the mornings so that when the maid came to do the room she wouldn't be alarmed by his pallor, his bright, glazed eyes, and his lack-lustre hair that stood up in tufts on his head, and inform the manager. The symptom that caused him most concern was that his testicles had lost their firm ovoid form and sagged shapelessly.

Having left the empty bottles at the shop and renewed his supply – he got through three or four a day – he walked slowly down the esplanade by the river, his malaise accentuated by the rude health around him, the purposeful strides of pedestrians, the quick pedalling of cyclists, the noise and speed of the cars.

Back in his bed at the hotel, he put the palm of his hand to his mouth and breathed on it to see if there was any sign of the fever going down. It still felt as if held to the spout of a steaming kettle. But in case this test was not conclusive, he tried another, holding his damp hand in the air outside the bedclothes. If it dried quickly but remained hot, that would confirm the first experiment, but if it was soon cool and moist, that would betoken an improvement.

The third or fourth evening about the hour of six, when the last race was over, the monks filed into their stalls for Vespers, c'est l'heure d'apéritif, chéri, prison supper was served, Lane had died, he started shivering and his teeth chattered.

He said a short prayer, not for his speedy recovery; that kind, which he'd made such desperate use of as a child, was now impossible. 'Lord of my chance engendering and Instigator of my fantasies, instruct me how, through the proper use of imagination, to break out from my restricted consciousness to wider glimpses of your nature, demonic or benign.'

By eight-thirty he was up, bathed, shaved, and dressed and sitting, weak and shaky, in the lounge of a big hotel on the river; his own was a smaller, commercial one in a side street.

The place was dim and deserted, it being too early in the season for tourists, for he'd just spent his Walpurgis Night thirty-seventh birthday in his sickbed, and only a few of the chandeliers were lit. H ordered a liqueur. After the quantities of apple juice he felt like something short, strong, and full-flavoured, and sat sipping it all alone in the enormous shadowy room.

Next morning H took a D-Zug, which he supposed was an express, for Berlin, via Cologne, and booked into a back-street hotel whose narrow, twisting passages were hung with pictures of old-fashioned, long-funnelled warships, and where there was a typewriter in the public room which, after the insertion of a two-mark piece, could be used for a stated period, after which it locked itself again.

On this machine H wrote a letter, after telephoning Kolbinsky, who asked him to start taking conversation classes right away, telling Iseult about his plans, which involved residing in Berlin till the end of term. He added, after having to put in another coin (he was a slow typist), that when he came home for the summer holidays they'd discuss the financial and other aspects of the new situation.

46

This was now one of H's chief concerns. Earning a salary for the first time in his life and with the prospect of what he thought of as his freedom, he resolved to do all in an orderly and proper fashion. When later he would talk matters over with Iseult, he must have sound arguments to convince her, and satisfy himself, that he could remain in Germany while she lived in Ireland with the children on the monthly sum, to be decided on, he would send her. His earnings as a novelist would also have to be allocated.

H went to the Humboldt Klub and asked Herr Eberstadt if he could find him a room in a private house or flat where he'd be given the evening meal.

H waited while the blond young man, already preparing to make the move to Oxford while it was still feasible, though H didn't know that, consulted his list of approved addresses and then telephoned to one of them. He heard himself referred to as 'the Irish poet', der irische Dichter, which possibly contributed to his being offered part-board and lodging at the first place Herr Eberstadt tried – most Germans, H thought, were cultural snobs – at the rate of 120 marks monthly.

The place was only a short walk away, across a corner of the Tiergarten and under an arch of the S-Bahn viaduct into Bachstrasse. In the second-floor flat he was shown the vacant front bedroom and the family living room also looking over the street to the elevated railway line. In his halting German H expressed himself satisfied with what he'd seen and paid Frau Möller a month's rent in advance.

He moved in the same evening and ate supper with the Möllers, father, mother, and two grown-up daughters, one plump, fair, and homely, the other slim, olive-skinned, doe-eyed.

H, feeling his way in the new milieu, wasn't sure at first what to make of his landlady, nor what she was making of him, the others were less concerned, and when, after he'd gone to his room, she appeared there and said something in which the only word, or syllable, he recognized was 'kiss', he wondered whether she was suggesting he bid her a warmer 'good-night' than the one he'd wished them phonetically before retiring. Then he saw she'd brought a cushion which she thought he might need under his pillow, the German for which it seemed was Kissen.

Alone at last, H became aware of a roar that recurred every couple of minutes as the trains went past at window level only a few yards away. How, for God's sake, would he get any rest till one or two in the morning, accustomed as he was to the mountain silence at home of which the wind in the fir trees was a part? But while worrying over this and regretting the sum paid in advance, he forgot the noise and was soon asleep.

The trains came to fascinate him, not the city ones but the D-Züge whose tracks ran alongside. Breakfasting in the warm May sun on the balcony with Frau Möller and the plump daughter – the others left the flat early – H read, as these went slowly by, the destinations displayed on the carriages: Warschau, Bukarest, Budapest, Köln. There could hardly have been a greater contrast between the solitude of Dineen and this balcony in the centre of Berlin, about halfway, he calculated, between Alexanderplatz in the east and Adolf-Hitler-Platz in the west, which itself was then at the hub of Europe.

The conversation class turned out to involve his sitting in a small room in the Englische Seminar wing of the university at a highly polished table that stood on equally shiny brown linoleum, with two, three, or four girl students, and keeping some kind of talk going for one and a half hours.

At first he treated it as a social occasion, an afternoon visit, even missed not being able to offer them refreshments and tried to make the conversation interesting, in spite of which a disconcerting expression that he interpreted as boredom appeared on the faces of two of the girls. But after a bit he grasped that they were listening with close attention, if not to what he was saying in itself, to turns of phrase and pronunciation.

When his landlady told him she was accompanying a rich acquaintance who was taking the cure at Bad Gastein and suggested his either eating out of an evening or getting his wife over for the time she'd be away, while the monthly payment would be reduced to eight marks, H's first thought was to ask Julia.

The idea delighted him, but would it be possible to pass her off as his wife in view of the forms she'd have to fill in and the one that Herr Möller would

243

probably have to sign in connection with obtaining ration coupons? Butter, coffee, and, H thought, soap were all in short supply.

The idea of being, to all intents and purposes, married to Julie for a few weeks in this foreign place fascinated him, but he abandoned the idea as involving too many problems.

Trains clattering by in the stifling nights, sudden afternoon storms, thunder crashing over the ornate balconies, white needles of rain fizzing on to warm pavements strewn with fallen chestnut blossoms, and, from atop a café table, a glimpse of the brown-jacketed, wooden-seeming idol, one arm thrust stiffly out, a short dark brushstroke under the nose, being carried along upright in the black open car with its blue spotlight piercing the noon glare of Unter den Linden.

In his conversation classes H was wary in discussing National Socialism. The dark girl with the name he hadn't yet managed to memorize brought up the subject in her fluent English and it crossed his mind that she might be an *agent provocateur* sent to test him before his appointment was ratified.

In answer to one of her questions he said, 'I agree that of two opposing political systems the less bad should be preferred, but as it is more and more widely accepted, then it can easily become the more dangerous, predetermining modes of thought and mental attitudes, its principles may even, if it triumphs over the other system, become dogmas.'

'But it can't be right to support a tyranny brutally enforced.'

'It depends what you mean by support. Personally, I'll always question mental attitudes, no matter how virtuous, that become so universal that they threaten the freedom of the imagination to delve and explore.'

'Isn't our first duty to take account of the truth or falsity of the conflicting outlooks?' the girls insisted.

To try to stress that the conversation was first and foremost an academic exercise, he corrected her way of expressing herself.

' "Can we form judgements irrespective of the intrinsic merits or demerits of the opposing ideas" would be a better way of putting it.'

The girl with the long name that he always forgot wasn't, of course, an agent of any kind, but belonged to a wealthy family with industrial interests in Silesia ('My father makes small machines to put under big ones to absorb vibration,' she told him) who found in his class, whenever the two dumb girls were absent, a substitute for the foreign travel that was becoming difficult. Though she did, at the last of the classes, mention that her mother had planned to take her to Greece in the holidays but had found that the ship didn't dock there; it was met by a tender on to which it wouldn't be possible to load their car. She added that she'd be back at the university for the winter semester.

On the hot last evening H called in at the awninged Konditorei in Bach-strasse on his way home and selected a dozen rich little pastries which the shopgirl picked from the tray with a silvery pair of tongs and placed in a carton over which she deftly folded the lid, tucking its winged corners into the slots in the cardboard sides. He was taking in all the odds and ends that made up the feel of Berlin which, in turn, was part of a wider awareness of being 'on the eve' – not just on the eve of departure, but of a still greater change.

The Möller girl arrived home a few moments after he had with a similar carton, and they sat in folding chairs on the balcony, she, her father, and H, with an enormous pile of Kuchen and the by now familiar china coffee pot on the table.

H was glad after the intense bouts of talk with the girl students, having left the money he had over with the dark one to keep for him till his return, to relax there over coffee and cakes – the ones with a spoonful of stiff whipped cream on top and damp, rum-flavoured centres were his favourites – and only have to put in a word or two now and then in German.

As the street lamps began to glimmer from the warm dusk of the street below and the first trains with lit windows clattered by, turning the sky beyond the elevated line an electric blue, father and daughter spoke sadly, with what H thought of as the German facility for sentiment, which for the moment he shared, of his coming departure. The last of the cakes had disappeared from the now faintly gleaming plate, and the last smoke from Herr Möller's cigar, one of the final associations for H with what was slipping away, drifted out over the balustrade.

47

After the hot refraction from the Berlin pavements, summer was filling the garden at home with a pallid light and cool, gorse-scented breeze. Sitting beside Iseult as she weeded one of her flower beds, H tried to answer her eager questions. Who was Hitler? Was he the Bright Avenger?

Why disappoint her? If it came to that, did he know the answers? He told her of Prince Biron von Kurland and about a big military parade in honour of the visit of Prince Paul of (he thought) Yugoslavia that had passed along the Ost-West-Achse near where he'd been staying and that Frau Möller had taken him to, securing them seats on a crowded stand by getting him to give her his Irish passport to show a policeman.

It was when they started to talk of his job at the university in Berlin in the autumn and, as she squatted on her haunches, her hands in the familiar dirty old gloves stopped probing with the trowel for the roots of the low-spreading, star-shaped weeds whose name he didn't know, that they reached the vital point in the discussion.

'You can stay here till we see how I get on, and how the international situation develops.'

'Oh, I'm not afraid of the international situation.'

'Of course not, Pet, but what about the children?'

She said nothing and he went on: 'War or no war, wouldn't you and they be better off here with the quiet countryside and garden, and where you've your mother?'

He went to his room and lay on his bed without their having come to a conclusion about the future. But one thing, on a quite different level, had become clear to him: the start that he'd made on a new novel while he'd been away was not good at all. It was a relief to tear up what he'd done of it.

Ah, what a really frightful struggle it was to find a way of saying, whatever its ultimate worth or relevance, what wouldn't be said at all if not by him! And wasn't it going to be even more difficult to write anywhere else but at the trestle table under the familiar damp stain and the picture of St Catherine on the wall?

But after the first few days, spent mostly with the children, he began to look forward to returning to Berlin in the autumn, taking a flat there, and at last beginning a life of his own. What it would be like wasn't clear to him, but anything was better than living in this state of the constant nervous abrasion that he and Iseult inflicted on each other.

He systematically set about preparing for his final departure. He sold the Welsummer breeding stock, the flocks of high egg-yield Leghorns, keeping only a few deep-bronze Barnevelders, then the appliances and huts. The various transactions were not without pain for him. What once had touched a nerve in his heart never became indifferent to him: the oily intestines of old cars, the sour whiff of laying sheds, rain clouds over the greensward of racecourses, secretive Dublin pubs, the smell of a monastery guesthouse, the sound of Gregorian chanting.

H handed Iseult half the proceeds, paid Deasey what he owed him, put aside the price of his fare to the Hook of Holland (he'd only been able to get a return ticket for marks from Berlin that far), bought a suit, a high-necked jersey to lessen laundry troubles later, but foolishly not a winter overcoat, and a wedding present in the shape of a first edition of *The Ballad of Reading Gaol*, to stand, if she saw fit, beside her *Vanity Fair*, for Julia. With what remained, roughly fifty pounds, he went in early August to the country meeting where they were running the filly.

Sulphurous-looking clouds sailed over the rather shabby stands. As soon as the first race, which H hardly saw for watching the sky, was over, he went to the stables. It was almost completely dark in the box where Matt Deasey had stood a bucket of water he was using to give the filly a sponge down. Mick came with saddle and number cloths from the weighing room and greeted H in the dusk with a few murmured words which he didn't catch; rain had started to drum on the corrugated roof, increasing his nervousness.

'What's that?'

But Deasey, busy saddling the filly, didn't repeat the remark. Only when he pulled tight the girth and was stooping to fasten it in the deep shadows under the filly's belly did he mutter: 'I told Chalk Lynch not to knock her about.' Lynch was the jockey Deasey had engaged, nicknamed 'Chalk' because he was still an apprentice and hadn't yet a printed nameplate to slide into the frame on which riders and runners were displayed.

While Matt led the filly to the parade ring, H and the trainer went to the bookmakers. Instead of the 100–8 or 20–1 that H had expected against Sunnymova – he always thought of her as 'the filly' and coming on the name repeated on the lists was like seeing 'Julia Jenners' in big letters outside the Victoria Palace – there were eights and an occasional nine.

'Chalk must have backed her,' Deasey said.

Deasey stood dejectedly, the rain dripping off the lowered brim of his hat, in front of one of the bookies and H guessed that, though he'd impressed on the trainer since his return that he wanted him to win with her, the discovery that Lynch, who'd ridden her at work and no doubt discussed the race with some of the other jockeys, had backed the filly upset him. He never seemed to wish to arrive at, what for H was, the moment of truth.

'We'd have put Corcoran up, if it wasn't for the seven pounds' allowance off her back that the lad can claim.'

While H would have got a thrill out of seeing the taciturn Corcoran, rider of the winner of an Irish Derby, huddled in the rain on the filly's back, he was quite satisfied with the way things had turned out.

The third of the Deasey brothers appeared out of the throng and had a few muttered words with Mick.

'Tom saw Mrs Mathews, our lad's sister-in-law, back the filly at 100–6,' the trainer told H, smiling his sad smile, under the drop on the end of his nose. 'I'd sooner not have had her exposed just yet, she's only a baby,' he added.

H decided to slip off and put thirty of the fifty pounds he had with him on his horse. Making a slow mental calculation he concluded that if he won two hundred and fifty pounds, plus the eighty or so the race was worth, less the present he'd give Lynch, he'd be able to keep the filly. Although he'd promised Iseult he'd sell her before returning to Germany, the disposal of the poultry had been an unexpected wrench and the prospect of having her another year would console him for the other loss. What of the loss of the children? But Ian was away at school anyhow, and he hadn't thought or felt much about it yet. The poultry and the filly involved simpler emotions.

When he'd placed his bet, further reducing the price to sixes and no doubt watched by Tom, who kept vigil for his brother on racecourses, he didn't rejoin Deasey but went up on the stand as far away as possible from the portion of it reserved for owners and trainers.

The race, a seven-furlong event, was run in the steadily falling rain; the watery element was present at times of crisis, H reflected, recalling the black raincoat Iseult had been wearing as she'd hastened, half an hour late, into Euston station, the steamy baths of Vienna, the thunderstorm on the drive with Weg and her sister, rescuing him from Rugby, to London, and the weather when he started on his first novel in the hut at Tintown.

In one of those desperate finishes in which two horses gallop side by side to the winning post, so close in this case that Lynch couldn't use his whip nor risk unbalancing his mount by transferring it to the other hand, nobody could tell whether Sunnymova or the other had won. H was anxiously trying to catch every opinion expressed by those around him. When the judge had reached a decision and the winning number went up – it was before the days of the photo finish – it wasn't the filly's.

At home H wrote in a large yellow copybook he'd bought in Berlin to serve as a diary and notebook: 'August 12th, 1939. Three weeks back and in that time I've scrapped the novel, got rid of most of the poultry, lost a race by a short bloody head, sold the filly, for a hundred and forty pounds, while the European situation has steadily deteriorated.' He added, 'On my way home through London a German friend of Stroud's told us the following story:

'A friend of his, Y, was having dinner in a restaurant in Prague (city of fog, patriotic fervour, overcharging, and music) early last year with his wife, when the proprietor, a friend of his, called him into a back room. Waiting there were a couple of characters whom Y knew were Nazi Fifth Columnists. One of them (I imagine a high complexion, dark blue eyes, black lashes) began asking Y some questions while the other, dumb, porcine, and gazing at the ceiling, stood at the door. While he was giving his answers, it was clear to Y that they weren't going to let him go. He'd disappear, as others had; he was going to be taken to Germany (he was German by birth) and wouldn't see his wife whom he loved, and never more tenderly than at that moment, for years.

'When this was clear to him his fatalism, patience, and resignation (he was in these respects not unlike myself) vanished, and he sprang towards the door, yelling Help! Nazi Swine! and so on, at the top of his voice. His wife and one or two of the other diners ran in from the restaurant as the two kidnappers were dragging him to the back entrance, where no doubt a van was waiting, and they had to release him. (End of Anecdote.)

'A little later Hitler occupied Czechoslovakia, after which Y could have shouted his head off and neither his wife nor anyone else would have heard him or, if they had, could have come to his help.

'Ponder on this event, true, tangible, and of which I can imagine the details, as if it had happened in Dublin. Reflect long and imaginatively on the terror of separation and kindred agonies. Be clear about what is going on, but be equally clear that the only final opposition comes from the private and pure conscience without any axe to grind. This nobody now has much chance of developing except, like Nick Peters, he is already shut away and beyond indoctrination. Then, and it may soon be only possible in an asylum, he makes the final act of dissociation from all public attitudes both criminal and righteous, which, if not interchangeable, sooner or later shade off into one another.'

Was he finding excuses for doing what it would be intolerable to give up? How far was his determination to return to Berlin influencing his spiritual judgement? What he thought of as the sap in his cells had always been impregnated with a fear of moral attitudes, the greater the more widely held they were. This was the same sort of instinct that urged him to write fiction about the exploration of every tenable, and sometimes even untenable, alternatives!

Whatever he would be accused of it would probably be unjustly, which was not to say that he wasn't guilty. Guilt of some sort was a necessary condition of his being, but there was a kind of evil that, if imaginatively participated in, could destroy him, which was what public ignominy could never do.

He received a letter telling him his appointment at Berlin university had been approved and one from Ulla Flickenschild – her name was on the back of the envelope – back from Greece.

She seemed convinced that war was imminent and wanted to warn him without running foul of possible censors. She told him his classes had been one of the few bright spots in the long sultry summer. 'My father believes the Führer is soon going to liberate Danzig, which will be a proud day for all of us.' And in case he might misunderstand her she added, 'Though the only reason for pride these days is to have none.' Let them work that out!

Ulla, or her father, had been right.

'*September 1st.* This morning as I sat at the trestle table trying, and failing as has happened each day for weeks, to find a tune to which the spirit can sing its own sweet, if somewhat discordant, song, Ian came in, his fair face flushed, having run up the hill from the village, and after waiting to get his breath, as well as perhaps with an idea of prefacing the announcement with a moment of silence to make it the more solemn, told me that Germany and Poland were at war.

'Stayed in my room most of the day, going down now and then to listen to the news bulletin on the radio and discuss the situation with Iseult. At six-thirty heard Chamberlain preparing the way for England's entry into the conflict.'

H spent much time in that warm early autumn about the place, alone or with the children. Sitting in a deck chair one late afternoon by the side of the 'castle' he heard a blackbird, or it might have been a thrush, for he wasn't conversant with birdsong, sing a few notes from high in the tall elm that, slightly bowed from the prevailing westerly wind, topped the battlements of the tower and blocked with leaves each autumn the lead valley, probably the cause of the damp in that part of the old house. As he listened with an intentness he'd never given to a bird's song, he recognized the echo of past tranquillity.

After a moment's pause the short song was repeated note for note, giving H another chance to try to interpret it as an obscure comment on his future. But though this he failed to do, the impact of the song caused the hour to be singled out and recalled for years to come. Afterwards the sun had shone more tenderly because its hours of falling on these old and unkempt lawns were nearly over.

With Ian gone back to school, H had only Kay to turn to with his plans. Iseult, though not adverse to his returning to Germany, had little belief in his being able to do so.

'Tomorrow we're going to Dublin to see if I can get a visa,' he told her as they sat on his bed.

'Right-o,' said the little girl, digging her nails into his palm in the excitement of having him confide his secrets to her, although H knew she had no clear idea of what a visa was.

They went by bus to town where Iseult left them to spend the day with her mother.

H went with Kay to the French Consulate where a girl clerk with red hair was busy with a group of quietly persistent nuns. When she at last turned to H, he came out with the sentence he had prepared: 'I've been advised to go to Switzerland for health reasons and I wish to apply for a transit visa through France.' He had obtained a certificate that he was tubercular from Miss Burnett's doctor, now her husband.

'But you're not sick, Daddy?' Kay said when the girl had gone to fetch a form for him to fill in.

'What did you expect me to say? I want to enlist in the Wehrmacht?' He pressed her sticky paw, in which was clasped some chocolate he'd bought her.

When he had filled in the form, not one of whose questions, except for his name and permanent residence, he considered it wise to answer truthfully, and handed it back to the red-haired girl, she announced, 'You'll have to have the Swiss visa before we can do anything.'

'If I come back with a Swiss visa will I then get the French one?'

'It can't be decided here. It could have been yesterday, but this morning we had a directive that all applications had to be forwarded to Paris.'

At the Swiss Consulate an elegant young man took down the details as if receiving them out of thin air and without seeming aware either of H or the child. Then he announced, nor was the remark addressed to anyone in particular, that the request would be sent to Bern and an answer could be expected in three weeks.

During the next days H made several applications for entry visas to neutral countries, afterwards being unable to recall which office had been which.

'Excuse my bringing my little girl with me, Consul.'

H gave a transaction with a publisher in Amsterdam, who had in fact brought out a translation of one of H's novels under the curious title of *De Weg Alleen*, as the reason for wishing to make this particular application.

'You don't require a visa to enter Holland,' the consul told him.

For a moment H was elated, but the bald little man added in the most friendly manner, 'All you need is an exit visa from the British.'

This was something that neither the girl at the French consulate nor the sleek young man at the Swiss embassy had thought fit to mention.

H took a taxi to one of the houses overlooking the river on the seaward side of O'Connell Bridge.

After listening to H explaining his desire for a winter sports holiday, the official said, 'If you care to give us your passport we'll have it sent to Oslo. It won't take more than a few days.'

'Now for the Hibernian Navigation Company,' H told Kay as they again traversed the four flights of dark stairs.

But at the shipping office it turned out that although cargo vessels might sail occasionally to Oslo and Stockholm, though even this much the clerk seemed reluctant to admit, passengers were now definitely barred.

A thought that had been worrying H now made him go to the Department of External Affairs to ask for a new passport, one that wouldn't have on it evidence of his recent visit to Germany.

For once H could explain his position straightforwardly.

251

'With thousands going over to work in England, I don't see why you haven't a right to take up your job at Berlin university, providing you can get there,' Mr Boland told him. 'That's in perfect keeping with our neutrality.'

H's spirits rose as it seemed the Government might even welcome his proposed trip as a small proof of their nonalignment.

'Let's have a look at your present passport.'

'I left it at the Norwegian consulate this morning.'

'Norwegian?' Mr Boland repeated incredulously. 'Then you must go and get it back at once. It will be lying in a drawer there.'

Having retrieved it (Mr Boland having been right about the drawer), H had just time to post the passport, sealed and registered, to the Department before catching the bus home.

Like her mother, Iseult was passionately pro-German and impressed by Hitler's threats of retribution, which were being backed up by the Wehrmacht's rapid advance through Poland. She told an Anglo-Irish neighbour, who was rumoured to have an air-raid shelter in her garden, that Churchill had had the *Athenia*, full of Americans returning home, sunk in order to involve the United States in the war right away.

The visitor turned pale, rose from the tea table, and, followed by H to the door with her handbag that she'd forgotten, left the house.

Iseult was astonished and contrite. 'She needn't have taken it personally,' she said.

'She didn't,' H explained. 'You could have been rude to her and she'd have overlooked it so long as she could think of you as "one of us". What she, and all those like her, won't tolerate is having doubts cast on the validity of their indulgence in their great passion of righteous indignation, and such a wonderful opportunity doesn't come very often.'

Then, just after Christmas, against all likelihood, came a note from the Swiss consulate saying that his visa had been granted and if he presented his passport it would be stamped in it. A few days later he heard that the French transit visa, valid for twenty-four hours, was also awaiting him.

48

H left Dineen on a still day in early January, when the smoke from the cottages hung in the air, and, after wiping the misted window of the bus, he had a glimpse of the children standing on the road on each side of the stooped figure of his mother.

That evening, sitting opposite him in the compartment they had to themselves on the short train journey from Dublin to Dun Laoghaire, Iseult remarked that should he fail to obtain an exit visa in London, as seemed quite likely, he'd just have to put up with spending the war with her. Her tone struck him as for once humble and almost suppliant. As they walked from the station to the pier, not having waited for the boat train, with his heavy suitcase, she noticed a rat in the shadow of a warehouse and crossed the street to chase it for some yards along the wall. Like the repeated birdsong and the bat on the night he was born, H took it as an omen of some sort, probably an ill one, and it became the last vivid memory he had of her.

While he waited in London to hear from the passport office in Petty France where he'd applied for an exit permit, and been interviewed by one of several officers sitting at tables in a big upstairs room, H stayed at a comfortable hotel near the Haymarket; an address befitting somebody on his way to spend part of the winter at a Swiss resort.

The war was present in unfamiliar signs and portents: the sandbagged entrance to an official building, a shop window crisscrossed with tape, the gas-mask case slung over a shoulder in the street, the snatches of French from the room next to his, the maid coming of an evening to pull down the blackout blind and, above all, the utter darkness of the streets at night.

In odd ways he had intimations of the coming doom: at his bedroom mirror brushing his hair that had lately become unruly and stuck up in all directions as if fanned by the wings of the Angel of Destruction; noticing displayed outside a cinema in the Haymarket the name of a film; *The Rains Came* – for a moment the word *rains* had a secret and terrible meaning.

He looked up none of his former friends (Julia was married and living in the Albany) except Stroud who, in between violent coughing bouts, talked of the prowess of the R.A.F., and, when they parted outside the pub, groped his way to the whirring of a hand-generated torch. He hadn't dared tell him where he was hoping to go and, in general, the meeting had been a mistake.

Coming down one morning he was handed a telephone message by the clerk at the reception desk asking him to call at the passport office at his earliest covenience. He went there not knowing whether the exit visa had been granted or not, was told to wait, and sat with others on one of several benches while from time to time the dark blue books came sliding down a chute from a room above.

He recognized his own green one from afar and was already on his feet when his name was called. When it was passed to him under the grille, he put it in his pocket and went out to the street before opening it.

It was only when he was through the French examination at Boulogne in the early hours of the bitterly cold January morning and seated in an unlit compartment of the Paris train, that he had a sensation of the great change taking place.

A day in wintry, waiting Paris with the *Abri* signs along the streets and where a more complete transformation than in London was apparent – or was it the one in his own life he'd become conscious of? He was not going to pass through without looking into the Dôme, not because he might see Lisette and Danielle with the little dog – or was it to the other girl he'd given it? – just arrived from the Hôtel de Royale Bretagne and sitting up at the counter, after eight long years, even longer in their lives than in his, but for a kind of solitary last supper in the company of ghosts with a bottle of Chianti, before taking a taxi to the Gare de l'Est.

Bern, city of dry, unmelting snow, of hot silvery radiators – after washing a pair of underpants, he hung them on the one in his hotel room – of arcades with lit shop windows, though it was morning, on one side, and on the other, through the arches, snow from a dark sky. At the big, pale police building H was given, with no fuss at all, a permit to stay, and then went to sit in an overheated little café, smelling of freshly ground coffee, a thick carpet absorbing the melting snow from his shoes, served by a big, blonde, handsome waitress in a frilly apron.

Dark-bright city of picturesque snow scenes observed from cosy interiors, the only one for a long way in any direction, H reflected, where coffee and cream or chocolate would go on being served at the morning hour of eleven while one by one the others shared the fate (it was softly snowing clichés) of Warsaw.

H took a taxi to the German embassy out in a suburb, and having stated his business and asked for the ambassador, getting here having cost him enough in perseverance and anxiety to justify this request, was shown into another warm room to wait. The time that elapsed before he was received by a sombrely attired official behind an antique desk was sufficient to make him suppose that this was the personage he'd asked for. Though the delay might have been due to their telephoning Berlin to have his story corroborated, the place being no doubt full of spies.

The official asked what kind of a journey H had had in good enough English to convey a tone of polite concern that went with the formal look of the suit, the buttonhole, and antique furnishings. When he said he was sending somebody with H in a car to the consulate where they'd give him the necessary documents and heard that H had had a taxi waiting all the time, he looked up with, for the first time, real concern, pressed a bell and gave directions to have it paid off, dismissing H's attempt to go out and do so himself.

That evening H was in another taxi being driven from one station to the other in Basel through the openings left in the street barricades, the most warlike preparations that H had yet seen. Inside the station he paused for a couple of moments, setting down his suitcase in the last well-lit and neutral spot he would encounter for many a day, between the Swiss and German control posts.

A few more steps and there'd be no turning back, he'd be on the other side of a wall that was going to become more impassable as time went on, where little or nothing could reach him from the place he'd left, and from where even if Kay – it was she who was in his thoughts – became ill he couldn't be summoned home.

Having missed the Berlin express, he could only get a train as far as Freiburg where he spent the night, showing the document signed by the ambassador, as well as his passport, to the two plainclothes policemen (Gestapo?) who came to the hotel in the morning to tell him he was in a forbidden frontier zone.

After a long day's journey through the desolate-seeming snow, with a glimpse of the frozen Rhine, he was back at the Hotel Habsburger Hof, where it was too late to eat, though once he'd dined much later after his long exploratory walk, and he was glad to buy a couple of apples from a bowl of them on the reception desk, an indication of how little was available without ration coupons.

Waking in the night and groping for the light-switch in order to eat the second of the apples in an attempt to allay his hunger, he hit his mouth on the marble edge of the bedside table and broke off a front tooth.

In the morning he rang up Kolbinsky who, after welcoming him back, and before going on to deal with the purpose of the call, disconcerted H, who was at best ill at ease on the phone, by inquiring how his work was going and expressing the hope of being allowed to see some of a new novel. Was this to indicate that there was no war fever here, or part of the German politeness that H felt he hadn't fully plumbed?

Later, walking from the hotel to Potsdamer Platz on his way to keep his appointment, an arctic wind blew through his light overcoat, the stump of the broken tooth ached painfully, and, for the one and only time, H wondered if his decision to return had been the right one. He came to remember this stretch of street as that where the iciest winds of wartime were always blowing.

Kolbinsky accompanied H to the university Kasse where he collected his back salary, which had been paid in regularly since his official appointment in the summer in spite of his delay in reappearing. Still cold and in pain, H stood dumbly in the office at the Englische Seminar while the secretary slipped a sheet of paper into her typewriter and waited for him to tell her the

255

general title of his weekly lectures, including the names of the writers he'd be dealing with.

With the unexpectedly large wad stowed away in an inside pocket, and doubled up in the bitter wind, he set out to find a dentist. Passing through an arctic square he saw a group of figures modelled in snow representing, among those he recognized, Chamberlain and Churchill, and dropped the coins that had been slid under the grille after the carefully counted hundred-mark notes into the street artist's box.

Extract from H's War Diary: 'Time: deepest winter, 1940. Situation: uncertain, compromised, companionless, cold to freezing, stump of broken front tooth needing attention. Alternatively: alone and free, passionately involved in my own living fiction, imaginative participation unimpaired, unpredictable possibilities.'

The plaque at the street door said 'Zahnärztin', but because he hadn't taken the last syllable into account it was a surprise to have a girl in a white coat looking into his mouth.

The 'Ach!' with which she greeted what she saw there, followed by the 'Ach!' when, answering her question, he told her his nationality, as well as all the later 'Achs!' became part of her image for him. It was one that he might have fictionalized in a novel had not these early wartime impressions been largely obliterated by the more intense ones later superimposed. Another thing that charmed him was how she held her hands an inch apart to show him the extent of her knowledge of English in which, nevertheless, she conversed with him, asking him about the Duke of Windsor, who, he guessed, symbolized for her all that was debonair and most un-German.

Then with another woman, apprentice or assistant, peering over her shoulder the little Zahnärztin started on the nerve-racking, to both of them, excavation of the stump.

A sharp cracking that indicated that the root had split into two, possibly more, pieces, followed an hour or two later, as time was being measured by H, by a crunch that meant, he dared hope, that at least part of the splintered stump had been wrenched from its anchorage in his upper jaw.

'Not nice, no?'

The gurgling of the glass bowl into which he was spitting mouthfuls of blood and water. The girl dentist holding her hands apart again, showing him, he supposed, though he'd lost the thread of what she was trying to say, the degree of nervous tension they'd both suffered, or perhaps the length of the extracted root.

Preoccupied by the ache in his mouth and, on another level, by the astonishing realization of where, after the months of struggle, he actually was, he went to the American Express in Unter den Linden to arrange for the monthly transfer of part of his salary to Iseult. His next call was to the office of an estate agency of which he'd taken note in the summer because of a notice, now removed, announcing, 'French and English spoken':

After explaining where he came from and what he wanted, H had his hand shaken by the huge gangster of a proprietor who then dipped his broad, padded shoulders over a ledger.

'Something commodious, eh? How about this?' he asked in a glib, accented American, 'beautiful fifth-floor apartment, large parlour and dining room, with, what-you-call-it? sunshine conservatory, one main and two secondary bedrooms, maid's room, bathroom, two toilets, all luxurious appointments. I know these people: high army officer, wife off to the country with the child.' He looked up and winked at H.

The rent, even after sending the equivalent of twenty pounds home each month, an arrangement that was going to take time to get going and needed a special permit, was within what H could now afford and the size of the place didn't deter him; it would add to the sense of freedom – he'd sleep in the rooms in rotation and make all the beds, say, once a week.

On the day H moved in he gave his first lecture at the university, had Ulla Flickenschild come up to the little rostrum and ask him to dinner one evening at her parents' house in Grünewald, was again charmed by Fräulein Dr Sonning when he went to be measured for a bridge for an artificial tooth, and was lent by Kolbinsky one of Kafka's works in German that he hadn't heard of.

So much to be absorbed and reflected on all at once, quite apart from the more general impressions, by him who seemed in retrospect to have lived so like a hermit at home that a bird's song had given him food for hours of thought!

He explored the flat, wandering from room to room and letting certain features of the place form an atmosphere: the frosted glass window of the big dark hall that gave on to an echoing interior well, the double sliding doors between the living rooms, the twin beds in the main bedroom, the glass cabinet full of china ornaments in the smaller drawing room, finally settling in a leather armchair in the middle of the largest room, beside the telephone; but who could possibly telephone him? On his knee was the book that Kolbinsky had lent him, and on the floor beside him, a dictionary. Having with some trouble translated the title page, containing as many words as that of his own first novel – *Reflections on Sin, Suffering, Hope, and the True Way*, by Franz Kafka – he foresaw that it was going to be vital for him to read it, even if it meant learning German to do so.

It turned out to be a collection of aphorisms or pensées. Having drawn the curtains across the three windows overlooking the wintry Platz four or five storeys below, H, after a long time that, in reverse ratio to the time spent while the girl dentist's hand, whose palm, he'd noted afterwards, was red with the pressure of the forceps, had struggled with the stump of tooth, seemed only a few minutes, had made out one of them: 'We too must suffer all the suffering round us. We have not all one body but we have one way of growing and this leads us through all anguish whether in this form or that ... There is no room for justice in this context, but neither is there any room for fear of suffering or for the interpretation of suffering as a merit.'

Amen, H commented.

He hadn't understood what he'd read, partly because of his difficulty with the language, but also, he knew, because he wasn't ready for what was being communicated. But, he'd found before, the fact that the sentences fascinated him was a sign that they belonged to a mode of perception that, though he hadn't reached, he was ripening towards.

Next day he was taken by Kolbinsky to meet a Dr Zimmermann, a round, pale-eyed little man with fair hair who also spoke perfect English though with a slight (Yorkshire?) intonation, and had been a lecturer at a university in the Midlands up to the outbreak of war. He struck H as wishing he was still there rather than here, and he asked H if he'd care to write some talks that could be broadcast to 'our English friends'; had 'chums' been on the tip of his tongue?

In agreeing, H was turning from the busy street to slink with thieves and petty criminals down dim alleys, leaving the lawful company to which he'd belonged to become, in its eyes, a traitor. He was thinking now of himself as a writer, published and, for the most part, read in England, rather than an Irishman. This was a kind of malefactor whose rejection was seldom rescinded because the crime was not merely against an individual but that society as a whole.

The deed was done. H's first reaction: relief at in the end it being so easy to take this step outside the moral Pale.

The advantage he had over the ordinary criminal was that in the prevailing conditions it was possible to act in a way that would evoke in his judges the same condemnation as the kind of peacetime crime of which he was incapable.

49

H was now fully occupied by the lectures and classes, the talks he'd agreed to write for Dr Zimmermann, the slow elucidation of Kafka, visits to the girl dentist, shopping and the apportioning of his coupons to the best advantage, cleaning the large flat, including carrying the two refuse buckets down five flights of backstairs to a shed in the yard, where he had to empty the pail with the food remains into one of the bins destined for what were known as Goering's pigs, and a couple of visits to the Flickenschilds.

As for the talks, it wasn't difficult to discredit the propaganda of the various combatants, with the possible exception of Poland which had been too busy retreating to strike attitudes, as fundamentally dishonest.

Of the British, who claimed to be engaged on a crusade against barbarism, as indeed, he pointed out, they'd always been according to their apologists, H recalled some of the former ones such as those against Kruger and the Boer farmers, Lenin, Trotsky, and the early Communists, Gandhi and his disciples, Pearse, Casement, and the men of Easter Week, whose photos, so effective was the indignation aroused in the press, his nurse couldn't bear to have in her room overnight.

H did think it necessary, however, to explain that none of these examples were looked on with pride by honest people in England, a fact that seemed to surprise the plump, pale-eyed Doktor, who suggested that in talks of this sort there was no room for fine distinctions, and who perhaps, H thought, was right. He didn't get his way in this, but he made H cut out the reference to the British intervention in the Russian Revolution.

In another talk H pointed out that by trying to extinguish the very private and personal insights in favour of a general acceptance of profitable (for the war effort) moral concepts, the Allied propagandists were corrupting the only sources by which the human spirit could come to its difficult judgements and register its personal, sovereign compassion.

Dr Zimmermann, having glanced through this one too, placed it in a drawer with the other, and H saw that it wasn't what he wanted.

All the same he paid H for the three and asked him to a meal at a restaurant that evening to meet a fellow countryman of H's who had also agreed to do some work, in the way of translation, for him.

'An Irishman?' H asked.

'An Irish woman, or so she says, but I'd like to have your opinion on that. Another thing I want to ask you: what impression did you get of the effects of the broadcasts of Lord How-How, as they call him – does that mean they're mystified as to his real identity? – were having?

'Oh, and one other question,' said the beaming Herr Doktor (H had now guessed for whom his talks were destined), 'what does "browned-off" mean? I hear speakers on the B.B.C. use the phrase which is a new one to me.'

At a big crowded restaurant – everybody seemed to eat out in Berlin – next evening, H, after searching through several rooms, getting in the way of waiters hurrying hither and thither with trays, and generally calling unwelcome attention to himself by his un-Central-European air and attire, especially his non-crease, unsoilable, turtleneck jersey, found Dr Zimmermann and a sick-looking girl at a table keeping a seat for him.

The little Doktor introduced her as Miss something-or-other; H was too distracted by all the faces he'd had to glance at to register names.

She looked, he thought, as though she might have been the daughter of a Spanish croupier, an Italian jockey – she seemed very small – or the owner of a back-street hotel in, say, Cyprus or Malta. What he was getting at was that, wherever she came from, she looked intriguing and far from respectable.

As they were studying the Speisekarte, a procedure complicated by the need to calculate the expenditure of coupons, it dawned on him of whom she reminded him: his idea of the girls chained to the railings. Not that he'd seen a photo of them at the time.

Intent on finding something without the mustard sauce in which most meat or fish dishes were smothered these days, he chose one which required more Reisemarken, or eating-out, detachable coupons, than he had left, the girl offered him some of hers.

'I've plenty.'

'How's that?' H was curious about her.

'I don't go to restaurants, don't go out much at all.'

'What *do* you do?'

'Play and read, read and play; the piano, I mean.'

'What kind of music?'

Her narrow face with shadows under the large luminous eyes closed up, and he saw he'd intruded into guarded privacies. Or it might be Dr Zimmermann's presence – he was listening to every word – that she resented.

Later she relented a little and said she'd been studying at the music conservatoire in Vienna (did he recall it?) and had stayed on in spite of the war, but trouble over her papers had forced her to come to Berlin.

'We gave her a Fremdenpass,' Dr Zimmermann put in.

'What's that?' H wanted to have it clear.

'A passport for friendly foreigners who, for one reason or another, haven't a valid one of their own. By the way,' he added to H, 'the first of your talks is being broadcast tomorrow night.'

'I'd like to hear it but I haven't a radio,' the girl said and H suggested she come and listen at his flat where there was a big set on which he could receive the B.B.C.; Germans, he'd heard, were forbidden to listen to it.

In the morning her coming was forgotten in his preoccupation with the lecture he was giving. He'd found that the English writers the students thought it correct to admire were the ones who, to him, were suspect. At first he tried to influence their judgement, but later abandoned any such aim and was content simply to air his thoughts and thus help get them straight, while giving the students the opportunity of hearing English well spoken with a few facts about the literary figures in England and Ireland with whom some show of familiarity might later prove a benefit thrown in. Some of them hoped to go to England when the war was over, either as *au pair* girls to cultured families or to a university. They nearly all looked up to England and the English.

There was Jane Austen in her fictional drawing room, the parochial spinster with the sharp eye and ready, though genteelly muted, wit, proving once more, if proof was needed, that the English novel was a safe retreat for those who didn't want to be reminded of the subterranean rumblings and other presages of disaster discernible beyond the vicarage garden.

In order to give more weight to them, he supported his views with other, more authoritative ones. He'd looked up Charlotte Brontë's opinion of Jane Austen in a book he'd got from the State Library and he opened it, first at the wrong page – he'd several books on the lectern in front of him with slips of paper sprouting from each – and read out to them: 'She does her business of delineating the surface of the lives of genteel English people curiously well ... What sees keenly, speaks aptly, moves flexibly, it suits her to study; but what throbs fast and full, though hidden, what the blood rushes through, what is the unseen seat of life and the sentient target of death – this Miss Austen ignores.'

'I'll read that last half-sentence again,' he said, 'and I'd like you to tell me to what you think it refers.'

When he looked up after doing so he was taken aback by their blank (bored? bewildered?) expressions and quickly began searching in another book, determined not to retreat but to involve himself in total war with them by a swift sortie on another of their idols: Bernard Shaw. Making things worse was the fact that instead of the clear, cultured enunciation they'd expected, because of the missing tooth his voice had a sibilant indistinctness.

'It is largely the sort of questions that anxious and imaginative people ask that determines the quality of the thinking of a particular period,' he began in his newly acquired, professional style. 'If these are the kind that raise doubts about the original premise on which it is based then all is probably well with the spiritual health of that society.

'What sort of questions did Shaw pose? Always ones to which there were neat, logical answers.

'His was a mental world where certain familiar concepts were placed upside-down, in a very orderly fashion, but no new concepts were introduced.'

He had almost forgotten that he had a visitor coming when, for the first time since he'd moved in, the bell rang in the silence of the flat. The girl stood on the landing – for a moment, in the dim light, H thought it was a child whom she'd sent to say she couldn't come – apparently exhausted after the long climb; as all lockable objects here, the lift required a key and could be used only by the residents.

He'd bought a selection of pastries that looked like those he recalled from the summer but had the indefinable taste he'd come to associate with the war. Susan Loyson, not Lawson, she explained, though that was what was on her new passport, sat on a settee with her shoes off and her feet tucked under her, sipping the real coffee he'd bought on the black market.

They talked somewhat warily. H wasn't sure whether she mightn't be an agent of some kind (British? Nazi?) and she seemed equally on her guard.

'Where do you live?'

'Some friends let me sleep at their flat; I'm out all day.'

'Practising the piano?'

If she'd agreed immediately his suspicion would have increased, but she shook her head and her eyes became even brighter as he turned away his glance in case it was with tears, reassured that she wasn't a spy.

What he'd meant to ask was not where she was staying here but where her home was. He tried again.

'Your family must be worrying about you.'

'All the family I've got is a grandfather in London. My mother's dead, and as for my father, I don't even know for sure who he was.'

This, or something like it, he sensed was true, and it partly accounted for her air of a lost child equally ready to melt or turn vicious.

'Neither do I,' H told her, 'know anything about mine.' She was eating the little tarts, ersatz jellified fruits on a cardboardy base, quite ravenously. 'It appeared he killed himself with drink, or perhaps more deliberately, in Townsville, Australia, shortly after I was born, but nobody ever said so, I had to sense it on my own.' Iseult had repeated what his Quintillan uncle had told her mother at the conference called when he and she eloped to London, suggesting that H had inherited the mental instability.

'No, they never speak of things that make them uncomfortable,' the girl said. 'I'm not even sure whether it was because my mother wasn't married that grandad disowned her or because my father was probably a Russian Communist.'

'Zimmermann said you were Irish.'

'I had to give them a good reason for my wanting to stay on here.'

'Ah!'

'You see, I'm going to have a baby.'

She glanced at him with a half-hostile, half-suppliant look. She couldn't have known she was going to be faced with a real Irishman when she'd told the Germans her story and, he wondered a little about what she'd just said (later she explained that her grandfather had taken his daughter with him on the first British diplomatic mission to Russia after the Revolution). She struck him as someone constantly having to defend herself as best she could against various kinds of authority.

He showed her over the flat and she looked, he thought, wistfully into each of the rooms; her normal expression was one of wary dissatisfaction relieved by an occasional flash of mirth, when her small drooping mouth turned upwards. In the bathroom she studied the map of Europe which he'd put up over the mirror so that he could meditate, as he pulled the razor through the soapy film of foam, on the long and difficult journey he'd made. Pressed up against the washbasin as she asked him to show her on what part of the island depicted in yellow on the left of the sheet he lived, H saw the hem of her petticoat showing at the back, indicating by the ill fit of her skirt, the bulge in front that he hadn't noticed.

When it was time for William Joyce's nightly broadcast, H turned on the set and they heard the English voice with the snarl in it announcing (twice over): 'Germany calling.' The tone was that of retribution being pronounced on a proud and stiff-necked people who had got away for too long with the role of the chosen ones.

Lord Haw Haw's polemics left H cold. It wasn't the political or military events that concerned him but the possible inner revolution that he hoped the war might bring about. Just as he had hoped long ago at school that the Russian Revolution and, later, the Irish Civil War, might be the first rumblings of a psychic earthquake.

'That'll make them squirm,' Susan, as he'd started calling her while they'd been studying the map, exclaimed as Lord Haw Haw read from the book of the recording angel. H didn't contradict. For him it was a public word game that had been going on for as long as he remembered and at which the British had always excelled up to now, and would, he imagined, have the last word.

The girl's delight in what she believed was the discomfiture of her own people, or at least her mother's, came, he thought, because of the hurts and slights, real or imagined, she had suffered as a child and adolescent.

Later she told H about meeting Hitler at a reception in Munich her grandfather had taken her to a couple of years ago. The dictator had patted her on the cheek in answer to something she'd said to him in German. H imagined her confiding to Hitler one of her girlhood fantasies such as the English having executed her Irish patriot father, after which the Furore had sucked in his mouth in the old-woman smile and strutted on.

On an afternoon shortly after Susan's visit H suffered his first, and, of that degree of intensity, last, bout of homesickness. Suddenly, forgotten familiarities were haunting him. He felt against his palm the loose handle of his bedroom door at home, caught, below the muted noises from Hochmeisterplatz, the peculiar rustle of the mountain wind in the fir trees outside his window, smelled the warm comforting odour from the row of hens perched in a laying shed with their heads under their wings when he opened the door at night and flashed his torch on them.

So strong were these signals as he stood by one of the sitting-room windows from which he had a view down Paulborner Strasse that led from the square below to Kurfürstendamm, that he thought at any moment he must catch sight of Iseult and the children coming along it, having just arrived in Berlin and walked from the Zoo instead of taking a taxi, after depositing their baggage.

If three figures were to appear in the distance not quite recognizable at first, conjured there by the intensity of his pain, he'd rush down, not waiting for a lift, and run along the pavement from which the snow had been newly swept to meet them before they could vanish. But all he saw, beyond the yellow bus waiting at the terminus, was a couple of dogs copulating in the street and a fur-coated woman who had stopped to watch them.

50

H sometimes went to the Flickenschild villa in Grünewald to sit holding Ulla's hand on the sofa in the big sitting room under a picture of a waxen, short-legged Adam and Eve by Cranach, talking of Kafka, Mann, Melville, Proust (compared to whom, H remarked, English novelists were a bunch of village gossips), and of 'our old boy,' as she called Hitler, and, occasionally, of Ulla herself.

'It's something I've never done,' she said in answer to a suggestion of H's.

'Not slept with a man?'

'Never, never,' she repeated, in a tone that he interpreted not so much as a direct refusal as an intimation that she was leaving it to him to decide whether to take the responsibility of her initiation.

Because of their rather intellectual relationship, the physical one resulting from their acting on his proposal was bound to be awkward, at least in the initial stages, she being a virgin, and all the harder for him to sustain under her mental scrutiny.

So he didn't grasp the possibly opportune moment, or at least postponed doing so, and, instead, when the weather was mild enough and most of the snow was off the links at Wannsee, played golf with her, her father, and a business associate of Herr Flickenschild's in a four-ball match.

Ulla's father was an expert player. 'He does only a very few things but all of them well,' Ulla commented.

When H got home after one such game he wrote in what he called his wartime diary: 'The three of us set out in steady rain under umbrellas (Herr F. is on the German international team and likes to practise in all weathers), playing what Herr F. called best ball, high ball, low ball, a system I didn't follow. Our handicaps: Herr F's, 3; U's, 10; Dr X's, 24; my own, as given by myself, 14.

'Was soaked through but played well, that's to say erratically, getting in some good shots (about five) and a number of poor ones. After continual calculation and adjustment Herr Doktor X announced a draw, though I've no idea how he arrived at it.'

Why did H note down trivialities in the midst of momentous events? Was it because, when not actually possessed by his demon, which was comparatively rarely and fleetingly and hardly for as long as it took to write an entire novel, his mind was neither diligent nor remarkably intelligent? This lack of a brilliant mind was undoubtedly one of the reasons, but these superficial interests helped dilute some of the more unprofitable hauntings that took place there.

There was, though, one incident on the golf links that had some significance and on which H meditated afterwards. One afternoon when they were playing alone Herr Flickenschild offered H a spare room in the big villa, suggesting that he might find it easier living with them than being all on his own in wartime Berlin.

When H told Ulla, she said her father feared part of the house might be requisitioned and that he'd prefer having H than a strange woman with several children. 'You could probably sublet your flat if you wanted to, though the contract is sure to forbid it. Everything is verboten with us that isn't obligatory.'

H thanked Herr Flickenschild and said he'd like to think it over. But he knew he wouldn't move to the villa even though it meant seeing more of Ulla whom he really liked very much.

It wasn't in the legend. Or, to abstain from what might be a tendency to self-glorification, he was more likely to attract to himself the kind of events his awkward psyche needed by remaining in the flat and, when he'd made up his mind to it, inviting Susan Loyson to share it with him; on a second visit she'd told him that she hadn't seen her baby's father since the time of its conception.

On his free afternoons he walked the streets within winter range of the Platz where the flat, as well as a Lutheran church, whose clock he heard striking the hours of day and night, was situated. Starting on the return journey at the far end of Kurfürstendamm with his back to the grim black pile of the Gedächtniskirche, the café Linden, whose candelabra Herr Eberstadt had disappointed H by mentioning as one of the first things to see here, was on his right and a few yards further was Mampe's where it was still possible to drink Bowle in one of the small well-heated rooms decorated with photographs of the early Zeppelin flights, to which, it seemed, the firm had been official caterers. Across the wide boulevard was Stöckler's, where he occasionally went for a half lobster, off the ration, and a bottle of white wine.

For the first time in his life he was living alone in a big flat, bathing and shaving every day, reading the paper at breakfast, punctually catching the same bus each morning, dining out when he felt like it, and in general acting the normal civilized, urban man from whom he'd never felt further removed.

Popular songs came over the radio between announcements of British shipping sunk, preceded by a fanfare of trumpets. His favourite was 'Es geht alles vorüber' which haunted him as Julia's pantomime duet, 'You may not be an angel . . .' had once done. 'Lili Marlen' came later, at least into H's ken. He even went to films, which he rarely had at home. He also listened every evening at the hour of six to the B.B.C. news which was almost his only link with the world he had left. So far he had had no letters from home.

The war had come to a temporary halt and nobody, least of all H, knew what would happen next. To the songs and the announcements of torpedoings was added the news that Molotov was in Berlin signing a treaty of eternal friendship, the effect of which, as far as H was concerned, was that two young Soviet Russians turned up at his conversation classes.

He saw Susan from time to time in a café in Viktoria-Luise-Platz which had been one of the squares he'd passed through on his first long exploration the previous summer. Although he was punctual, she was always waiting and told him that it was in such places she spent her days rather than make herself a nuisance by hanging around the tiny flat whose owners, an elderly couple, let her sleep in the sitting room.

'I return at nine when they go to bed,' she said. 'I tell them I work at the radio.'

'But you don't?'

'I read the news in French a few times till they got hold of Michel; that's where I met him.'

In which case she hadn't stayed on after the outbreak of war because of not daring to return pregnant to her grandfather, as H had understood, unless she was talking about a period just before the war and of the Vienna radio station. But he wasn't going to cross-examine her.

'Did your friend return to France?'

'Oh no, he's a Breton nationalist and he's here to get the Germans to give Brittany independence if they win the war.'

H presented her with a just-opened red rose on a long stalk that he'd bought at one of the numerous florists that were now the only shops with prewar window displays. He thought she regarded it with surprise as if such tokens weren't for her. But again he put off suggesting she move into the flat.

In the end he made the offer one evening at supper in a restaurant in Kurfürstendamm, not Stöckler's where she wouldn't have fitted in among prosperous German business executives and their well-dressed women.

Would she refuse, as he'd declined the Flickenschilds' invitation to stay with them? She too might have her own legend to create. But for him the alternative hadn't been to sit in the corners of cafés drinking cups of malt coffee, and counting the Pfennige, all the long winter days.

'I could have a room with you?'

'Several, a whole wing.'

'I won't be able to pay anything.'

'I didn't suppose you would.'

She was turning over the flakes of some indeterminate fish in mustard sauce with her fork.

'It's really O.K.?' she asked.

'Oh, yes. Move in any time you like.'

'The day after tomorrow?'

She'd have liked, he guessed, to have come tomorrow, or even today, but didn't want to seem in too desperate a hurry.

A man at the next table was watching them, no doubt to see who was speaking English. When H stared boldly back at him, he returned his attention to his food. Surprisingly, only a couple of times when H was talking in his native tongue in public, as he did throughout the war, was an objection raised, and at least on one of these occasions an apology was made when H's companion, not Susan by then, indignantly defended his right to do so.

Susan moved in with two blue soft-leather suitcases; her few belongings, H noted, looked to be of good quality, but uncared for. He gave her the big room with the twin beds; he slept in one of the smaller bedrooms.

For the first few days H didn't see much of her; she stayed in her room; when he looked in the second evening to ask her to come out with him to dinner she was lying on one of the beds studying a paperbound music book, one of several she'd piled on it.

'I can't afford eating out.'

Rebuffed by her tone and annoyed that she seemed to think he expected her to pay for herself, he shut her door again and went out alone.

Often, when he was reading, still slowly struggling through the Kafka, he heard her padding about in her stockinged feet. She seemed to live on snacks, mostly bread and tomatoes, which she neither ate at the kitchen table or took to her room. He'd found a whole sheet of traveller's ration coupons one evening on the desk by the telephone. When he asked her about them, not thanking her straight off in case she'd merely forgotten them there after making a call, she told him they were of no use to her.

H occasionally heard her telephoning, and although he didn't eavesdrop, for he wasn't curious, at least not at that time, and she spoke in German, some of the calls seemed to be to an official to whom she was giving the information that would enable him to make out a maintenance order for the support of the baby when it was born.

Sometimes whole days passed and they only met in the kitchen or passage. H had hung another map, of Eastern Europe, on which was shown the much-diminished Poland coloured a paler shade of red than the German Reich and across which was written 'General Gouvernement', in the dark hall, and coming home one afternoon he found her studying it, having first had to switch on the light. After peering at it beside her and trying to envisage the sort of desolate occupied places the towns with their Germanized names (Lemberg, Litzmannstadt) were like, they turned as of one accord and crossed the hall to the frosted window.

He opened it and they stood looking down the inner well where their voices echoed as in a cave and they breathed the dusty scent. While they leaned over the sill with nothing to see but the other hall windows below and the bottom of the shaft, he kissed her.

When he woke up in the big room next morning, she was already sitting up in the next bed in a torn nightdress, pushing aside dark strands of straggly hair as she sucked at a tomato, looking like a girl of fourteen or fifteen from a back street in a southern town.

Sensing him watching her, she wiped her mouth on the end of the sheet, stretched herself and lay back on the pillows with her thin brown arms behind her head and her belly making a slight bulge under the bedclothes.

'With no aunt or grandfather to watch what time we come in at night or when we get up, we could stay in bed all day,' she murmured.

It seemed she was still delighting in having freed herself from the regime of the house in St John's Wood which had quite failed to turn her into the sort of marriageable young lady, with a gift for music and languages, that her grandfather had probably hoped to make of her; there were, H imagined, and later heard about from her, signs of early delinquency.

H was back in a world of disorderliness. But this one wasn't like Iseult's; Susan's carelessness didn't come from apathy but from the completeness with which she gave herself to the dreams reflecting in her large, luminous eyes and which, H guessed, were about becoming a concert pianist as well as the even more secret ones of healing the real or imagined childhood wounds with a series of spellbound lovers.

Now she also used the other part of the flat; when he returned from the university he'd find her, her feet tucked under her, hair uncombed, curtains drawn, though it was still daylight, table lamp lit, with her music, munching a piece of cheese or end of sausage, perhaps making up for months of semi-starvation.

51

When Susan took it into her head, she did the shopping and cooking, but some days she spent on her bed with her music scores, that were stained with tomato juice, or she padded about in an old red dressing gown down to her bare feet, an abducted child half-reconciled to her captivity.

She'd come and huddle beside him on the settee in the smaller sitting room, her feet tucked under her, and talk of her past, which, however, never became at all clear to him, with a nostalgia and melancholy that nothing but love-making roused her out of.

By the time the new and active phase of the war started, H had sunk into an obsessive existence in the big flat with the moody, pregnant girl. He heard the news one morning at the Foreign Office where he'd gone early with a talk for Dr Zimmermann. The Doktor hadn't yet arrived in his office, but his assistant in the British section gave H the news about the invasion of Denmark and Norway quite apologetically as if it was an ungentlemanly act, a breaking in at the back door just when both sides had seemed set in token postures of hostility; the young man was one of the always immaculately dressed anglophiles whose prevalence had surprised H on his prewar visit.

H and Susan discussed the new aspect of the war and the possibility of the Allies, and especially the English, being defeated.

'They'll still be the good children of the postwar world, win or lose,' she said, 'heroes and heroines, writing their glorious war memories with wreaths being laid everywhere and everyone being more righteous than ever. Nobody has ever managed to combine superiority with self-interest so well.'

As it drew into summer, Susan drooped and swelled and looked like a starved and tousled-haired stray who'd escaped, if somewhat late, from a brigand's lair. Indeed the flat itself seemed a thieves' kitchen in which they hid like a couple of malefactors while the B.B.C. broadcasts assumed a tone of moral grandeur as the defeats multiplied and Churchill's ringing phrases were repeated.

The days grew hotter and she sat silent and exhausted-looking in one of the big armchairs. He supposed the prospect of having the baby frightened her, but when he tried to reassure her she looked scornful and shook her head: 'It's not that.'

'What, then?'

'Can't you guess?'

If she wanted him to draw her secrets out of her, this was a game he didn't care for. Just as he was getting ready to go to the university, she said, 'My fingers are losing their touch.'

H sat down on the settee beside her again.

'And I can't even blame the war for bringing my life down in ruins, that's how it began.'

'It's not in ruins, Susie.'

'Don't call me that.'

'What am I to call you?'

'Can't you find some other name? That's what they called me at home and usually disapprovingly.'

'What would you like to be called?'

'Don't know.'

She looked at him reproachfully out of her wet, luminous eyes as though he were to blame for not having another name ready. H meditated for a few moments. 'I'll call you Katusha.'

If he wasn't to be late for his class he had to hurry down to the waiting bus. As he boarded it he looked up at the three windows of the big room and saw the pallid oval of her face at the middle one as she waved to him and then formed the syllables with her mouth: 'Ka-tush-a'.

H was always fully occupied keeping the class or lecture going; but upstairs in the lecturers' room between classes the tense compulsive atmosphere of the flat would come flooding back over him. When the telephone on his table rang he would grasp the receiver and wait anxiously while she asked him to bring back some item from the shops till, before ringing off, she would ask, 'Still love me?' or 'Miss me?' – phrases that she repeated in and out of season.

H hadn't yet had any letters from home. He had a feeling of precarious freedom; nobody knew where they were. Their state had something in common with that of Siobahn and Nicky in his novel.

She sometimes kept the curtains drawn and the lights burning in the big living room all day, saying she couldn't stand the summer glare through the windows, hummed sombre melodies, made telephone calls (about the maintenance order? to the maternity clinic?), replacing the receiver as he came in from fetching their evening beer.

It was half in relief that H went to Frankfurt to meet a British prisoner of war who had asked to see him, having heard in a letter from home or through a newspaper report that H was in Germany. This officer, who bore the possibly Jewish name of Manville was, according to Dr Zimmermann, himself a writer, though H had never heard of him.

Zimmermann wanted H to go. What he hoped would be gained by the meeting H didn't know. He himself was at first reluctant but then agreed, partly to have a short breathing space from the erotic, neurotic trance of the flat.

Dr Zimmermann sent a young Foreign Office official with him, in case, he explained, the commandant of the camp should, in spite of the telephone message, become suspicious if he arrived alone, in his rather shabby suit (though this Zimmermann didn't mention), and, in his poor German, asked for an interview with one of his prisoners.

H met the emissary from the Auswärtige Amt one evening at the Potsdamer Bahnhof where the places had been reserved for them on the Frankfurt-am-Main express. He was just as H had expected: tall, solemn, balding, and speaking a precise, accentless English. One of his first remarks when they were settled in their corner seats was to ask if he was a military man, and when H, taken aback, shook his head, added, 'I thought you might have been in one of the services,' and H realized that he'd mixed him up with a British ex-officer who'd defected to Germany before the war; there was a slight similarity in their names.

Leaning back and looking out of the window as the train pulled out, H intimated his disinclination for conversation and began thinking of Susan alone in the flat, with nobody to go down to the Kneipe for cold beer for supper, and imagined her, not having bothered to make herself a solitary meal, stretched on the settee in one of her old satin nightgowns, shiny-tight over her belly, devouring fruit and doing her finger exercises. At the last moment she'd clung to him, murmuring, 'Love me?' and when he'd given a perhaps impatient nod, her eyes had shone with the increased brightness that presaged tears.

They were driven to the Stalag in the Taunus hills outside Frankfurt in the

271

inevitable black Mercedes, after putting in time after their very early arrival by having hot baths at the station.

There they were welcomed by the commandant, Major Rumpel, at his house in an orchard, a big man in a white mess jacket who, H's companion had told him, was a friend of Goering's and had a telephone line direct to the Reichsmarschall.

H and the Foreign Office official, whom H soon saw had been an unnecessary precaution on Zimmermann's part, sat down to a table spread with a chequered cloth and laid with two big blue pots of real coffee and platefuls of bread and slices of sausage, with the commandant and his staff.

It was a relief to hear Major Rumpel speak English with a pronounced accent; H distrusted Germans who spoke it perfectly as either secret anglophiles or, conversely, rabid Hitlerites, though hadn't he spoken it at all it would have meant the balding young man, to whom H had taken a dislike, acting as interpreter.

H was soon put at ease by the major, who didn't ask him any questions at all, with his easygoing, but not too genial, air, his homely establishment, and the handsome young members of his staff around the collar of one of whom H noticed the Knight's Cross.

After breakfast, if that was what the meal was, the commandant sent for Captain Manville and suggested to H's companion that he might like to take a deck chair into the orchard. So, rather to his surprise, though in keeping with his impression of Major Rumpel, H was left alone in the sunny room to await the prisoner of war.

A short, sun-bronzed man of around H's age (thirty-eight), in khaki shirt whose sleeves were rolled high, well-creased trousers, and soft leather footwear that H envied, and that he thought were called flying boots, entered the room.

The first moments had in them some tension which the British airman tried to lessen by offering H an English cigarette, an attempt that H, by having to refuse (he didn't smoke), frustrated.

'I didn't know whether they'd give you my message,' Captain Manville was saying, 'or, if they did, whether you'd care to come.'

'Here I am,' H answered, aware of the inadequacy of the remark but still feeling his way.

'I'd better tell you right away that I've no political or ideologist purpose in meeting you; what I want to talk to you about is your books.'

This was what H had hoped and why he had risked coming. Several English prisoners of war had expressed sympathy for the German war aims and some had been released and were, he'd read, employed in translating or other work. He knew Dr Zimmermann had equated Captain Manville with these, though, in asking to see H, his approach was more wary, as might be expected in the case of someone of his rank. Because the captain would be an exceptional prize and Zimmermann didn't consider H a reliable envoy, he'd sent along one of his staff.

'My books,' H repeated.

H wasn't exactly surprised, but this interpenetration by fiction of so factual a situation came as a shock. Because of creatures of his imagination Zimmermann had made arrangements at the Auswärtige Amt, seats had been booked on the train, Major Rumpel had issued orders, his staff, including a Ritterkreuzträger, had clicked heels and shaken hands.

'I've just read, *I Won't be Wearing Shamrock* ... for the second time,' Captain Manville was saying, 'and I took the chance you wouldn't think my asking to see you an impertinence.'

A hesitant smile flickered over his bronzed face.

'No, Captain, on the contrary. They've put up notices at all the stations, saying "Räder müssen rollen für den Sieg!" to discourage people travelling for private reasons, but could there be any more private journey than this one of mine to discuss imaginary inmates of an Irish asylum with a prisoner of war?'

He'd launched himself into the long sentence without knowing precisely how he was going to end it, trusting to his intensified emotion at meeting somebody to whom, with reservations, he could open his heart to inspire the right conclusion.

Captain Manville, evidently still under the spell of the novel, started talking about Siobahn's attempts to cure Nicky of his sexual inhibitions, manifested in his caressing of silky tresses detached from their owners in his solitary room at night, by pretending to be teaching him the movements of ice-skating, without, of course, skates or ice, at their secret trysts behind the asylum fuel shed.

'There's another aspect of all this I'd like to discuss with you,' Captain Manville said, 'but first I want to say how touching I found your heroine's telling Nicky that once she had cured him of his impotence he'd feel like rushing up to the first girl he saw – after his release from the asylum, I think she meant – and saying – wait a minute, it's one of the passages I copied out, I've got it here.'

The prisoner of war produced a pocket diary filled with what appeared to be extracts from books he'd been reading, some in French, as H could see over his shoulder, and, finding the right page, read out: 'For the blessed love of Christ let me undress you! Not all at once, I couldn't stand the shock, but bit by bit, starting at the blouse buttons, and, if you've the patience and all goes well, if I don't faint, get sick or otherwise disgrace myself ('I can guess what other disaster he was afraid of,' Captain Manville paused in the reading to remark, 'I too was afflicted with that particular disability as a youth, never

273

getting within inches of the girl without being overtaken by a premature orgasm') let me strip you to the skin. Then, after a pause for refreshments and to come to myself, I shall be in a position to push on and complete the breathtaking leap (not a pas-de-deux on an imaginary ice rink but in an actual bed) that joins man and woman.'

'But I know of course that these passages, however, appealing,' the captain went on, shutting and replacing the diary in the breast pocket of his shirt, 'are incidental to the main current of the story in your novels. And it's in connection with this that I'm puzzled. Not by anything in the books themselves, they strike me as marvellously all of a piece, but in your own attitude, Mr Ruark, as expressed, tacitly but unmistakenly, in your coming here to Germany.'

'Of which you disapprove, Captain.'

'I've no right to approve or disapprove. But as a writer you've given me so much that I'm puzzled and wanted to put the straight question. You're the last person I'd have imagined siding with the enemy.'

'Whose enemy?' H couldn't help asking, though he knew the question was disingenuous.

'Oh, I know that as an Irishman they're not your enemy technically. But aren't they proving themselves the enemy of mankind, I mean of those very human and irrational attitudes and the freedom of thought that you're so committed to in your novels.'

'The last thing I can, or want to do, Captain, is justify my being here in moral terms. Whatever the motives for my coming here, and they were complex and far from pure, I've begun to realize that it's here in the company of the guilty that with my peculiar and, if you like, flawed kind of imagination, I belong. The situation I've involved myself in, however disastrous for my reputation, and perhaps because it *is* disastrous, gives me a chance of becoming the only sort of writer it's in my power to be.'

'I'd understand it if you told me you'd be at home among the defeated but surely not among these victorious brutes.'

H didn't answer. Captain Manville had touched a vital spot. If the setup here really triumphed, as seemed likely enough, H saw quite clearly by now that for himself it would mean inner disaster. To be acclaimed by a pseudo-élite in a triumphant Reich as a foreign writer of genius would hardly be a bearable situation. In the case of a German disaster, which even then he didn't rule out, having thrown in his lot with the losing side would certainly turn out to be of immense value in his growth as an imaginative writer. Though being branded as a Nazi by those from whom most of his readers would have to come, scarcely argued well for his future, no matter how his work developed.

52

After lunch with Major Rumpel and his staff, H, at the Major's suggestion, had gone for a stroll in the wooded hills with Captain Manville; the officer prisoners were allowed out for walks on parole.

Not wanting to spend another sleepless night in a stifling train, he'd decided to stay in Frankfurt and get the morning D-Zug. He tried to phone Susan but got no reply from the flat, which didn't worry him because she sometimes went to sit on a bench on the strip of grass opposite, where the lawn sprinklers were whirring, in the comparative cool of the evening. His travelling companion, who had failed to persuade H to come to supper with a married sister who lived in the town, took the night express back to Berlin.

H's meeting with the R.A.F. officer was one of those events that went on developing in his imagination long after it had taken place. For in the end the R.A.F. man had shown how intimately he grasped things not quite clear to H himself such as (to the captain) the dangerously close identification of H with his fictions.

One possibility: the captain belonged to those – H had heard there was one or two in every prisoner of war camp – who reported to the British Intelligence Service on prison morale and also such matters as general conditions, the prompt delivery of Red Cross parcels, plans for escape, etc. As a special duty he'd been instructed to investigate H and his activities for future reference. But anybody capable of entering so deeply into H's subterranean world was surely too contaminated by it to return with a practical report to his superiors.

Captain Manville had explained what he called 'the criminal urge' as in some ways similar to that of certain writers who only live significantly in their work and remarked in passing that Raskolnikov had murdered the old woman in reaction against his image of himself as a nonentity and had only been saved from the resulting destructive pride by Sonia.

The moment H entered the flat he knew it was empty. From the silent hall he called Susan's pet name, although he knew there'd be only deepest silence. Her bed was unmade; had it remained so from the day before? The crumpled sheet was stained with what might have been spots of blood but was more likely juice from a tomato. The smaller of her suitcases, the limp blue one, was gone, but none, as far as he could see, of her few prized possessions, not the sickle-shaped silver ornament like a miniature breastplate, nor her black party dress in which he had naturally not yet seen her.

Had she gone to the maternity home suddenly (in the night?) without having time (bothered?) to leave a message? H went to the desk where the telephone stood and examined the list of numbers that, in one of her short-lived practical moods, she'd scribbled on a sheet of paper, and that included those of the Englische Seminar, Dr Zimmermann's extension at the Auswärtiges Amt, as well as a couple without any names beside them. On the chance that one of these was that of the clinic, he dialled the first and a man's voice answered with the completely un-German 'Allo!'

He sank into one of the big leather armchairs. He was due at the university in a couple of hours, having obtained two days' leave at the request of Dr Zimmermann, and until then he was free for solitary meditation of the kind there'd been little opportunity for lately.

The thing that the sunburnt captain had said that, at least in the short term, affected him most was the suggestion that if H had the need to escape from the company of the morally justified, as he put it, he should have gone to Russia. H was inclined to agree and perhaps it was not too late.

Whatever might have altered since the early days when Mayakovsky, Essenin, Gorky, and other poets and novelists had greeted the Revolution, Stalin struck H as a monster in the Dostoevskyan tradition. If Hitler was a mongrel barking and snarling at closed doors – had they been opened to him he'd have crawled in wagging his tail – Stalin was silent, solitary, contemptuous both of his enemies and allies.

H was glad to have the university work to rouse him from this trance in which visions of Moscow were mixed with anxiety over Susan. His lecture this week was about the state of literary criticism in England to illustrate which he had two clippings, one from the *Sunday Times* and one from the *Observer* on the same book. The first began, 'A glorious historical novel ... the most gifted writer of his generation,' and the second, 'It is a very bad book, so bad that one doesn't want to write about it.'

'Which do you think was right?' he asked the rows of girl-faces. 'More likely the second because even in the sentence I've quoted there's a touch of sensitivity, a shrinking from something crude or hackneyed, while the first review starts off with a falsely resounding ring.'

The point he wanted to make was that the praising of the trivial and mediocre that goes on all the time is even more damaging to the formation of true values than the neglect of books of some originality. Only if there was anything approaching even a rough concept accepted by reviewers of what had no connection with literary art, could there be some basis for critical discussion.

As long as he was in one of the ugly classrooms talking to the girls, these problems, which were crucial to him on one level, formed an insulation

276

between him and his painful preoccupation. But back in the lecturers' room he could think of nothing but Susan, half expecting the telephone, standing beside the adjustable reading lamp with the green enamel shade, to ring and to hear her voice; she might recall the time that on this day of the week he was up here between classes.

When she did telephone it was early one morning to say that she'd be back that day with the baby girl. H didn't ask why she hadn't let him know where she was all this time; the waiting was over, she was coming back, a new life was beginning for them.

The bell rang that evening after hours of uncertainty, of going to the window to watch for a taxi approaching from any of three possible directions, and there she was, her now slight figure more of a weary child's than ever, her face on the dark landing all gleaming eyes and wry smile as she held the wrapped bundle.

As though to avoid immediate questions, not that H was going to ask any, she sent him to bring up the things she'd left in the entrance hall, which, besides her suitcase, included a folded cot. After making a couple of journeys in the lift, he found her on her bed suckling the baby, her face screwed up in pain.

'It hurts,' she said.

'What does?'

She looked away. She expected him to grasp everything without explanations: why she'd gone off without leaving a word, why she hadn't let him know where she was, and now what sort of pain feeding the baby was causing her.

She set up the cot in the small bedroom that looked on to the yard at the back, spread an oil sheet on the table and placed the baby on it to change its diapers and clean and powder its pink underparts. While doing this with her rapid, nervous energy she inquired: 'Missed me, darling?'

He was waiting to see whether she was moving in here too, but when she'd put the baby in the cot, she shut the door, returned to the big bedroom, dragged the blue suitcase on to her bed and, as she started to unpack, asked, 'Aren't you going to kiss me?' He had been shy of touching this strange slim girl.

He put his arms round her gingerly, not sure where she was tender, and she clung to him, with her face turned away as the tears welled up in her eyes.

'Eeii, it was horrible there!'

'Poor Katusha.'

'It's all right now, isn't it?'

'Of course.'

'Even better than before?'

'If we make it.'

'Why are my breasts so sore?'

'Didn't you ask them that?'

She shook her head impatiently; he guessed she'd had as little as possible to do with the nurses.

He slept with her in her new slimness for the first time on a thundery afternoon when the sitting room was so dark that they turned on the light after watching the downpour from the window, the water sweeping along the gutters and out halfway across the street with the dusty clock face on its iron pedestal at the bus terminus washed clean and bright.

After they had dressed and Susan had attended to the baby, which she had called Dominique, they went out and sat at a café terrace on the Kurfürstendamm drinking shallow glasses of the Bowle that could still be got there, in the cooler evening air.

H told her about the captain from the prisoner-of-war camp whom she lightly dismissed as an agent. Instead of contradicting her he asked: 'Why didn't you leave a couple of words on a scrap of paper?'

Her face clouded, shadows creeping over her olive-tinted skin, gathering in her eyes, and, as H watched her the answer was suggested to him as surely as if it was whispered, just above the noise of the passing traffic, in his ear: the Breton called and took her to the maternity clinic. This explained the cot, the woolly toys in the suitcase and the name: Dominique.

He ordered two more glasses of Bowle and saw her wave gaily to the bus that they should have caught; it was getting late and the ones on the route whose Endstation was outside the flat only passed at long intervals.

He asked if she'd let Dominique's father know of her arrival and she gave a quick, nervous shake of her head.

'He paid the expenses though, didn't he?'

'That's all free here.'

'He bought you the cot and the baby clothes.'

'It's not true, not true, not true!' she cried, while those at neighbouring tables stared at the astonishing spectacle of a couple drunkenly quarrelling in English.

53

Left alone, H sat on where he was, drinking and making up his mind to go to Russia. He imagined the room in Moscow with its ancient, faded wallpaper and worn velvet curtains from which he'd set out to explore the city where more private obsessions, actual and fictional intensities, to him interchangeable, legends, visions, and agonies had been experienced than anywhere else, except possibly Petersburg, which he'd also visit.

He'd meditate before the entrance to the old houses where every door was hallowed by the past, perhaps contemplating the very building that had housed the English club where Levin had waited impatiently while Sasha had ordered an elaborate lunch starting with Flensburg oysters; walk through the streets and alleyways, there or in Petersburg, where, at one time or another, the great ones of the earth had passed on their desperate or joyous missions, to historic encounters or merely, like Gogol's clerk, to and from some government office: Nikolay Lenin, on his way to address one of the sessions of the Soviet Parliament in the former restaurant of the Hotel Metropole; Raskolnikov, to his fateful meeting with Sonia; Chaliapin and Andreyev at the turn of the century to a session of the 'Wednesday' club; Essenin and Isadora Duncan, no more than a few years ago, in their bridal droshky; and Rozanov, with his short quick steps, hurrying home to another scene with Suslova.

He would see the Kremlin and the Peter and Paul fortress where, in the Trubetskoy Bastion, Dostoevsky had been kept before the sham execution, where Gorky had languished, and the Decembrists, Bakunin and Pisarev, had heard, at noon and midnight, the clock tower chime a Byzantine hymn; now, he had read, it played the 'Internationale'.

Each time the waiter came swaying with his elevated tray down the aisle between the pavement tables and, leaning over the empty chair, placed another glass of the pale gold-green drink before him, H was impelled on ever deeper explorations of a time he'd missed and cities he'd never been in. He was now intent on the more secret and sombre northern one, shrouded in the cold mists of the Neva, whose dark curtained rooms with their horselike sofas, old tiled stoves, fly-blown mirrors, and discoloured tablecloths and bedspreads (ink-stains? blood stains?) were less easily penetrated.

When he left the café it was dark, and on his way home under the dim illuminations – violet-coloured fairy lights on top of invisible Christmas trees that glowed far above the street – he called in at a Kneipe and drank several Schnapps that plunged him into the final phase of drunkenness. In this state, where thought is narrowed to a small intense spot of consciousness, beyond which all is blurred and irrelevant, he let himself into the flat.

Entering the first and smallest of the three communicating living rooms – he'd an idea of stealthily passing this way instead of by the passage to the bedroom – and without turning on the light in case the blackout blinds were not down, H started to pull on what he thought was the end of one of the sliding glass doors. When it did not open, he pulled harder and, with the crash of breaking glass it occurred to him in passing, as a vague possibility that in any case hardly concerned him, that it might be the china cabinet that he had overturned.

As he reached the bedroom by his circuitous route, Susan, awakened by the noise, asked him what it was.

'What was what?'

'Sounded as if you'd fallen through a window.'

'Nothing of the kind.'

'What's that on your hand?'

He wiped it on the pillow.

'It's blood. Better come to bed before you do more damage.'

They spent the next morning patiently, in a mood of reconciliation, sorting the various ornaments and knick-knacks, discarding those broken beyond repair, putting on one side the few that had escaped and gathering and fitting together, for gluing later, the pieces that remained.

That afternoon before his lecture H spoke to the Russian student about the possibility of getting a visa to visit the Soviet Union, and was advised to apply at the embassy in Unter den Linden.

Then, still impelled by the peculiar, nervous energy generated by certain hangovers, he called at Dr Zimmermann's office in the big Wilhelmstrasse building to make his report on his meeting with the British air-force officer. Of course, H's version of the talk had nothing to do with what they'd actually discussed, and was sufficiently irrelevant and confused to prevent Zimmermann supposing the captain was of any use for propaganda purposes.

'He's one of those English crackpots with all sorts of crazy notions that they've got to air to anybody they can get hold of.'

'Herr Schwartz said you spent some hours with him.'

'I daresay he timed it on his watch. He's a pedantic little jack-in-office whom, with Major Rumpel's cooperation, I managed to shake off as soon as I got there.'

H knew that, should he need it, he'd have the camp commandant's backing; the major, because he was a friend of Goering's, could afford to show his independence of the various bureaucracies.

But the pallid, smiling little Doktor wasn't going to make an issue of it. There was something more important he wanted to talk to H about; they needed someone capable of translating the items broadcast in the news service to Britain into something like the B.B.C. English they all admired. If H agreed, he'd have an office and a typist at the Drahtlose Dienst where he could work a few hours each evening after leaving the university.

Several considerations inclined H to accept. It would enable him to save enough to ensure the continuation of the sending of money home, which he'd heard through the Irish Legation was arriving safely, for several months after he went to Russia, should he succeed in this endeavour. Or, if he didn't, Susan could get someone to look after the baby and do the housework; she resented becoming a Hausfrau.

Their times of idyllic domesticity never lasted more than a few days and nights. Then a tense exhaustion seemed to build up in her, deepening the shadows under her eyes which grew bigger and shone threateningly till finally the storm burst over some trifle.

Susan was delighted to earn what seemed to her, after the almost penniless months, a lot of money, though not nearly so much as what H was paid, by sharing the cubbyhole of a room with him every evening and typing the news reports as he translated them. She engaged a woman as babysitter who was also supposed to have a warm meal ready for them when they came home around ten, and wanted to give him the rest of her pay towards the house-keeping and rent, which H, with for once as much money as he knew what to do with, didn't take.

One of his average afternoons and evenings during the autumn and winter of 1940: punctual arrival at the Englische Seminar. A few minutes respite; the classes, particularly the lectures, never ceased to be an ordeal. Leaving the last refuge of the lecturers' study, the walk to the main university block and the heavy-hearted climb up the wide stone stairway to one of the lecture halls. The vain attempt to sow doubts in the minds, most of them closed and impervious, of the students about the English writers with their orthodox insular mores and emotional poverty they'd learned to admire, and an equally unsuccessful effort to persuade them that it was the deeply disturbed and disturbing ones like Emily Brontë, Keats, at his peak, and Lawrence, whom H was at last ready for, were the true soothsayers.

Free at last from a task for which he was quite unsuited, and relaxed, the walk in the warm evening across Unter den Linden and up the long Charlot-tenstrasse to his next, less arduous, assignment, with a call on the way at a Kneipe where it was still possible to get a drink other than beer, if only a glass of sweet liqueur, with which to counter the dusty aftertaste of the lecture in his mouth. Then to the Drahtlose Dienst building, a meaningless name to him he learned to pronounce parrotlike until, once seeing it written, he realized it was the German equivalent of the English 'wireless', as old-fashioned a designation as 'horseless carriages', where a sheaf of news items were awaiting him on his desk.

The door of the tiny office opening without the knock that heralded the directress of the service with more sheets, and Susan in her faded summer dress, her black handbag tightly gripped under her thin brown arm, slipping quickly, and as though surreptitiously, in.

'Glad to see me?'

A quick embrace and then to work, her fragile-seeming fingers clattering the typewriter keys in what struck him as a semi-distraught fashion which resulted in mistakes that pretty, plump, efficient Fräulein Gloth had some-times to complain of.

The hours in the brightly lit cubbyhole together, H, on one level, intent on turning the ungainly German war reports – all written German struck him as ponderous except Kafka's and Rilke's – into imitation B.B.C. English. 'In the course of the last forty-eight hours, our submarines operating in the Atlantic and North Sea areas have sunk X thousand gross registered tonnage of enemy shipping...In Crete (or Greece or Yugoslavia) the remaining pockets of enemy resistance are being cleared up by our air-borne (armoured) divisions.'

He would pause, conscious of Susan's erratic typing that she interrupted for snatched kisses and caresses. She expected these at odd moments when-ever they were alone together outside the flat; walking home in the blackout, in the lift, and especially here. Their violent quarrels were also indulged in here when no typing got done and he couldn't concentrate on the translating.

A retirement, after one of these, to the lavatory at the end of the corridor to come to himself, sluice his face burning with misery, and rinse his parched mouth in cold water. Inadvertently swallowing a few drops – he didn't trust it for drinking – he coughed and spat into the basin and noticed a trace of blood there. Fever, headache, reddish expectoration: signs that, worn out by too many private fevers and pains, the tubercular virus was established in his lungs?

The journey home by crowded U-Bahn, through the bright, tiled stations, each of which became linked for him with some point reached in the constant emotional crises they lived in, emerging from underground at the wide network of dimly lit rails at Gleisdreick, which he'd crossed by footbridge on his first exploration of the city, the suddenly darkened compartment in which he held her hot little hand (or was it his that was still fevered?) and her whispering, 'Love me?'

H in the bathroom sucking up saliva, washing it around his mouth, and expectorating to see whether, without coughing, there was blood in the spit, as there was – it came from his gum – while he heard Susan rowing with the babysitter – he realized she'd be forever at loggerheads with maids as she was with officials – over the cabbagy stew she'd prepared for them. Only in bed in his arms did she uncoil and relax.

54

When they engaged a daily maid, nothing went more smoothly nor became easier. H's one good suit, dark blue with thin grey stripes, double-breasted, disappeared from a drawer of the sideboard in the dining room; the owners of the flat had locked the wardrobe in the bedroom where they'd evidently left part of the huge stock of clothes that all Germans seemed to possess. In a panic, for he was tense, nervy, at having nothing to wear but his old flannel suit, he went to the police around the corner – announcing the loss might make it easier to obtain extra clothes coupons – who took down what he told them in longhand, asked some questions, and assured him and Susan, who'd insisted on coming too, they'd recover his property.

The fat, elderly nurse, reigning sluggishly in her starched regalia in the back bedroom, complained that she wasn't a friend of cabbage, which formed a substantial part of the dishes she was served. And the elderly help, whom they sometimes saw late at night in a corner by herself in a nearby Kneipe they called at on their way home, often failed to turn up, causing Susan what seemed to H exaggerated apprehension at the prospect of having to tell the nurse she'd have to do a small amount of housework and perhaps prepare her own evening meal.

She'd cling to him as if to protect her from daily helps, nurses, Fräulein Gloth, and various others from the past: landladies, domestics, and governesses who, she said, had all taken an immediate dislike to her.

Sometimes she let him soothe her down and caress away her cares. But once, in the bathroom, when she'd knocked and asked him to shelter her after an early morning row with one or both of the women, she flung her arms around him as he was pulling on his trousers, and when he told her to calm down for the love of God she thrust her distraught face, with wide, near-manic eyes, forward and instead of kissing, bit him. Two shallow punctures broke one of the creases from the outside of his nostrils to the corners of his mouth.

The conversation classes, but not the lectures, were a respite from the stormy days and nights with Susan. The tranquillity of impersonal discussion with a half dozen or so civilized girls, not a savage among them, in their fresh summer dresses came as a relief from the constant scenes.

When he told Susan that he was thinking of applying for a visa to go to Moscow at Christmas, she said he should first consult a White Russian friend of hers; it was he and his wife who'd let her sleep in their living room before she'd come to live with H. This old man, who, it seemed, had known her grandfather in Petersburg before the Revolution, would warn him of the dangers that threatened an English-speaking foreigner in Russia.

It was the hope of getting back his suit in which to present himself at the Soviet Embassy, rather than to hear what the old White Russian had to say, that caused H to delay making his application. But one afternoon when he was taking the kitchen pail across the courtyard to the shed where the refuse was dumped, he saw a green-uniformed policeman emerge from the entrance to the cellar under the block of flats. He reported this to Susan after he'd climbed the back stairs, and heard her jeer to the daily help who, on account of her varicose veins, was excused taking down the rubbish, at this typically useless display of German thoroughness – no doubt hurting the woman's feelings – as he rinsed out the pail at the sink.

Next morning the suit reappeared in the drawer of the dresser, which H found left half-open as if to call attention to its presence, and the woman confessed to him that she'd pawned it to pay her landlord (at the Kneipe? Ha! ha!) and had gone by taxi to redeem it the moment he'd paid her her weekly wage – having heard about the policeman? He assured her that, if necessary, he'd tell the police that he'd discovered the suit in a case where he'd packed it away with other things and forgotten it. 'But what about Frau Loyson?' she asked. They didn't pretend they were married. With all the identity cards, permits, and ration coupons this would have anyhow been difficult.

'Frau Loyson won't say a word.'

One day a week they had off from the Drahtlose Dienst, and he'd chosen it to coincide with the afternoon he'd no classes and also with the domestics' free day. Dressed in the recovered suit, he made use of the next one to go to the Russian Embassy.

On the way he called at the Café Viktoria at the corner of Unter den Linden and Friedrichstrasse for jam omelette, one of the only coupon-free dishes left that he ate with relish, and because in the S-Bahn, from which just after Bahnhof Tiergarten he caught a glimpse of some of the Möller family on their balcony, he'd decided that he wanted a little more time to make up his mind whether he really wanted to go to Russia.

Was he deterred by the suggestion made by Susan's friend, that, after having been assured by the Moscow University authorities, where he hoped to get a similar post to the one he had here, that they'd find him a suitable lodging, he'd wake up one morning in Lubianka prison or the Peter and Paul Fortress to the chiming by the bells of the 'Internationale'?

No. That was a risk, at a time when risks were thick in the air, that he'd take.

It was that he was still under the physical-neurological spell (was it love?) exerted on him by Susan. This was strongest not when they were together but at such moments as when he returned to the flat and she was putting down the phone, or she wasn't there and the maid told him she'd gone out soon after him. And sometimes, as now, when he'd been away from her an hour or so, it overcame him with a promise of their relationship becoming a peaceful, joyous, and trusting one.

H hurried home to tell her the good news, but at the flat there was no answer to his ring; the daily help had one key, Susan had kept the other so that she could slip down to the dairy next door for the full-cream milk she was entitled to as a nursing mother.

H rang and listened, rang and listened. Then he stood outside the door without ringing; waiting for the lift to be summoned down as she returned from the dairy? To let those instincts that registered danger and shock before the mind had the time, or courage, to do so, take in the situation?

He descended in the lift and had a look up and down the street, not for Susan whom he knew didn't like to leave the baby even for the few minutes it took to fetch the milk but, though not quite consciously, for somebody emerging out of one of the two passageways that led from the courtyard at the back.

As he stood there what he took in was not anyone hurrying guiltily away, but that the sky had receded and faded slightly and that the breeze that was cooler was making a faint sibilant sound in the lime trees. Autumn had come while, until this moment of forced perceptivity, he'd been too preoccupied to notice it.

H reascended in the lift and a moment after he pressed the bell, Susan, in her dressing gown, opened the door.

'I've been ringing for ages.'

'Ringing? Not true! I've been here all the time.'

He knew less than ever what was reflected in her wide, luminous eyes (surprise? incredulity? excitement? anxiety?).

'For five or six minutes.'

'Dominique was yelling so while I was changing her just now that I mustn't have heard.'

'For Christ's sweet sake! I listened each time I rang the bloody bell and the place was silent as the tomb.' This he didn't say. For one thing he wasn't ready for the shock to both of them pressing his suspicion too far.

She led him into the smallest of the living rooms, that he always thought of as the ill-omened one, where the china cabinet stood, which they'd had new glass put in but whose contents were noticeably depleted. As she sat beside him on the settee, ostensibly to hear about his visit to the Soviet Embassy, she wilted like a chastised child and turned a distressed face to him. Then she was in his arms and all doubts were excluded from the precarious certitude of the moment which he'd have liked to prolong indefinitely.

Was it the fragility of their relationship that kept it painfully intense, or had their cellular protoplasm some rare chemical deficiency (or excess) that, signalled from one to the other in all sorts of ways, made them cousins in the midst of strangers? He became most nearly conscious of the kinship when the indefinable bond was nearest snapping, as when, a week or two later, from the top of a bus on his way home from a morning at the university he caught sight of her strolling up Wittenbergstrasse towards the Romanisches Café with a tall man of about his own age. On her return Susan admitted without prevarication having met Vialatoux, calling the Breton by his surname as if he was already famous as a national liberator, to discuss with him the payments for his daughter.

It was a relief to H, as when he'd wakened one morning from one of his mysterious childhood illnesses with a mind clear of feverish images, to realize next day the incident no longer worried him. For several days he didn't give it a thought and then it obsessed him again and, at the lunch hour break, he took a taxi all the way from the university to the Romanisches Café right across the city, stood inside the door looking for Susan and Vialatoux, didn't see them, and got another taxi back just in time for the next class.

By now H knew (had she known all along?) their days together were numbered. They spent much of their free time on the settee in the small room with the sliding glass doors closed, tentatively exploring possible changes and trying to gauge their own and each other's reactions. Susan said she'd like to give up her job at the Drahtlose Dienst and devote more time to her music, though how she'd do that without a piano H didn't ask.

'I bet there are plenty of your students who'd love to take it on.' But at the back of both their minds he sensed thoughts of a more drastic upheaval.

'I might move to the pension where I was before.'

'Before what?'

Nervy, distracted, she seemed not to take in what he was saying, though this he couldn't be sure of. It might be that she didn't wish to show her relief at his suggestion.

At one of his next classes H said he'd soon need a secretary for a few hours every evening and a fair girl with glasses, who'd once written him a long love-letter, shyly offered herself. He told her the directress at the radio news service in English would have to do the engaging, hoping that Fräulein Gloth wouldn't find her a proficient enough typist.

286

Shortly after that – all was now going with frightening speed – a middle-aged woman, who though not a university student, had enrolled for his course, asked H to an Advent party she was giving for the members of his class.

Though it turned out that she lived quite close, H was doubtful if he'd go till the last possible moment on the November Sunday afternoon. Deep in a long, inconclusive discussion with Susan, he was hoping they were about to reach a miraculous solution to their troubles. But finally he left her huddled up on the settee and hurried across the already wintry Platz.

55

That night as H was undressing in what they called, though hadn't used as, the dining room, into which he'd lately moved his bed, the telephone rang in the big room next door.

He was trying to put a face to the unexpected voice out of the receiver as the girl was telling him her name, Halka Witebsk, and reminding him that she'd been at the party. She'd heard he was looking for a typist and inquired if she might take on the job.

H stood in the big room with the blackout blinds over the three windows and only the table lamp lit, one cup of the instrument by his mouth the other turned to his ear, hearing the low, foreignly accented words echo out of the ebony shell.

There were two or three library books on the big desk, a glass-stoppered ink bottle standing on the base of its own shadow, a handful of brassy Pfennige, mark and two-mark pieces with a dim silver sheen in a china bowl, and these he saw not as usual submerged in the present flowing over them, but suddenly exposed and made unique by a shift in the tide of time. He was momentarily aware of them no longer as part of a Berlin room on a wartime night but as they'd always appear in the light of his backward vision.

H arranged to meet Fräulein Witebsk next afternoon at the corner of Unter den Linden and Charlottenstrasse, accompany her to the Drahtlose Dienst and introduce her to Fräulein Gloth as his new secretary.

Back in his new bedroom – he and Susan no longer shared the big one – he tried to recall the girl, but all that he could evoke of her was the bright, wondering glance, turning her brown eyes black as she listened to the Chinese student, Chuan Tee, hold forth in the conversation class, as he did when a topic roused him from his golden lizardlike basking.

The day that she started sharing the little office with him, H left the flat and moved to the pension. For most of the first week he spent his free time sitting idle in an armchair in the middle of his room waiting for the old-fashioned telephone on its upright stand to emit its shrill tinkle, or one of the No. 14 trams that ran past the flat and through Nikolsburger Platz, on to which his balcony looked, to bring Susan.

It ended by his going to visit her, arriving at the flat one afternoon as though to see how she was getting on; they hadn't parted after a quarrel or, as far as he was aware, on a note of finality. Susan opened the door in her old red dressing gown, her lank hair about her narrow shoulders that seemed to droop – at the sight of him? Inside the dark hall he thought he caught a morose gleam as she took a quick second glance and dropped her luminous eyes again.

She brought him into the fatal small room with the glass doors and the china cabinet from where it was only a few steps across the hall to the kitchen where she was preparing something (for Dominique? for an expected visitor?) which was distracting her from giving him her full attention; the daily help had been impudent, she explained, and she'd had to get rid of her.

H saw that his presence made her nervous, but he kept sitting where he was on the settee with the gilt wicker back, unable to get up and go. The shock of realizing that she was waiting for him to leave was too much for him to adjust to at once; he had to have a little more time either to face it or to satisfy himself that her apparent concern about what she had on the cooker and her keeping the talk to impersonal things had some other cause.

This is the end, he said to himself during one of her absences in the kitchen. What was he reminded of? Or rather, for the terrifying sensation was a new one, how to transform it into an image whose pain was more capable of being grasped?

He'd been walking with her down a path through a wood that if, in spite of all difficulties and doubts, they pushed on along he believed would lead them to a quiet, sunny clearing where all that was wrong could come well. Now, turning a corner, the path had come to an end in impenetrable forest.

Back in his room at the pension, the flow of time no longer carried him in any purposeful direction and for want of significant movement the days filled up with the unbearable details of mechanical existence.

The best part of the day were the hours at the Drahtlose Dienst realizing in Halka Witebsk's presence the fact, that left to himself would have been long obscured from him, that his psyche, caged within this neurosis, hadn't been able to stretch its wings and that what he was feeling was the fear of flying again into wide, free spaces.

It was during these weeks that H received the first letter from home, apart from a note through the Irish Legation. Iseult wrote in reply to one from him

– she seemed to have had several – affectionately, with news of the children, the garden; it had been written in summer. It referred cautiously – the envelope bore the British censorship stamp – to the war which she evidently thought would end with a German victory in a not-very-distant future when, as she put it, 'We'll all be together again in more propitious circumstances and your old Pet, who is going grey at the temples, will turn over a brand new leaf.'

As if he hadn't enough emotional complications, the letter evoked home and his wife vividly. She seemed to imply they might live in Germany after the war with him appointed to some diplomatic post! He put the letter in his inside pocket. By carrying it with him he felt he was leaving the final decision about the future open.

One Sunday afternoon, which he had told her was now his free day, he heard the outer door of his room being opened, there was a tap on the inner one, and Susan, in her thin coat was peeping in and saying, 'Hello, darling!'

She had brought a bottle of white wine which they stood to cool in the snow on the balcony where a blackbird with his feathers puffed out against the cold was perched on the stone balustrade.

'Don't laugh at him, poor thing,' Susan said, as H was refastening the French windows. She was worked up as always, but now her nerviness impelled her to him, and when he embraced her her eyes shone with tears (because of the blackbird? her own unsolved problems? their being together again?).

Drinking the wine later she spoke with childish naïveté of herself, asking him if he thought she was depraved; was she referring to her unadmitted lovemaking with somebody else that day he'd been locked out? And just before she left said shyly: 'I've got to get out of that awful place, darling.'

'You mean the flat?'

'I wonder whether we could find a room where you'd come and live with me and Dominique. She's a very well-behaved baby.'

Although the moments of lucidity in regard to the hopelessness of his obsession had been becoming more frequent and there were still several months of the lease of the flat to run, in the new year they moved into a big back room let by a tall, plump, languorous Yugoslav, Olga Mihailovich.

All went well for a bit, with Susan once again the vulnerable, delinquent adolescent at odds with the rest of the world, who submitted herself, body and wounded spirit, only to him. In no time she alienated their charming landlady's humbler and older sister, who did all the work, including cleaning their room, and came to H to comfort her for the things this woman had, Susan said, called her; because of the registration forms which the landlady had to sign, the Mihailovichs knew they weren't married.

Besides her new dependence on him, Susan seemed to have got over her distaste for housework and did the cooking on a single-ring electric cooker in the corner just inside the door; further along the wall a big window looked on to the courtyard in which a single, now bare, chestnut tree grew, a third corner contained the baby's cot, the fourth the divan bed. In the centre was a table covered by a red cloth that served for all the purposes for which there had been so many different pieces of furniture in the flat.

But soon the old tensions returned and new ones were added. Their room with its two doors had formerly been the only way of passing from the front to the rear of the flat – a common arrangement in old-fashioned Berlin apartments – but now a flimsy partition divided it from a passage to the back premises, behind which it turned out their landlady had her couch. At night they heard whispers, whimpers, and faint moanings.

Susan surprised him by resenting these. She'd have knocked on the wall if he hadn't restrained her by keeping his arms around her.

'They're being as quiet as they can,' he whispered, 'there's nothing to make such a fuss about.'

'Filthy beasts!'

He felt her trembling. What she seemed especially to resent was that the beautiful Yugoslav had a constant change of lovers, though from the indistinct murmurs H didn't know how she could be so sure of this.

When he was tired of reasoning with her and she wouldn't let him sleep, he got out of bed and started to dress, saying he was going out till things had quieted down.

At that, she jumped out too, and he grasped her to prevent her scratching or biting him. They remained standing in silence, she naked and imprisoned by the wrists, he half-dressed and breathing quickly from the effort of keeping a tight hold on her, while the baby slept peacefully in its cot and the faint sounds of lovemaking continued from the next room.

At times he felt he'd been lured to depths where this sea nymph who thrived in the submarine shadows was drowning him. But the facts, as far as he could regard them objectively, didn't fit the fairy tale of the waylaid, infatuated prince.

While they were together the dream still compelled him, but after a few hours absence from her it had begun to fade. And he had now often a longing to be returning to where he'd be alone as he walked towards their room along Achenbachstrasse from the U-Bahn in Nürnbergerstrasse of an evening.

He never knew what state Susan would be in. When he opened the door and found her behind it at the electric ring preparing his supper it was an ill omen; he suspected she hurried there on hearing him open the door in the flat in order to avoid having him look at her too closely. But she fired querulous questions at him over her shoulder such as 'Glad to be back?' 'Longing for Katusha?' 'Still love me?' from the corner.

She might tell him at supper of a visit to her agent who'd promised and failed to get any engagement, even one with a café orchestra, or about a slight she'd received from the landlady's sister, or she'd huddle on the couch, watching him eat with wide wet eyes and not speaking at all.

He saw that their life together had again become a shared neurosis that was precious and that he both longed and feared to escape from.

The fear wasn't sexual, for he had never felt sexual desire isolated from emotion, and what would he do, deprived of these emotional extremes which set the rhythm of his consciousness? He had a foretaste of the miseries of deprivation, and when at Easter she suggested their going to Vienna, having found a place in the country where Dominique would be looked after, it seemed that this was the solution.

They attended the Easter morning ceremonies in the Russian church nearby with a superstitious idea, which he sensed she shared too, that this would be a propitious start to the holiday.

In Munich where Susan had an unnamed someone in the concert world to see – she was secretive about all that concerned her music – they spent a night, and the next day arrived late in the evening at the Hauptbahnhof in Vienna, from which Iseult and he had been seen off by Fräu Sczeky and old Hansen nearly twenty years before, and took a room at a hotel beside the station.

In the morning Susan had a row with the chambermaid and started the day with eyes made enormous by the deepening of the bruiselike shadows under them. Waiting with their suitcase at the tram-stop in Mariahilfstrasse, she told him which number they must take and a little later, standing on the front platform, explained what ticket to ask for in a tone that indicated that this was her city which she was going to guide him through, except for certain of her secret sanctuaries.

She conducted him to a part of it that, when he admitted he didn't know, she told him was never seen by tourists, and in the Wiener Hauptstrasse booked them in at an ancient looking hotel called 'Goldenes Lamm' where, she said, Liszt used to stay and where they were given a long narrow room in an annexe whose door opened directly on to a strip of snow.

Without waiting to unpack, they went out again on a pilgrimage to places with which she had, usually painful, ties from the past. She took him to gaze at the peeling grey and yellow façade of the Theater am Markt, closed and deserted, where, she explained, Beethoven had conducted the first performance of one of his symphonies, then to the café Giraldi nearby for a belated breakfast of Malzkaffee and black bread; after the upset at the hotel where they'd stayed the night, nothing would have made her eat there.

Still letting him have glimpses of a fabulous past, though not as yet hers, about which he was more curious, she spoke of her heroes (Raimundo, Josef Kainz, Grillparzer) as she took H to see the view from the top of the Hochhaus, the city's one skyscraper, built since H's stay in Vienna, which, though she knew of, he didn't mention.

But when the lift had taken them to the top, it wasn't the view of the distant Danube, nor St Stefan's spire, nor the great wheel of the Prater she showed him, but pointed to another part of the big block itself, where, she said, in the penthouse on a wing below where they stood she'd lived when she was seventeen with a Bulgarian, a man who'd drunk huge quantities of wine, given wild parties, and made love to her constantly and on all occasions. A pair of heavy curtains had been kept drawn across one end of the sitting room (those were its windows at this side) so that in the midst of festivities he could retire with her behind them.

'Is he there still?'

'I heard he'd gone back to Bulgaria just before the war; I wasn't with him anymore by then. He might have kept on the flat, though; let's see if his name is still beside the door.'

They descended and, in another part of the building, again took a lift, and there sure enough by the door she led him to was a rather dirty card with a Bulgarian-looking name on it, and Susan squatted down and peered through the keyhole. Straightening herself she smiled her musing, self-absorbed smile that made him feel an outsider, without commenting on what she'd seen. H had a look for himself and beyond the hall, through an open door, got a glimpse of what he took to be the living room, but the place seemed to be unfurnished and there were no signs of the curtains, which, from Susan's expression was what he'd supposed she must have had a glimpse of.

She took him to places where she'd once spent what she cherished as fateful hours (in her musical career? her relationship with various lovers?). Her short past seemed to H to have been a constant crisis. These were mostly cafés – the Café Landsmann opposite the Burgtheater, the Café Mozart at the back of the Opera – and, of course, the Conservatoire where, when H put his arm around her on one of its gloomy corridors to remind her of his presence, she'd quickly freed herself and protested, as if at an unseemly advance, 'Oh no, not here!'

In the evening, instead of eating out, Susan suggested their buying what she said she'd often got for her supper on her way home from the music lessons. In a commemorative spirit she purchased the raw herrings in a vinegary sauce with chopped onions, and brought them back to their room in a dripping carton, with a bottle of wine, for supper.

The little repast was eaten on the bed, the coverlet over their shoulders, for it was bitterly cold in the room, the wet carton in a towel between them, taking alternate swallows of the raw-tasting wine from a toothglass. Afterwards Susan went across to the hotel proper to see about having a bath.

After trying to wash the reek of the fish off his fingers in cold water, H lay on the bed and evoked the other Vienna of long ago, his city of precarious car-drives along snowy or gale-swept streets, of bifteck tartar eaten in warm cellars to the strains of gypsy music, of jewellers' windows at which they'd pause while Mr Isaacs ran his shrewd eyes over the rings, of the steamy, echoing Diana Bad, of Iseult, sad and homesick, of traffic-polished snow glinting blue with a promise that after all these years was still unfulfilled.

Susan returned in tears with a tale about a housemaid, or housekeeper, having told her that couples weren't permitted to use the bathroom together.

'And I hadn't said a word about wanting to take a bath with anyone! The old bitch must have heard we'd registered in different names and made up her mind to spoil what she imagined was a night out for us!'

No good telling her that with her morose, delinquent air she'd always arouse all sorts of extreme reactions from suspicion and dislike to fascination.

56

Beethoven's house on a rampart above the Ring, the Burgtheater, where a certain Katerina Schratt was the presiding spirit from the past, the Theater-an-der-Wien, the Theater-in-der-Leopoldsstadt and Schönbrunn, she showed him all her shrines. Thought he never actually saw the inside of the latter, for, as they left the tram, she was attracted to a grassy plot outside the gates from which the snow had thawed and where a profusion of small wild flowers were growing. From where he waited near the tram terminus she looked like a child bent eagerly over its treasures, and by the time she'd gathered a big bunch was too exhausted and there was too much tension in the air, each having too many separate memories, too many present doubts, for a sightseeing tour of palace and park. They took a tram back and before they had reached the city centre, the bunch of white flowers were wilting in her hot hand.

Sometimes he went off on his own to try to regain his own image of a Vienna that had nothing to do with its theatres and concert halls, still less with the private happenings in various dwellings. She had also pointed out to him the places where a very young girl, who was both herself and a mythical creature, had cast a spell over a series of lawyers, car salesmen, theatre directors, and musicians.

Back in Berlin H guessed by her long absences from their room as well as by the shadows that gathered in her face and that only their sensual interludes seemed to disperse, that their life together had become as painful for her as it was for him.

She had still the key of the flat and often went there, saying she wanted a piece of music or a book, and didn't return till evening. One day H took the key and went there himself. The floor of her room was littered with her things, odds and ends of clothing, a couple of pairs of tiny socks, now too small for Dominique, articles of make-up, and some school exercise books which she had used as diaries. H opened one that was evidently from her school days and read a sentence about another girl whose tongue, that she had put out at Susan, was compared to a moist, pink little animal that dwelt in a warm cave and wanted to be taken into hers. When he put down the book guiltily without reading more, a scrap of paper, with a telephone number on one corner and scrawled across another the name, Robert Brassilach, fell out of it.

Dominique, back from the babies' home in the country, had taken to pulling herself up by the rails of the cot, standing in her ankle-length flannel nightdress, looking over the top and howling in the early summer mornings, a habit that at last brought a protest from a young man in the room next door, the one on the other side of theirs to their landlady's. And Olga Mihailovich came with her silent, catlike walk to tell him (Susan was out) that the lodger had complained.

'He's a foreigner,' she said, to indicate that his complaint couldn't be dismissed as German unpleasantness.

'I hear your baby crying too, you know,' she added.

'She isn't my baby.'

'You're not her father, Mr Ruark?'

'No.'

Apparently the registration forms had not contained this piece of information.

'It did surprise me that you and Miss Loyson had been that long together.'

He saw that Olga Mihailovich had been puzzled by the relationship; she'd no doubt overheard their quarrels – it wasn't only a one-way communication through the thin wall. It might be a matter of surprise to those who knew him as polite, considerate, self-effacing, things that Susan certainly wasn't. But what somebody like the landlady wasn't aware of was that he too had his quieter disruptive tendencies.

Often awake till late at night, she refused to settle to sleep till all was quiet in the landlady's room, and having to keep Dominique occupied from early morning, Susan started the day tired and tense. Some mornings she was in such a state that she dreaded being left alone for the short time it took him to fetch the milk and rolls in case, she said, Olga Mihailovich should come in with fresh complaints about the baby, or the state of the bathroom, where Susan washed out the nappies and hung them to dry, or 'just to show herself off to me after an all-night carousal with her latest lover.' So then they took the baby and went to a café at the junction of their street with the Kaiser Allee kept by a big burly Swiss, to breakfast under the chestnut trees in the warm, summer morning with the radio playing popular songs from inside.

One morning on his way to the dairy H met Halka hurrying along the Kaiser Allee to the Zoo underground station on her way to the university. Although he knew that she lived with her widowed mother and sister not far away in a street on the other side of the monument crowned by the hand with upward-pointing finger at which he'd paused on his first long walk through the unknown city, her sudden appearance astonished him. While intent on the flickering embers of the fire he was tending in his shadowy abode, an angel had appeared momentarily in the cave mouth.

One morning, before they were out of bed or Dominique had become bored with the toys in her cot, there came whispers of solemn-sounding declamation from open windows across the court, beyond the thick chestnut trees, the tall wax-white blossoms of which had crumbled, and still lay on the ground, and in at the big window of their room. Neither of them, intent on the minor details of starting the day, took much note of the radios being turned on at this unusual hour; it was only as they were on their way to the Swiss café that Susan said, 'Something must be up again.'

The Swiss proprietor told them the news as he brought them each a boiled egg, which he sometimes treated them to, perhaps feeling a bond with them as neutrals like himself.

He waited by their table a moment, shaking his cropped head very slightly and H, not to be outdone in expressing an independent, if cautious, opinion, and also to show he appreciated the eggs, murmured his disapproval and looked grave. His first thought was that he'd never now stand at the corner of Sadovaya and Vosnesensky streets or walk by the Fontanka canal where, on a mist-shrouded evening, Raskolnikov had entered the hotel to drink a glass of tea and scan the paper for some mention of crime.

Nor would he see Lubyansky Lane, now called Serov Lane, as he'd learned from one of the Russian students in his conversation class, where Maya-kovsky had lived when he wrote a poem containing the lines: 'The day burned out like a white page: a little/smoke, a little ash.'

Meanwhile there were the respites with Halka when he spoke of things that

Susan wouldn't have cared to listen to. In the pauses between bouts of translations and typing – Fräulein Gloth was glad of the change of secretaries – while she listened with her tranquil frown, he talked of the past in which was the halcyon time of peace, which he never really regretted.

He told her of his aunt's house by the bridge and the view at dusk from the upstairs window across the railway line and over the commons to the cluster of squat walls, still luminous, under tall columns of blue smoke-haze, and especially of the corner field flooded in rainy seasons, which, in retrospect, seemed to have been constant, where there was always a flock of starlings that rose in a black whirring wheel which, darker at the centre, spun off crazily into the silvery evening; when he was homesick now, it was for this one field. He told her of these tranquil things while she leaned her bare brown elbows on the table in front of her, one on each side of the typewriter, her face cupped in her palms.

When H mentioned going away – the only means of ensuring a break with Susan – in the long vacation, she said she'd have to look for another job in order to have some money to give her mother. But Fräulein Gloth told her that with her knowledge of English and typing ability they'd be glad of her in the Englische Redaktion up at the Rundfunkhaus at the other end of the city.

H gave up his translation work when the university term finished; he still wasn't sure what to do or how to expedite the end that he and Susan knew was on the way. Soon after Halka started her new job, he took her to supper at a restaurant in Adolf-Hitler-Platz patronized by the foreigners who worked at the big circular red-brick radio building at the western, fashionable end of the new East-West avenue through Berlin.

They had a surprisingly good meal with a bottle of red wine, celebrating their first evening together outside the office, though there'd been a Kneipe next door to the Drahtlose Dienst where they had sometimes sneaked down to when work was slack.

He saw that, with its carpets, red-plush curtains, and table lamps, the place might be for her luxury undreamed of, but that this was something secondary and that she'd have been equally happy with him anywhere. Her eyes tilted up at the outside corners and lit with the black intentness that had first made him notice her in his class when Chuan Tee was holding forth. She pointed out William Joyce to him at a table with others in an inner room, round reddish face with a scar down the cheek, whom she occasionally typed for, and, because of the awe in which he seemed to be held, supposed must be somebody of great importance in England who was here on a peace mission. She had no idea of what the war was about nor of its growing fury.

Waiting at the underground for the train that would take them both to the station nearest their respective homes, she said that only one thing clouded for her the wonderful evening. Had she had a glimpse of his darkness of spirit, from the lucid depths of hers? But no, it was the ten marks which the meal had cost him that was worrying her, an expenditure whose consequences in her experience were bound to be felt later.

The next day when they were sitting at a café terrace in Kurfürstendamm, H told Susan he was going to Munich. Why not Vienna? His feelings about Vienna were painfully complicated as a result of his last visit there with her and he wanted to go somewhere where there'd be no such associations.

Neither brought up the question of what would happen when he returned. He ordered a couple more glasses of Bowle – the last he ever drank; when he returned to Berlin such luxuries had disappeared – and out of the sudden lightness of heart, which he shared with her, though he was apprehensive too. Susan told him she'd written to Furtwängler, whose address her agent had given her, begging him to let her play for him at his home and tell her honestly whether her great ambitions had any justification.

That night she clung to him with a kind of desperation, and when at last he'd gone to sleep woke him to ask if he really loved her. In the morning, instead of her old blue blouse and faded summer skirt she put on her black dress and stockings and then, shortly before it was time for him to leave, pulled him down beside her on the bed and asked if she shouldn't come too.

'What about Dominique?'

'I know people in Munich who'd look after her.'

'And Furtwängler?'

'Nothing will come of that.'

He saw she was waiting for some encouragement, but he didn't say anything, one way or the other, but put his things into a suitcase, and she threw in a few clothes of her own. But just as he thought she was really coming, she changed her mind and kissed him good-bye.

In Munich H took a room from which he could hear the Rathaus bells chiming the hours as the painted figures revolved in slow procession on the clock tower, though its window gave only on to the stairway well of the building of which the pension formed the top floor.

Next morning he sent Susan a telegram wishing her well in her attempt to contact the famous conductor and then wandered the wide streets where he'd once walked with Polenskaya. The day was hot, long, and empty, and even after an evening meal in a restaurant – eating out was now an art and he didn't know the right places here – he was still hungry.

He went to bed early in the warm stuffy room to continue reading *Crime and Punishment* which he'd borrowed from the Englische Seminar library before leaving. He read very late with short breaks in which he rubbed his tired eyes, heard the hours and half hours chime from the Rathaus, and recalled with a chill his loneliness.

When he closed the book in its faded red cover, he lay hearing occasional steps echoing up the stone stairway, still in the company of Svidrigaylov and Sonia, the two characters between which the story seemed polarized. Both fascinated him more than Raskolnikov whose attitude after the murder H failed to understand. What especially struck him at this rereading was that the time was past (things have gone too far, was how he put it to himself) for any such humble confession as Raskolnikov's and especially his bowing down to the mob. Did this feeling come from that pride of his that Captain Manville had seemed to fear might corrupt H's psyche and damage his work?

The days, partly occupied in trying to get enough to eat, passed with painful slowness. By studying the midday menus as soon as they appeared in their frames outside the restaurants, with the required ration coupons marked against the dishes, he could decide in good time where the best value was offered. These were the most crowded places where he had to queue and, as soon as the doors opened, wait at a table with a paper, keeping the Russian novel to occupy him in the nights, until lunchtime. In the evenings it was the same.

One morning there was a surprise: a parcel delivered to him in his lonely pension room. It was from Susan, and it contained a tin of meat, one of evaporated milk (from Dominique, she wrote in a short, noncommittal note), a cake, a shirt of his she had washed and ironed, and a tattered copy of Thomas Mann's *Death in Venice* in English that she'd picked up at a secondhand bookstall despite its being banned.

H sat on his bed with the opened parcel, pleased and gloomy, touched and resolved to face the fact that the break was final: he took the arrival of the parcel as an intimation of this.

In the end he went to Vienna. Better there where memory would lurk at street corners, outside cafés – none of the interiors where it might be especially painful need be revisited – than hang around here in a place that wasn't a vital part of the complex pattern being woven, he liked to imagine, out of the past and future.

Another room in the long series, this one at the Hotel Stefan, König von Ungarn, in a narrow street, and looking on to an even narrower cobbled alley at the back, close to the cathedral to which Iseult, in her fake sealskin coat, had gone off one snowy Sunday morning, pale and estranged, to Mass.

57

Installed in the old hotel with its arched and panelled doors, each inscribed with what he took to be the name of a Hungarian saint, in Gothic script, and wall telephones of an even more ancient type than the one whose ringing he had sat for hours waiting for in his room in the Berlin pension, H, after a breakfast of Ersatzkaffee, Kunsthonig (artificial honey), two fragile petals of fat, and a couple of slices of sourish black bread, tried to occupy himself with a new novel.

When he left the hotel around noon, having invariably torn up whatever he'd written, he started off briskly enough, but by the time he'd turned the corner into Stefan's Platz his pace had become sluggish and anyone trailing him and seeing the way he loitered around it would have supposed he was keeping a rendezvous.

He couldn't make up his mind where to go; as soon as he set out towards a particular café, eating place, or bathhouse, it struck him that no possible good could befall him there; it was a matter of time passing and slowly effacing the most acute of the memory-feelings.

The two places most conducive to the slow psychic diminishing of his obsession was a bath establishment where he could lie in a sunken green tub of steaming water, and a bathing pavilion, a section of the Donaukanal, screened off by a floating platform of wooden cubicles, where hours could be spent in the semi-stupor of sun basking.

There were trotting races in a suburb called the Molkerei near the Prater; there was also flat racing of a sort at Freudenau, which he only discovered shortly before leaving when he'd no longer any desperate need of distraction. But it was to the Trabrennen at Baden, some miles from the city, that he went, setting out after his morning's abortive work. Cooped up in the tram on the hour-and-a-half drive through what seemed a dreary landscape, with nothing to distract him from his neurosis, resulted in his arriving at the baroque little spa in a condition in which every incident and sight was distorted into intimations of his loss.

H wandered about the enclosure waiting for the time to drag by between the races, though at the races themselves he hardly looked, standing impatiently behind a wire fence on ground level, anxious for the afternoon to pass and to be back in Vienna, and more aware of a woman and two men nearby than of the horses pulling the buggies round the track. Each of the men had given the girl a handful of tickets which she had put in her bag, and H followed them after the race, keeping an eye on them from afar, afraid to let them out of his sight, because these intimate, trustful transactions were both comforting and, at the same time, the cause of further acute pangs.

On the return journey he sat in his corner – the compartment was that of a train rather than a tram – and with the summer evening fading from what he thought was beyond the Danube, which remained out of sight, he had an intimation of horrors taking place not so far away, in, roughly, the direction that, till now, the intensity of his own private life had kept him largely insulated from. Later, he thought of this afternoon and evening as the, up to then, most wretched evening he had ever spent. He had lately read of the encirclement of whole Red Army units without its registering except as another piece of war news at a time when sensation after sensation of that sort had produced in him a certain degree of indifference. The situation of these hundreds of thousands of Russians marched off to prisoner-of-war camps where they would slowly starve to death or be ravaged by epidemics was one of the signs that conditions on a vast scale were being created in which not only were the victims deprived of any kind of compassion, but also of hope. The despair of vast numbers of people somewhere not very far away as pain flies (the phrase came unsought) across the darkening plain was identified by him with his own sense of desolation, and thus made real imaginatively.

Back in Vienna he kept walking aimlessly through the streets that, unlike those in Berlin, remained lit until ten. He felt it here too: the city was contaminated by the plague of despair that these lands were in the grip of.

That night in bed he read in the Tauchnitz edition of *Death in Venice* that Susan had sent him to Munich a sentence or two that had a bearing on his thoughts of the evening. But he knew that when a state of mind becomes intense enough almost anything read has a special significance. Thomas Mann, more conscious than Yeats of the contradiction between his life and work, put the matter clearly: 'There he sat, the master: this was he who had found a way to reconcile art and honours; who had written 'The Abject', and in a style of classic purity renounced Bohemianism and all its works, all sympathy with the abyss and the troubled depths of the outcast human soul.' The next sentence that had caught H's tired attention – he read late because he feared the moment of turning out the light and laying his head on the pillow: 'Knowledge is all-knowing, understanding, forgiving; it takes up no position, sets no store by form. It has compassion with the abyss – it *is* the abyss.'

One evening as he was crossing the square in front of the Café Mozart, he looked upwards and saw in the deep incandescent blue, high above the weathered red roofs and the dome of the Opera House, a new moon. He used it, as he'd used the words in *Death in Venice*, as a confirmation of a certain state of consciousness in himself, this time one of very fragile hope.

He started to visit the places he remembered from long ago and on which, on his last visit, Susan had superimposed her own more obsessive memories. He went to the furrier's café where he'd breakfasted every morning with Mr Isaacs, to the one in Praterstrasse in which he'd drunk Tee mit Himbeersaft with Iseult and Frau Sczeky while Hansen had come and gone on his black-market errands, and outside which he now tried to conjure up the grey Opel Darracq as it had stood in the slush of a winter's day. He had a long meditative look at the hotel annexe in Mohrengasse where they'd lived for two or three months, at the steep ramp that had once led down to an underground garage, up which he'd had difficulties in driving the two-cylinder car, at the Diana Bad and the Hotel Bristol.

He re-explored the sad and impoverished city. Was it war or his having awoken from his former dream that had stripped it of much of its aura? He gave up his attempt at writing, enjoyed swimming again, lying in the sun, and sitting for hours in cellars and cafés, and wrote to Halka. He'd have liked her to come to Vienna, but this was impossible because her mother kept a strict eye on her and even made a scene if she stayed out after ten.

One morning he woke up and realized the time for lingering on here was past and went to a ticket agency in Kärntnerstrasse to book a seat on a plane to Berlin. But when he handed in his passport the clerk told H, apologetically, that foreigners weren't permitted to travel by air. He postponed his departure for several days; then one August evening he took farewell of the ever-haunted streets from the tram to the station.

In Berlin H took a room in a pension on an upper floor of a building at the corner of Kurfürstendamm and Kaiser Allee, and a little later met Halka at another corner nearer her home at the hour they'd arranged by letter.

They strolled along side streets under chestnut trees and balconies bright with coloured awnings, and although nothing was said, and he was as shy as she, he sensed or imagined – it came to the same – that in place of their separate physical auras they were enveloped in one, which could only mean that they were soon to become lovers.

H brought her back to the pension, managing to shepherd her along the corridor to his room without their being seen; he wasn't sure what was permitted here and was afraid of an incident that might upset the delicate balance between them.

H had brought a bottle of white wine from Vienna and left it under a dripping cold tap in the basin. But he saw that Halka didn't need any stimulant. She was ready, for whatever shocks were in store; she mightn't enjoy it, but she was going to let nothing stand in the way. It was H who was

301

becoming self-conscious at having to take the initiative, something that it seemed he'd never done before.

After some kissing that, because both knew what was in the offing, wasn't prolonged, H brought out the fatal words, 'Come to bed,' and, catching her quick nod, took the bottle from the basin and a glass from the shelf above it, placed them where they wouldn't be knocked over on the floor at the far side of the bed and, with his back turned, took off his jacket and trousers. When he went to pull down the bed clothes she was already naked, and he took her by the hand and got with her under the sheet with which he covered them, though the heat was stifling.

He lay with her in the dim room – she'd pulled the curtain – with the sound of cars and trams from Kurfürstendamm filling the hot breathless silence, kissing her and feeling her tense with anxiety and, perhaps, curiosity, and possibly even some excited expectation.

'Well, here goes,' he said, so that there could be no turning back.

'Ach ...'

'All right?'

'It aches.'

Her face was damp against his mouth; sweat was also gathering in the hollow of his chest.

H was still hanging back to spare her the probings whose purpose she couldn't yet feel, when she intimated by the pressure of breasts and belly: 'For the love of God, go on!' Even though what she wanted was to have it over and done with, it was enough to produce in him the preliminary thaw that precedes the final central melting and orgiastic flooding.

Next day H rang Susan. She was immersed in problems of her own, more or less desperate, more or less hopeless, of which she cleared her thoughts sufficiently to tell him he could have the room at the Mihailovichs as she was moving elsewhere. And after a couple more nights at the pension, where he didn't dare bring Halka again, he moved back into the familiar room.

That evening, without unpacking, H lay on the couch, the table lamp beside him, constructing a lit island of tranquillity in the big dark room where so many miseries had lurked, in a state of calm he'd forgotten, waiting to meet Halka around midnight and stroll (yes, he could stroll again instead of rushing) with his arm about her, under the blue-white searchlights, from the U-Bahn station to her door.

58

After the second or third time with Halka it was as if they'd been lovemaking for years. She came in the late afternoons, between leaving the university and going to the Rundfunk, and as soon as they'd embraced, she took off her shoes and when he returned from locking the door was already stretched on the couch with her dress pulled up, delighting him by thus displaying the same impatience as his own.

Afterwards they stayed on the couch while the water boiled on the much-patched electric ring in the corner for the black-market coffee H bought from Olga Mihailovich, and he read to her some of Keats's poems; raptly she listens, he reflected, his thoughts echoing the cadence of what he'd been reading out. Before she had to leave they made love again.

The first lovemaking in the afternoon involved the transition from the non-sexual world in which both had been caught up, but the second or third time they started from inside their sensual consciousness and, not having far to go, could take their time, savouring the eternal strangeness of the act.

In the hushed aftermath, where for a little while nothing is as it was before and objects are not quite set in their pre-orgasm outlines after their obscuration in the general physical melting, she took the used contraceptive and dangling it by the neck gave it one of her dark-eyed scrutinies before returning it to him to dispose of.

At the start of the winter semester, Olga Mihailovich glided in one evening and, with her ambiguous smile, offered him a piece of gold made up in a thick, crude-looking ring for one and a half thousand marks. The sum, large as it was, he could just afford to pay. And the next day, after withdrawing the amount from the American Express, as he counted the notes into her plump white hands, she suggested he might like a smaller room, the one next door that the young man whom Dominique's crying had disturbed had previously occupied.

Though the move was only a matter of a couple of yards, it was part of more subtle changes. It marked the end of his and Halka's honeymoon. There was no lessening of sexual intensity but, on recovering from the sensual trances, she began to take a closer look at him and what concerned him. She became jealous over some of the girls in his classes, 'brazen little witches', of Susan when she'd come around to fetch the rest of her things, 'what right has she to call you "darling"?' or of his not having told her something she considered important.

She sulked for a day or so, removed her few belongings, as well as a photo

303

she'd given him, and only came around the second or third evening, white-faced and shadowy-browed. Then the wounds were healed in a bout of lovemaking which reached a delirious pitch in ratio to the degree and duration of their estrangement.

A week or two after one such reconciliation she told him at the last minute of one of her visits when, having got into her overcoat, she'd turned to the wardrobe mirror, that she thought she was pregnant.

Lightheartedly, to reassure her, and hide his shock, H, from behind, laid his hand on her belly and boldly assured her, 'There's nothing there.' His touch excited them all the more for being made without sensual intent. He drew her back on to the couch and, still in her overcoat, made love to her over again.

As well as the physical contact, there was his reading aloud to her, mainly from Keats. Her enjoyment of this too was instinctive – she didn't always understand the poems – but he saw it as a bond of a different kind without which their relationship would have been even more precarious.

Though he didn't care for the overblown diction of many of the poems, what still fascinated H in Keats was his very personal sort of insights. Like himself, Keats was aware of intellectual limitations, which in H's case amounted to certain blind spots.

> What though I am not wealthy in the dower
> Of spanning wisdom, though I do not know
> The shiftings of the mighty winds that blow
> Hither and thither all the changing thoughts
> Of man, though no great ministering reason sorts
> Out the dark mysteries of human souls
> To clear conceiving; yet there ever rolls
> A vast idea before me, and I glean
> Therefrom my liberty: thence too I've seen
> The end and aim of Poesy.

One Sunday Halka invited him home to lunch with her mother and sister. Because of what he'd heard of Frau Witebsk's strict Catholicism and of the rules she laid down for the girls for their meetings with men, H was doubtful about accepting.

'What will she think of you having a married admirer?'

'She won't think anything.'

'She's angry if you come home half an hour later than usual.'

'She's suspicious of soldiers and the sort of men she thinks Lise and I might pick up in cafés. She'll believe anything I tell her about what she imagines as the wonderful world of writers and university lecturers.'

None of this put H at ease. But when he arrived at the rather dark ground-floor flat he saw that Frau Witebsk wouldn't overawe him as his mother-in-law had. She was a small, prematurely white-haired woman in whom he noticed hints of Halka's innocence and passion.

All went well and H was touched by Frau Witebsk's apparent liking for, and even trust in, him. Halka's sister had evidently troubles enough of her own and kept silent most of the time. He came away wishing, for the first time seriously, that he wasn't married. Not for Halka's sake, though later they were to regret it because of the added dangers the lack of official sanction for being together exposed them to, but so that Frau Witebsk, dressed in her Sunday black could go to church and see the priest pronounce the hallowed words over them that would efface some of the anxieties that marked her forehead and drew her mouth tight.

Suddenly the warring world intruded into the hidden life that H was living, not yet in the way of air raids or much reduced rations but involving him more closely. In answer to a phone call he went to see Dr Zimmermann who told him about a plan to broadcast to Ireland and asked him to contribute a weekly talk.

H guessed that the Herr Doktor, or his superiors, was afraid that America's entry into the conflict would influence Ireland to abandon her neutrality, though this seemed to H a very slight threat in the light of the powerful forces the Germans had managed to line up against them.

H returned to his room, aware that he wasn't going to refuse. For one thing, when he'd agreed to write talks soon after coming here he'd made the crucial decision even if he hadn't delivered them himself. In any case, what he told the professor in his study at Bad Godesberg before the war was his only criterion for deciding how far to go in his dissent.

Would it have been better to have had nothing to do with them now that he was here? Probably; but not simply in order to escape a formal guilt. He saw guilt in relation to the writer not so much as an involvement with malefactors as a sharing in universal attitudes for the sake of easing imagination's lonely ache. And it was not a question of how far these could be morally justified. Better the infected sovereign psyche than one that shared in a general righteousness that didn't belong to it.

59

What was he to say in these talks? And who would listen? Iseult and his mother-in-law? Molly's uncles? The Deasey brothers? Some of his former jailmates? He could condemn such Allied atrocities as he'd heard of – the indiscriminate bombing was only just beginning – but that would involve him in the same deception as the propagandists who presented the war as a moral conflict.

The harshest judgement passed on him would not be entirely undeserved even though he didn't accept the jurisdiction of the court. Could he express his belief that the only possible good that could now arise out of it was if it ended by bringing the whole structure, ideological, cultural, moral, crashing down about the heads of whoever was left with whole ones? Hardly.

Extract from H's wartime diary on a date in early 1942: 'An alert this afternoon as I was sitting reading at the window. So far the raids have been confined mostly to the city outskirts though a few incendiaries have dropped around the town, not yet on the block where I had the flat, unfortunately, which, if burnt out before the owners return would preclude troubles over the business of the china cabinet.

'After a few minutes saw what I took to be a solitary Russian plane flying slowly from the east and shining softly in the frosty light (a tiny silver cross horizontal against the pale sky and fringed around by ghostly pink and white rosettes). Watched it for five minutes or more till it turned south and slowly disappeared. Had it not been for Halka would have longed to be in it on its long, long homeward flight.'

H didn't want to end the war among the victors whoever they turned out to be. Russia in defeat would be infinitely preferable to a triumphant Nazi Germany, which still seemed a possible outcome.

From the radio on the folding table with the green baize top came, between the popular songs (Lala Anderson's lilting 'Lili Marlene', Zarah Leander's throaty sex moanings) the announcements of the defeat of Russian armies, at Bryansk and Taganrog, by the Don and Donetz. Other news came slipped under the door in the form of an occasional letter from home, with Iseult writing as if, for her, time had stood still, or even reversed itself to the days before their estrangement, his mother weaving a web of small local placidities, Kay with dutiful notes from the mould of the convent school to which she'd been sent, shy, clumsy ones from Ian, and Aunt Jenny's, which were the sharpest evocations of the past.

Along the hallway in late afternoon came the quick tap of Halka's wooden soles – he'd given her a duplicate key to the outside door – and, a scarf wound into a turban over her head and ears, her thin coat, into which her mother had sewn a rabbit-fur lining, smelling of icy winds, she'd appear in the warm room, where only a tablelamp was burning.

To the excitement of her wintry apparition in the small haven, she added, while she undressed, odds and ends of her own news: increasing trouble between her sister and mother, a remark of her English professor about Blake that she wanted elucidated later, the welcome return of her period, the announcement of a gift for H in the way of a half-sheet of the ration coupons issued to soldiers on leave that her sister had got from her sergeant.

One night a week H went to the Rundfunkhaus with Halka and was directed to one of the soundproof cubicles where they sat before a microphone and waited for the red light to come on. Then she announced him and he read the talk from the script. Sometimes somebody from the Irische Redaktion came and listened, but they were mostly alone, and he doubted whether Dr Zimmermann or anybody else monitored what he said.

The talks were more difficult than he'd expected. He was supposed to be speaking to his own people, but who were they? He could try to stress the other reasons, beside material advantage, for Irish neutrality. One of these was that those who thought for themselves were free to come to certain conclusions about the war without feeling they were letting down their fellow countrymen who were taking the risks and doing the fighting.

They could question the Allied posture of moral grandeur, and in particular Churchill's, without giving comfort to the enemy. And they'd be able to dissociate themselves, in spirit, at least, from whoever proved the victors, and to forgo participation in the celebrations ushering a peace that, not being the chastened kind born out of near-despair, would soon turn brash and complacent.

Dr Zimmermann asked H to come and see him and suggested he might not be laying enough stress on Hitler's war against communism – H had purposely never mentioned it – which, he said, must have much Irish support.

'Not from the sort of people I'm talking to,' H told him, 'some of them may be anti-British but none are anti-Russian.'

Dr Zimmermann said no more, though H saw he wasn't convinced but instead showed him a report from Dublin in an English magazine, *Picture Post*, saying that the Irish weren't impressed by the promises H was broadcasting from Germany.

'What promises?' H asked, though he knew there was no sense in resenting the paragraph.

'I thought you'd better see it,' Dr Zimmermann said. 'But don't let it worry you, you'll never have to give an account of yourself to these people.'

Zimmermann's other suggestion was that the talks should be given after ten o'clock when, he said, the Athlone station closed down, so that it couldn't be used as a guide to targets in Northern Ireland by German raiders, and H was glad for once to be able to agree.

On Saturdays he and Halka took the S-Bahn through suburbs of white stucco, red-and-green-roofed villas and neat lawns over which sprinklers were casting rainbow spray in the early morning sun and, further out, through sandy allotments with their wooden weekend shacks, screened by lilacs and silver birches, to several of which H imagined retiring with Halka. There they would live (on what?) far from the rest of the world and the war (was it over?) and, at the end of the hot day, after watering their beans and asparagus, lie on their couch by the frame window with the swallows darting and dipping against the clear, washed-out sky.

Not that he was taken in by this or other fantasies. The sight of the shacks behind their leafy screens – huts had always fascinated him – evoked a sensation of felicity that he couldn't resist enjoying for a few moments, but he knew it had little to do with what was in front of them. He also knew – but that was subconscious knowledge – that such a tranquil existence would be disastrous for them.

Iseult and the children were confidently waiting for him to return when the war was over. In an effort to make some sort of plan he told Halka that he'd bring her home with him and they'd all live together at Dineen.

'What about your wife? What would she say to that?'

'After the war a lot will be possible that wouldn't have been before.'

This might become true of those who would survive some of the worst horrors, but he knew that to imagine the postwar world as a place where fundamental changes would be general was an illusion.

Halka nodded – it was in the train on the way to the lakes that they first seriously discussed the future – and put her hand over his. 'I wouldn't mind as long as I could be with you. We'd go for walks alone together, wouldn't we?'

All was well, he needn't worry about what would happen if he survived the war; as long as he didn't ask himself how Iseult would take his going for walks with this girl, something he'd never done with her herself for years, or what it would feel like to be shut up in his room at night with Halka in the one downstairs that had been Miss Burnett's.

Once on the lake (Müggelsee or Sakrower See) the immediate sensations, of hot sun on his chest and arms, the plop of oar blades lifting leisurely and, finally, in a cove surrounded by rushes, her body, brown and crossed by the two paler sections usually hidden by her swim suit, stretched along the bottom of the boat that was gently rocking as he let himself down on to her, banished thought of the future. Late on these summer Saturday nights, back in his room from the Rundfunkhaus – her mother didn't know the exact hour of his broadcast – Halka still kept a scent of the hot tarry bottom of the boat where she'd lain sweaty and naked and, later, cool and smeared with sun lotion while they'd picnicked.

One of the passages Halka had him read to her and discuss was the letter in which Keats reflects on the purpose manifest in animals intent on their prey, and writes of the man who also 'hath a purpose and his eye is bright with it.'

By 'purpose' Keats seemed to mean what H called obsession, and Keats's obsession with poetry enabled him in the end to give up his feverish desire for fame, for Fanny, even for 'a life of sensation', and live out his destined legend to his early and agonizing death.

H had his own 'vast ideas', even if he didn't mistake them as being of the same magnitude. And compared to them most of the news on which he commented in his talks were passing sensations soon overtaken by the next in the series.

Sometimes, by way of a change, he presented news items of his own. One of these was the recording of the deaths, in mysterious circumstances, of certain individualists embarrassing to the Allies: Cudahy, whom H had come across when he was American ambassador in Dublin and who, transferred to Brussels, had got himself into the news by welcoming the Germans there, had resigned, or been sacked, come to Berlin for an American paper, asked H to a drink at the Adlon and told him of an interview in which he'd warned Hitler not to continue to provoke Roosevelt by careless attacks on United States shipping, and had died suddenly in Switzerland shortly afterwards; a young Englishman, whose name H had forgotten, who'd written a novel called *This Above All* that Kolbinsky had lent him, about the adventures of a soldier who'd deserted after Dunkirk, and had himself, as H had read in an old English newspaper in Zimmermann's office, been killed in a car accident in South America.

With the setting in of the long nights, the war loomed directly overhead out of the moonless sky and street after street crumbled into hillocks of white rubble that soon weathered into a gritty mud that sprouted weeds, between which paths were trodden and new landmarks appeared to replace the old: the floor of a room balanced between two solitary upright walls; a cellar that they passed on their way to the only restaurant in the neighbourhood still serving fish off the ration, gaping from under a pile of bricks from which came the stench of death and disinfectant. Then with the coming of another summer, women and girls, stocky and sallow-skinned, their hair bound in dusty scarfs, appeared from nowhere to shift the rubble. A colony of them, with their children and a few old men, lived in the only cluster of still standing but badly battered houses in the same street and, on the way back from the restaurant, passing them as they gathered in the warm dusk outside their dwellings – as formerly in their villages? – H imagined himself and Halka among these deserted Russians living in one of the rooms behind the boarded-up windows, fetching water from the hydrant down the street, cooking supper over a wood fire in the yard. In his fantasies they always hid, so that when the war ended they couldn't be found.

The constant disruption of the transport service and of the university schedules, the long queues outside shops and the delays everywhere, made it difficult for her mother to keep a close watch over Halka's comings and goings. So that when, on account of the air raids, Frau Witebsk went to stay with relations in East Prussia, it didn't, at least at first, cause any great change in their way of life except that sometimes when Halka came to his room from the Rundfunkhaus, instead of having to get up and dress again, she stayed the night.

One night H was having supper with her, her sister, and her sister's sergeant on night leave from his barracks, when a bomb burst a few yards away from the Witebsks' flat. The crockery jumped on the table, plaster showered down, the double glass doors, long locked and stuffed with paper against draughts, flew open, the window panes broke behind the velvet curtains; this they only noted later. In the silence that was sucked back into the vacuum left by the roar they stood around the table on which Halka's birthday candle still burned – H didn't recall jumping up – waited a moment (for the house to cave in?) and then, not hurriedly but as if sleepwalking, made for the cellar, shepherded by the Feldwebel.

Those from other flats already sitting on benches hardly looked up as they entered, and H, once seated beside Halka, soon felt this reluctance to make any but the most circumspect movement as if the quiet between the explosions was too fragile to risk disturbing.

Here he was, her prophet, as she sometimes called him in the biblical terminology that came natural to her, and what could he say to her? It wasn't a matter of the death that comes from illness, old age, or even accident, in which the spirit is given a little time to make its retreat. It was destruction, utter and instantaneous, with no time for the psyche to sniff the oncoming of death and lay itself down in its own bed or whatever rags or straw it had gathered against that hour. This psyche, as the consciousness thought of itself, imagination's unique locale, its beautiful pattern of roots in the deoxyribonucleic acid, drawing up its 'vast ideas' from deep in the past, could it be annulled, reduced to a spot of slime on a collapsing wall?

Not that he felt any resentment against those who were doing the bombing. It was the apparent vulnerability of the nucleus at the core of the cosmic structure that appalled him.

Though apropos of the Allied bombing, an English airforce officer whom he met in a French transit camp after the war told him they hadn't been allowed to bomb the gas chambers in the concentration camps because the evidence of the enemy's guilt was far too valuable to destroy.

When the electric bulbs shining through the dust haze at the end of their cords had ceased to swing slowly, and the hunched shoulders began to straighten, the sweet tones of distant sirens (did they only sound faint after the explosion? or had the neighbouring ones been all destroyed?) gave the all clear.

Swiftly the sensations of living flowed back and before they were up the cellar stairs H was impelled by an urge to make love to Halka with the bodies that had been just restored to them. But wasn't this desire peculiar to his own kind of sexuality, that was stimulated by contrasts and incongruities, and something she wouldn't be likely to feel so soon after the shock of the raid? Better put it from his thoughts, be patient and let her come to herself in her own time.

With Lise and Kurt he was looking around for cracks in the walls and other signs of damage when he missed Halka who he thought had followed them into the living room. Her sister said she was reheating the coffee that they'd been drinking with their interrupted meal, but he found her at the door of her room waiting.

'Come,' she said and beckoned him in.

60

Along pavements scarred with the star-shaped cracks made by phosphor bombs and stacked with salvaged furniture, past a pile of steaming rubble at the corner that neither commented on immediately because, he sensed, she, like himself, required a little time to take in what had become of the six or eight-storey block at the moment they'd jumped up from her birthday table, wearing their gas masks to traverse the dark billows of smoke that came rushing out of the shell of a big school in the Kaiser Allee, they reached the hardly recognizable square from which branched the street where H had his room. Ahead, in a patch of wintry sunlight, where the fires were mostly out, they saw the two Mihailovich women and Olga's Polish lover in the armchairs where they'd spent the night beside an upright piano draped in oriental rugs. H was touched to find, when they arrived at the forlorn-looking little group, that they'd brought out his good suit, once before lost and recovered, and his books: the prohibited Thomas Mann and Kafka side by side with the unbanned but even more subversive Keats on top of the rugs.

H and Halka climbed the stairs and entered the abandoned flat. The place seemed as usual – Olga had told them only the top floor had burned – and in his room where it was almost the same as ever except for a damp spot in the centre where water had dripped from the ceiling, they lay down; the second-phase sensuality had set in, the morning trance after a night of desolation-copulation. Afterwards, still half-drugged, she murmured, 'No need for polite habits anymore,' and squatted down on the already wet carpet.

They made a couple of trips to the street with more of his belongings, but on the third ascent were too tired and out of breath to salvage anything further. Before abandoning the portable gramophone, they put on a record and left the flat, with its doors all open, to the music of one of the popular tunes of the moment.

Leaving what they'd saved in the care of the Mihailovichs to be collected on their way back, they took the S-Bahn which had miraculously been got running again, the viaduct shored up with timber, H noted, in the vicinity of Nollendorfplatz, to the university.

Nothing but a couple of walls, on one of which the board with the schedule and notices still hung, remained of the Englische Seminar building and H felt relief that his role as lecturer on English literature was at an end.

'What are you going to do now?' she asked.

'Make love to you soon as we get back to your place.'

'Klar! But what will you live on if you don't get paid?'

'On the money in the bank saved from the translation and the talks.'

'Stay with us and share my room, Luke.'

She called him Luke either when sulky or at moments, like this, when she was really thinking of something else. At other times she had other names, biblical ones, and all sorts of endearments for him.

H spent the winter at her and her sister's flat while Halka worked on for her degree, in English, Spanish, German, and Philosophy, poring over books from the still-standing Staatsbibliothek, among which Francis Bacon and Cervantes caught his eye, with her head in her hands and a finger in each ear to shut out the talk of her sister and the Feldwebel, for her own room was too cold to remain in for long, and later travelling on the continually patched-up underground to the suburban houses of professors where groups of students were examined.

Many nights they sat cowering in the cellar while H tried to think his way through the mystery of the apparent extinction of the psyche – one of the names the mind, looking into its mirror, gives itself – by means of high explosive.

Was it a fledgling that couldn't survive the tearing down of its biochemical nest? Or a wild and wary bird that had flown from the tree before the great bang that never reached the ear?

Then, nothing consciously resolved, up the cellar stairs and into her bed to a first quick coming with Halka, exacerbated nerves needing hardly more than the other's touch, without the use of what she called an antibaby device which seemed superfluous with so many infinitely more effective anti-everything devices in operation all around.

He lay in bed long after Halka had got up and gone to huddle near the tiled stove in the living room with her books. He was always suffering from lack of sleep; in the trams and U-Bahn trains everyone looked as if they were coming from orgies, heavy lids dropping over the eyes of young and old, and shadows under them all.

Later he'd walk about the dead and dying city, noting how the skeleton was becoming visible as block after block collapsed, revealing long vistas over low hillocks from street to parallel street, and how these areas of desolation, restricted and isolated at first, gradually spread and joined together, so that there were vast spaces, such as that formed by the jungle between Tauenzienstrasse and Kaiser Allee, of pale, hump-backed deserts.

In the early evenings he'd drag Halka from her books, which she clung to as an antidote to the constant fury of the raids, and take her to some boarded-up café among the ruins where there was nothing to drink but the hot black brew that took the place of coffee, and try to beguile her with tales of peace and plenty. He told her about the filly, adding the concrete details that made the scene dense before a race, drawing out the suspense to transport her temporarily into that small, self-contained world. Or he spoke of the races for the Derby he'd watched: one with Liam O'Flaherty, one with Stroud.

'Tell me what else,' she pleaded, not to have to return too soon to their rather desperate situation.

He explained to her that these odd tales had become more intense in the telling because of the pain they were adding to them. And one day he ended by saying that the time was coming when they'd have to leave Berlin; and this came as a surprise to her because her sister's lover, the Feldwebel, was still confident that the German advance, halted at Stalingrad, and since become a steady retreat, would soon be resumed. H was asking Halka to leave home – though it might now be a precarious one, it was the only haven she had – to come with him whose standing wouldn't be high in the now certain event of a German defeat, a writer who had ruined his prospects in the postwar world, with a wife who wouldn't, outside his fantasies, be likely to welcome her, even should he manage to get her over several closed frontiers.

While from the radio salvaged from H's room came announcements, at half-hour intervals, that no raiders had crossed the German frontiers, they had a supper prepared by Lise from what she'd been able to get on her way home from the dress shop where she worked, with either her soldier's leave ration coupons or their own meagre supply.

As the critical hour, on moonless nights, approached, Lise lay on her bed with the evening paper, disconsolate because the Feldwebel's military-police duties kept him at one or other of the mainline stations, and H and Halka talked in low tones by the stove. Among the things they discussed were plans for the summer should they survive; H didn't contemplate so difficult a move in the middle of winter. He had several ideas, none of them very sound, but this she couldn't distinguish, the one that he favoured at the moment being, as long as there was no second front in the West, to go to France, try to get to the Breton coast and there pay a fisherman, perhaps with the gold ring, to take them to Ireland. Alone, he might have remained where he was till the Russians arrived – he still thought of their leaders as the least culpable of those directing the vast slaughter – but he feared for Halka with her Polish background, which fact could be gleaned from her papers.

At intervals the news was repeated that 'There are no enemy formations over the Reich,' ending with, 'We'll be back shortly,' a promise that, the story went, had sent the elderly couple from the flat above, just as they'd returned from the cellar, hurrying down again. Towards midnight Halka would bring her feather eiderdown to warm at the stove. When he saw her almost too tired to keep her arms raised as she pressed the big bundle to the hot tiles, he could hardly wait for the approaching moment when he'd kindle her shadowy face to a glow of response with kisses raining down on her in relief at being spared for that night the half hour's ordeal in the basement.

In early summer the pattern changed, and though there were less frequent night attacks, by Mosquitos that he imagined as small, swift aircraft capable of carrying one or two large bombs each to Berlin even in the shorter hours of darkness, there were big-scale daylight raids by American Flying Fortresses.

'There's a subject for one of your talks,' Zimmermann told H. 'Systemized area bombing: planned extermination of civilian populations.'

But H was determined not to start moralizing. Other commentators were concerned to prove their side had a monopoly of public ethics, a claim which he, having no side, had no intention of contesting, any more than his fictional hero, Nick Peters, would have dreamed of protesting to the asylum authorities, or any other body, about his treatment. But he let Zimmermann think the idea appealed to him – by now he was pretty sure that nobody here listened to the talks – because he was soon going to need travel permits for himself and Halka which would be hard to come by if he antagonzied the smiling little Doktor.

Anyhow, he foresaw the broadcasts soon coming to an end. Half the time he couldn't get to the station at the appointed hour because an alert was on and transport had come to a stop, or it hadn't yet been got going again after a raid. Sometimes there was a raid while he was there and he was given a microphone with a tightly fitting rubber mouthpiece that was supposed to shut out the sound of the bombs.

When that finally happened, Halka having meanwhile received a document, not with the printed heading she'd expected on top because the Sekretariat wasn't functioning, but rubber-stamped with the name of the university and a swastika, testifying to her having passed her exams, and, as a further indication that the time was ripe, they had come to the end of their study of Keats, they left Berlin. Lise and the Feldwebel, wearing the metal military-policeman's plaque on a chain from his neck and thus ensuring them seats in the crowded train, saw them off, and as they passed through the ruined suburbs H took farewell of the city where he'd just spent the most intense five years of his life.

At the station in Munich, where he'd decided on going now that they couldn't get to France, a hut had been set up at which the influx of bombed-out refugees seeking shelter could be dealt with. While H waited in the background, more conscious of himself as an outsider than in Berlin where, with his post at the university and Zimmermann to put in a word for him, he'd been a privileged foreigner, Halka joined the queue in front of the wooden shed.

Unused to practical matters and dealing with officials – her mother and later her sister had had that responsibility – she returned from the window with her brows marked by the ordeal, but grasping a slip with the address of a hotel on it.

The way there led them along a path trodden in the dusty remains of what was just discernible as a street, and it appeared that this city had had its share of bombs: a fact he hadn't been prepared for. When, at the damaged hotel, H was shown his room with a badly cracked wall and boarded-up window and Halka was taken further down the passage to one she was to share with another woman, he thought she might question his wisdom in bringing them here and abandoning the shelter of her room in Berlin. But, though downcast from the realization that from now on their not being married would make difficulties for them, she didn't say a word as they went out again into the warm autumn morning; they'd travelled overnight.

Crossing the town, they emerged into the big park of the Englische Garten, where H recalled once sitting dreaming on a bench when he'd wandered from the hotel where he was staying with Iseult and her mother. There they rested in the shade of a row of beech trees and from the attaché case that he always carried with him H took the *Oxford Book of English Verse*, borrowed from the library of the Englische Seminar before its destruction, and opened it at Wordsworth. It was these nature poems which had once bored him that served as their daily prayers in this new phase of existence: the liturgical expression of their faith in surviving to reach the promised land, as she called the place he was supposed to be leading her towards.

They fell asleep and when, hours later, he dizzily opened his eyes on the wide sunny meadow he was back at Dineen, just after hearing that faraway bird carefully repeat its song, and the countryside, so often irksome to him then, was enchanting in its quietness. But the sirens were sounding and they crossed a corner of the park to the gallery built by Hitler to house the modern paintings in the naturalistic style approved by all high authorities, under which was an air-raid shelter. When they came out it was time to start looking for a place to eat; he recalled the necessity of studying the menus and queuing up early, and took her to the Rathaus. A look inside the Keller showed them the futility of trying to find a place there, and they turned into the narrow old streets around the Frauenkirche where, in a once-fashionable restaurant called the Schwarzwald, they got a small table to themselves.

But when H managed to get hold of a waiter his accent attracted attention and he was told he'd have to wait. An officer chimed in to say that camps were where the pack of refugees who had overrun the Reich should be, and Halka retorted that H, far from being a refugee, had left the peace and plenty of his native land to come here . . . etc.

'What land, for the love of God?' asked an incredulous lady at the next table.

Though she'd marched head high from the place, Halka stood trembling outside. 'That couldn't have happened in Berlin,' she said.

H was inclined to agree; he'd come to the conclusion that it wasn't the Prussians but the Germans more popular with prewar tourists, the Bavarians, who'd be most vindictive towards the weak, and the loudest with their anti-Nazi protestations when the enemy arrived. Later they were in the hotel cellar where there was a crack in the vaulted ceiling at one end that H, with a sure instinct for direction, saw extended under the street, and afterwards, for fear of another humiliation, they didn't dare spend the rest of the night together in H's room.

But the unpropitious start to what Halka in her biblical phraseology called 'The Flight', a phase that covered the time from their leaving Berlin to the end of the war the following spring, though only the last few months were actually spent in homeless wandering, didn't set the tone, as he'd feared, for the whole of their stay in Munich.

61

After various shifts – there was a limit on the duration of a stay in any one hotel – on the last day of September they managed to get accommodation on the top floor of a pension which at night they had to themselves, the other rooms on it being occupied as offices by a business firm. This was such a stroke of luck that Halka noted the date at the back of a holy picture she kept in her missal.

In order to avoid being conscripted for war work in a factory, she enrolled in a course for English interpreters – that this was given priority seemed an open admission of the coming defeat – which she'd only to turn up at a few afternoons a week.

In the mornings they climbed on one of the open wagons pulled by a small locomotive emitting clouds of smoke that ran from the triumphal arch, but not the same one under which H had once met Polenskaya, on a narrow-gauge rail laid to replace the twisted tram tracks, to the centre of town. In a café near a big public shelter they sat reading Wordsworth till the alarm sounded as it usually did punctually at eleven. They'd been driven from the cellar at the pension by the behaviour of a family who spread themselves over it with a portable radio and at each announcement of new waves of bombers approaching had put on their steel helmets, recorked their Thermos flasks, placed their electric torch and first-aid kit on the bench they'd requisitioned for their belongings, and glared at Halka and H huddled, devoid of protective paraphernalia, in the opposite corner.

On the afternoon that Halka took off – as a star pupil she was allowed a lot of latitude – they walked in the Englische Garten, near which the pension was situated, fascinated by the stillness of the autumn-tinted trees. In the aftermath of the explosions a leaf falling and turning slowly in the still air was a peculiar balm, as were the nature poems.

In the clear evenings of winter they called at a kiosk further up the long, wide street on which they lived and H, in the queue for the evening paper, watched the red sun sink at its far end, a star just above, as the cyclists streamed along it from work. It struck H that this (setting sun and the evening star) was one of the mysterious eternal words being spoken to those in need of them. But more immediate was the need to scan the daily war report on their way to the restaurant in the park where they had their meals for news of the Russian advance.

When there was news of further German withdrawals and they were each served with a portion of mussel hash in a slender ring of mashed potatoes, which was now their favourite dish, the evening was one of those full of a precarious bliss, the only kind still possible.

On their way home from supper or, later still, returning from the trenches in the park where they sheltered during night attacks, they had further intimations of a reality that seemed to balance without annulling the one they were involved in. Looking up at the night sky above the park and gazing into the black gaps in the pale shoal that ran across it, they glimpsed depths that weren't completely strange to them, and were conscious of contemplating reflections of abysses in themselves. The constellations were on the move, slowly spinning with the faint whirring that was the just audible beat of the silence they were in such need of.

When the worst of winter set in, they went to cinemas or stayed in bed fully dressed, ready to hurry to the Englische Garten when the sirens started. But when they climbed out of the deep trench across which felled logs had been laid and covered in earth, in a daze – both the din and the tremors were increased by the frozen earth – they had no longer the urge to make love.

At last they were being worn down by the constant onslaught on the nerves. These had become permanently bruised by the harsh song of the falling bombs. At the moment of hearing the all-clear they no longer had the urge to hurry to their room to make love. Instead they rose and walked home wearily arm-in-arm as if they were an aging couple in whom the fiery passions have burned out, leaving a residue of white ash in the blood.

This state, which he saw as the foretaste of a possible time to come, was not without its unexpected rewards. There was a new tenderness between them, unrelated, at least consciously, to sex.

He still hadn't any plan for after the war but the one of his bringing her home. And now, in the sober mood brought about by hunger, sleeplessness, cold, as well as the culminative effect of nervous tension, it appeared completely unrealistic. But rather than admit this and return to Berlin, in February he decided it was time to move towards the Swiss frontier which it might be possible to cross; he would forge Halka's name as that of his wife on his passport.

They left from a suburban station on a chill morning before it was light and travelled the fifty kilometres beyond which nobody without a special permit was allowed to journey from their last registered abode. Setting off at a brisk pace to walk the rest of the way, they were slowed down by the wind in their faces over the wide, rolling Allgäu plain and made so little headway that he began to wonder if to have left the shelter of their Munich rooms wasn't another, and possibly final, mistake of his.

They went into a pine wood to rest and there H took stock of the situation. Present provisions and means of replenishing them: the sausage sandwiches they'd brought with them and that Halka was too exhausted to eat, some travellers' coupons; they wouldn't get new ration cards until they had a residence permit and a permanent address in the new district, where they'd be lucky even to find beds for one night in a hotel. Stock of clothes and personal effects: all in the suitcase which, labelled and directed to the left-luggage office at Lindau station, he'd hopefully put into the guard's van of the train they'd got off; what chance there was of recovering it at the other end he didn't know. Financial position: he'd been receiving his salary from the university and, with what he'd saved in Berlin, had with him several thousand marks, that there was nothing to buy with, as well as the heavy gold ring that Halka was wearing.

'Are you sorry we left the pension?' she asked.

'Not for a moment.'

'I can't walk much further; the little express has run down.'

It now dawned on him that it was at the time of buying the ticket and not on the train that the permit for a longer journey would be asked for. They could book to any place fifty kilometres beyond the next station they came to.

It was dark again when they got the next train, and they decided to stay on it till it reached Lake Constance, although they hadn't tickets that far. Huddled together for warmth in their corner of the unlit compartment they became aware, through the gaps in the roughly boarded-up window, that the horizon was aglow, not with a wall of fire, as it had been through the trees of the park when they'd come out of the trench, but with a festive white illumination. They contemplated the vision in bewilderment till a fellow traveller told them that these were the lights of Switzerland across the lake.

The station at Lindau was undamaged, clean, and spruce-looking after all the patched-up places they were accustomed to, and they paid the excess fare without being asked for their permit; and at the left-luggage office, when the name on his passport had been compared to that on the label, they were given the suitcase.

There began another new phase of existence; Lindau station which, with its miniature harbour, served in peacetime as the terminal for the lake steamers, became the base to which they returned every few days to spend a night in the comparative comfort of its big waiting room. Police checks on the homeless hordes that were sleeping in stations made it advisable to be able to show tickets for an early morning train and, to avoid trouble, to take it to a neighbouring town and not reappear till a couple of evenings later.

Their return there was always a kind of homecoming at which they got out the miraculously restored suitcase, took from it what they needed in the way of clean clothes, or merely had a look through its contents, had a wash at the gleaming row of basins in the station lavatory, made use of its well-kept w.c.s and then went to the station restaurant, with its view of Lake Constance, where there was always one dish available without coupons.

After the meagre meal they stayed on at the table, for it was still too early to settle for the night on one of the white, garden-style seats in the waiting room, and the background noise of German faded, in H's ears, to a hushed murmur that ceased altogether for moments and then, breaking back in a roar, kept casting him up and carrying him away from the shores of the exterior world.

He had always a pocketful of railway tickets; which ones they used depended on whether there'd been a police check and at what time, and he couldn't have recalled to which of the various towns they'd travelled in any preceding week. They were constantly coming and going with all the others: Italian workers whose factories had been destroyed, refugees from the Baltic states, Hungarians, and Rumanians.

During these last days (against all likelihood) he'd hit on the theme he needed for a novel.

Scraps of incident and dialogue came to him in these apparent unpropitious circumstances; he hadn't even an old copybook among the odds and ends in the attaché case in which to note them down. Lying on a hillside above the lake while Halka cut the couple of thin slices of black bread that was two-thirds of their daily ration – she, but not H, having a temporary permit to stay in the district could obtain ration cards – and placed on each a small portion of cheese; in the crowded station restaurant buzzing with constantly excited talk, for rumours were ripe, or at night in the waiting room for the lake steamers, where now was a longer wait than had been provided for, he had found a theme wherein to explore the further states of consciousness that the experiences of the last years had opened up.

It would be about somebody (X) in one of the Allied cities, all V-signs and flags, celebrating the triumph of the forty-two crusading nations, not just over the Nazis, but, it seemed to X, over his, and the other personal modes of thought that went counter to the popular and victorious one.

Of course he'd have to work an imaginative miracle to persuade anyone that X was anything than a psychopath. And he realized that the chances of finding a publisher were nil.

As soon as they got back to Lindau after a night or two in small stations to the north along the shores of the lake, or from a trip up one of the lines that ran eastwards, they hurried, before retiring to the toilets, to a news-agent's shop in a back street in the window of which the latest of the daily communiqués issued by the army High Command were displayed.

They peered through the glass, sometimes only just making out the type-

320

script in the spring dusk; to have returned earlier would have deprived them of the excuse, should there be a check, that they were waiting for a morning connection. H might be gaining insights into the sort of novel that he and probably nobody else (fortunately for the literary watchdogs!) could, at the moment, write, but he knew that there was a limit to how long they could hold out.

When the communiqué reported further Russian advances, they turned back towards the station and the wide-gleaming lake feeling that the un-known wonders of peace were about to be given them. In this state of expectancy, when even the prospect of the supper of soup, and whatever extra they might come by – and once an officer at their table had had to leave before the meat dish he'd ordered had been served and it was passed on to them – was an excitement, they passed the rest of the evening.

They were equally vulnerable to the occasional reports that seemed to indicate a prolongation of the war. The evening after they'd read of the German advance in the Ardennes they stayed leaning on the parapet at the tiny harbour, with its stone lions guarding the narrow entrance, reluctant to enter the station for another long night spent on one of the garden seats, painted the same gay colours as the steamers.

'Should I not try to get back to Berlin, and you to your legation and ask to be repatriated?' Halka suggested.

'There'd not be much chance of finding you again.'

Towards sunset the day after this serious setback they arrived at a small town called Dornbirn a few miles south of the lake, and sat on the platform eating up the rolls which they'd bought in a baker's in another town and which should have lasted for two days, their careful schedule now abandoned. While H waited with the reddish light shining in under the station roof across the flat fields and between the poplars in the direction of the Rhine, Halka went to apply at a camp for German refugees that they'd heard had been opened there.

As she crossed the square in front of the station, H saw by Halka's face that something had been achieved; it wasn't radiant, but neither were the brows dark with a foreboding that she was hurrying to share with him.

Now she had a bunk in a requisitioned school where she could keep the suitcase with their belongings, was assured of two meals a day and could spend the morning and afternoon with H whenever he returned; as a foreigner he wasn't allowed in the prohibited frontier zone. During his constant journeys in crowded trains he had much to absorb him: the novel, his secret obsession with which was increased rather than diminished by the apparently insurmountable problems involved, which might be got in the town he was going to – as the Allied armies approached the stocks of all

321

kinds were being distributed to those who queued for them – and, above all, the prospect of the return to Dornbirn, each of which was a miraculous homecoming.

One sultry evening Halka suggested that, instead of starting off on his evening excursions, he wait outside the camp till all was quiet and then creep in in the dark past the double-tiered bunks to one beside hers that was unoccupied. He hung about as a thunderstorm was gathering over the mountains, sheltering against the wall of the school building when it burst, from where he could see far off through the rain the lights of Swiss villages like strings of diamonds against black velvet along the lake. This was one of the hours, another had been the one spent leaning over the harbour wall, when he was most conscious of exterior reality penetrating the fragile, deeply imagined one of the embryo fiction.

The nearest room into which he could walk openly and be given food and shelter was hundreds of miles away beyond impenetrable frontiers. He was risking arrest by being where he was and when the Allies arrived – though better the French than the British – his situation would hardly be more secure.

62

One day when H had made a longer trip than usual, for the first time in all his wanderings the train by which he meant to return was very late and, while he waited with an anxious group of the homeless who were his constant travelling companions, there were rumours that it wouldn't arrive because the French had reached the town to the north from which it was due. When finally he got back to Dornbirn, having joined in the general murmur of relief as the ancient-looking engine had at last come puffing wood smoke around the bend, he found Halka, tense and pale beneath the tan, waiting in the crowded café where they met. She'd been at the station several times but not knowing where he was coming from hadn't been able to decide from the various scraps of information about the cancellation of services whether or not he'd be able to get back.

But there was little time to reflect on how near they'd been to being separated with not much chance of finding each other again in the chaos following the end of hostilities, for she was excitedly showing him a couple of keys, though it took him a moment to grasp that her turn had come to be allotted a room in a private house.

H carried the big suitcase from the camp to a tall building on the market square on one side of whose hallway was the entrance to a bank and on the other a glass door which she proudly unlocked. Across the small entrance hall she opened another door and showed him the tiny room, even smaller than the one in Berlin, with just space for a bed along the wall and a table under the window that looked on to the market square.

The room in the empty ground-floor flat – the owners, the bank manager and his wife, lived in the one above – came to have for H the haunting tranquillity that gathers in certain places, such as the hut in Glenmaroon, that, for whatever reason, lie outside the lines of communication between even the minor centres of this world.

They spent a half hour in it together in peace and relief, and Halka somewhat hesitantly asked him if he didn't think, as a first tentative attempt to prepare for the time when he'd take her back to his home in Ireland, that they should forgo lying on the bed together. In his present state H was ready to agree. Being alone in a room with her for the first time since leaving Munich didn't cause him to remember with an excited shock the act that circumstances had been pushing out of his mind.

Now he never went further than Lindau to the north, though he sometimes travelled as far as Feldkirch and the Liechtenstein frontier in the direction away from the advancing French. They'd trudged to the frontier together a few days before, and H had handed his passport, with Halka's photo pasted in the unused space for a wife's and indistinctly marked with a rubber stamp he'd got hold of in Berlin for the purpose, to the Swiss sentry at the gate in the barbed-wire fence who'd told them that a car with Pétain and Laval in it had just been turned back. H had remarked that he didn't see that as in any way a precedent affecting them, and the soldier had taken the document to his superior in a nearby barracks but had come out again and returned it almost at once with a shake of the head.

He was seldom far from the lake. Strolling back, in the warm dusk of that sun-drenched April, towards some station, he often caught a distant flash of silvery light from the open end of a narrow street.

One evening as he walked from the station at Dornbirn where he was now spending the nights with Halka in the one bed without, however – impossible as it would have seemed to him a few months earlier – making love to her, he joined a crowd in the square where leaflets were being distributed. He paused as he entered the bank building to read: 'Our Führer has fallen before the enemy.'

Later, when he pondered on the actual facts, he tried to gauge the degree of despair that had preceded the suicide; despair and disaster fascinated H in direct ratio to his recoil from moral jubilation and victory. Had Hitler been capable of sinking, at the very last, to the incommunicable darkness of the irredeemably lost? This, H believed, was a prerogative of certain drunkards and drug addicts, condemned criminals, and inmates of asylums, bestowing on them a mysterious grace that nobody who is still in some kind of contact with his fellowmen can imagine. H believed that Hitler's experience in the bunker had been shared by few other men. He had fallen through a spectrum of mental states from one of high manic exaltation to a realization of utter disaster in a short space of time. He'd been forced to the confines of what thought can bear by a calamity that in its outward magnitude and personal culpability had surely no counterpart.

What could a human being in that unique and terrible situation not have achieved, outside all norms of experience, by a profound acceptance of his own ruin, so horrible and irreversible because it had involved millions of others? This was a supposition dependent upon the correctness of H's view of pain, guilt, and disaster as offering a means of escape from self-imprisonment. The chances of Hitler having taken it were, of course, almost nil. (It was not for H to rule it out completely.) Instead of preparing himself for the humanly inconceivable, saving miracle, he had almost certainly spent his last hours accusing his own suffering people of betrayal.

He showed Halka the leaflet, which she only glanced at before going up to her landlady's kitchen where she was allowed to cook the gruel that she shared with him for supper. This they ate at the table by the window, dipping their spoons into the bowl alternately in silence, but for the buzzing of the flies in the bushes just outside, and only when she'd washed their solitary dish at the sink of the unused, ground-floor kitchen, in which there wasn't a cooker, and given it him to dry, did he start telling her where he'd been and what he'd seen in the course of his wanderings.

Today, his birthday, Walpurgis Night, and he'd an idea – though nobody had ever said so – the anniversary of his father's death, there'd been the sound of another storm gathering over the lake which the warm mouth of evening was misting with its breath.

They didn't leave the house again – what he'd taken for distant thunder turned out to be the rumble of artillery – until a couple of days after the French troops, young and smart-looking with their American-provided uniforms after the middle-aged, tattered Germans, had come stalking into the square where white sheets were hanging from the top windows of the hotel.

H, relieved of the necessity of keeping as far as possible out of sight, had now only the Austrian landlady's Catholicism – it turned out that this was Austria and that the frontier ran between Dornbirn and Lindau – to consider by not too openly seeming to live with Halka, while not, ironically, techni-cally doing so at all. But Frau Altdorf solved the problem by letting him sleep on a camp bed in a big attic at the top of the building where, on shelves around the walls, the bank files were stored.

There was neither post nor newspaper, no cafés, all being shut, no cinemas, no shops; but they'd a supply of the food from the last-minute clearances stored in the suitcase under the bed. Their state of chastity deepened the sense of living in a monastery, and Halka added her own biblical note to the atmosphere by reading out each evening, at the dormer window of the attic where they'd climbed to escape the gaze of the Algerian soldiers stealthily prowling the streets and peering into ground-floor rooms, from the psalms in her missal.

While he listened to the praise, complaints, hopes, prophecies, and occasional cries of anguish directed to a very personal Protector conceived in an inward-turned isolation similar in some respects to his own and Halka's, H had a view of pale, distant crags that rose high into the evening sky. When she read the verses in the, to H, doubly veiled language of the German translation of the Old Testament about the holy Mount Hermon ('Einziges Gebirge'), these snowy peaks became an image of the unexpected state of tranquillity they had entered.

A week later they learned that the war was over without, at first, the news having much effect on their absorbed and hungry existence; with manna sometimes falling from the sky in the shape of a hunk of cheese that rolled out of a passing jeep or a tin of sardines that an elderly woman neighbour, having heard of the 'stranded Englishman', handed in at their glass door.

H sat in the shade in the small dusty garden thinking out parts of his novel – other parts remained obscure for want of background detail which at the moment he'd no way of obtaining – while Halka mended their worn clothing or helped Frau Altdorf in her kitchen upstairs.

In the long afternoons they remained in her tiny, ground-floor room full of the hot sound of flies buzzing in the small-leafed, tiny bushes that screened the window from the street and the rumble of military vehicles passing southward from the other side of the square.

Victory was being greeted with jubilation in the great world; even here there were signs of it as the Algerian troops, a couple of whom, they'd heard, had been already shot for rape, were roasting whole sheep in a field at the end of the town.

Every evening after supper as H dried their single dish, standing in the little hallway between her room and the unused kitchen, the piece of earthenware with its pale sheen inside and brown outer glaze in his hands, he was conscious of performing a ritual in which his hidden life with Halka was celebrated in secret.

He didn't remain long in this blessed state of seclusion, as he thought of it, without the intrusion of more worldly longings. He thought of Europe in which the barricades were coming down and the cities beginning to offer again their sensational satisfactions to the starved exile.

He didn't mention his restlessness to Halka and hardly admitted it to himself, but persuaded her that they couldn't live idly here indefinitely and that Frau Altdorf would need the ground-floor flat when her son returned from the front, though she hadn't said anything about it.

The plan he proposed was to get himself taken on one of the transports that he'd heard were leaving Bregenz, the nearest large town, each week for Paris, made up mostly of French men and women being repatriated. From Paris he'd write to Iseult about bringing Halka to Ireland and at the same time see if arrangements could be made through his embassy for getting her out of Austria.

Halka listened and reassured him by agreeing to all he said; how should she not agree, he reflected uneasily, knowing nothing about such matters? She told him that it worried her that he'd given up making notes for his novel, and when they switched on the too-bright, naked bulb in the attic – under which Herr Altdorf studied the files on winter evenings? – and, with their evening prayers, she read out the Psalmist's complaint, 'How can I sing Jehovah's song in a strange land?' she suggested that that was how he felt.

After several delays and much phoning from the town commandant to the Centre de Repatriment in Bregenz on H's behalf, he was told one morning to present himself at the camp there. He put a few things into the attaché case and, with Halka, took the first train he'd been on in months, after never seeming to be out of one, for the short journey.

She sat in the corner on the side where the lake would appear, holding his hand.

'It's best to go to Paris; from here I can do nothing, not even write a letter.' Not that she had ever queried the wisdom of his decision.

At the camp, in a big, red-brick former technical college, H showed his passport, was allotted a bunk in a dormitory and directed to a tiled room with a row of showers where an old woman stuck the nozzle of a spray inside his trousers and blew powder down them. When she asked Halka to pull up her skirt they explained that it was only H who was entering the camp, and it seemed to H that was when the final decision was taken and the separation made inevitable.

Halka went with him to his bunk in a big upstairs room whose windows looked over the lake, and having left the small case, that he seemed to have been carrying for years into endless cellars, makeshift shelters, bunkers, and trenches, on it, they went into the town and sat in a café till it was time for her train to Dornbirn. They'd been told at the camp that the next transport for France might leave any morning and that the names of those being sent on it would be posted up in the hall the night before. She promised to come on the midday train the following day and H said he'd be waiting outside the station, but when they parted it was a provisional farewell because they couldn't be sure whether he mightn't have already left by then.

Soon he was eating the first full meal he'd had since they'd left Berlin nearly a year ago and, after finishing his own plateful, devouring the portion that a Greek woman next to him left almost untouched. Later, on his way from his dormitory to the toilets as he passed the passage window he was brought to a painful halt as if he'd walked into a sharp point that pierced him in the region of his chest. He stood gazing at the pale peaks of the Säntis range, that Frau Altdorf had told them the name of, cutting into the limpid depths of evening, then returned to his bunk and, carrying his case walked in a trance of indecision to the top of the stone staircase. He remained there for some minutes (there was still time to catch the last train to Dornbirn) waiting for the recollection of what he now thought of as the blessed time that the sight of the mountains had evoked to grow stronger and more definite, but in the end he went back to his bunk with the attaché case. Before climbing on to the bunk for the night, he descended to the hall to read the list of names for the transport in the morning and was relieved not to find his name among them. Next day he was waiting when Halka, in a red skirt that she'd made herself out of some bunting from past Nazi celebrations, was the first from the train to come running from the station.

They walked along the promenade under the plane trees by the lake and she gave him a booklet she'd sewn together out of odd pieces of paper in which she'd copied the psalms she used to read out of her missal. As H put the small book with its green cardboard cover – from one of the bank files? – in an inside pocket with his passport and empty wallet, having left her what remained of the German marks, she told him she'd heard on the Altdorfs' radio that an atomic bomb had been dropped on Japan. As they walked in the thin patches of shade cast by the dark canopies on top of the row of smooth pillarlike tree trunks at the edge of the shimmering water, H recognized by its impact on deep centred nerves that would take time to assimilate it that this was one of those rare pieces of news – that of the Russian Revolution had been another – that was going to have some profound consequences that he could only indistinctly foresee.

Later they sat in a café in the street separated from the lake by the railway line, and before it was time for her train, and for H to troop to the dining hut with the others for supper, she recited in a low voice, which he leaned across the table to catch above the buzz of conversation, the prayers of their

327

Vespers. Afterwards they said the provisional farewell, though a transport having left that morning it was unlikely that another would go next day, that repetition made the more painful, and he crossed the road with her to the station.

63

H had protested to the French woman responsible for making out the lists for the transports when he hadn't seen his name on the following one and she'd given him a plausible-sounding reason, as he was finding was always so with explanations in French, for the omission. But in the morning before it was light he was awakened and told to get dressed quickly and join the others already taking their places in the two buses.

They set out on the long drive to Strasbourg; were the first traces of atomic dust falling in the steady August rain? If so, like everyone else, H was still ignorant of it and his worry over the weather had to do with its probable effect on the flimsy suitcase on top of the bus he'd bought as his first postwar purchase.

Halka would be waking up, her day still unclouded, but at noon she'd come running out of the station, fail to see him in the small throng always meeting the trains, in expectation of relatives returning from prisoner-of-war camps, know he had gone, and, all the same, look into their café, then make her way slowly to the big red building, climb the stone stairs, and find, on his bunk, the note that he'd left there.

At about which time the first bus stopped on a winding country road, having taken a wrong turn, and waited for the other to catch up. The passengers trooped out after the six-hour, nonstop drive, the men turning their backs and the women pulling up their skirts and squatting in the rain at the roadside in view of the few who remained in the bus, a Ukrainian priest and, astonishingly, H, whose bladder always functioned unpredictably, among them.

A thin finger of grey up-pointed from the flat countryside through the misty evening and the Ukrainian patriarch turning his bearded face to H to announce: 'Strasbourg Cathedral.' Then the bus bumping over an improvised track to a point at the bank of the Rhine where a pontoon structure replaced the damaged road-bridge downstream and a placard in French, 'You are now entering the land of freedom', which evoked a jeer from a section of the expatriates. A night in a transit camp in Strasbourg with a festive supper at small tables with white cloths in one of the former exhibition

328

buildings, and afterwards opening a French Red Cross parcel on his bunk in another big hall discovering long-forgotten luxuries like the honey cake called pain d'épice, blue packets of Gauloise cigarettes, tins of corned beef, and handfuls of raisins. Next morning, after attending, all alone, a mass celebrated by the Ukrainian patriarch in a pavilion, the slow train-journey in a straw-carpeted goods wagon, with a stop at Nancy for a supper provided for the repatriates by a café near the station.

In the early morning of the second day, the Marne winding below the half-open door, the patriarch saying mass at the end of the goods wagon and H both sick with longing for what he'd left behind and with excitement at the thought of Paris. After a long wait outside the Gare de l'Est they were met by a reception committee, among which was a young man with painted fingernails who struck H as the first authentic sign of peace, and shepherded into old green Paris buses; all except one Frenchman who, as a forced deportee, was being accorded the doubtful honour of being sent to a hotel. Then the second – third, counting the couple of nights clandestinely spent in Halka's in Dornbirn – in the series of camps, prison cells, and cellars in which, with a couple of short interludes, H was to spend the next year.

The repatriation centre in the narrow, fashionable rue Leonardo da Vinci was simply a big villa in which the rooms, the only traces of whose elegance remained in the moulded ceilings, were filled out with the usual tiers of bunks, and with trestle tables set up on the courtyard under a huge chestnut tree.

H started off by having his first proper wash in months with a piece of real soap from the Red Cross parcel in a downstairs apartment that had been converted by hanging showers from the ceiling and cementing part of the parquet floor; in spite of which the handbasins upstairs seemed the preferred place for ablutions and the room was always awash with water that seeped out along the adjoining corridor. When he was cleaned up, and after getting the address from one of the uniformed Yugoslavs, with the red star prominent above the peak of their caps, who appeared to run the place – officially in charge of a young French sergeant who padded ineffectually about the drier parts of the house in sharply creased khaki slacks and sandals – he presented himself at the Irish embassy in a nearby street and was told it was already closed till the following day. That evening H wrote a letter to Halka care of a Swiss address supplied by Frau Altdorf, from where he hoped it would be brought to her by someone who came regularly to Dornbirn on business. And in the morning he was received by the First Secretary in the sort of well-furnished room that both fascinated and made him aware of his own semiragged, if now clean, and impecunious state; a black homburg with a curl to the brim on a coatrack behind the desk struck him a minor blow.

At the interview H learned that there wasn't the 'foggiest' chance of getting Halka out of Austria, and that his appearance in Paris wasn't a matter for official rejoicing by the representatives of his native land because he might well be 'picked up' by the American Military Police and 'taken in' for questioning, thus involving his own government, and also because there was at present no way of returning him to Ireland except via England where he was likely to be detained and cause even greater embarrassment to those who, after having managed to stay neutral throughout the war, hoped for no further trouble between themselves and the victors.

The First Secretary said he'd cable to Dublin for advice, asked how H was off for money and whether he'd a bank account at home – of all possible questions to H the most irrelevant – and told him to come back in a couple of days. Just as he was leaving, the official recalled a letter that had been left at the embassy for H some months earlier and, after a search through the drawers of the desk, handed him an envelope addressed in a script that H recognized as Susan's.

She wrote from an address in Seine et Oise where she was staying at a convent. She was rarely in Paris, she said, but if he got her note as he passed through Paris on his way home and would like to see her she'd come in. Before he thought of Susan and what he'd answer, there was the much more difficult letter to write to Iseult. This he laboriously composed on his bulk, the third on the left from the door of the ground-floor room which was the one on the left as you entered the portico from the street, as he told Susan in the note that, in an interlude from the complex business of explaining the situation to his wife, he sent her, suggesting she call at the camp on her next visit to town.

H knew when he'd at last finished the letter home that he'd said too much about Halka and dwelt too fleetingly on his own immediate plans. All the time he'd been writing he'd been aware of a fellow apatriate two bunks away sitting with his dark head in his hands. And when the midday meal was served at the wooden tables in the courtyard he remained there, bowed and motionless.

Macaroni ladled on to the enamel plate, the steamy, ivory coils topped with magenta-coloured sauce and a tin dipper filled from a wooden pail of red wine and poured into whatever containers the apatriates had managed to provide themselves with; in H's case an American mess can he'd found in the station at Nancy.

His neighbours at the trestle table were a flirtatious young Jewess, whom H had no intention to become involved with, and a thin individual of indeterminate origin who inelegantly sucked the strands of macaroni into his mouth and whose jacket was smeared above the breast pocket with the piece of soap he apparently kept in it.

He and H were among those to linger on at the wooden board, slimy with spilt macaroni, in the shade of the big tree and receive a second measure of wine while they talked in German, the common language of the camp. H's companion produced a surprisingly clean card from another pocket on which H read 'Dr phil. Ludovic Weiss' and an address in Budapest. They hadn't been talking long before it appeared that Dr Weiss had been in Paris a year ago at the liberation – he'd since worked in the mines in the Ardennes as well as having been to the South of France – and could give H the details he needed to make a start on his novel.

By now H saw that the fiction he had in mind would be regarded as an affront by somebody who had put himself outside the common pale. The theme would be anathema to almost all possible readers and, if it had any relevance at all it could only be for a new generation.

It hadn't needed the First Secretary's mention of the American Military Police for H to realize that in the eyes of the people in the street here, and of the others in the camp, he belonged, if they guessed his secret, to those who were at last being brought to justice at Nuremberg and elsewhere. The plague that for years had ravaged Europe had at last been brought under control and the infected, as well as those who'd been the original carriers, were all safely isolated. It seemed to H that only he had slipped through the decontamination squads and was here with the sound and wholesome, keeping his shameful secret to himself but likely to be discovered at any time.

He imagined the contempt of the whole healthy world about to be turned on him. But he never doubted that the piece of fiction must not be an attempt at self-justification, nor, on the other hand, a gesture of defiance, though that might be more difficult to forgo.

When he recalled some of his semi-serious fantasies at the time of his first coming to Berlin, in one of which he'd tried to persuade Hitler to use his unique powers to bring about a real revolution, he couldn't be certain he hadn't been infected by the plague, however unusual his symptoms.

Whether this was so or not, and he resolved never to attempt to exculpate himself, his situation was the right one, if he had the gift, out of which to write the novel that his others had been an exercise for.

After a second visit to his embassy where he asked for, and was given, the writing materials he needed, as well as being told that his wife had been in touch with the Department in Dublin about getting him to Ireland, which news he didn't comment on, as neither, to his relief, did the First Secretary – H sensed he had here a support in his resolve to try to return to Austria – he made a start on his story.

Thematic outline of this fiction, the unlikelihood of whose publication within the foreseeable future was confirmed by a list of writers, mostly French, but with Ezra Pound's and his own name among them, whom the columnist proposed should be blacklisted, in a newspaper he was shown at the embassy.

Sam Morrison, from a neutral country, in Paris in August 1944 in the flat of his girl friend, Monique, takes up with the blond young Sacha, who'd become a member of the Latvian S.S. in the early days of the war and now, for reasons of his own, had stayed on when the unit to which he was attached pulled out of Paris. Together they take to the rooftops armed with a sniper's Mauser and a Schmeisser, ammunition for both (supplied by Sacha), cold veal (provided by Monique's black-marketeer father), rolls, and some bottles of wine, returning at odd hours of the day and night to Monique's flat through the skylight.

Through his hero H hoped to elucidate some of his own complex feelings that ranged from the constant fear of being discovered, arrested, and stood among the minor monsters at the trials being currently staged, to immersion in the counter-current of his subversive thoughts about the only kind of freedom worth fighting to preserve.

H spent much of the day at work on his bunk, recalling the writing of his first, unpublished novel on a cot in another camp, with the dark apatriate sitting motionless a couple of beds away, usually with his head in his hands. He established his hero and his blond, laughing, dimple-chinned companion from the faraway Baltic on the hot slates (those August days, Dr Weiss told him, had been as sultry as these). They were drinking the warm wine, reclining with bare feet in the runnel of tepid water left by the last thunderstorm in the lead gutter above the Place Vendôme, and interrupting their siesta to take a potshot at a patrol of arm-banded Fifis or a German jeep in front of the Ritz.

He might not have been able to give an account of what he meant by his fiction beyond the suggestion that he was more at home with Monique and Sacha than sharing in the exploits of the liberators.

Had he not been born with this preference for the company of outlaws? Was it not his task as a writer, not to justify this to his critics but to relate it, if he could, to a wider kind of consciousness? He was also preoccupied by fiction of another kind, and sitting in the Café Scossa on the Place Victor Hugo at the other end of the narrow street from the villa, he imagined catching sight of Halka among the passersby, having somehow managed to get herself to Paris. So disturbing was the shock of seeing her face among the strange and potentially hostile ones that the reality, he thought, couldn't have cut deeper.

One afternoon, returning from one of these vigils at the café (For what was he waiting? To be picked up by the French or the Americans? To suddenly see Halka, who'd been brought his letter with the address of the camp and had smuggled herself here by way of Switzerland?), the big Yugoslav at the table in the villa portico handed him a letter from Iseult which he retired to his bunk with and didn't at once open. He realized he'd written to her at a moment of weakness immediately on his arrival here when his hopes had still been high in expectation of her coming to his help, and this, he now saw, he'd no right to expect. He'd opened his heart to her because of his fears for Halka and she'd sense that the emotion, which his letter had been too full of, hadn't been for her.

Iseult was brought sharply back to him as he read. She was still on the moon or, rather, on an outer planet of her own whose surface had a pure, frosty sparkle. She wrote how relieved they were to have news of him at last and hear that he was safely in Paris. When was he coming home? Not a word about the difficulties his letter had been explicit about! Towards the end she did mention Halka, but incidentally as one of the lesser complications which, in her detached way – H was conscious of the old antagonism – she could take lightly. She ended by saying she was arranging with his aunt to send him some money while he was waiting for a means of getting home; she'd heard the direct air service would shortly be reopened.

The last bit of news, that about the money, not the air service, was the one glimmer in the letter. It was difficult to work in a place full, especially towards evening, of the coming and going, the arguments and laughter, the surreptitious love-making, of the other occupants, and he'd asked about the possibility of getting a room at a hotel while continuing to have his meals at the villa. The big weather-beaten Yugoslav partisan had told him nothing was simpler and had given him the name of a cheap hotel in a street at the other side of the Place Victor Hugo.

All the same, bitten by bugs, distracted by all kinds of noises from the stridently quarrelsome to the sweetly caressing, H, supplied by Dr Weiss with the necessary background, was working away feverishly.

Extract: 'The Judgement Day atmosphere in the air had brought quite a few civilians into the streets. Sacha was a joker who couldn't keep his big perpetually turned-up mouth shut in what he saw as such humorous circumstances. Defeat appeared to delight him. As he marched along beside Sam Morrison in the uniform of the Latvian S.S. (the only members of the Division to have managed to get to Paris?) with his Schmeisser under his arm, his lips were forming a new pleasantry. Passing a girl in a passageway (a darkly aristocratic-looking creature) he blurted out in a tone of mock dismay, "Fräulein, wir sind kaputt!"

'Rounding the corner of the rue de Rivoli, Sam saw that Sacha was about to put on another little act in front of an approaching Frenchman (one of those lean, handsome, cynical-looking types whom he himself was in awe of).

' "For God's sake cut out the horseplay, Sacha! Our situation isn't the best in the world!"

'But nothing could have stopped his companion. He came to a halt in front of the young Frenchman who had side-stepped off the pavement and announced, "Es ist wahr, mein Herr, wir sind besiegt, kaputtgemacht." [The rumours are quite correct, my dear sir; we're done for, washed up].

' "If we can't take part in the victory charade we can put on our private one of glorious bloody ruination," Sacha announced.

'The oppressive August drawing to a close. The police had taken over the Prefecture on the 20th without much ado now that the Americans were only a few miles away. Shortly afterwards the Fifi occupied the Hotel de Ville and many of the good citizens of Paris flocked to join them and fasten the F.F.I. brassard on their arms.

'Rain fell in torrents on the morning of Thursday, August 24th. The roof valleys behind the low parapets were turned to rivulets and Tiger tanks were making a few last sorties from the direction of the rue de Rivoli. General Choltitz was at his headquarters in the Hôtel Meurice and the Grand Palais was burning, while Sam and Sacha remained at their self-appointed post, sniping at Fifis, "Septembrisards" (as the latter-day Resistance was afterwards called), Germans, de Gaullists, Milice, and Communists indiscriminately.'

Pedestrian, descriptive stuff, H reflected, during a bout of leg scratching. He was hurrying on to what he saw as the highlight.

'On Friday the 25th Leclerc's main force entered the city at the Porte d'Orleans and Sam saw newly hoisted tricolours on the Tour Eiffel and Arc de Triomphe. He'd spent the night with Monique (like the earlier girls she had later had her head shaved) while Sacha had been busy reconnoitring (as he called it), using some of the gold watches (of which he'd a briefcase full) to bribe electricians who had got the Notre Dame lift that, in normal times, takes sightseers to the top of one of the twin towers, working again.'

64

H had a note from Susan saying she couldn't come to Paris and asking him to visit her at the convent: not the sort of place he could imagine her. He took a train to the small riverside town (Seine? Oise?), having meanwhile received the first instalment of the weekly sum that Iseult had promised him. It worried him that he was taking it under what might be false pretences, but not to the point of his refusing to take it.

They met in the convent parlour and with his gift for taking what he wanted to in at hardly a glance, he saw it was much the same Susan: the olive skin, ink-tinted under the eyes with their luminous egg-white, hair brushed for the occasion but still limp and straggly.

She suggested they go for a walk and, as they strolled by the river, she with her handbag clamped tight under her arm just as he remembered, she told him of how she'd been 'liberated' by the British in the Ruhr, who hadn't taken particular note of her until, having to register for something or other, it came out that she hadn't any identification papers. After some interrogating she told them the name of her grandfather, who she thought would disown her but, though he didn't want her back in England, had intervened on her behalf and had her sent to the English hospital in Paris.

'Were you ill?'

'I was having a baby.'

The baby had died and Susan had had puerperal fever – was that what had also been wrong after the first baby? – and later she'd come to the convent where the nuns had been taking care of Dominique.

'And you, Luke, you're on your way home?'

H said that on the contrary he was trying to get back where he'd come from; he was encountering a lot of trouble in going in the other direction to the general flow.

'My God, how I wish I could get to Germany too, but they wouldn't let me!'

They had tea alone in the parlour and she turned on the radio that she'd tuned to a German station. And while he ate the bread, butter, jam, and biscuits, a change from the macaroni and sauce at the camp, she clasped her child's hands on her lap, her shoulders sagged and her eyes filled with tears. She reminded him of how she'd been when she'd first moved into the big flat in Berlin, as he caught sight of her padding between her room and the kitchen: a delinquent, abandoned, rebellious, homesick child. She had involved him in a strange acute kind of pain and she was one of the people who would always haunt the past for him.

The German tunes evoked for H too a time that was precious and which he was afraid that he might have lost. The longer he listened, as if Susan's presence must always provoke in him a neurosis, the more intense became his feeling that he shouldn't have come here because, by interrupting his constant preoccupation with Halka, he might dissipate some inner energy and diminish his chances of returning to her.

'You know they shot Robert Brassillach?' she asked, switching off the radio as a lay sister came to clear the tea things.

For a moment H thought she was referring to Dominique's father, then remembered he'd seen the name, at a moment when it had made an un- forgettable impact, in her pocket diary on the floor of the bedroom when he'd gone back to the flat.

'Who's that?'

'They killed him,' she repeated, not answering the question, 'at Fort Valerien, where the Germans executed all the others, and he cried out just like them, "Vive la liberté!". If you'd been a Breton they'd have shot you too,' she added, regarding him with the downward pull of her mouth he'd never been quite sure how to interpret.

'Not as a nationalist. But there was a time when I half-expected they'd shoot me to oblige the British.'

'He was a friend of Vialatoux. (Yes, that was the name that had once made H rush by taxi from the university to the Romanisches Café and back!) He wrote things in his poems that aren't permissible.'

Back in Paris H felt that he might at any moment be discovered and denounced. In the intervals of intensive work on his novel, when, sitting on his bunk of an evening, he heard more hurried steps on the cobbles of the portico, where the carriages had once driven in, than those of the leisurely apatriates, he waited for his name to be called by the Yugoslav at the entrance. Partly because of this but also to have more quiet, not to mention the bugs, H took a room in the hotel whose name he'd been given.

Extract from H's fictional memoir: 'The pallid, fleshy, comic-looking Sacha came to pick up Sam in a mud-coloured Volkswagen that he'd "organized" in much the same way, Sam imagined, as he'd have arranged in peacetime an outing, with a couple of Lulus and a bottle of Aquavit, to a beach at the Baltic. Sam couldn't refuse to go with him, although, apart from the greater risk involved, he'd sooner have remained on the familiar roofs with the possibility of a nightly return to Monique's arms.

'With a store of provisions to last several days, Sam and Sacha took up their position on one of the twin towers of Notre Dame. The Latvian youth was in the highest spirits and, having changed to pyjamas (the sun was blazing down) fired a burst from the sub-machine-gun (he'd a pile of spare

336

clips for it) in the direction of an F.F.I. position across the left-bank channel of the river. He confided to H that he'd heard there was to be a victory parade on Sunday to the cathedral, headed by De Gaulle and Leclerc, and slapping his plump white hand to his pyjama-clad thigh, he exclaimed in his limited English: "Boy, what you say to that!"

'Sam didn't admit to not sharing in his delight at the prospect of having a shot at one of the French generals (if that was really Sacha's intention). His comrade-in-arms was lolling around, between spells at the parapet, enjoying himself tremendously, determined to score another point or two in this private war of his, keeping his blistered nose out of the sun, curling up his mouth, laying his big, soft hand on Sam's knee, and regarding him in all innocence to make sure, every hour or so, that they were the brothers he took them to be.'

At the hotel H was given a room with a large red-quilted bed and a washbasin at the end of a narrow, twisting passage which for several days he didn't leave except to go for the midday and evening meal to the villa. His sense of isolation not only from the other apatriates, but even more from the people on the streets and in the cars that thronged them and circled this way and that about the Arc de Triomphe as if there'd never been a war, made him avoid much going out. Each time he returned to the hotel, took his key from its numbered hook, looked at the green baize board where letters were slipped under the cross-braiding and climbed the rickety stairs, he imagined a joy more intense than any he'd ever experienced as he reached the corner of the passage of his room: the sight of the big, leather suitcase he'd left with her standing outside his door as a sign that Halka had come and was either gone out for a few minutes or was waiting in the room next to his. His longing to see this was so excessive and the possibility so slender that as he climbed the stairs he felt he was in a state close to dementia.

By the third or fourth day after the move he'd reached one of the highlights of the novel in the arrival of the victory parade at Notre Dame on the previous twenty-eighth of August:

'As he saw the archbishop of Paris come out to greet the two generals, Sacha's dancing blue eyes froze, and Sam realized he was one of those born Catholics in whom the Church evokes a kind of fury, springing, no doubt from bitter disillusion. As for Sam, he edged the telescopic-sighted barrel out over the parapet with a mixture of terror and excitement, determined to establish himself irretrievably among the vanquished by firing at one of the security patrol men who (alerted by Sacha's shots) were scanning the house-tops with field glasses.'

H was startled by a knock on the door; he'd forgotten that he'd asked Dr Weiss around that evening. The long, stooped figure let himself rather gingerly on to a chair, as if it might be some kind of trap, and took the glass of sourish wine that H poured for him.

Dr Weiss had news of a transport that he'd heard was leaving for Germany shortly; he'd been several times with H to a French girl, a lieutenant, who had her office in a neighbouring villa to the camp, and who was supposed to be arranging the repatriation of some German civilians, including several Fräuleins whom returning Frenchmen had brought back under solemn declaration of intentions to marry. These tidings, though he didn't place too much trust in them, lightened H's heavy heart, and it seemed fitting that it was Dr Weiss who brought them; he'd become one of H's heroes, along with Lane, O'Flaherty, and Hilliard from the days of his youth.

The Hungarian (Polish?) Jew was ready to leave after living over a year in France and Belgium at, except for a short spell as a miner, various camps and repatriation centres, and he'd had his name put on the list for an eastbound transport by the girl lieutenant at the same time as H.

'You want to go home to Poland?'

'To Germany, my dear young lady.'

'Excuse me, I understood you were Polish.'

'Certainly. But I'll only return when my native land is free.'

'Where do you really want to go?' H asked him afterwards.

Dr Weiss had scratched the inside of his leg – although the rooms had been sealed and the bugs gassed, some had survived – and at the same time moved his shoulders in a shrug: 'I may spend the winter in Graz where the British have a camp for Czechoslovak refugees from the Russians.'

He was now answering some questions H put to him about incidents during the solemn Te Deum in Notre Dame in thanksgiving for victory when, he told H, shots had been fired from one of the galleries.

But what he really wanted to talk about were certain tendencies in himself that, he said, he'd only noticed lately. 'Sitting on a bench in the Place Victor Hugo of an evening I find that the passing females that I watch closely are the ones under sixteen.'

The light flickered out, as it did for periods every night, and Dr Weiss went on: 'My most delightful fantasy these days is to imagine paying some gangster friends to kidnap a couple of these little girls and take them to a house in the country where they'd handcuff them to me, on the pretext of preventing excape while allowing them some freedom of movement. For three or four heavenly days I'd share the most intimate moments with them while they saw in me nothing worse than an unfortunate fellow prisoner.'

When Dr Weiss had left and the light had flickered on again, H turned to chapter ten, the one in which the Te Deum is being duly sung in the cathedral and, high above, Sacha is lying in a small patch of shade with the wine bottle to his mouth while he pisses into the lead gutter ('That's the beauty of pyjamas, boy, no fussing with fly buttons!').

Before he went to bed H stood at the window, the light failing again having prevented him from working, looking for one of the constellations whose name he'd learned from Halka in the Englische Garten in Munich. He saw the stars as, with the psalms he read from the booklet she'd given him, the only link he had with her, no answer having come to his letters, two to the Swiss address, one dispatched through the Red Cross.

From Iseult, on the other hand, letters came every few days telling him of what she'd been hearing about possible ways of his returning – in the last she repeated that the Paris-Dublin air service would shortly be reopened – and never, since the first one, as much as mentioning Halka.

H was glad when it got dark and he could walk the streets between the hotel in the rue Copernic and the requisitioned villa in the rue Leonardo da Vinci without the feeling that a keen eye might spot him as one whose place was not here among the healthy but with those who'd been stricken with the plague.

Returning one autumn evening a few days after Dr Weiss's news about the transport, which hadn't materialized, from supper in what had formerly been the villa's basement kitchen – with the row of old-fashioned bells on the wall labelled: 'Salle de Monsieur, le Baron, Boudoir de Madame, la Baronne,' etc. – there was on the green board an envelope with a Swiss stamp in Halka's writing.

It was a subdued letter of fear and longing. All Germans had to leave Austria, she wrote; the men had already gone to transit camps and the women would be taken shortly. He had best return home because once in Germany she couldn't get in touch with him and there'd be no way of him finding her.

There was also a letter from Iseult, in answer to one in which he had made it clear he wouldn't return without Halka, saying she didn't see how she could go on getting his aunt to give her the money to keep him in Paris if he intended to prolong his stay there quite unnecessarily. He wrote her a note in reply, telling her not to send any more remittances, and that he'd either go back to live at the camp or return to Austria. The next evening, after what had perhaps been the most frightful day of all, on his way to supper, Sous-lieutenant Courcelles called out to him in passing, with her were a couple of smart male officers – he hadn't recognized her in the ill-lit rue Leonardo da Vinci – that an eastbound transport was leaving the villa at eight in the morning.

65

A bus brought them to the Gare de l'Est where they had *laissez-passers* that allowed them on to a train taking United States servicemen on leave back to their units in Frankfurt. But because these were valid only in France, they had to disembark at Metz, though a G.I. with whom H had been talking told him, if he really wanted to go to Germany, simply to stay where he was; H was impressed by the easygoing American attitude, but too apprehensive of calling attention to himself to take the advice.

At Metz they were lodged in an ancient barracks, Fort Moselle, on the banks of the sluggish, muddy-looking river, in the rest of which were ragged German prisoners of war for whom Dr Weiss, having talked to some of them across the wire, brought back loaves of bread, lately off the ration, from his expeditions into the town with H.

H's sense of suffering from a complaint that would have put an end to his freedom if discovered intensified as he sat with his friend in one of the cafés on whose walls hung pictures of De Gaulle, Roosevelt, and Churchill, and in some also of Stalin. Any moment he might be taken to the American commandant's office, handed over to the French – the prisoner-of-war camp was under their jurisdiction – and placed among the Germans, thus putting an end to any chance of rejoining Halka.

He'd never spoken to Dr Weiss about the war years, though they'd shared in other attempts to cross into Germany; they'd reached a Rhine bridge together a few weeks before with documents stamped by the new young mayor of Strasbourg only to be turned back by the French military police, who demanded passes signed by the military governor. But he thought that his guide and companion guessed his precarious position just as he sensed that Dr Weiss had some secret of his own to hide and imagined him with a crime like Stavrogin's on his conscience, recalling what the other had told him when he'd visited H in his hotel. What was he fleeing from or seeking as he roamed Europe in straw-filled cattle trucks from camp to camp, his belongings bundled together in a dirty towel?

Dr Weiss now spent the long overcast afternoons in fishing, and on Halloween, a feast that, with Walpurgis Night, H always took private note of, he brought to the dormitory, which they shared with a dozen other various nationals, both men and women, including a Swedish couple, five or six small fish, mud-coloured like the water they'd come from.

Days had passed in queuing up midday and evening for a canteen of thick pea soup made from a chemical-smelling yellow powder which H developed a craving for after the diet of macaroni, in visits to the town for extra bread, the Paris edition of the *New York Herald Tribune*, full of the trials of war criminals, and for a few glasses of wine with Dr Weiss in a café. On Halloween, after the additional supper of fish baked on top of the stove, H went and sat for an hour in the big Gothic barn of a cathedral.

A week later, on the morning of November the eighth, from the intercom loudspeaker came an almost intelligible announcement in French that the expatriates interpreted as an order to descend to the compound with their baggage.

Suddenly all went swiftly; they joined a trainload of Yugoslavs being sent home, and after H had been reclining for some hours in the straw of the jolting wagon he was roused by Dr Weiss who brought him to the door of the truck.

'We're crossing the Rhine!'

H stood beside his friend, who was fumbling in his pocket, not the breast one where he kept his soap but a lower pocket bulging with various other belongings, regarding the war-scarred buildings on the east bank of the river. He was experiencing not only relief in now having no closed frontiers between himself and Halka, but an unexpected delight in being back in a land which showed all the signs of defeat.

Dr Weiss extracted the two packets of French cigarettes he'd been looking for, the most negotiable of present currency, and handed them to H, looking away again immediately, his eyes, with their pale lashes, screwed up as if he was intent on scanning the distance.

The train was being stopped by a signal outside a small station whose name, Appenweiler, H made out on the distant partially demolished platform, and the four or five Germans in the wagon were getting ready to leave it.

'You'd better get off while you can,' Dr Weiss told him, 'or you may find yourself carried on to Yugoslavia.'

H took off the nearly new fawn raincoat he was wearing, received from the Quakers in the rue des Martyres to cover his rags, and gave it to his friend, in no sense to make up for the Gauloises, but in what he now saw as his contribution to the exchange of farewells – tokens of a brief relationship that there was no other way of commemorating. As he climbed across the tracks with his cheap suitcase in his arms, it having lost its handle, he could see from the corner of his eye Dr Weiss, who'd put on the pale-coloured garment, watching him from the open door of the wagon.

Across the station square a yellow building with a faded sign, 'Gasthaus,' above one boarded window through which came the sound of a piano playing what H, unmusical as he was, knew could only be a Beethoven

341

concerto. After a glass of watery beer he spent his happiest night for months on one of a row of mattresses in a dormitory with the returning Germans.

H found there was a train that ran daily from Strasbourg to Innsbruck, stopping at Appenweiler en route, and boarded it in the morning, glad to stand with the crowd of Germans in the corridor; most compartments were occupied by French troops.

After the long climb into the hills of the Schwarzwald, H, wedged in between the two sexy Fräuleins whose tentative pressures he was too preoccupied to be more than just aware of, noticed that the train was coming to a halt. It stopped at a deserted-looking station in the mountains, and when after five minutes there was still no sign of the journey being resumed, his old fears returned. Had the Deuxième Bureau, having been just too late to find him in Metz, telegraphed to the French military police at this Black Forest station to stop the train and, should he be on it – he'd stated his destination on the travel permit signed by the officer at Fort Moselle – have him taken off and brought back under guard to Paris?

While the others, including the two girls who'd long since got in with a bull-necked business type, were speculating over the delay, H's conviction that he was the cause of it increased. When there was a jostling among the throng at the far end of the corridor as two soldiers made their way along it from the next carriage, he decided that the moment that for the last three months he'd been expecting had arrived. But before they had reached his end of the corridor – what they were looking for, it turned out, wasn't at all what he'd feared, and they had stopped beside the two German girls who, however, ignored them in favour of their elderly fellow countryman – the train restarted with a series of reassuring jerks.

Around nine o'clock of that November night he got out at Dornbirn and left the station between two rows of townspeople who gathered there each evening in the hope of meeting relatives returning from prisoner-of-war camps, and, as he started up the Bahnhofstrasse towards the marketplace, Frau Altdorf caught up with him.

H didn't ask if Halka was still there, and each successive moment that passed without Frau Altdorf saying that she'd been sent away was blessed with the growing promise of reunion. When they came to the bank building she put out her hand in the dark and took the attaché case from him and, while he waited outside the door behind whose frosted glass was no glimmer of light, went upstairs with it.

H stood in the hall taking in the reality, after so many imaginative returns, of being back, though still not quite reassured by the landlady's behaviour. Then on the landing above appeared a plump-seeming girl looking down at him. Before he'd visually identified her with the longed-for image, his senses had registered a shock of joy; without appearing to touch the stairs, she flew down the last flight into his arms.

The initial strangeness was accentuated by Halka's having filled out on the quantities of pears and plums that, she explained, she'd eaten while helping her landlady to pick and preserve.

Around midnight they went to bed together without interrupting the talk that had been going on for hours. H counted the strokes he'd feared he'd never hear again as the clock in the market square struck three and, at last, the talking stopped. The silence between them was the almost imperceptible pause that intervenes between ebb and flow, daylight and dusk. The pressures to communicate had been spent; there was a moment when nothing stirred, then the other movement below that of thoughts and their expression set in.

In the intense relief of opening their hearts to each other, unburdening them of the loneliness and fear, the sensation of dumb touch had been forgotten and now rushed back in a shock of delight out of the blue.

In the morning they went through snowy streets to a yard where big, tight-leaved cabbages were being distributed. Halka received a cleanly sliced-through portion as her ration, and as H carried back the icy half-orb with the flat, cut side uppermost with a few snowflakes falling on to the intricate yellow-green pattern, he felt he was holding in his freezing hands a symbol of what he had regained.

A few wintry days of bliss, devoid of almost all normal activity or amenity, between two periods of darkness and dread; not that H foresaw the suddenness of the oncoming of the second of these.

Small happenings that long ago would not have registered now echoed clearly and magically in this pure atmosphere. The one occasion when they left the little room of an evening to attend a recital by a French pianist in a wooden hall a few yards away down a side lane from the bank, they prepared themselves as for an event demanding the most faithful responses. And that is what it turned out, even for H who normally would have dreaded having to sit through a concert or recital. The music of Schumann, Chopin, and Liszt, especially Chopin's 'Barcarole' and the 'Ballade', Opus 47 – he kept the flimsy, single-sheet programme and studied it afterwards – introduced him, as previously only certain works of fiction had done, to new states of perception. Back to the cold room and, hunger forgotten, into bed where her body became a sexual extension of the music and sensations were spiritual-sensual, sacred-obscene, complete as never before.

They had one bad morning when he told her about meeting Susan in Paris, and Halka made him anxious, for he'd an inkling that time was short, by sulking for several hours. And in fact they had hardly recovered from the intensity of the reconciliation when they were startled by a shrill ring of the usually silent bell. A young French lieutenant asked H if his name was Ruark and if Mlle. Witebsk lived here too. He then told them to come with him to the street where his *copain* was waiting.

He took them to a car that was stopped, not in front of the bank, but in the market square and spoke to the driver who got out and, as H and Halka returned to the house, followed by the two soldiers, she asked him, 'What's all this about?'

'It's bad,' he said, to prepare her for what was coming.

The quiet room seemed outraged by the presence of the two intelligence officers, as H guessed they were, and questions were put to him in a curiously desultory manner, as if the lieutenant didn't know what to ask and the order had come from Paris or even London, and in French that Halka grasped better than H. He was asked where he came from, had he a gun, how long was he living here; the Frenchman seemed surprised when H said he'd returned from Paris the previous week. He asked Halka if she had been in Marseille during the war, told her to repeat her Christian name and surname, compared them to what was written on the slip he had with him, and then with the same casual air suggested they take a few things with them as they'd be going away for a couple of days.

They were put in the back of the car and driven along the road that for most of the way ran close to the railway line on which they'd so often journeyed to and fro. At Bregenz they were brought to a second-floor office in a building at whose door H had read the sign, 'Sécurité Territoriale" and Halka was told to take everything out of her handbag; a cutting she'd kept about the trial of William Joyce was studied and commented on in low voices, but H's letters to her care of a Swiss address were ignored. After H had cleared out his pockets and had the contents, including the green booklet of hand-copied psalms, returned to him, a soldier was summoned and, after he was ostentatiously handed a revolver by the lieutenant, they were ordered to accompany him.

They trudged beside their guard – he was carrying a rifle, the revolver had disappeared into his pocket – up a steep street to a part of the town on the hill they had never explored.

'I'm thirsty,' Halka said. What hauntings the word evoked for H!

A high wall full of small, lit windows loomed over them, a barred gate was unlocked and in a stone-flagged, whitewashed hallway they were handed over to Austrian prison warders; Halka at once requested not to be separated from H and was told that this wasn't a hotel.

She turned to wave a good-bye as she was taken by her humorous jailer, in a ski suit, up the ancient, winding stairs, and H, after giving up his passport, money, pen and shoelaces in a tiny office, was also conducted upstairs and down a passage with a red-tiled floor to the last of the metal doors which, unlocked by the stocky little warder, revealed a heavy wooden one – in it, at the level of H's chest, was a small aperture – through which, after a further jingling of keys, H stepped into a cell whose two inmates were waiting in curiosity at this unexpected intrusion.

Sitting on his cot, H answered the tactful questions of the elder of his two fellow prisoners, a tall handsome man in a French uniform from which the insignia had been stripped, who introduced himself as Kestner, whom H later learned from Matukat, his other cellmate, was a colonel of the Algerian regiment who'd done most of the fighting on the way here.

In perfect German Kestner (an Alsatian?) was inquiring the age of H's fiancée as he'd described Halka, and hearing she was in her late twenties, remarked reassuringly, 'Old enough to take what's happened sensibly,' as if that point, rather than curiosity, had prompted the question. He didn't ask H why they had been arrested, nor even his nationality which H mentioned of his own accord.

Kestner returned to a pile of documents on the small table near the wire-guarded bulb over the cell door which, it turned out, the office of the Sécurité de Territoire gave him to annotate late into the night, and which he was taken there to return during the day – his added notes on the lists of French *collaborateurs*? Every half hour or so, his bladder reacting predictably again, H had to get up and take the few steps past his chair to the bucket in the corner. When at last H settled himself for the night, Kestner got up and showed him how to arrange his two blankets to the best advantage, remarking that it was an art he'd learned during a North African campaign.

He slept for short intervals and at each awakening re-experiencing the shock of their arrest and incarceration. In the morning at exercise with the other prisoners he had a glimpse of Halka's face behind the bars of one of the second-floor windows and signalled back to her without the warder who stood at the top of the steps from the yard to the back door, or the other stationed under the high outer wall watching the cells, remarking it.

Endless days emptied of all certainty except the fact that they'd fallen into the retributive hands of the victors. H, and Halka because she was involved with him, had been rounded up as one of the plague-ridden in the countries being cleaned out. He was not interrogated beyond the brief questioning at their arrest and it did not occur to him to question their right to imprison him, nor even Halka. It wasn't hard for him to see his state of mind as signalling him out from the healthy norm at a time when divergence and dissent was doubly suspect. That his inner state was obviously not the factual reason for their imprisonment was irrelevant.

345

Imperceptibly H got used to the life of the cell, by patience and learning to live on the smallest scraps of reassurance. Listening to Matukat's constant appeals to Kestner, to whom he looked up as someone in authority, a tendency among many Germans that H despised, to examine his dossier at the Sécurité office, H was encouraged to ask the colonel (ex-colonel?) to try to find out something about his own and Halka's case. He also sent a message to Halka by Matukat, who worked in the kitchen where the women prisoners sometimes peeled potatoes: H described her to his cellmate who dropped the note into her lap as he passed with his buckets. And a few days later a letter came from her in a flimsy bit of paper stuffed into the back binding of her missal, which she was able to send him by the stocky warder known as Pappa Masson, thanks to a benevolence hidden beneath the brisk severity of his exterior.

In the evenings of the days when Kestner had been taken down to the town H waited anxiously for his return. But after the ex-officer had given his usual ambiguous replies to Matukat's importunate questionings, during which he'd have taken off his uniform jacket and stretched on his cot, an ironical smile flickering, it struck H, below his close-cropped moustache, and occasionally farting, he'd take up a book and, while reading, start humming an old German tune. The sentimental words of this song, popular before H's time, about, of all things, a mother swallow and her fledglings, came to haunt H from having to listen to Kestner singing it below his breath, while seeming to read – to discourage Matukat? – as his hope of hearing something about his and Halka's probable fate dwindled.

Some first prison-impressions: the jingle of keys, the clap of the warder's ski boots on the tiled passage, the cry 'Kübel raus!' at the hour of putting the heavy slop bucket outside the cell, and the refrain of the song:

> Immerzu, immerzu,
> Fliegt die Schwalbenmutter zu,
> Ohne Rast und Ruh...

which H translated to himself as:

> To and fro, to and fro,
> Flies the mother swallow
> Without rest or peace...

The power of obsessive hunger to give trivialities vital significance: when the shutter in the inner door was slapped down and the tins of gruel or thin soup, containing a few pieces of potato, were passed through to Matukat, H took in exactly how full the one handed on to him was compared with the other two, and a fraction of an inch on the wrong side – Matukat always

346

seemed to manage to put aside the fullest for himself – caused him a pang of disappointment.

The correspondence with Halka, now carried on entirely by missal, which Pappa Masson was not indisposed to take back and forth between their cells, impressed by the pious connotation of the exchange – or pretending to be? – was at first confined to exhortations, on H's part, for her to continue to cling to the somewhat obscure promises of their favourite psalms and not give in to despair. Then, as nothing more drastic happened to them, they began, half-shyly at first, to express love and longing for each other and finally, ever regaining a little more outspokenness, there were frank expressions of desire and, finally, of the hope of Halka becoming pregnant at the first opportunity; this bold new idea was an especial reassurance.

When H at last brought himself to ask Kestner if he'd been able to glean anything about their case, he was told, 'They themselves at the Sécurité are in the dark; the orders for your arrest came from Paris and they're waiting for further instructions.'

H interpreted this as bad news; otherwise why hadn't Kestner volunteered it of his own accord? He was half-convinced that the British had asked the French to arrest and, after a short delay, quietly execute him; this, if questioned, could later be explained as failure in liaison. The idea was strengthened during one of his attempts at what he thought of as facing what was in store by the sensation of the blood gushing from his chest wounds in spurts rather than in a constant flow. Reflecting on this unexpected physical detail, he saw it as an authentic premonition, the effect of the pumping action of the heart which itself hadn't been mortally wounded, and which he thought had been mentioned by the prisoner who'd witnessed the executions at Maryborough.

One morning as he filed with the others back into the building after exercise, he was told to collect his belongings together in readiness to be moved to another cell.

After waiting apprehensively most of the day, for any change that wasn't the essential one was to be dreaded, H was conducted on a winter afternoon to a ground-floor cell that struck him as horribly crowded the moment the door was opened. Unlike the one he'd left, there were no cots in it, but half a dozen straw mattresses lay side by side on a raised and slightly sloping platform at the further end. The warder indicated his as the vacant one on the stone floor.

H had been assimilated into the little community of three in his previous cell, being made to feel somewhat less vulnerable by this tentative solidarity. He'd imagined that Kestner had a certain regard for him, as he didn't treat him with the amused contempt he showed for Matukat; and with Matukat, largely preoccupied with hero worship for Kestner, H had established a kind of understanding. But here he'd no contacts; he was with a gang of strange men, all young except for a farmer in for selling produce on the black market, who played cards and conversed together in an unfamiliar dialect.

At exercise he looked with nostalgia towards Kestner, when not down at Sécurité headquarters, and Matukat, and one day managed to join them, by pausing to adjust a piece of purposely torn boot sole, in their part of the slowly perambulating ring. As he did so, a paper pellet fell into the yard not far from them, and Kestner drew H's attention to a shadowy head and shoulders behind the bars of what he said was a punishment cell. On the next circuit H stepped out of line, stooped quickly and picked up the bit of paper.

'Bloody silly taking a risk like that,' Kestner told H; the warder hadn't spotted him.

H was trying to determine whether the woman at the window was or wasn't Halka. He'd only a moment or two at each round of the yard to make up his mind; he daren't draw attention to her by turning his head. Another paper pellet fell into the yard, still miraculously unremarked by Pappa Masson, who'd just been brought the morning's post from the front gate by the female warder.

Unscrewing the first piece of paper before attempting to pick up the second, H found it blank – because her pencil had been taken from her? Had she been able to scribble or scratch a word on the other bit of paper? He was about to try to retrieve that too, but Kestner laid a hand on his arm.

'You're only encouraging the crazy bitch!'

It evidently hadn't crossed Kestner's mind it might be H's 'fiancée' up there, or was he suggesting that as she must be temporarily out of her senses, there was nothing to be gained by H getting himself locked up in another punishment cell?

For nights H was haunted by the apparition at the window. As he lay awake on the floor, everything seemed to indicate that it was Halka; one night he interpreted unaccustomed sounds overhead, where he thought the punishment cells were situated, as the result of her having been found by the warder on his nocturnal rounds, hanging from a window bar. In the mornings he was less sure that it had been her; no one had appeared at the window during exercise again.

At last for the first time since he'd been moved to the new cell, the reason for which he supposed had been the interception of one of their notes, her missal was handed in to him through the aperture in the door. Waiting till his cellmates had returned to their cards, after the expectant pause that always accompanied an unscheduled opening of the Judas hole, he felt inside the back binding with his little finger – a contact that sometimes, but not on this occasion, had for him a subtly sensual connotation – and extracted the piece of toilet paper on which she wrote that she'd heard he would be taken with a transport of prisoners to Paris in a few days.

'I've been promised that we'll be allowed to meet before that happens. But that will be with a warder and we'll have to speak German, so this is to say a few last words of real good-bye.'

With such life-and-death messages and intimations crowding in on him, he gave little thought to a constant need to scratch, registered by what seemed a nerve far away on the fringes of consciousness. But one evening after taking off his trousers before slipping under the blankets he saw that his thigh was covered with burning, itching pimples, still without much concern. He thought that a body already taken over by powerful poisons, as it seemed to him, in the way of psychological by-products wouldn't for long afford a feeding ground for germs.

This theory wasn't borne out, and it was just during the long hours while he waited to be summoned to the prison governor's office to take leave of Halka before joining the batch of French and Belgian prisoners – the latter followers of the Nazi leader Degrelle – whom he'd overheard his cellmates confirm were being sent home for trial, that the rash spread.

When both legs, from hip bones to knees, were covered by tiny, ooozing sores he reported his condition, and the following evening at six, which, as at certain other fateful times in the legend, was now the hour when, after an outwardly empty day, the vital events took place, the doors were opened and Pappa Masson accompanied a bespectacled girl into the cell.

Keeping his shirt tucked between his legs, H lowered his trousers and the girl stooped and scrutinized the red pustules. Straightening up, she looked into his face with a fraternal regard that H understood as between two of the contaminated and, after naming the skin disease, told him, in English, that before the war she'd been a medical student in Brussels. Meanwhile the black-market farmer was protesting to the warder at being exposed to an infectious complaint and demanded that H be isolated in a cell where he couldn't give it to the rest of them.

Now it seemed to H he was shunned by the others in the cell, though it was only the elderly prisoner who folded a sheet of newspaper over the rim of the bucket before he used it. While he spread the black greasy ointment over his thighs and awaited, with increased dread towards evening, the order to put together his belongings, he was aware of having reached the furthest point of loss. All was ending in disaster; he was about to lose Halka, and as for becoming the kind of writer he had hoped to, the prospects might be better than ever but, even if he survived, it seemed it would have to be in a future too remote and unforeseeable to be contemplated except in the fantasies that he sometimes indulged in.

He was again preoccupied by the particular kind of isolation extreme examples of which had obsessed him long ago in Paris when his mind had been attuned for such reflection by the early evening hangovers. He imagined himself relieving the thirst that seemed always suffered by those who, through a misgearing or mistiming that prevented the intermeshing of their consciousness with the ones around them, were exposed either to public or self-condemnation.

In the most frequent fantasy he constructed a machine out of which, like Moses with Aaron's rod, he could cause a sparkling stream to flow. He saw himself trundling his mobile dispenser into precincts reached through a bolted door at the end of tiled corridors, or alongside institutional beds in the endless nights. There were also recipients of the long, cool, citron-flavoured drinks whose faces were not those of complete strangers, though H never defined them too closely.

The second evening after starting the treatment he heard an unusual clamour coming from the window high in the wall and one of the prisoners, by standing on the table and grasping the bars, drew his head level with it and reported that the transport had assembled on the steps; the window overlooked the prison entrance.

Until his muscles couldn't support him any longer, the watcher at the window described the scene under the lights above the front gate as an officer addressed (inspected?) the prisoners and the guards stood below the steps with sub-machine-guns cradled in their arms. Then another of H's cellmates replaced the first and continued the commentary, naming those in the assembled group he recognized.

One was the Belgian girl who'd prescribed the ointment that was already proving efficacious, but the greater shock came with the news that Kestner, known throughout the prison as its most distinguished inmate, was there with the others and, what was more, the only one to be handcuffed.

H was aware of relief that he wasn't after all waiting out there to be taken somewhere where there'd begin an endless legalistic process to decide whether he was to be publicly branded with the sign of the guilty, which couldn't, he thought, have detached him more completely from the community of the just than he now was.

Shortly after the departure of the French and Belgians, on a clear spring morning – he and Halka had now been six months in prison – those in his and the adjoining cells were sent into the vegetable garden at the back of the building to shake out the straw in their mattresses and air their blankets. The impact of the blinding light – under its high walls the exercise yard was in comparison, in perpetual twilight – was almost intolerable. After he'd accustomed himself to it he pulled his hand from the slit in the material into which it had been thrust to loosen the straw, and as he straightened his back he saw, floating high above the distant horizon, the pure pale peaks of the Säntis range. In that moment the intimation that the previous summer in the transit camp in Bregenz he'd been on the verge of grasping, but hadn't had the courage for, was being repeated to him.

The cell, on his return, appeared dim and shabby to the point of being uninhabitable, and it was hard to see how he'd ever looked on it, or his own corner of its floor, as a tolerable shelter. But soon he was reconciled to it again. Although he was still far from coming to understand the necessity for what had happened to them, he did begin to see the silence that he had entered as the deep divide between the past and what was still to come. Whatever it was that was at the other end there was no way of telling. It might be a howl of final despair or the profound silence might be broken by certain words that he didn't yet know how to listen for.